Praise for *Castle Danger*

The second book in the Matt Lanier series is just as much a page turner as the first. Chris Norbury spins a complex, fast-paced plot with a wonderful cast of characters—both empathetic and dangerous. I love the setting of this book, which is a much of a foe at times as the actual bad guys. - **Valerie Biel, author of the *Circle of Nine* series and *Beyond the Cemetery Gate: The Secret Keeper's Daughter***

I get chills thinking about this book—not just because it is so suspenseful, but because the author so skillfully set the winter scape for this North Shore novel. – **Maren Cooper, author of *A Better Next, Finding Grace*, and *Behind the Lies*.**

Castle Danger is a suspenseful, engaging read. Taking place in northwest Minnesota in a frightful winter, the setting comes alive, menacing and life-threatening to any who lack the foresight and skills to survive. . . . Well-paced with an interesting plot, *Castle Danger* kept me on the edge of my seat. I'd recommend *Castle Danger* to fans of thrillers and suspense. - **Leigh Holland, author and book review blogger**

Books by Chris Norbury

Straight River (Matt Lanier #1)
Castle Danger (Matt Lanier #2)
Dangerous Straits (Matt Lanier #3)

For Middle Grade and Older Readers
Little Mountain, Big Trouble

CASTLE DANGER

CHRIS NORBURY

CSN
Press

To Mom: You are the embodiment of unconditional mother's love.
To Dad: Your generous, expert feedback inspired me to believe in my writing ability.
To Sandra: You've lovingly allowed me to follow my many and varied muses since the day we were married.

Chapter 1

Matt Lanier stood on the middle of Snowfall Lake, gasping for air, wobbling on his snowshoes. His leg muscles quivered on the verge of collapse. His pulse pounded like double-time timpani beats in his chest and temples. Each icy inhale rasped his throat. Gusts of wind threatened to knock him off balance. If he fell, he doubted he could stand again, let alone walk. Microdiamonds of snow whirled across the open expanse of white and crackled against the hood of his parka. He'd hit the wall many marathon runners experience after about twenty miles, except his wall was made of ice.

The last few ominous measures of Bach's Toccata and Fugue echoed in his brain. His choices were unequivocal: keep walking or die.

If he'd ignored the emergency flare he'd seen and heard yesterday, he certainly wouldn't be risking his life for the stranger lying at his feet. Instead, he'd wrestled with his conscience a hundred times today about whether he should've feigned ignorance.

If he jettisoned the bleeding, unconscious trapper here in the middle of this large, oval-shaped lake in the heart of the Arrowhead region of northeast Minnesota, he would quickly reach safety by himself. If wolves didn't feast on the remains, or a Forest Service plane didn't discover the body before ice out, it would sink to the bottom. No one else would ever know what had happened out here.

He looked back at the mummy-shaped load on the makeshift sled tethered to his waist. Wisps of breath vapor rose slowly through a frosted patch of the black scarf covering the mummy's face. Incredulous, Matt snorted and shook his head. "I'll be damned," he said to his cargo. Even his voice sounded iced over. "Looks like we keep walking."

The temperature felt like minus twenty Fahrenheit. The wind-chill? Too cold to compute. At his last rest stop, two hours ago, he'd burned his remaining fuel. Building a fire and shelter to warm up would take time he didn't possess. His high-tech clothing couldn't protect him indefinitely from the lethal cold, and the deer hide cloaking his shoulders and torso would only buy him a few extra minutes of warmth.

Since leaving his campsite in the pre-dawn light, he'd covered approximately eight of the ten miles he needed to travel to reach safety. Sunlight reflecting off the crystalline snowpack stung his eyes as he gauged the angle of the impotent January sun. Mid-afternoon. He'd badly miscalculated his travel time. *Good plan, genius.* Two hours of light. Two miles to safety. Too much to ask of his body?

After dropping his ski poles, he pulled off the Gore-Tex outer mitt and the insulated inner glove from his right hand. He fumbled in the outer pocket of his parka with stiff fingers for the last of his venison jerky. The few bites of dried deer meat comprised his only energy source for this final push. Crusted ice cracked off his ski mask when he opened his mouth. Chewing the jerky was easy once it broke into small, icy meat chips. After eating the last salty but otherwise tasteless bite, he donned his glove and mitt. A handful of snow helped him swallow the food but numbed his mouth and his throat and did little to ease his thirst.

He glanced at the head of his human cargo. "You damn well better stay alive," he said, angry at the man for intruding on his life, "because I'll get royally pissed if I do all this work for nothing."

His unconscious passenger replied with more breath vapors. Matt had wrapped him in all the warm layers of clothing and materials he could spare. Every piece of exposed skin was covered, but he made sure the face coverings were loose enough to allow air to get to the man.

To make the sled, Matt had cobbled together his cross-country skis, a nylon tarp, driftwood, rope, bungee cords, and straps cut from a spare Duluth pack. He pulled the sled with a rope looped around his torso. To brake the sled on down slopes, he'd fastened his ski poles to the tips of his skis with duct tape on the basket ends. He pushed backward on the poles when he needed to stop the sled from crashing into his heels. The rig was cumbersome and clumsy but worked well enough.

His passenger tended to slide off the sled when Matt dragged it across slanted terrains such as portage trails or snowdrifts. Repositioning the man several times per hour had been the main time waster and a major pain in the ass. Alone and with no gear to carry, he could've traversed anywhere in the Boundary Waters at about three miles per hour. Dragging two hundred fifty pounds of dead weight through snow-drifted lakes and across rugged, rocky portages, he traveled little more than one mile per hour.

He picked up his ski poles, checked his towrope, and found his guide point, a long narrow peninsula jutting out from the southeast shore a mile away. Once he reached the point, he'd turn southward and travel downwind to Olson's Wilderness Canoe Outfitters.

Matt tried to take a step, but the motion electrified his nerves with pained fatigue. "Damn. Don't give out now, body." A jolt of adrenaline called up from a hidden reserve of survival instincts steadied Matt's rubbery muscles. He breathed deeper, slower, willing oxygen to saturate his blood.

He forced his body back into work mode and groaned from the exertion. He was almost ready to give up when the sled grudgingly moved from the deep powder. He took a step, then another, and he was under way. A feeling of triumph surged through him.

He set his concentration on ignoring the fatigue, ignoring the searing pain in his muscles, ignoring their pleas to give up. To help maintain his energy and pace, he hummed Ella Fitzgerald's smoking hot version of "How High the Moon" with Count Basie's band. With every step, he dreamed of warmth, rest, food, and gulping quarts of water instead of chewing handfuls of snow. He plodded on, fighting for balance as the raging northwest wind tried to topple him.

The wind had scoured most of the loose snow from the surface of certain spots on Snowfall Lake. Matt rejoiced when he hit those spots because he maintained a faster, steadier pace—almost two miles per hour. The sled skimmed across the hard-packed snow, and he could almost run in his clumsy snowshoes. Then he'd hit a patch of deep powder, and his spirits sank as his pace slowed.

He cleared the peninsula as the sun touched the tops of the tallest trees in the southwest sky. Shadows stretched across the snow-covered lake and deepened the green of the pines and the brown of the aspens and tamaracks, which in turn highlighted the white birches. Angling to the south, he finally got the damned wind out of his face. Although it was an enormous psychological boost, the tail wind added nothing to his speed.

Matt intuitively set his course for the boat dock, still unseen through the whorls of loose, powdery snow. He'd worked several summers for Ferdie Olson in high school and college, guided dozens of canoe trips, and knew his way back to this place as well as he knew the way back to anywhere he'd ever lived. Sweating now, he dug deep for extra energy and quickened his pace. The finish line of his marathon was in sight. A quick glance back at the injured trapper revealed he was still breathing.

Despite the sweat dampening his body, Matt couldn't remember the last time he hadn't been shivering. Rigid with numbness, his face felt like an ice mask. The wind continued to swirl microscopic snow particles into his eyes, blurring his vision. Above all, his stomach growled non-stop. He hadn't eaten a full meal since an early breakfast of walleye garnished with dried morel mushrooms he'd harvested in the fall. Since then, he'd burned thousands of calories.

Matt slogged on toward Olson's Outfitters, head down to maintain forward momentum. He estimated his remaining distance every few minutes. One thousand yards. One yard equals two steps. Two thousand steps. He hummed Tchaikovsky's *Marche Slave* in an attempt to maintain a steady pace and because the title seemed appropriate for the situation.

A faint outline of the main building, the lodge, appeared. *Ignore the deadly cold.* He hummed louder. *Ignore the pain.* Five hundred yards left. *Rise above the agony. Balance. Breathe.*

He glanced back at his passenger. "Dying ain't allowed today, pal."

Unless what awaited Matt at Olson's was a cop with a nervous trigger finger.

Chapter 2

Matt's muscles spasmed as he inched his way toward the lakeside entrance to the lodge at Olson's Outfitters. Compared to traversing the flat lake, the gentle thirty-yard incline from the boat dock seemed like scaling a mountain. The urge to collapse into the snow and die chilled his brain. He sagged but then steadied himself. *No. Finish the job.* He remembered what his mother used to drum into her children's minds almost daily: *Family takes care of family. End of story.* He couldn't stop doing the right thing merely because it was too painful. The man lying on his sled wasn't family, but he was a fellow outdoorsman. Matt wanted to believe the stranger would've done the same for him if their situations were reversed.

He unleashed a long primal scream that was swallowed by the wind. Straightening, he summoned his last ounce of energy and inhaled deeply. Leaning forward, every muscle as taut as piano wire tuned to double-high C, he pulled. The pressure in his head made it feel as if it would explode. *Save this man instead of watching him die like you watched ... her... die.* He gained an inch. Then another. Then a foot. Traveling those final thirty yards to the back door took two minutes.

He collapsed against the door, gasping. After catching his breath, he shed his backpack and snowshoes and crawled to the front of the lodge. With no load to bear, he felt weightless but was too weak to stand. He struggled up the steps and across the porch to the wooden bird feeder hanging from a bracket jutting out from a porch post. After leveraging himself up to a standing position, he removed an outer mitt and groped the narrow space between the feeder and the post. The key to the front door hung from a nail tacked into the backside of the bird feeder, just as it had ever since Ferdie Olson opened for business four decades earlier. *Good ol' slave to habit Ferdie.*

After fumbling the key off the nail with frostbitten fingers, Matt glanced at the big thermometer mounted on another post. Minus twenty-eight degrees. *Son of a bitch.* Colder than he'd imagined. To keep his spirits positive during the trek, he hadn't dwelled on the temperature. The number of degrees below zero made little difference. Zero would kill a man only a few minutes slower than minus twenty-eight would.

He worked the key into the lock and opened the front door. Ferdie had lowered the heat to maintenance level for the winter to keep the pipes from freezing. Still, the blast of forty-degree air that slapped him as he entered was the equivalent of walking from a refrigerator into a hot sauna. The lodge smelled of musty pine and ancient wood smoke. He closed the door, turned on a fluorescent ceiling fixture, staggered to the back door, and dragged his human cargo inside.

Matt peeled off the scarf, towel, and ski mask with which he'd covered his passenger's face for protection. The man's skin looked ghostly white with a tinge of blue. He then removed the space blanket and tarp he'd wrapped around the man's body, which exposed the bloodstained sleeping bag. He leaned down and put his ear to the man's face. Shallow, steady breaths came every few seconds.

Tears welled up from the bottom of his gut. He sat back against the door and patted the man's shoulder as if he'd been an equal partner in the journey.

With the trapper out of imminent danger, Matt could think more than five minutes ahead. *Heat. Call for help. Eat.* The liquid propane heating system would take too long to warm the spacious lodge, so he headed for the massive fireplace in the main room.

Built from large stones of Arrowhead granite and framed with varnished red pine boards, the firebox stood four feet high and eight feet wide. Matt remembered the summers he'd worked here. He and his cohorts, all students, would bask in front of the fire on many chilly summer nights after they had completed the day's chores. Standard topics of discussion were nightmare trip-guiding stories, lying about trophy fish catches, and complaining about their gruff, benevolent dictator, their Lord and Master, King Ferdinand S. Olson.

The wood laid across the andirons by Ferdie had enjoyed two extra months of inside drying time, so Matt got the fire crackling nicely in minutes. As the heat hit his face, tension drained from his body. He extended his palms to the warmth, wanting to curl up here and sleep for a week.

Instead, he trudged to the back room and dragged the trapper into the great room on the tarp. He muscled the trapper onto the large, rustic, leather-and-wood sofa in front of the fire. The man groaned and opened his eyes for a moment and stared blankly as Matt laid him down. He wrestled the bloodstained sleeping bag off the man and draped it over him.

After walking into Ferdie's office, Matt sat in the creaky wooden desk chair and picked up the phone. The dial tone hummed its one-note melody. He let out a sigh of relief and tapped three numbers into the keypad.

"Nine-one-one. What's your emergency?" The professional, reassuring male voice on the line took him aback. The moment he'd dreamed about all day, but thought would never arrive, was here.

Matt said, "I need an ambulance at Olson's Outfitters on Snowfall Lake."

"What happened, sir?"

Matt almost said, "I found an injured trapper in the Boundary Waters and brought him here," but his mind flashed danger signals and he hesitated. "Uh, yeah, I was trapping a few miles east of here and got my hand caught in a trap. Lost a lot of blood." Because his mouth and lips were still numb, he had little trouble sounding exhausted and half-frozen. He put more pain into his voice, more disorientation. "Broke my damn leg too. Almost … didn't make it. Got frostbite for sure."

"Okay, sir, we'll get someone out right away. But it'll take longer than usual because of yesterday's blizzard. Need to send a plow out to lead the ambulance to Ferdie's."

The access from Fernberg Road, east of Ely, to Ferdie's was about one mile long, so the delay from plowing would buy Matt several extra minutes. "Thanks," Matt said.

"What's your name, sir?"

Matt's face flushed hotly. He hadn't thought the dispatcher might ask for the trapper's name. Hadn't thought to check the man for identification. Hadn't thought about anything but surviving until now. He stalled. "Getting dizzy ... damn hand bleeding bad ... head hurts like a sumbitch."

"Stay with me, sir." The dispatcher's voice rose and tensed.

Matt dropped the phone on the desk and walked to the doorway.

"Sir? You still there?" The voice sounded muffled and tinny from across the room. "Sir? Stay on the line."

Matt softly closed the office door behind him and headed for the retail area of the lodge—a combination mini-grocery, hardware, and camping and fishing gear store. Anything a wilderness canoeist or kayaker might need at the last minute during paddling season.

He opened a package of sliced ham and another of flour tortillas from the freezer and nuked them in the microwave in the back-room kitchenette. In minutes, he'd made two large burritos flavored with frozen shredded cheese and a jar of salsa. While he wolfed down the burritos, he heated water in the microwave and found packets of instant soup and instant coffee. In two minutes, he had a bowl of hot soup and a cup of hot coffee. He took the meal to the fireplace, where he ate and drank a little slower. The hot food acted as a heater core in his gut, warming him from the inside out.

The temperature had risen enough that he couldn't see his breath as he exhaled. He added two logs to the fire. Matt's next task was to pull the ski mask off his face and head. He winced as the ice gave way, ripping out numerous beard hairs. He shook out his sweat-matted hair and slicked it back, letting it hang down to his shoulders. The warmer the fire grew, the more he wished he could lie down and thaw for two days.

Energized by the simple act of eating, he checked the trapper's wounds. The bandage on his hand was blood-soaked but had slowed the rate of bleeding. Matt couldn't apply a new bandage to the puncture wounds because he didn't want the rescuers to become suspicious if they noticed a fresh bandage on an unconscious man. He did manage to give the man a few sips of warm soup broth.

After carefully exposing the trapper's lower leg, Matt studied the broken limb. The trapper's shin was a swollen, grotesque, purple, green, yellow disaster. Matt's first aid skills excluded setting broken bones, so he'd only dared to put a splint on the leg last night.

He went back to the grocery area. The fresh food was long gone, but the freezer contained remnants of last season's products. He withdrew a few pounds each of hamburger, chicken breasts, steaks, and some of Ferdie's homemade venison sausage, then piled them on the checkout counter along with an assortment of condiments, staples, and a handful of freeze-dried meals. He loaded a large Duluth pack with the groceries and set it near the back door.

Next, he went to the back supply room of the outfitter section and found a sleeping bag to replace the one in which he'd wrapped the trapper. He loaded the new sleeping bag and the items he'd used to keep the trapper warm into the Duluth pack on top of the food, then topped it off with fuel canisters, matches, and several packs of flashlight and lantern batteries. Satisfied he'd gotten most of the items he needed, he cinched the pack tight, took it outside, and secured it on his sled.

The wind still whooshed through the pines and tossed puffs of powdery snow across the tops of the snowdrifts. He listened for the rumble of a snowplow or the wail of an ambulance siren but heard nothing.

The western sky glowed with a fiery, purplish-red that implied a sultry summer sunset, incongruous considering the thirty-below-zero temperature. He breathed deep and let the cold air sting his nostrils and lungs. It dawned on him that it was so cold he hadn't smelled anything outdoors the entire day. In the distance, a pack of wolves serenaded the moon. Except for the whistling wind, their haunting chorus was the only sound of nature he'd heard all day.

After washing and replacing the dishes he'd used and transferring the opened packages of food he'd used for his meal to his backpack, Matt returned to Ferdie's office, moving noiselessly because the emergency dispatcher was still on the line, asking for a response. He found paper and pen in a desk drawer and wrote for a few minutes. After he'd folded the paper, inserted it into an envelope, and written *Ferdie* on the front, he placed the envelope in the middle drawer of the desk.

He returned to the great room and slid a sofa pillow under the trapper's head, then tucked the sleeping bag down behind his body to absorb more heat from the fire. He could think of nothing else to do that would help the poor, unfortunate bastard.

Matt went out the front door and listened for the plow and the ambulance. Still nothing. After replacing the key on its hook behind the bird feeder, he returned to the door. With one short, sharp motion, he rammed his elbow through the window next to the door, making a jagged, six-inch-wide hole, and stepped inside. He closed the door but left it unlocked.

Matt fetched a paper towel from the kitchenette and came back to the trapper. He found a spot of wet blood on the bandages and dabbed it with the towel, then smeared blood on the door to Ferdie's office and dabbed some on the desk and phone. He tossed the paper towel into the fire and made sure it burned to ashes.

When he heard the distant growl of the plow engine, Matt stood, zipped his parka, and donned a replacement ski mask he'd borrowed from Ferdie's stock. He knelt and rested a hand on the trapper's shoulder. The man's eyelids fluttered half-open. Matt noticed a glimmer of awareness.

"Good luck, stranger. I did the best I could for you." Matt's voice cracked not from emotion as much as full-body fatigue. "I hope it was enough."

Would saving this man's life make up for the deaths he'd caused last spring? The cold emptiness in his gut told him it hadn't yet. *Maybe someday.*

Blinking yellow and red lights through the window indicated the plow had led the ambulance almost to Olson's parking lot. He walked out the back door, strapped on his snowshoes, put on his inner gloves and outer mitts, and harnessed the sled to his waist. As the emergency personnel entered the front door of the lodge, Matt retraced his steps onto Snowfall Lake. He disappeared into the starlit darkness as a whirlwind of blowing snow enveloped him and covered his tracks.

Chapter 3

Blustery northwest winds buffeted Allyson Clifford's rickety Chevy Suburban as she white-knuckled up Highway 61 from Duluth. Returning from her weekly grocery run, the cargo area contained more than a dozen plastic bins full of fresh fruits, vegetables, poultry, meat, and as much fresh fish as she expected to sell over the weekend at her restaurant.

Her fingers hurt from choking the wheel for the past hour. She anticipated losing traction on every patch of glare ice on the road. She was grateful the road crews had quickly plowed the highway, but sand and salt were useless at subzero temperatures. At this rate, she might arrive in Castle Danger too late to prepare adequately for the lunch rush.

After ten more tense minutes, she turned onto Halcyon Drive and sighed with relief. She drove the final one hundred yards up the narrow road and parked behind her restaurant, which was perched a safe distance from a rocky outcrop fifty feet above Lake Superior.

As she got out, Josh raced out to greet her wearing a red down jacket, red mittens, and clunky winter boots. "Mama, Mama! Did you bring me something?"

He spoke with the joyous delight of an eight-year-old that always melted her heart. Josh was home from school on a weekday due to a teachers' training day. She beamed and knelt down as he approached. Never in a million years would she tire of her son's youthful enthusiasm for life. "As a matter of fact, Joshie, I did."

She pulled a small bag from her jacket pocket and dangled it in front of him. Josh grabbed the package and almost ripped it to shreds. "Awesome. A Hot Wheels race car." He threw his arms around her. "Thanks, Mama. You're the best."

She hugged him tightly and absorbed his love as if he were a heating pad thawing her cold limbs. Then she gave him a big, embarrassing kiss on the cheek and buried her nose in his shaggy blond hair while he squirmed to get away.

A Hot Wheels car was a slam-dunk present for Josh because his favorite play activity this year was to set up his massively long Hot Wheels racetrack and race his growing collection of cars. He invented all sorts of contests, such as measuring the distances the cars flew off jumps or rolled across the restaurant's wood floor. The winner was awarded the parking place of honor on his bedside table, lit up by his nightlight.

Allyson stood. "Help with the groceries before you play."

She handed him the lightest bin, and he dragged it into the restaurant's kitchen. As she lugged another bin inside, she spotted Hannah Boudreaux folding napkins and wrapping them around silverware sets.

"Morning," Hannah said with a smile and far too much fake cheer.

Usually, Allyson expected a sour expression and a noise akin to a grunt. This meant only one thing. She turned on her "boss" voice: crisp, clear, commanding, all business. "What did I tell you about letting Dean into my restaurant before we open?"

Hannah's expression flipped from a smile to a surprised frown, and her voice spiked from mature young-adult cheerful to hormonal adolescent whiny. "How did you know?"

"The Halcyon is not your personal love shack. Where is he?"

"Restroom."

Allyson shook her head. "Get him out."

"Aw." Hannah started to pout, then seemed to remember that copping an attitude never worked on her boss. Instead, she headed for the restroom.

Louder, Allyson said, "When he's completely out the door, help me with the food."

Hannah was a typically moody teenager made more mercurial by the fact she was madly in love with her sleazy boyfriend, Dean Sobolik. She took every opportunity to meet with Dean anywhere but her own house because her parents liked Dean even less than Allyson did.

Despite her questionable taste in young men, Hannah was an excellent waitress. She hustled, paid attention to details, and after the first week, grudgingly stopped texting on her cell phone while working. She'd already discovered how to exploit her recently blossomed body to attract boys. Her petite figure, pleasantly naughty smile, and lilting voice paid off in generous tips from her male customers. With her long brown hair tied into a ponytail, she played the girl-next-door card as well as anyone Allyson had ever seen.

When Hannah came back from shooing Dean out the door, Allyson said, "Did Josh behave?"

Hannah smiled at Josh, who was running his new Hot Wheels car across the floor and making racecar noises such as *Vroom*. "Of course. He always behaves perfectly for me."

"That's because he's in love with you. Thanks for watching him." In a more guarded tone, she said, "Is Gary here yet?"

"Yep."

"Sober?"

Hannah shrugged. "Maybe."

Allyson's cheery mood dropped a level. *Maybe* usually meant *No*.

"*Won*derful," she said, not bothering to hide her disappointment.

Decent cooks were hard to find this far north because of the remoteness. She'd been lucky to land Gary Soukkala two years ago. He arrived in the area to accommodate a woman he loved around the time the chef she'd inherited from the previous owners also retired after helping her transition for a year after she took over. Allyson read his resume, saw he was a graduate of the Culinary Institute of America, had worked as a sous chef at one of the top restaurants in Chicago, and hired him on the spot.

Gary slouched at the bar with his head in his hands. A glass of clear, bubbly liquid Allyson hoped was club soda sat on the bar. His black hair looked as if he'd slept on one side of his head all night. His face sported a three-day stubble. She noticed he'd worn the same clothes yesterday—fashionably torn blue jeans and a black T-shirt with the Willie Nelson song title, "Roll Me Up and Smoke Me When I Die," screen-printed on the front.

Locking onto his eyes, she searched for hints of a hangover. "Hi, Gary. Ready to go?"

He looked at her too casually, and his eyes seemed to take an extra second to focus. "Aces today, Allyson. What's the special?"

He spoke in the deliberate style of someone trying to mask a hangover. She decided immediately. "Split pea and ham soup with choice of Panini-grilled sandwich. There's still a few gallons in the freezer."

A soup-and-sandwich special ensured Gary would work a minimal amount with knives. He wouldn't need to chop large quantities of food in rapid sequence and risk slicing off a finger. She hoped this would avert another mini disaster.

Gary's face reddened. His eyes avoided hers. "I'll thaw the soup."

She crossed her arms and lowered her chin. "You're teetering on the edge."

"Only had a few last night. Couldn't sleep."

Gee, he'd only used that excuse twice before this week. "Get some coffee first."

Gary poured coffee and walked unsteadily to the kitchen. Allyson went to the front host station and mulled over her options for the rest of the daily specials.

Although the Halcyon didn't officially open until eleven, the locals knew the coffee pot was always on. As long as the customers sat at the bar and stayed out of the staff's way, they were welcome to stop in early and exchange the latest gossip over a hot beverage and a day-old pastry. Therefore, she wasn't surprised when the front door opened. Brent Wilner, her full-time busboy, blew in on the wind-whipped snow.

"Hi, Ms. Clifford," Brent said with his perpetual cheeriness and a lopsided smile as he removed his jacket and headed for the kitchen.

"Hi, Brent," Allyson said with the motherly softness she always got when Brent was alone with her. Because Brent suffered from Asperger's Syndrome, strangers and narrow-minded locals subtly ostracized him. Allyson didn't care. Brent was the Halcyon's most conscientious worker. He loved bussing tables and washing dishes because the job was so finite and self-contained. Even though Josh was normal, whatever that meant, she would've been equally proud to have Brent for a son.

She was wiping off the large black chalkboard sitting on an easel near the hosting station when he came back to get his marching orders for the day. "Want to write the specials?"

She held out the box of colored chalk. Brent smiled and took the chalk from her hand. "Yes, I'd like that."

She handed him the piece of paper with the daily specials and their prices listed. "You remember the rule for writing menus?"

He stared at the ceiling for a moment with an intensity that always unnerved her. "Menu items in big letters, descriptions in medium letters, prices in small numbers." He lowered his volume with each phrase, almost whispering the word *prices*.

She patted his shoulder. "That's right. Put some of your special flair on the board today too. A nasty day like this could use some of your sunshine, honey."

Brent blushed. He either did a task to one hundred percent of his ability or refused to try, so she knew his art would at least be colorful, maybe even weirdly eye-catching.

She glanced at the clock over the door. "Ten minutes, people," she announced. "Let's get in gear."

Allyson began her pre-opening routine but pushed the pace because of her late start. The usual nervous gurgle revved in her stomach. Running a restaurant was like acting in a long-running stage play. Each day required a new performance. Each customer expected the same high-quality food and service the previous nine hundred ninety-nine had received. She flipped the switch to the gas fireplace that formed a wall between the bar and the main dining room, then checked the till, making sure it contained plenty of coins and paper money.

Next, she turned on the background music, a smooth jazz station from satellite radio that played tunes conducive to dining and quiet conversation; the warm, cozy atmosphere for which she strived. She wanted customers who appreciated quality food and a relaxing dining experience.

Allyson went to the specials board to check Brent's work. He'd written the specials in large, neat block letters. The descriptions of the dishes underneath each item were written in a smaller, more feminine cursive. The prices were smallest of all but still visible from a short distance. Brent's flair this time was a dozen snowflakes sprinkled throughout the bare spaces on the chalkboard to signify the current weather. More astoundingly, each one seemed identical, but upon closer inspection, each was unique, like a real snowflake. More of Brent's special gift—attention to detail.

Winter always slowed business at restaurants in the Far North, so Allyson was down to her core staff. Gary was prepping food in the back. Hannah was finishing her place settings. Brent was organizing his bussing station. The music played at the perfect background volume.

She made one last check. The dining room looked perfect. Warm beige tablecloths complemented the maple trim and earth-toned walls. Lake Superior, or just plain "The Lake" to everyone who lived on the North Shore, was at its magnificent best through the huge picture window along the row of booths. Rolling steel-blue waves shimmered beneath a cloud-flecked sky. The Lake drove the entire North Shore economy: tourism, recreation, fishing, and shipping of taconite ore, coal, timber, and grain from the west. The Lake was so large, it influenced weather in the Arrowhead Region—the so-called Lake Effect.

After a deep breath, Allyson recited in a bare whisper the prayer she'd recited every day for the past five years. "God, please give me the strength to resist all that is bad for me. Give me the wisdom to do what's best for Josh. Give me the faith to know that tomorrow will be better for us than today."

Praying did little to calm her jittery nerves, but each prayer added a block to a spiritual and emotional wall between today and her past life. At eleven o'clock, she flipped the switch on the *Open* sign and checked the front door to make sure it was unlocked. The Halcyon Bar & Grill was open for business.

Chapter 4

That evening, the small band Allyson had hired for the weekend had finished their last set and started packing their instruments on the Halcyon's small stage. One couple lingered over dessert and coffee. Her friend Pauline Allen sat at a window table nursing a decaf and staring out at the blackness above the Lake. Hannah loitered near the kitchen with Brent and Gary. Allyson tended bar for three men seated there watching the Halcyon's large, flat-screen TV.

She didn't advertise the Halcyon as a sports bar, but her satellite connection received more sports stations than the local cable network, so a small group of regulars would occasionally stop by to watch sports. Or so they told their wives.

Especially on weekends, she sold more booze by dressing sexier than usual and flirting a little with the guys. All it took was a V-neck blouse showing a hint of cleavage paired with slacks that were just tight enough. The men pretended to watch University of Minnesota-Duluth hockey or whatever other sport was on TV. Thanks to the mirror behind the bar, she knew they ogled her ass and legs as much as they watched the games. When she faced the customers, they divided their surreptitious glances above and below her neck.

Tonight, one man studied her face much more than her body. The curiosity in his stare unnerved her. She studied the puzzled expression on his face to determine how drunk he might be, then caught his eye. "Is anything wrong, sir?"

"Oh, no, it's just that you remind me of someone. Have we ever met?" His voice ignited a vague memory. Faux classy, with a touch of ignorant slimeball. La-la Land meets New Joisey. He was big and thick, like a football lineman. Not unattractive, but not someone she would've remembered for his looks.

"I don't think so."

"You sure?"

"Pretty sure."

He squinted and pursed his lips. "There's something about you." He wagged his finger. "Damn, this pisses me off. Ever been to Vegas?"

Her hand dropped to her lower abdomen in response to a dull ache that flared up. "No." Her throat felt so tight she barely got the word out. "Ready for a refill?"

He waved her off. "Drivin' me nuts that I can't remember where I met a gorgeous chick like you."

The burning pain spread upward. She forced the tension from her voice. "Everyone's got a twin somewhere in the world, right?" If she had seen him in Vegas, she didn't want to remember the details. "Excuse me for a moment."

She walked toward the kitchen and stood next to Hannah, who waited for the last couple to signal for their check.

Hannah looked at her expectantly. She'd been glancing at the clock and fiddling with her order pad and pen, which usually meant a hot date with Dean Sobolik right after work. "Closing soon?"

Allyson glanced over her shoulder at the bar. The man had resumed conversing with his friends.

"I hope so," she said and walked over to Pauline's table. "Girlfriend," Allyson stage whispered.

Pauline turned from looking out the window. Short and housewifely, she made everyone smile merely by her presence. The first thing strangers noticed were her clothes. The brighter the colors, the better. Tonight she wore lime green tights under a black miniskirt and Sorel boots, a look that didn't flatter her generous behind. Above that, a fuzzy, multi-colored, knitted sweater made her look like a giant psychedelic caterpillar. A pink beret at a jaunty angle atop her short, bottle-blond hair completed the ensemble.

The second thing people noticed was her voice—a squeaky version of northern Minnesota Lutheran, helium-tinged and bubbly. She took pride in being a faux-sexy, fun-loving smartass and Castle Danger's resident busybody.

"What's up, Allie?"

"Don't look now, but check out the dark-haired, stocky man at the bar on the left."

Pauline grinned like a horny co-conspirator and leaned over to see past Allyson. "Why? You gonna hit on him tonight?"

Allyson's frown cooled her expression. "Of course not. He said he recognizes me from Las Vegas."

Pauline flicked her wrist. "Don't worry, honey, I'm your wing woman if you need me." She kept shooting glances toward the bar.

Allyson glanced at the man, then back at Pauline. "I hope he's mistaken, but I want you to remember him just in case."

Pauline finally got a good look at the man when he turned toward her table. Her eyes got dreamy, as did her voice. "Mmm, he's sorta cute, Allie. Looks harmless to me, other than he could probably bench press me with one hand." She quickly added, "Naked, of course."

The ache in Allyson's stomach intensified. "It's probably nothing, but I've been too relaxed lately. I need to keep my guard up. If you see him hanging around town tomorrow, let me know."

"Sure thing. I'll throw myself on that hunk like I was diving onto a live grenade if it'll keep him from bothering you."

Allyson forced a casual chuckle. "Thanks."

Inside, she wasn't laughing. Returning to the bar, she concentrated on the Vegas stranger, urged her brain to make some sort of identification connection. Unfortunately, most of that lost weekend in Las Vegas was a fuzzy, drug-hazed memory at best.

Chapter 5

Matt awoke to the most unnatural sound one expects to hear in the wilderness during winter—an airplane engine. He freed his ears from inside his mummy sleeping bag and sat up. The noise was from a United States Forest Service plane. They made routine runs over the Boundary Waters Canoe Area Wilderness (BWCAW) during summer, especially if fire danger was high. Occasionally, they performed search and rescue missions for stranded canoeists or hikers. He shook his head to clear his mind. A rescue mission in winter? Almost no one went to the Boundary Waters in winter. The plane's sound faded to nothing.

He gauged the sun's location through the tent fabric. Late afternoon. He'd gotten back from Olson's before midnight, making excellent time without the added load and worry of the trapper.

Every muscle and joint had ached for a long rest, and he'd obliged his body. When he awoke, he felt almost as stiff as if he'd frozen to death, but he'd held up under the stress of the marathon rescue and survived with only minor bumps, bruises, and muscle pulls.

He opened his canteen and drained the water into his throat as he heard the plane engine approach again. It was tracking more to the east this time. A few minutes later, the plane returned and was further east but heading north instead of south. Then it dawned on him. The plane was searching the terrain in a grid pattern radiating from Olson's to the north, east, and south. They were looking for him.

He lay back on his sleeping pad and slammed the ground with his fists. Had Ferdie read his IOU and deduced Matt Lanier had written it? Had trackers followed his trail partway back to camp? The wind would've blown snow over the tracks in mere hours, so he hadn't worried about leaving a trail. He assumed the authorities would've stabilized the trapper at the hospital and not questioned him until he was lucid, which was good because it meant the trapper had survived.

When the plane returned for the fourth time in twenty minutes, Matt's spirits fell, and he sighed. It was time to leave the wilderness. He'd camouflaged his campsite well, tucking his tent under a thick copse of white pines away from the shoreline and only burning small campfires with his driest wood during daylight. Now the authorities knew someone was out here, and the trapper had told them where he'd sustained his injuries. Based on the events of last spring, they might deduce that the rescuer was Matt Lanier, which meant they wouldn't stop looking until they found him.

He'd known he'd go back to civilization eventually, but this was still too soon. His stomach knotted into a dull ache, partly from ravenous hunger but mostly because he didn't want to make this decision. No matter what might come in the future, he was done playing Good Samaritan. Saving the trapper had forced his hand by putting him back on the run. Once again, he found no upside to being a nice guy.

He dug out his maps of the BWCAW and the Minnesota road map he'd taken great pains to preserve for this moment. He spread the BWCA maps across his lap and the tent floor, used a flashlight to study lakes, portages, and routes to pockets of civilization. Then he laid the Minnesota map atop the BWCA maps and studied the Arrowhead region. He'd have to go on foot since he assumed the police had found his abandoned truck months ago. He mulled over several possibilities but quickly eliminated Ely and points west. Too close to Olson's Outfitters and the deaths he'd precipitated last spring.

That left the southeastern half of Minnesota's Arrowhead region. It featured many small towns along the north shore of Lake Superior, or just inland, where a man looking to stay anonymous could find a room or a small cabin in the woods and blend in with the other refugees from big-city life.

Matt's eyes kept going back to the big lake. Superior. *Gitchi-Gami* in the Ojibwe language. Shining Big-Sea-Water according to Longfellow's classic poem *The Song of Hiawatha*. He'd always loved Lake Superior. One of his most vivid childhood memories was first beholding *The Lake* from the hilltops of Duluth and believing the water spread V-shaped to infinity. Lake Superior had seemed as grand as an ocean.

The North Shore. Rugged coastlines. Small cozy bays. Quiet little towns. Isolated cabins. Live-and-let-live people. That settled the first part of the question.

Now it became a matter of which town. He refocused on the Minnesota road map. Stay away from Duluth. That's where ... she ... had died. His eye caught another town name. He smiled and nodded. He returned to the BWCA maps and plotted a route to Lake Superior. A buzz ran down his spine—part fear, part excitement. The orchestra in the back of his consciousness began the Largo movement of Dvorak's Ninth Symphony. Matt absentmindedly hummed the English horn solo. *Goin' home, goin' home, I'm a goin' home.* He'd leave tomorrow at dawn and start his new life. But was he going to a place that might actually become his home?

Chapter 6

Fifteen minutes before closing time the next evening, the Halcyon was empty of customers except for Pauline. She wandered up to the bar, coffee cup in hand, and flashed a mischievous smile at Allyson, who was loading glasses into the bar's sanitizing machine.

"Want to watch a movie tonight?" Pauline said with energetic encouragement and then set her cup on the bar.

Allyson gave her a quizzical look as she put the cup into the sanitizer. "You're here two nights in a row? Don't you have kids and a husband to go home to?"

"I'm a bachelorette for at least one more day. Darrell's driving a long haul to Texas and the boys are at his mother's for as long as she can stand the little bast—whoops." She feigned a devout expression and pressed her palms together, fingers pointed heavenward. "I mean, little darlings."

Darrell Allen hadn't been Pauline's first choice for a husband. She had gotten pregnant by him two years after high school. Seeing no better options for marriage in her future, she decided Darrell was close enough to the real thing. He was a hard worker, loved his two sons, and tried hard to please his miniature dynamo.

Allyson chuckled. "A glass of wine with that movie might be fun."

Pauline's eyes brightened. "Ooh, and some chocolate too. Perfect with a rom-com."

"Okay, you convinced me," Allyson said. "I'll close up here. You run home and get chocolate and a tearjerker from your collection, then meet me at my house." She picked up the TV remote and flipped to the local news station.

"Sounds good," said Pauline. She stood and put on her coat.

Allyson's full attention went to the TV when an artist rendering of some sort of abominable snowman flashed onto the screen. A few seconds later, the on-screen announcer reappeared. Then the picture cut to a camera shot of a reporter standing in front of the Ely hospital. The caption below read "Tess Keating-Live." Tess Keating was an attractive Nordic blonde bundled in a fur-lined hooded parka.

Pauline said, "How about I bring three or four movies and we can decide what goes best with the—"

"Shh." Allyson thrust her hand up and out to silence her friend. She turned up the volume.

"… is a remarkable story," the voiceover said. "What can you tell us, Tess?"

Keating glanced at her notes. "Ely resident Joseph Backstrom was trapping small game in the Boundary Waters Canoe Area recently when he accidentally caught his hand in a trap. While returning to his snowmobile, he stepped in a snow-covered hole and broke his leg. When he reached his snowmobile, which is illegal to operate in the Boundary Waters, it wouldn't start. Knowing he'd never be able to walk to safety in the below-zero temperatures, he fired a flare gun as a distress signal, then passed out from loss of blood."

The video went to a photo of a haggard young man lying in a hospital bed with one leg in a cast, a bandaged hand, and ointment smeared on his face.

"What makes this a remarkable survival story is the fact that Backstrom claims a stranger who looked more like a wild creature hauled him back to Olson's Canoe Outfitters on Snowfall Lake east of Ely."

The picture returned to the drawing of the creature.

"The rescuer is obviously human," Keating continued, "because the emergency dispatcher talked to a male caller who reported the injury. But when Backstrom regained consciousness, he was adamant he never called nine-one-one or talked to anyone."

The picture returned to Keating. "I spoke with Backstrom a short time ago. He described his rescuer in vague terms because he was mostly unconscious during the approximately ten-mile trek from where he'd been trapping to Olson's Outfitters. Backstrom remembers the man was bundled in a deerskin hide wrapped over his outerwear. He had long hair and a long beard, but wore a ski mask as protection from the weather. Backstrom believes his rescuer transported him on some sort of sled. Hospital staff treated him for a broken leg and severe frostbite. His mangled hand required seventeen stitches. Backstrom may lose a few fingers or toes, but he considers himself lucky and blessed to be alive."

By this time, Gary, Hannah, and Brent had gathered near the bar to watch.

The screen split into two shots. Anchorman Ron Romasko spoke from the second screen. "Tess, do the authorities have any explanation as to why Backstrom's rescuer didn't stay with Backstrom until the ambulance arrived?"

Keating shook her head. "They are just as bewildered as anyone. Perhaps the mystery man was also doing something illegal in the Boundary Waters and feared arrest. Perhaps he's publicity shy. County sheriffs and the U.S. Forest Service questioned Backstrom about his location when he was injured. They began searching for the mystery rescuer earlier today, if only to make sure he was safe out in the elements. Reporting live from Ely, this is Tess Keating."

Allyson and Pauline exchanged amazed expressions. "Wow," was all Allyson could get out.

"That's some story," Gary said. "I know I couldn't hack it outside for more than a few hours in that sort of weather."

Brent feigned interest but appeared more intent on watching the subsequent news story.

"Cool," Hannah said. "I always wondered how many nut jobs secretly live in the Boundary Waters. Now we know there's at least one."

"Mmm, a Sasquatch in Minnesota," Pauline said. Her face turned upward with a dreamy expression. "Imagine hauling an injured man all that way through the wilderness in thirty-below weather. He must be some hunk. Superhero material."

Allyson said, "You'd better get those movies so we can get your mind on some *normal* hunky males."

Chapter 7

The next evening, a group of eight women up from the Twin Cities on a quilting retreat came to the Halcyon for dinner and drinks. After their fourth round of white zinfandels and light beers, they insisted on singing karaoke even though the Halcyon didn't own a karaoke machine. They'd gotten rather rowdy for a bunch of middle-aged grandmothers, but Allyson figured they were harmless and let them get their grooves on.

One woman commandeered the ancient electronic keyboard Allyson kept in the small stage area in case one of the bands she often booked to play on weekends needed a spare. She also kept it around, hoping Josh would take an interest in music, something she'd loved as a child but was never allowed to do except for singing in the church choir.

The half-drunk pianist played consistent with her inebriation, and the women who sung were worse. At least the two who tried to dance suggestively, like middle-aged, fully clothed strippers, were too busy busting their moves to add to the painful noise. The quilt club called it a night soon after ten o'clock, but not before running up the biggest bar tab of the week and leaving a generous tip.

Gary had gone home fifteen minutes earlier after preparing the last food order of the night and doing his usual barely adequate cleanup of the kitchen equipment. Brent was mopping the kitchen floor. Hannah was counting her tips at one of the back tables.

Allyson sat at the bar reconciling the receipts for the day when she heard a muffled thud near the front entrance. She looked out the window but saw nothing. She turned back to the receipts but heard another thud a few seconds later. She walked to the door and peered out the window into the snowstorm. Looking down through the window at the front steps, she saw a pair of Sorel-booted feet lying on the concrete entryway.

She opened the door. A man lay flat out on her doorstep, motionless. Her throat tightened and panic coursed through her veins. He wore winter clothing. Longish hair protruded from under his hat, and a frost-coated ski mask covered his face. A backpack and some sort of sled lay a few feet away in the snow.

"Hannah! Brent! Get out here now!" She used her commandant's voice and immediately heard two sets of footsteps rushing up behind her. She knelt. "Sir, are you okay?" She shook his shoulder.

The man grunted in response.

Thank God, he's still alive. "Brent, give me a hand here."

"Yes, ma'am." Brent stepped outside and rolled the man onto his back.

Ice and snow covered most of his face. Brent sat him up, and then he and Allyson helped him to his feet. He stood for a second, then his knees gave out, and he collapsed.

Hannah let out a quick yelp of surprised fear.

"Brent, get his feet," Allyson ordered. "Hannah, take one arm. I'll get the other. Drag him inside."

The trio shuffled him into the foyer of the Halcyon and laid him down. Brent kicked the door shut behind them, but snow blown in from the wind and falling off the man littered the floor.

Allyson knelt. "Sir, can you hear me?" She shook him.

"Diane?" he murmured and opened his eyes to slits. They tried to focus but seemed to object to the relative brightness of the Halcyon compared with the stormy night. He closed them after a moment.

"No, I'm not Diane." Allyson exchanged puzzled glances with Hannah, who knitted her brow and shook her head, indicating she didn't know anyone around here named Diane.

Allyson knew little first aid, but at least she didn't see any blood. "Are you injured, sir? Any broken bones? Frostbite? A concussion?"

The man lay still, his breathing shallow but steady.

"Hannah, bring some warm water. He might be hypothermic."

"I'm on it." Hannah scurried to the kitchen.

"Brent, help me get his outerwear off. We need to see if he's injured."

Brent took the man's boots off while Allyson removed his gloves and hat, then unzipped his jacket. Together they sat him up and worked the jacket off his arms before laying him back down.

"Get a chair cushion for his head, Brent." She gently removed the frosty ski mask, revealing a scraggly beard. His skin was whitish from the cold but had a basecoat of darker brown, indicating he had spent a lot of time outdoors. His cheeks were cracked and reddened. She guessed he worked outdoors for a living.

Brent came back with the cushion. They slid it under the man's head. He mumbled and moaned. She felt his hands and gasped. If he'd stayed outside much longer, it might have been too late to save him.

Allyson faced Brent. "Let's get him over next to the fireplace. We've got to warm him up fast." The man was lighter without his boots and outerwear, and the first part of the haul was over the polished wood floor of the foyer, so they more easily manhandled the stranger over to the fireplace and laid him down in front.

Hannah returned with a tumbler of warm water and knelt beside Allyson, who was rubbing one of the stranger's hands between hers. "Is he going to die?"

"I don't think so," Allyson said. "Brent, hold him upright." As Brent supported the man's torso, Allyson took the man's cheeks between her fingers and squeezed. "Hey, buddy," she said loudly and deliberately, "drink some of this. You need to warm up."

His eyes half-opened and he stared at her, dazed and unaware. He opened his mouth as Allyson put the glass to his lips. He sipped, closed his eyes, and leaned back into Brent's arms. If this stranger indeed was hypothermic, at least he hadn't lost consciousness. But he was close.

"Put him down. He's out of it. You two go find some blankets," Allyson said, then stood. Hannah and Brent hustled off. Allyson turned up the flame in the fireplace. She sat in the nearest chair and stared at the man as he lay motionless. Where the hell had he come from?

Chapter 8

Matt awoke when the sunbeams streaming onto his face became too bright to ignore. He rolled onto his back, opened his eyes, and realized he was indoors, in a real bed, and he was *warm*. He couldn't remember the last time he'd woken up and not been cold. He absorbed the comfort as if he were a sponge.

When he turned his head to study the room, he flinched in surprise.

A foot from his face, a little boy sat on a chair with his elbows on his knees, his chin propped in his hands, staring at him with a child's intensity. Matt half-expected the boy to poke him with a pudgy finger. A mop of straight blond hair and clear blue eyes framed a face most doting grandmothers would describe as *darling*.

"Who the hell are you?" Matt asked in a croaky voice.

The boy's mouth formed an *O* under bugged out eyes. "You swore. I'm telling."

"Sorry, I've had a rough year."

"Oh." The boy furrowed his forehead. "I'm Joshua, but you can call me Josh. Everybody does, 'cept Mama calls me Joshie sometimes. I hate it, but she's my mom, so what can you do, right?" His voice sounded high, reedy, a cross between a clarinet and an oboe. Expressive. Relaxed. Confident. Impressive for a child.

Matt studied Josh's intelligent gaze. "Uh, yeah, moms are like that."

"Who are you?" Josh said with a matter-of-factness that implied a stranger stumbling into his life after a dark and stormy night was commonplace.

Matt tried to remember the final thirty minutes of his journey last night. "Am I in Castle Danger?"

"Yep," Josh said with boastful pride. "Home of the Halcyon Bar and Grill, voted the number one North Shore restaurant by *Minnesota Monthly* magazine." He spoke like a practiced pitchman. "Mama owns the Halcyon. I help her run it."

Matt nodded, despite his confusion. "Got it."

He sat up slowly and began pushing off the bedcovers—several handmade quilts. The room spun, and he became painfully aware of his exhausted state. He sank back down on the bed. Not only was his body spent, he hadn't eaten in ... when had he last eaten? "Are your mom and dad around? I'd like to talk to one of them." He realized he was as parched as a man stranded in the desert. "Also, I'd sure appreciate a big glass of water."

Josh sprang to his feet. "I'll get Mama, then some water." The little ball of energy ran out of the room. "Mama! The popsicle man's awake!"

Matt smiled. Moments later, he heard adult footsteps.

"He wants water too," Josh said. "I'm bringing it for him. And he swore."

"Okay, Joshie. Thanks." The female voice sounded soft, yet strong.

Josh's mom appeared in the doorway, and Matt's head cleared measurably. No older than thirty, she wore gray sweatpants and a maroon-and-gold Minnesota Gophers sweatshirt with the sleeves pushed up to her elbows. She held a screwdriver and a greasy rag. A navy blue bandana covered dark brown hair pulled back in a long ponytail. Dirt smudged her face. A face that, despite her sloppy appearance, exuded sensuality. Yet it also showed a faint wariness. She looked at him with a combination of warmth and suspicion in her tight smile and narrowed eyes.

The conflicting signals confused him. "I guess I have you to thank for saving my life. I owe you big time."

"You're welcome. But it was nothing really." Now her voice sounded flat but edgy. "Everyone around here helps each other." She crossed her arms and analyzed him like an antique dealer trying to decide whether to restore an old piece of junk.

"I didn't mean to fall into your place so late."

"Yeah ... well." Her hesitation and neutral expression implied he'd been a major inconvenience.

Uh-oh. "Look, if it's not okay for me to be here, just point me to the nearest motel."

Josh returned with a glass of water.

"Thanks, Josh." Matt propped himself up on an elbow and drained the full glass with several large gulps while Josh sat cross-legged on the floor, mesmerized by this stranger. Matt couldn't remember the last time a glass of water had tasted so delicious, so energizing. "I'll get my gear and hit the road."

He tried to sit, wavered, then collapsed back onto the bed. His muscles were on strike.

Josh's mom tipped her head back and shook it, obviously annoyed by his lack of mobility. "Just lay there for a while." Her tone was stern and commanding, its softness gone. "I don't open my restaurant for another two hours. You can stay here until then."

"Thank you, ma'am." What was it about her voice that confused him? It contained so many simultaneous nuances and tones, like the individual instruments of a symphony orchestra. Or a virtuoso singer who can sing any part, evoke any emotion.

Matt looked at Josh. "You okay with me hanging out for a while?" He added a conspiratorial wink, hoping to curry some favor with Josh.

Josh's eyes widened. "Heck, yeah."

"Joshie," she said, "I have some adult things to talk over with our guest. Go read your book in your bedroom, okay?"

Josh frowned. "Okay," he said and trudged from the room.

She smiled at her son, then faced Matt. "He seems to like you. I wonder why?"

Matt smiled meekly from under the quilts. "Because I remind him of a teddy bear?"

"More like a real bear—extremely hairy and scary looking."

"Sorry." The only personal grooming he'd done in almost nine months was to hack off as much of his long beard and hair as he could with his hunting knife before he set out for Castle Danger. That way he'd look the part of a regular guy roughing it out in the wilderness for two weeks.

"We gave you a warm bath to thaw you out."

"We?"

"Two of my staff. Don't worry. We closed our eyes."

"Really?"

She gave him a look that was simultaneously disdainful and sexy. "*Pfft.* Of course not. You were nearly frozen." Her tone turned sardonic. "Who worries about nudity at a time like that? We didn't scrub down your private parts, although you certainly need scrubbing ... everywhere." She wrinkled her nose.

"Yeah ... sorry about that. I go *au naturel* in the woods."

"Let's get down to business." She narrowed her gaze to laser-beam status. "Who are you, and why did you almost die on my doorstep last night?"

He avoided her stare. "Matt Johnson." A second later, he glanced back to gauge her reaction to his lie. Her facial muscles tensed a minuscule amount.

He fought to suppress the involuntary rush of blood to his face. Had he hidden his wallet well enough? Throwing it into the woods hadn't been an option because he'd want his relatives to be informed in case he died. He didn't use a fake first name because he didn't trust himself to answer to anything but *Matt* when someone addressed him.

"I'm thru-hiking the Superior Hiking Trail. Doing the whole thing, Grand Portage to Duluth. I was making decent progress until I twisted my ankle up near Lutsen." He locked eyes with her, knowing he'd need to look and sound the part of a free-spirited winter survivalist out for some adventure. He hoped his confident look didn't come across as crazy. "When the blizzard hit, I busted my ass to get someplace warm before I got frostbite. I was damn lucky you were still open last night. It was last night, wasn't it?"

She nodded. "The blizzard closed the roads; otherwise, I would've called an ambulance. We thought you had hypothermia at first because you were nearly unconscious, but I don't believe you were frostbitten."

"I was mainly exhausted. Not much sleep, slogging through deep snow, bum ankle slowing me down. I was cold and numb, but not quite an ice cube."

"Ah, that explains your delusion and disorientation. I figured you weren't going to die, so even though I thought you were frostbitten, I took a chance you wouldn't develop gangrene and start dropping fingers and toes all over my floor."

His empty stomach churned at the thought of his blackened fingers strewn about the floor.

"You've got some nasty scars on your back."

Matt looked away.

"And those two fingers on your left hand must've been torn up pretty bad not too long ago."

Time to end this line of questioning immediately. He shrugged. "Hey, shit happens." He looked back at her, hoping his icy frown would dissuade her from more interrogation.

She glanced quickly over her shoulder at the doorway, then turned and pointed the screwdriver at him. "Please don't swear anywhere near Josh."

"Sorry. It won't happen again. I'm used to talking to myself a lot."

"So you *are* mentally disturbed. You expect me to believe that crazy tale?"

Nine months ago, he had decided self-preservation was paramount. Until he could walk in public without fearing for his life, he'd lie any time he believed it would keep him alive. "I'm just an extreme sports aficionado, pushing my limits and—"

"An aficionado?" She contemplated his word choice with pursed lips. "Why do you have several detailed maps of the Boundary Waters in your gear and no maps of the Superior Hiking Trail?" She folded her arms across her chest and raised her chin.

Damn. Did she know he'd lied about his real name and was playing it cool? If so, why not confront him? "It's not polite to look through someone's personal belongings without permission."

"If you had died, we wanted to see if you had contact information for next of kin. A wife?" She asked the question with a hint of disbelief.

"I'm sorry; Josh didn't tell me your name."

"Allyson Clifford."

"Well then, Allyson Clifford, I'm grateful for your care. Give me another few minutes, and I'll get dressed and split." She seemed too suspicious.

Better to go to a motel or bed-and-breakfast and play his Superior Hiking Trail alibi cleanly from the start.

He'd severely underestimated the energy drain of the daylong ordeal to Olson's with the trapper. One day of rest hadn't sufficed before his fifty-mile walking, skiing, snowshoeing marathon to Castle Danger. Both trips had been made in brutal winter weather and with very little food or rest. He'd traveled from his Solitude Lake encampment in the heart of the Boundary Waters to the North Shore in less than twenty-four hours, hoping to reach civilization at least a day sooner than would seem humanly possible on foot. That way, no one looking for him because of the injured trapper would consider someone that far from Ely to be the rescuer.

"Use the guest bath to take a shower. Down the hall to your left," she said. "There's only one problem with you leaving now, Matt Johnson, Mister Extreme Sports. Highway sixty-one from Two Harbors to Grand Marais is impassable. That means you're stuck here." Her last sentence sounded anything but pleased.

"Last time I checked, snowshoes work just fine in blizzards too."

Surprise registered in her expression for a moment, then switched to comprehension. "Based on your immediate history, do you think that's a good idea?"

Matt considered the wisdom of leaving in such hostile weather. "If I could trouble you for a meal before I leave, that might restore my energy. I'll pay. I've got some cash stowed in my gear." Matt glanced around the bedroom. "Where is it?"

"In the garage." She turned to leave, but stopped and looked over her shoulder at him. "Do you like white bean pheasant chili? That's our lunch special today. We'll have plenty." Her voice softened to a tone that almost sounded friendly.

"Sounds better than the *Boeuf Bourguignon* at *Chez d'Or* in Minneap—"

Her eyebrows flared upward.

Damn. Matt wanted to bite his tongue off for blurting out something so out of character for his jock persona. "I mean, any kind of chili sounds wonderful. I appreciate your kindness."

Allyson's cell phone rang. Her body sagged as if she knew what was coming. She pulled the phone from the pocket of her sweatpants and answered.

"Hi, Gary ... yeah, I figured you'd have trouble ... No, no, stay there, I'll be fine." She hung up and mouthed the word *shit* so Josh wouldn't hear. The look on her face made Matt want to go back out into the blizzard and take his chances with hypothermia.

"Problem?"

"My chef. As I expected, he's snowbound." She sounded frustrated and angry. Her expression was a multiple of those two emotions.

"Sorry to hear that. Maybe it's better for me to leave right now, get out of your hair."

She recoiled a few inches when she appeared to notice her mood and tone, then relaxed her pose. "Sorry, it's not you." Her tone softened. "I've been stressed with other things. A broken furnace here," she raised the screwdriver and rag, "a leaky toilet and late deliveries at the Halcyon. Plus, bad weather makes for hectic days. Locals are too tired from digging out to cook, so a lot of them come in for lunch and the latest gossip. On top of that, I comp all the emergency crews with sandwiches and coffee when we have a crisis, and I stay open as long as they keep coming in. I'll probably be up all night."

So the attractive witch possessed at minimum a small heart. Matt softened his tone as well. "That's very generous of you. I understand. I'll stay out of your way."

She lowered her chin and looked at him through upward slanting eyes. "Will you play Hot Wheels with Josh at least once? That'll be payment enough for a meal." The soft, warm, sensual tone in her voice sounded like low notes on a violin.

A shudder of attraction ran down Matt's spine. "I'd be glad to. Thank you," he said with emphatic sincerity.

"Oh boy," Josh said and dashed down the hallway. The adults smiled at his delight. He'd been lurking in the doorway for several minutes, but hadn't moved or made a sound until now.

Seconds later, Josh returned lugging a suitcase-shaped box with the bright red and yellow flaming Hot Wheels logo printed on the cover. "I keep all my cars in here, Matt. I have twenty-two. Plus a zillion miles of track. The cars go super fast and I set up jumps and loops and sometimes I crash all the cars together and it's a blast. We can use my Secret Super Garage at the Halcyon to park 'em, then take 'em out one at a time and see which one goes the farthest off the jump."

"Secret Super Garage? Wow, Josh, you're a real aficionado."

"A fishin' what?" Josh's blank look was expected. Allyson's fight to suppress a smile was not.

"Ask your mom what it means." Matt shot a disdainful look at Allyson.

She forced seriousness back into her expression. "Joshie, Mr. Johnson needs to clean up first. But I have an important job for you. Stay here until he's showered and dressed, then bring him over to the Halcyon."

Josh's eyes brightened. "Okay. Can I play—"

"*May* I," Allyson corrected.

Josh looked at Matt and gave him a Moms-always-have-to-correct-your-words-don't-they look. "May I play Hot Wheels while he gets ready?"

Matt gave him another conspiratorial wink.

In that condescending tone only a mother can pull off, Allyson said, "Yes, you may."

"Thanks, Mama." He disappeared down the hallway with rapid-fire footsteps.

Fully awake now, Matt contemplated Allyson's attractiveness despite her grubby handywoman look. Her baggy clothes hid a trim hourglass figure. Notwithstanding that he hadn't seen a woman in nine months, he easily imagined that when dressed up for an evening out, she would look stunning. With her high cheekbones, wide-set eyes, long legs, and makeup, she might pass for a movie star.

He struggled to sit up, taking care to keep his lower body covered. He hoped to maintain his equilibrium by focusing on her eyes, but he noticed she wouldn't meet his gaze. She glanced in several directions, more than once focusing on his bare chest.

After an awkward moment of silence, she looked at her feet and said, "Yeah, well, I'd better get back to my furnace."

Chapter 9

Two thousand miles away in a spacious office near Beverly Hills, California, Donnie Vossler sat in his leather executive chair, thinking fast, hoping he'd find some magic words to close this sale. The asshole customer, haggling over a measly one hundred bucks on a ten-thousand-dollar deal, was acting all macho, like he wanted Donnie to cave so he could act like a hero in front of his woman—a butt ugly shrew if he'd ever seen one, with a sour face and dumpy figure.

"Don't forget, Mr. Stein, I already threw in the extra six months on the warranty. The Blue Book value is right here in black and white. I'm a grand under that, and she's got five thousand fewer miles than average. Plus, it's a BMW, for goodness' sake."

What the Steins didn't know was that a month ago, the car had been in a flood. Because of that, most of the electronics went into spasms of irrational activity once the car had been driven for more than thirty minutes. Of course, their two test drives, on different days, had lasted less than fifteen minutes each.

"Well, I don't know...." Stein was probably recalculating the numbers in his tiny brain. His expression was one of a bad actor trying to look thoughtful.

Donnie assumed the man's brain was tiny because his head was so small. Only a pair of black horn-rimmed glasses added any width to his countenance. Stein looked at his wife for assurance, agreement, some sign.

Surprised to be called upon for an opinion, Mrs. Stein sank farther into her chair. She smiled meekly, like someone who'd always trusted her man to handle the *man jobs* such as buying automobiles or mowing the lawn.

"I like the color. And we deserve a BMW. Everyone else we know owns a fancy car. It's time we got one too."

Donnie locked eyes with Stein and pasted on his I-know-when-I've-been-out-negotiated smile. "I tell you what. I don't want a paltry one hundred dollars to be a deal breaker, so I'll come down to your price. What do you say?" *Crunch time. Don't blink now or I lose. He can't claim I screwed him if I agree to his final offer.*

Stein's eyes darted back and forth, up and down.

Donnie's eyes began to water, but he held steady. All that angst over a five-year-old BMW. *Yeah, right, that'll impress your moron friends.*

Stein looked once more at his wife, who gave him the tiniest of nods. He sighed and faced Donnie. "Okay. Deal."

Donnie beamed at his two victims as if they had just made the wisest purchase of their lives. "You drive a hard bargain, Walter. May I call you Walter now?" He thrust his right hand across his desk.

Stein nodded. "Sure." They shook hands.

"My assistant will handle the paperwork. It'll only take a few minutes. You two get yourself a couple of lattes in the lounge. I'll make sure the Beamer is in cherry condition inside and out before you drive her away."

He led the couple out his door, clapping his new best buddy Walter on the back and smiling so charmingly at Mrs. Stein that, for a second, he thought she might swoon. He rarely had trouble closing a deal when a woman was involved. So many women customers had flirted with him over the years, even bedded him, that his good looks were a foregone conclusion.

"Thank you for doing business with Vossler Motors. You'll be glad you did." The Steins already looked as though they believed him.

Donnie walked toward the service area, computing the profit on this sale in his head. He'd make an extra two thousand since he'd paid that much less for the car because of the flood damage. That detail wouldn't come back to bite him in the ass when the Steins discovered their little electrical problem and complained because the extra warranty he'd thrown in covered drivetrain only, not body condition or electronics.

As he reached the service bay, his cell phone rang. He pulled it out but didn't recognize the number. *Let 'em wait.* "Hey, Miguel, get the topaz blue Beamer prettied up for its new owners."

Miguel was a short, solid Hispanic from East Los Angeles who possessed a gift for fixing up any car you put in front of him just well enough to fool naïve customers into thinking the vehicle was in perfect condition. He looked up from behind the counter and broke into a shark's grin—sharp, ruthless, deadly. "You da man, boss."

Donnie responded with a fist pump. Some days, this job was way too easy.

Chapter 10

When Matt heard Allyson descend the basement stairs, he rose and hobbled into the guest bathroom, wincing with every step on his twisted ankle and holding a pillow in front of his bare private parts in case Josh was within sight. He closed the bathroom door, turned, dropped the pillow, and was confronted by the first mirror image of himself he'd seen in nine months. He flinched and caught a sharp breath.

The soft, doughy body of a professional musician and teacher had been transformed into the physique of the *after* picture for a weight loss and exercise program advertisement: rock hard abdomen, bulging biceps and triceps, no flabby bicycle tire around his midsection, firm leg muscles.

Matt hadn't thought his daily routine was anything special. He merely did what he needed to do to survive. Almost daily he chopped and sawed firewood, gathered branches and kindling, hunted or fished, set snares for small game, bushwhacked through the woods and marshes to forage for edible plants, canoed on Solitude and a few neighboring lakes, and built and weatherproofed his shelter before winter's onset. To cool off, ease his sore muscles, and add some variety to his routine, he swam daily until late September.

In addition, his diet had radically changed. No doughnuts and coffee for breakfast. No burgers and fries for lunch and dinner. No high-fat, high-sugar, low-nutrition food. And no more nightly glass or two of wine, or drinks before, during, and after a gig.

Other than a few indulgences he'd borrowed from Olson's Outfitters, he ate mostly fish, lean game such as venison and rabbit, morel mushrooms, blueberries, and other berries in season, and some edible greens such as dandelions and fiddlehead ferns. When fall arrived, he survived on stored dried berries, meat, and fish; the frozen deer's carcass he'd providentially found and hoisted into a nearby tree before the wolves had arrived; and a crude version of pemmican he'd vaguely remembered how to make from his Boy Scout days.

Now he understood Allyson's surreptitious glances at his bare chest. He smiled confidently at his reflection. Not since college had any girl or woman looked at his body that lustfully.

After a hot shower and a grooming session for his long, scraggly hair and beard, Matt dressed and went into the main part of the house to find Josh. His legs were still shaky, but he was damned if he would be a burden to Allyson Clifford. He might only be able to walk to the next building in town, but he wouldn't put up with her venting upon him or her personal and business problems.

He heard rolling noises on a hard floor and peered into the kitchen.

Josh had set up some Hot Wheels track and was playing with a car in each hand.

"Where's my gear, Josh? I need to take inventory."

"I'll show you." Josh grabbed his hand and led him into the attached garage.

His gear sat against the back wall. "Help me get this into the light. I need to find my money."

"Okay." Josh grabbed the largest portage pack by one strap and pulled as hard as he could, leaning almost parallel to the floor in an attempt to drag it into the kitchen.

"Let's haul together, buddy." Matt grabbed the other strap and pretended to strain as hard as Josh against the weight as they moved the pack into the sunlit part of the room. Josh's eyes lit up when he giggled at Matt for acting so silly.

While Josh watched with fascination, Matt unstrapped the pack. He removed what amounted to the essence of his life. Those things he used to survive every day: compact cook stove, fuel, matches, first aid kit, mess kit, sleeping bag and pad, tent, tarp, ax, hatchet, folding saw, water filtration system, and other small necessities. Everything but his Glock 17. Matt panicked for a moment but then realized he'd been carrying it in a pocket of his parka.

He stood and went to the hooks on the wall where the Cliffords' winter coats hung. He found his parka, patted down the pockets, but found nothing.

He spun around to face Josh. "Were you looking in my parka this morning?"

Josh gave him a blank expression. "No. Why?"

Matt fumbled through the pockets again. Had Allyson found his weapon? "I'm looking for something that wasn't in my gear."

"I didn't play with anything," Josh said.

Matt sat down and rechecked his gear. Maybe he'd forgotten and buried his only weapon deep in his clothes bag.

"What's wrong with your hand?" Josh pointed to Matt's left hand and leaned in to get a closer look. "Those fingers are bent funny."

Matt instinctively clenched his fist to hide his injury and tried to sound matter-of-fact. "I damaged a tendon."

"Oh. What's a tendon?"

"It's a stretchy cord that connects your muscles to your bones. If the cord is cut, the doctor sews it back together, but it's shorter and doesn't let your fingers move normally."

"Oh. How did your tendon get cut?"

"On some broken glass."

"Oh. Does it hurt?"

"It's just stiff." He wiggled the fingers of both hands. The two injured fingers only had about half their normal range of motion. "See?"

"Oh." Josh returned his attention to handling everything Matt pulled from his pack. He examined some items as if they were from another planet.

Matt pulled out the last item in the pack, a waterproof bag that contained his spare clothes, wallet, and a few other items. No Glock. His wallet was exactly where he'd left it, buttoned inside a shirt pocket. If Allyson had found his wallet and learned his identity, she'd replaced it well enough that he couldn't be sure she'd tampered with it.

Matt sat back and opened his wallet. He hadn't started with a lot of money, but didn't think he'd spent much over the past nine months, either. He'd bought most of his gear before going into the Boundary Waters. Then he'd turned to surreptitiously borrowing from Ferdie Olson's Outfitters for food to augment his hunting kills and expendable items like propane tanks for his cook stove.

He fanned the meager pile of bills like a hand of playing cards and dropped his chin to his chest. He'd need to stay at least one more night indoors, but even the cheapest motel room in town would use a sizeable chunk. He should've realized he'd need a sizeable sum of cash to pay rent, buy food, get some new clothes, and start looking for a job.

"Whatsa matter, Matt?" Josh seemed eager to console his new friend.

Matt smiled and tousled Josh's hair. "Just a little cash flow problem. Do you suppose there's an odd job I can do for your mother?"

"Most of our jobs are pretty normal."

Matt chuckled. "No, I don't mean weird jobs. An odd job is a job that anybody can do, especially if the person who normally does it is too busy or is absent for some reason."

"Ohhh." Josh seemed pleased by all the new words and phrases he was learning. "I'll ask Mama if you can clean my room or take out the trash. Those are my jobs, but I always wish I was too busy to do them. That's why I play with my Hot Wheels. Makes me look busy."

Matt stifled another chuckle. "I don't think I should do your jobs. I'll talk to your mom. If there's nothing to do, I guess I'll go hungry for a day or two. No big deal."

Josh's mouth opened. "You mean you don't have enough money for food?"

Matt waved his tiny wad of cash. "I'll buy a bag of beef jerky and some fruit. I can make that last for several days."

Josh's lips quivered, and his voice turned to a whimper. "That's not fair … you were in the blizzard … maybe some of your money blew away."

Matt patted Josh's shoulder. "I'll be fine." Inside, he was far from sure he'd be fine. "Let's go to the Halcyon."

"Okay." Josh seemed to regain his composure. They donned their winter clothing, and Josh led him on the short walk to the back door of the Halcyon Bar and Grill through deep, fresh snow in the blue sky and frigid cold. As they entered and removed their jackets and caps, the warm aromas of cooking food caused Matt to salivate.

Allyson turned when she heard them stomping their boots on the floor. She appraised Matt as if he were a male beauty contestant. "You clean up decent." Then she frowned. "Not sure the mustache combined with the stubble is your best look, but hey, we just met. Maybe you have the kind of face that grows on people."

She sounded sarcastic, but Matt caught a brief flare of attraction in her eyes. He suppressed a smile.

"Mama," Josh said in a woeful tone, "Matt's poor, but I don't want him to go hungry. Can I buy him some food with my money?"

Josh's offer caught Matt off guard. His face flared hot.

The look on Allyson's face showed it was all she could do to not scoop Josh into her arms and smother him with hugs and kisses for being so compassionate. But there was more, an intensity that implied Josh was special in another way. Represented a significant time in her past? Reminded her of a memory? Or a bad memory? Why was he getting these insights? He was baffled by the new talent for perception he seemed to possess, at least when it came to Allyson Clifford. He dismissed it as his imagination being in overdrive now that he was interacting with people after nine months of isolation.

Before she could speak, Matt jumped in. "That's okay, Josh. I can get more money later, but it'll take time since I think my credit card has expired."

Josh nodded. "Oh. Okay." The crisis was over in his mind, and he bounced out of the kitchen toward the dining room.

He lowered his voice and confronted Allyson. "Did you find a pistol in my parka last night?"

Her look changed to indignation. "You didn't expect me to leave it around for Josh to find, did you? Do you know how much damage an eight-year-old could do with a seventeen-shot Glock?"

"Sorry, I wasn't expecting to meet any kids on my trip."

"I hid it out of his reach. I'll give it back when you go."

"Fair enough." Matt would feel naked until he got his weapon back. "You're familiar with handguns?"

"I'm no expert, but I've taken a gun safety class and done some target shooting."

That fact helped him realize he needed to proceed with caution around her in case she got angry and pulled his own weapon on him. "Is that why you trusted me alone with your son, because you had my weapon and would shoot me if I tried anything funny?"

She gave him a haughty look. "Yep. Besides, in your condition, I figured Josh could've overpowered you all by himself."

Touché. He still felt barely strong enough to move, let alone harm a little boy in any way. He turned his thoughts back to fixing his money woes. "I *am* a little short on cash, but I'm willing to work for a meal, maybe two. I'm weaker than I thought, so I reconsidered leaving today. Since we're snowed in, I figured I'd find a cheap room, rest up a day, then move on."

"I see."

"I'm happy to do anything for you to help out—shovel snow, haul firewood, wash the floors. Just name it."

She contemplated his offer. "Can you cook?"

That was the last question he expected, yet he could see she wasn't joking. "I cook for myself all the time."

"I don't mean boiling water for a meal in a bag or gutting a fish and cooking it on a stick over a campfire. I mean—"

Here we go again. "I know what you mean." He tightened his tone but kept his face relaxed. "Being a bachelor with a low tolerance for rubber pizza and lukewarm Chinese takeout forced me to make my own dinners occasionally. I'm self-taught, but I can follow a gourmet recipe and get it right the first time."

"Very impressive, Mister Extreme Sports." She eased the tension in her voice. "Our cuisine is gourmet comfort food—dishes everyone connects with their mother or grandmother. We use the best ingredients, simply but perfectly prepared. My twist is amped up ingredients: ground elk, lamb, or veal instead of ground beef, artisanal cheeses, morel and shiitake mushrooms, fresh caught lake trout and walleye, pretzel rolls or brioche, organics and local whenever possible. Can you grill a decent steak or burger, cook al dente pasta, construct a respectable sandwich, and work fast if you need to?"

Matt considered her request. "I can't guarantee the fast part. Most of the time, I cook with a glass of wine in one hand while I chat with my guests."

Allyson sighed. "I don't have the luxury of giving you a tryout. If you're willing to do exactly what I say, I'll feed you and pay you minimum wage until Gary can get down here. If the highway is cleared by tonight, the plows should clear the road up to his place a few hours later. Maybe by tomorrow morning. Is it a deal?"

"Not so fast." He wanted her to dangle. Partly to piss her off. Partly to pay her back for her cool welcome. Partly to maintain his self-respect. He didn't want to grovel.

She put her hands on her hips and gave him a wary, bemused look. "What?"

"When we first met, I felt lucky you didn't sweep me out with last night's trash. All of a sudden, you're desperate to keep me. That tells me your stranded cook is a bigger deal than you let on earlier." He stared her down.

She lowered her head. "Yes. He's an alcoholic pothead, but he's brilliant. We've become a destination restaurant in addition to our travel business and town regulars." She re-engaged his eyes. "I can't match his speed. If we get extra busy, maybe the two of us can cook as fast as one tortured genius."

"So you're not just feeling sorry for me and throwing me a charity bone?"

"No. I really need a cook for the day."

"I see." He felt sorry for her—just a little. Her situation was similar to the days when he had to hire someone to sub for him on a gig because a better gig came up for him. He wanted to make sure the sub was competent so the bandleader would keep his trust in Matt. "You've got yourself a deal."

She smiled tightly, as if not enthused at all, and extended her right hand.

Matt shook her hand. Her soft, warm touch supercharged his body. He beat down an involuntary shudder of pleasure. *Easy, Matt, it's just a woman's hand.* After a mind-clearing deep breath, he said, "Show me what to do," without sounding like a crush-stricken fourteen-year-old.

Chapter 11

When his cell phone rang again, Donnie was in his office signing off on the paperwork for the Stein deal. Caller ID showed it was the same unknown number he'd ignored earlier. He answered just before the sixth ring, which is when his voice mail would have kicked in. He wanted to give his callers the impression he was in no hurry to talk.

"Vossler. Who's calling?"

"I got something big for you, Vossler, but it's gonna cost."

The voice sounded like someone Donnie should know, but he couldn't place it. "Why don't you tell me who the fuck you are and how you got this number?"

"I need to know if you're interested first. You and I didn't part on the best of terms the last time we met."

"Okay, I'm interested. You got thirty seconds to hook me."

"You sittin' down? What I'm gonna say might knock you on your ass."

Donnie looked at the ceiling with frustration. This guy was a fucking drama queen. "Look pal, I don't shake easily. Spill it already, or I hang up."

"Alright, alright." The caller paused.

Donnie felt a burst of annoyance. *Quit stalling, damn it.*

"I found your wife."

Donnie's jaw dropped simultaneously with his phone hand. His face flushed and his insides boiled. That *was* one of the few statements capable of knocking him on his ass. He inhaled a slow, calming breath.

"Who am I talking to?"

"Bobby Galvin. My boss at the Black Opal did a lot of business with you back in the day. Said you ran a first-rate operation."

The Black Opal? Shit, that was when he was flying so high he never thought he'd touch the ground.

"He rewarded me once with her ... Susannah." Galvin spoke the name with lustful reverence.

Hearing her name again brought long-suppressed rage rising from Donnie's feet to his brain as if he were being lowered into a vat of boiling oil. "Where is the bitch?" He could barely spit out the words without screaming into the phone.

"That's where my finder's fee comes in, Vossler. I figured this would be kinda important to you."

"Finder's fee? What the hell, you want money for this information?"

"Damn straight."

Not surprised, but also not wanting to queer this negotiation, he resisted the urge to tell Galvin where he could shove it. "Give me a number."

"Ten large."

Donnie gripped his phone so tight he thought it might snap into pieces. A sour taste built in his mouth. He swallowed with difficulty. "Too funny. Finding the bitch ain't worth a tenth of that."

"I beg to differ," Galvin said, trying to sound erudite but not succeeding.

Vague memories of Galvin came back to Donnie. This guy was second-class muscle for some small-time casino owner in Las Vegas. He was one of the mooks who stood around looking tough while—what was his name? Carter? Yeah, Vince Carter—sat in his office and pretended he was Bugsy Segal. Galvin occasionally roughed up a client who was too violent with Carter's women, or a gambler who hadn't brought enough cash to cover his inevitable debts.

Galvin might be telling the truth but asking for ten thousand dollars right off the bat showed he had no clue what information was worth to men like Donnie. "Sorry, Galvin, I might go a couple thou, but you'd have to bring her to me yourself before I give you ten."

Silence for a moment. Then Galvin spoke. "What am I, stupid? I bring her to you; that's kidnapping. She ain't worth jail time. Seven."

Donnie stifled his annoyance with a deep breath. "Look, we both know you'll be ecstatic with four, so let's just call that the magic number, okay?"

A pause. "Deal."

"Smart boy. I still know a few wise guys in Vegas, so if you're fucking with me, I'll make sure you're hurt bad. Understand?"

"This is legit. I swear."

Yeah, like the word of a two-bit thug means more than a gift-wrapped sack of dog shit. "How do you want to work this? I ain't giving you dollar one until I see her myself, in person."

"I figured that. I wouldn't have called if I didn't have rock-solid proof."

"What kind of proof?"

"Give me your email address."

"What the hell for?"

"I got art."

"In English?"

"I snapped a picture of her with my cell phone when she wasn't looking."

Donnie sat forward in his chair, incredulous. His pulse sped up at the prospect of seeing an image of his wife. Mixed emotions flooded to the surface in a burst of heat on his skin. He'd actually loved her once. She was the mother of his beautiful son. However, she'd also caused him unbearable pain when she'd kidnapped the boy.

He gave Galvin his email address and called up his email account on his desktop computer. His voice trembled. "This better be good."

"The light was low, but the photo's not blurry at all." Galvin paused. "Okay, it's sent."

"How'd you find her, anyway?"

"Funniest thing. This mulyak I know owns a place in Minnesota. Says the ice fishing is great. Plus, he owes me for a deal I did for him. I go up there, but the fishing sucks, not even enough for a decent meal. So we head into this local joint to warm up our asses. Great chow, a decent band. The place was rockin', considering we were in the middle of Boringville."

"I checked my email. No picture yet." Donnie studied the framed photo on his desk of his wife and young son, taken more than five years ago, wondering what they both looked like now.

"It's comin', honest. Takes a while sometimes." Galvin cleared his throat. "So anyway, I toss back a few and all of a sudden, the hot babe tending bar starts to look familiar. I ask her if she's ever been to Las Vegas. She plays cool and denies it, but she looks a little nervous. Then it clicks in my brain. Susannah. I think of you, pull out my phone, and when she's not looking, click."

Donnie checked his email again. "It's here. Hold on." He opened the email and clicked on the attached jpeg file. The thumbnail image of a young woman appeared. He enlarged the image and sat back in his chair as a tidal wave of old memories assaulted his brain. This woman's lips were thinner. She might've had a nose job. Her hair was shorter and darker—not a trace of blonde—but it was her. *Damn, she's still smoking hot. Maybe sexier than ever, if that was possible.*

"Fuckin' A, Galvin, you got something here."

"Told ya."

Donnie could almost hear the man smiling through the phone. "I assume your fee is for disclosing her location."

"You assume correct. But to show you what a nice guy I am, I'll throw in her new name, no charge, after you commit to the deal. Save you some time."

"Jesus. Sounds like you're running for Pope."

"You had a sweet gig going until she fucked things up for you. Call it a favor."

"I call it you trying to get an easy payday."

"Sometimes information is more valuable than product. Word on the street is she took your kid a few years ago, and you want him back. I figure if that's true, it's worth some serious cash from you. This may be the only chance you get to get him back."

Vossler reached for the framed photo on his desk, a little boy posed angelically by a studio photographer. *How long has it been, son?* "I ain't paying until I get up there and confirm. She's had some plastic surgery. The photo might be airbrushed. This could be one big scam."

"I thought about that, and I figured you'd go for a middleman holding your dough until you confirm she's your woman."

"Gotta be someone we both trust."

"How about my boss, Vince Carter?"

Donnie mulled it over. Carter wasn't stupid enough to conspire with Galvin on a penny-ante swindle like this. Carter had a rep to maintain, but he also knew Carter trusted him and wouldn't take sides either way. "You think he'd go for it?"

"I checked with him this morning. When I said 'Susannah,' he jumped all over the idea. I think he's hot to do more business with you if she's involved."

"Okay. How's this? I give him my word I'll pay if you're playing straight with me. Then after I see her myself, I send him the dough, and he pays you. But if you're fucking with me, he offs you, because why would he want to keep a fucking liar on his payroll, right?"

Another pause. Then a nervous-sounding Galvin said, "I swear on St. Patrick's shillelagh, this is on the level."

"I'll let your boss confirm it for me."

"You won't be sorry, Vossler."

I'd better not be. Donnie hung up and dialed the Black Opal Hotel and Casino.

Chapter 12

Matt learned the lay of the Halcyon's kitchen from Allyson as she briefed him on the dishes he'd have to prepare. The kitchen had an open design so the kitchen staff could see the dining area from the kitchen's large pass-through window. Conversely, the diners could see whoever occupied the kitchen; even watch their meal being prepared if they stood next to the stainless steel order counter.

Four booths lined the glass wall overlooking Lake Superior. Six movable tables and a ten-stool granite-topped bar completed the seating. Four taupe leather easy chairs with cocktail tables between them formed a semi-circle around the bar side of the central fireplace wall. One corner served as a stage for small musical groups. Decorated in a modern rustic style with an earth tone palette of colors accented with polished maple trim, the Halcyon exuded cozy and warm, with a spectacular daytime view.

Allyson explained the lunch business might suffer because of the waning blizzard. A few brave or foolish souls with four-wheel-drive vehicles might crawl through the drifts on Highway 61 and stop for a meal, but business wouldn't return to normal until the roads were plowed. However, more locals and emergency responders stopping in would offset that.

Hannah and Brent lived in town, so they'd walked to work. Allyson officially introduced them to Matt. He got an instant positive vibe about both young people. Everyone immediately set to work preparing for the open. Matt drifted into the kitchen to await his virgin order and discreetly size up his new boss.

When the first customers came in, a couple in their forties, Allyson greeted them with a cheery, "Welcome to the Halcyon. I'm so glad you found your way in through the snowdrifts. Old George sure is good about plowing the sidewalks, isn't he?" Her tone was sugar and spice, mellifluous, self-assured. She sounded genuinely pleased they chose her restaurant. Nothing like what Matt had heard during his brief conversations with her.

As they sat, she asked, "What can I get you to start? Coffee, tea, something stronger?"

"Coffee," the couple said in unison.

"Coming right up, two of the best coffees on the North Shore." She smiled, put a gentle hand on the man's shoulder, and left.

The woman eyed her suspiciously.

When Allyson returned with two cups and a coffee carafe and set them on the table, she addressed the woman as she poured. "Is this gentleman showing you a good time up here, hon? A pretty woman like you deserves nothing but the best." This new, more intimate voice was mellow, fluid, like a solo on a vintage Gibson Les Paul guitar played by a jazz master.

The woman, who Matt thought looked rather plain, beamed. "So far, so good. He picked the most romantic bed-and-breakfast for us."

"You must be staying at the Shoreline Inn."

The woman nodded, surprised. "How'd you know?"

Allyson waved a hand. "Sandy's the best. All the rave reviews are spot on. She doesn't let any guest go home with less than a stellar experience."

"I'll vouch for that," the man said.

Allyson acknowledged him with a quick glance. "Did the blizzard make things more romantic last night?" She winked knowingly at the woman.

The woman flashed a look at her man. "It sure did."

He blushed and smiled.

"I could tell," Allyson said. "Look at the menus, and Hannah here will do her best to keep you two satisfied. Gotta keep your energy up, right?" She smiled at both, but this time patted the woman's shoulder. Hannah presented the menus and began reciting the specials.

Allyson was fascinating to watch in action. She seemed to be a natural restaurateur. But as she walked back to the kitchen, her genuine smile flattened into a tight, thin line. "I know you're new, but you aren't here to eavesdrop until an order comes in. Check that fryer oil. The temperature has to be exactly three hundred seventy-five degrees. And we never have enough sliced onions. You can do two or three before Hannah comes back with her order." She veered off to the bar, leaving Matt chastised at her sudden change in temperament and voice, from mellow jazz to edgy rock.

Hannah came back a minute later with her order and stuck it onto a clip on the order wire. "French dip with fries and a spinach salad, chicken breast sandwich with apple-fennel slaw and rings." She chewed a large wad of gum and watched Matt for confirmation that he understood.

"Dip, fries, salad, chick sand, slaw, rings, got it." He tried to sound experienced and confident.

Hannah looked at him as if he were trying too hard, then gave him a perfectly executed skyward eye roll and exaggerated a chew of her gum.

Matt set to work, as nervous as he'd ever felt for a music audition. Allyson wasn't going to cut him any slack. *It's just like cooking at home only with bigger toys to play with, right?* He put a large potato through the fry slicer. Presto. An order of fries was now ready to dunk in the hot peanut oil—another of the Halcyon's secrets, he guessed. He started on the rest of the order, and a moment later, noticed Allyson watching him from the bar. It wasn't merely the look of a supervisor watching a new employee. She also looked at him the way a woman looks at a man, sizing up his potential. Matt's cheeks warmed, and the knife in his hand slipped, nearly slicing off a fingertip.

As the lunch hour progressed, Matt decided his growing physical attraction for her was not wise. He'd been alone so long he was afraid he'd do something stupid such as allow his emotions to hinder his survival instincts. Until he'd found a job, a place to live, then somehow obtained a new identity, his best course of action was to avoid all amorous temptations and remain alert. He mentally prepared to hit the road after finishing this shift and getting a hot meal.

Chapter 13

The lunch rush was over. They served fifteen meals between eleven and two, along with a handful of coffee and sandwich comps for the road crews and emergency personnel. "Actually decent for a blizzard," Allyson said as she prepared four Halcyon burgers, one of the signature items on the menu. Now that they all could relax, Allyson's demeanor changed to that of a beautiful, charming hostess entertaining guests in her home kitchen. Matt was impressed by how quickly she could change her outward persona.

When the burgers were ready, Allyson served them to Hannah, Brent, and Matt. They all sat at a back table with a view of the front door in case a customer wandered in. Josh had eaten a peanut butter sandwich along with an apple and was now busily running his Hot Wheels cars in and out of his Secret Super Garage, the far-left booth against the windows, humming a surprisingly melodic made up song. The kid might be a budding musician.

Matt had turned down a pre-lunch offer of white bean pheasant chili since he wasn't sure his stomach could handle something that corrosive after months of bland food. While in the wilderness, he'd trapped or hunted numerous small animals for food—squirrels, rabbits, ruffed grouse, as well as his one frozen deer—supplemented by fish, along with dried berries and nuts he'd harvested last summer and fall. Exotic but bland since he had no seasonings except salt and pepper borrowed from Ferdie Olson.

Matt bit into his Halcyon burger and stopped after a few chews. It was the best hamburger he could remember eating. Juicy, intense meat flavor along with a beguiling scent of herbs and spices, the center layer a heavenly slice of an indefinable cheese. Something in the blue family, so subtle and earthy that it complemented the meat to perfection. The combinations were as intricate and perfectly meshed as a contrapuntal theme and variations by Bach. He let out a long, low moan as he chewed and swallowed.

The others exchanged knowing glances.

Brent said, "Pretty good, huh?"

"This tastes incredible," Matt said after swallowing his second bite. "It's way too good to be called a burger."

Allyson leaned back in her chair and sipped a club soda. "Gary's recipe. He uses ground elk."

"Even the bun is off the charts," Matt said.

"It's a pretzel roll," Hannah said, "toasted with truffle oil."

"Wow." Matt took another bite, chewed deliberately, savored the flavors. "This is magic. Like Port, Stilton, and walnuts; lobster and Chablis; mussels and Pernod."

Allyson's eyebrows lifted. "Listen to you, the gourmand. You do extreme sports and know fine food?"

Damn. He'd blurted out too much again. Any hint of his past could botch his alibi. "I had rich friends who liked gourmet food and invited me to fancy restaurants with them for laughs."

"I'll bet," Allyson said. A flirtatious smile curled her lips, but she didn't press him further.

They'd nearly finished their meals when the front door opened. A man wearing a uniform cap and jacket walked in with a distressed look on his face.

Allyson stood and walked toward him. "Hi, can I help you?"

The man sounded more distressed than he looked. "My bus slid off the road trying to turn off the highway. I got a busload of senior citizens who aren't too mobile. Can you help me get them from the bus to here?"

"You were driving in this mess?" Allyson said in disbelief.

"Yeah, I know. Stupid of me, but we're already behind schedule. We were supposed to get up to the Grand Portage Casino this afternoon. The old folks get mad when they can't play their damn slot machines. The leader offered me an extra hundred bucks if I got 'em there by dinner. Looks like that ain't gonna happen." He frowned and looked at the others for sympathy.

Allyson took charge. "Brent, you and Matt get out there and help the folks inside. Hannah, get some coffee started." She turned to the bus driver. "How many passengers?"

"Forty-two."

"Okay. Hannah, after you start the coffee, set up enough places with napkins and silverware for everyone." She asked the driver, "Is anyone hurt or distressed in any way?"

"No. Some of the ladies were scared, but we didn't roll over. A few might have trouble getting out of the bus."

"Joshie?" Allyson called.

"Yes, Mama?" he replied from the coatroom.

"I need your help. Put on your busboy apron."

"Oh boy!" Rapid-fire footsteps preceded Josh's appearance in the dining room. He streaked into the kitchen and came out with his apron in his hand.

"Do whatever Brent tells you," Allyson said.

"I will." Josh looked expectantly at Brent.

Brent's smile was as big as Josh's. "Clear the dishwasher." He probably enjoyed the rare times he had an assistant. "I'll return in a few minutes."

As Josh darted off to the kitchen, Matt and Brent donned their outer-wear and headed to the bus with the driver in Allyson's Suburban.

Allyson turned her attention to feeding forty-three people at once. No small feat since her average dinner crowd numbered only fifty or so for an entire evening. Four hours later, the seniors had been fed and warmed up. The bus driver called his boss, who told him the bus couldn't be dug out until a large enough tow truck arrived from Duluth the next morning.

The senior citizens were a genial lot once they realized the gambling part of their trip wouldn't happen until tomorrow. They enjoyed the adventure of being marooned in a blizzard. The drinkers in the bunch migrated to the bar, where they drank a surprising amount of beer, wine, and liquor.

After the last meal had been brought to table, Allyson made a few quick phone calls to the proprietors of the two local motels and three bed-and-breakfast houses. They assured her there was enough room for all.

She went to the front of the fireplace facing the dining room and announced to the diners. "Ladies and gentlemen, we've found rooms for everyone in town tonight as long as some of you are willing to double up. And to thank you for your patience for our slow service because of your unexpected appearance, I'm giving everyone a ten percent discount on your meals tonight."

This elicited several appreciative *Oohs* from the patrons.

"And if you come back on your way home, I'll give everyone twenty percent off your food order ..."

This elicited several boisterous cheers.

"... as long as the group leader calls me first so we can bring in extra help."

The group laughed and applauded at their fortune.

Allyson offered the bus driver the use of her Suburban to shuttle passengers to the lodgings, and the crowd slowly thinned out.

As the last customers were escorted to a motel and the regular dinner crowd—a few couples who'd braved the storm—finished their dessert and coffee, Matt felt drained of energy. He wished he could sleep in a warm bed again, but was sure of his decision to leave Castle Danger tonight. Gary would return to work tomorrow, so Matt wouldn't leave Allyson shorthanded.

Allyson seemed to be a truly generous person despite their initial friction. He knew restaurant profit margins were tight, so twenty percent off an entire evening's worth of food charges probably meant Allyson would take a loss if the group returned. She'd probably only net a small profit tonight despite the nearly full house. The hoped-for payoff would be great word-of-mouth advertising.

As he watched her and worked with her throughout the evening, his physical urges kept crawling to the front of his mind. He hadn't slept with a woman in a long time—more than a year if he remembered the correct month of his last brief fling. The more he studied Allyson, the more he realized how stunning she was. She hid it well, not wearing overtly sexy clothing or using excessive makeup, but her sensual aura captivated him. Even though he'd picked up a vibe of attraction from her as well, he worried he'd make a complete fool of himself if he acted on his feelings.

When all the customers were gone, Allyson and Hannah came toward him as he chatted with Brent in the kitchen.

Hannah held out a small pile of cash. "Here," she said, "your share of the tips tonight." She smiled and glanced at Allyson, then gave a larger pile to Brent.

"The old folks were *very* appreciative of us feeding them on short notice and especially liked the discount," Hannah said. "One table left a hundred-dollar tip." She was clearly pleased with herself. "You deserve something for getting the meals out so fast under pressure."

He accepted the cash and counted it. Almost one hundred dollars. His bankroll had more than doubled. He looked at Hannah. "Thanks."

"You did well, Matt." Allyson offered her hand. "Thank you."

He shook her hand with reluctance. He got the same jolt he experienced the first time they'd touched. *Yep, definitely time to leave.* "Glad to help, and thanks again for saving me last night. But I'm moving on as soon as you close."

Allyson's mouth dropped open. "Tonight? In this weather? Mister Extreme Sports rides again?"

He shook his head. "Doesn't matter day or night with this weather. Cold is cold. I feel much better now that I've been indoors for a day. I've got a headlamp, so dark isn't a problem."

The bewilderment in her eyes pained Matt and confirmed his suspicion that she was attracted to him. "Are you sure?" she asked with a tinge of doubt. "You can stay in my guest room again since all the rooms in town are taken tonight."

"Yeah, I'm sure." He looked at her without making eye contact, afraid he wouldn't be able to leave if he made a personal connection.

They finished closing the restaurant in silence. Josh was asleep on one of the booth benches. He'd worked hard for an eight-year-old. Allyson had apparently trained her son well in the basics of bussing tables, and Josh appeared to love working with the adults and acting cute and cuddly for the oldsters. When he wasn't helping Brent, Josh had stayed in the kitchen and "helped" Matt, as well as talked nearly non-stop about his life, friends, school, and Hot Wheels. But he'd never hindered Matt from working, which struck Matt as incredibly mature for an eight-year-old boy and completely endearing.

Matt knelt next to the sleeping boy and stroked his hair.

Allyson glanced at Josh, then back at Matt. "He'll miss you. He hasn't been this energized about anyone in a long time."

"Sorry," was all Matt could say, sad that he'd made such a positive impression on Josh but wouldn't be around to develop their friendship.

"Will you carry him home for me? I hate to wake him."

"Gladly." Matt helped Allyson put Josh's jacket on him and picked up the sleeping bundle.

Josh woke long enough to realize Matt was carrying him, then wrapped his arms tightly around Matt's neck.

Matt's heart fluttered and warmed. *Is this how it feels to be a father?*

At the house, Matt put Josh down on his bed. He retrieved his gear from the garage, loaded his makeshift sled, and shouldered his pack.

Allyson had gone inside for a moment and was reentering the garage. She held out her hand. In it was Matt's Glock. "You might need this." She held his gaze as he took it from her. "Last chance for a warm bed tonight." It came out almost as a question.

"No. Best for me to go." He put his pistol into the front chest pocket of his parka. "Even one day in the same place seems like a long time. Maybe I'll come back some day. Buy another Halcyon burger."

She forced a wan smile. "Where are you going?"

"South. I'll go down sixty-one until I find an access road to the Superior Hiking Trail."

She nodded, pursed her lips, fidgeted with her hands. "Well then. Good luck. Stay safe."

They stood in awkward silence. Matt wanted to say more, but wasn't sure what.

She noticed his hesitation but reached for the garage door opener button. "Might as well go out this way. Easier with snowshoes."

He strapped them on, tethered his ski pole harness to his waist, and trudged down her driveway to Halcyon Road, where he turned toward Highway 61.

Ten minutes later, as he neared the intersection of Main Street and the highway, Matt heard an engine and saw headlights reflecting off the waning snowflakes. He edged toward the side of the road to allow the vehicle to pass.

When it stopped next to him, he stopped and turned to face the vehicle, a Chevy Suburban. The window rolled down, and Allyson's face appeared, grim but hesitant.

"If you're offering me a ride, you're crazy. I'm safer walking."

She shook her head. "I'm not offering you a ride. I'm offering you a job."

Stunned, he needed a moment to process the situation. "Ahh, Gary, right?"

She nodded. "He just called. This storm is the last straw. His girlfriend got sick of winter and talked him into moving to Phoenix with her. He plans to get a job as a sous chef. Then he'll save up some money, get some backers, and open his own place in a low-rent neighborhood."

"Why me? I'm sure you'll find someone more qualified."

"Gary's leaving tomorrow. No two-week notice, no nothing. I need someone immediately. Just until I can hire an experienced chef."

He shifted his weight and stared south down the highway. The vow he'd taken at Solitude Lake to stop helping others was fresh in his mind. The urge to keep going was powerful. Yet some force deep inside kept him from moving. His mother's spirit? He looked at Allyson.

Clearly uncomfortable, she held his gaze with resolve. "Please."

The way she said *please* touched his core. He stared upward, letting a few snowflakes drop onto his face. He desperately wanted not to care, but his resolve to look out for himself above all others flagged. With no chef and business likely to return to normal tomorrow after the highways were plowed, Allyson stood to take a major hit, perhaps enough to shut her down. Helping her would only delay his plans for a few weeks at most.

Matt looked back at the Suburban. The open window framed her face. She did a convincing impression of puppy dog eyes.

He sagged with resignation. "Two weeks max."

Allyson closed her eyes as relief washed over her face. "Thank you."

Chapter 14

Long after closing time the next day, Matt locked the back door of the Halcyon and trudged toward Allyson's house a block away. The modest three-bedroom, two-bathroom rambler had been included in her deal to buy the Halcyon. Allyson had generously offered him the guest room free of charge as long as he agreed to play Hot Wheels with Josh each day. He'd stayed late under the pretense of doing some serious grease removal in the kitchen. In truth, he needed time alone to reconsider his decision to stay and help her until she could hire a new chef. If he left, all she'd risk were some lost profits. If he stayed, he'd risk his freedom.

He was in danger only if Allyson knew his real last name. If so, and she made the connection to the deaths last spring, she might call the authorities. Or she could mention his real last name to someone else who'd make the connection. Almost to her driveway, he still hadn't decided, so he headed for the path that ran from the back of the house to Lake Superior. Maybe the dull whoosh of the waves would help him think.

The path—a well-worn trail used by Allyson and Josh for access to the Lake—wound around her house and down a gradual slope to the rocky beach. When he reached the head of the trail behind the house, he noticed a light from one room illuminating the snow-covered path. Turning right, he headed across the entire length of the building. When he drew even with the lit room, he glanced over, saw movement through a sheer curtain, and stopped.

Allyson stood in her bedroom. Naked. Drying herself with a towel.

Shocked, he turned away, walked another step, and stopped. Torn between leaving and staying, Matt's libido won, and he stayed. He rationalized he wasn't spying on her because she was the one who'd left her shade up.

He glanced around to make sure no one else was in the vicinity. Being busted for voyeurism and, by extension, the crimes from last year for which he was wanted, would've been a monumental blunder. He saw no one and turned back to look at her. The soft-white ceiling light gave her skin a golden hue. Her limbs, especially her legs, seemed longer without clothing.

She was applying lotion to her arms. Oil, perhaps, since he noticed a luminous shine on her skin. After finishing her arms, she raised her left leg, put her foot on the bed, and squirted a generous handful of oil onto her taut thigh. She rubbed the oil into her flesh, working deliberately from buttock to thigh to knee to calf, even rubbing oil into her foot. After straightening and switching legs, she repeated the procedure. She took extra time massaging a particular spot on her right gluteus maximus, which caused him no small amount of sensual anguish as her hands kneaded the generous but firm hip.

Matt had enjoyed the pleasures of sex with several women in his life and experienced his share of fantasies and debauchery, but this ... *Whew*. He'd never witnessed anything so simply, purely erotic. Knowing he was an inadvertent voyeur, and she was oblivious to his presence, made the moment over-the-top hot. His thoughts were confirmed by his growing erection. He realized he'd been holding his breath all this time and exhaled with a shiver.

Done oiling her legs, she straightened and rubbed oil into her neck, down her chest, then massaged some into each breast.

He gulped and shifted his position, growing more uncomfortably aroused by the second.

Then she froze, with a hand on each breast, her head up, as if she'd heard a noise.

Matt first thought an intruder was breaking into her house.

She looked toward the door to her room, then slid her hands to her shoulders, forming an *X* across her chest.

Statue still, sensing rather than moving, she reminded him of a deer trying to detect a wolf on the hunt. After an interminable moment, she looked toward the window, lips parted, eyes peering into the blackness. Initially, he thought she could see him, but he stood well beyond the weak beam of light thrown off by the ceiling fixture.

He was certain she'd pull the shade down, certain her woman's intuition had warned her to act more modestly. Even in tiny Castle Danger, on the edge of town, with no other houses within a quarter mile, somebody could be watching her. She either was uninhibited or had seen no one walking the path in the years she'd lived in the house, and didn't think it necessary to pull her shades.

After licking her lips and giving her head a small toss to flick wet hair off her face, she resumed oiling her breasts, tilting her head back to expose her neck, massaging harder, squeezing, applying more oil. Never had a woman so completely mesmerized him. Finished massaging her breasts, she did a final all over rub, making sure she hadn't missed a bit of skin before walking to the door and snapping off the ceiling light. The faint glow of a bedside lamp remained. She pulled the covers back, climbed into bed, and disappeared from view.

He sucked in a long, shaky breath and resumed his walk to the Lake, not wanting to arouse her suspicion by entering the house so soon after her unwitting show. The sensual urban soul of a Sonny Rollins tenor sax solo echoed in his head. He'd been looking forward to sleeping long and hard tonight. Now all he'd be capable of was replaying this scene in his memory a few dozen times.

Chapter 15

The bus from downtown Duluth to the West End was thirty minutes late thanks to the heavy snow, which added to Ben Nowitzki's steadily worsening day. His car was still in the shop, necessitating one more day of public transportation. He'd missed most of his favorite TV show, *Jeopardy*. He was already in a foul mood despite having won his small claims court case against a client who'd stiffed him. The client was a no-show in court, but Ben had little hope of collecting from an unemployed husband who'd hired him to track his wife for a week to see if she was cheating on him.

Ben clomped down the bus steps onto the sidewalk, slipped on some snow-covered ice, and landed hard on his ass. Wincing, he slammed the ground with his fists, partly in anger, partly to mask the sharp pain in his tailbone and low back. "Fucking great," he said through clenched teeth. Not only was he never going to be paid for a week's work, but he might also have an emergency room bill added to his steadily growing debt. He rolled over onto his knees and slowly climbed to a standing position. His entire lower abdominal area throbbed with pain, but at least he hadn't aggravated his sciatica ... yet.

He limped home and arrived a few minutes later at his duplex two blocks off Grand Avenue. The Nowitzki family had owned the two-story, 1920s Craftsman-style double bungalow since before Ben and his two older sisters—who had left long ago for warmer climates—were born back in the 1970s. Ben's father had died from a heart attack ten years ago. His mother had left the house to him when she passed away from a stroke two years ago.

Of course Ben had been grief stricken by his mother's death, but his second strongest emotion was annoyance. He became the property owner and now had to do his mother's work of keeping the upstairs unit rented and maintained. Luckily, he'd found a long-term renter last year, a widow with four cats who worked nights as a registered nurse. She was quiet, paid her rent on time, and kept her unit spotlessly clean. If Ben ever managed to attract a woman enough to get her to come over to his place, he was considering making a deal with Nurse Mary to lower her rent in exchange for cleaning his house the day before any hot dates.

Ben cleared snow from his sign—Nowitzki Detective Agency—and gingerly navigated the icy front steps of the porch. Once inside, he stomped snow from his shoes, brushed off his polyester winter jacket, and tossed his gloves and keys on the small occasional table near the front door.

After hanging up his jacket and retrieving a can of Busch Light from the refrigerator, Ben checked his single phone message. A voice he didn't recognize said, "I want to hire you, and I'll pay you well for your services. The work may be dangerous. If you're interested in hearing the details, be near your phone tomorrow at ten a.m. I will call then."

Ben checked caller ID for the incoming number. Blocked. "Fucking teenage pranks." He deleted the message and went to the living room to watch the last few minutes of *Jeopardy*. He sipped his beer while sitting in his BarcaLounger waiting for the commercials to finish. The final *Jeopardy* answer under the category *19th-Century British Literature* was "This famous character said, 'I ought to be thy Adam, but I am rather the fallen angel ...'"

Immediately, Ben said, "Pfft. Who is Frankenstein's Creature?" He tossed back the rest of his beer and crushed the can in his hand. "How 'bout a hard one next time?"

Chapter 16

The Halcyon was closed on Mondays. Matt was glad for the break after completing his first week of work. Physically, working in a kitchen was effortless compared to surviving in the wilderness in freezing temperatures with few tools or comforts. Mentally, he was exhausted, mainly from dealing with people again. Even the background noise level of a busy restaurant disconcerted him because he was so used to absolute silence. The cacophony had sounded like an amateur orchestra tuning up before a performance.

Allyson had mentioned she did paperwork there most Monday mornings, and he was welcome to use the kitchen to make breakfast for himself. As he walked in the Halcyon's back door, he headed for the coffee machine.

She noticed him through the open door of her office and came out to greet him. "Any coffee left?" She smiled, seemed relaxed.

"Yeah, still looks hot." He refilled the cup she held out and poured one for himself. "Judging from your smiley mood, can I infer my culinary skills justified my hiring?"

"Hardly. That was my at-least-I-can-afford-to-keep-you-one-more-day smile."

"Good to know. I'll tell my resume service they have one more day to embellish mine."

She opened her mouth to no doubt fire a wisecrack at him when a knock came at the front door.

"Be there in a second," Matt called out automatically, as if he were at his own home and expecting the visitor. He started toward the door and said over his shoulder, "You expecting someone?"

"No." Her expression turned cautious. "Wait." She crept to a side window and peeked out from behind the curtain. Her mouth dropped open, and she inhaled sharply, almost a gasp. One hand went to her lower abdomen as if she'd felt a sharp pain.

He tensed.

She returned to the bar and motioned him back toward the kitchen. "Don't answer." Her voice was a tight whisper.

"But they know someone's here."

"Shit." She glanced around as if looking for an escape route.

"What's wrong?"

"Just tell him I'm in Duluth for the day getting supplies. If he asks about Josh, don't say anything." The look in her eye was one of a mother bear ready to protect her cub at all costs. "Whatever you do, do not let him inside." Panic crept into her voice.

"Allyson—"

She waved her hand downward in a dismissive gesture and started back to her office. "Get rid of him," she said with a hint of desperation.

Confused, he shrugged and went to the door, now worried the visitor might try to charge past him into the Halcyon.

A dark-clad figure, blurred from the frost on the window, bounced up and down, toe-to-heel, presumably in reaction to the icy wind and near-zero temperature.

Matt cracked the door open enough to clearly see the stranger clearly. A tall, good-looking man with thick dark hair, wearing all black and underdressed for the weather in a leather coat, thin gloves, and no hat, shivered with a cold-induced grimace on his face.

"We're closed," Matt said. He pointed to the sign in the window that gave the Halcyon's hours of operation.

The man glanced from side to side, seeming nervous. "I'm not here to eat. I'm looking for Allyson Clifford."

The man's voice had a sinister edge—a rumbling string bass tinged with ominous, low-register bassoon. *Trust no one.* "Allyson's in Duluth all day buying supplies. What do you want?"

The man smiled—charming, but with a twinge of cynical or cocky. As if he knew he could use that charm to get what he wanted from someone. "It's personal." Then his expression became suspicious. "Why are you here if the place is closed today?"

"I work here. Just minding the store."

"You got a name?"

Matt crossed his arms and stood tall in the doorway. "You first."

The man turned away, then back, then raised his hands, palms up, and refocused on Matt. "Hey, I'm freezing my ass off out here. What happened to Minnesota Nice? I just want to know when Allyson will return, but you can't even invite me inside to tell me?"

"Maybe I'm not from Minnesota. You don't look like you're from here either. More like a guy who got lost on his way to someplace a thousand miles south of here." Matt stepped back and started to close the door.

The visitor's eyes lit up with anger. "Look, pal, I only want to talk to her. Why you making this a federal case?"

"Next time, call first." Matt slammed the door and made a show of engaging the handle lock and the deadbolt. Something about this guy chilled him to his toes. He was trouble. Maybe not trouble for him, but trouble for Allyson.

The man shook his head, incredulous that he'd just gotten a door slammed in his face, and walked away. Matt memorized the license plate number of the man's vehicle—a red, late model, full-size Cadillac SUV—before he drove away. It might come in handy for confirming this guy's real identity if that became necessary. His stomach churned as he returned to the bar. He was about to sit down when Allyson appeared from her office.

She looked as if her world had crashed around her. So small, helpless, shoulders slumped, disbelief in her half-open mouth, desperation in her eyes, which glistened with tears.

Matt's heart rose into his throat. "What's wrong? Who was that guy?"

She went to the front window and watched the red SUV turn onto Highway 61 and head toward downtown.

He went to her and started to put his hand on her shoulder, but was stopped by conflict in his mind between caring about someone and his vow to look out for himself first and stay out of everyone else's business. He'd already lied for her. Even that was too much involvement. He pulled his hand back but tilted his head, trying to engage her eyes. He lowered his voice and said as soothingly as he could, "You can talk to me."

Without warning, she stormed to the coatroom and put on her coat and gloves, a pink stocking cap, and a pair of large sunglasses.

"Where are you going?"

"To get Josh."

"Is he sick? Can I help?"

She vigorously shook her head. "This is my problem. Just stay here. If he comes back, don't let him in. Don't even talk to him."

"Why the panic? Do you want me to call the police? You look like you're afraid for your life." This time, he stuck out his arm to stop her, daring to touch her shoulder, forcing down the pangs of attraction that surged up his arm to his brain.

They both froze for a moment.

She wrenched away. "I don't have time to explain." She went outside, got into her Suburban, and sped off.

Chapter 17

After hanging around the Halcyon all afternoon waiting for Allyson to return, Matt gave up, locked the place, and walked toward Castle Danger's compact downtown for an early dinner. The only other places to eat were a coffee shop that closed at two p.m. and a McDonald's on the west side, just off Highway 61. The town seemed spookily quiet on a mid-winter Monday, even though the handful of cars and pedestrians seemed like a huge crowd compared to the solitude of the Boundary Waters.

By the time he'd finished his brisk one-mile walk to McDonald's, twilight had become night. As he walked through the parking lot, he noticed the black-clad man who'd stopped by the Halcyon sitting in a booth next to a window.

A teenaged boy sat across from the man, listening intently. He wore a black leather biker jacket over a white t-shirt. His long brown hair was cut in a punk style, one side six inches longer than the other side and hiding half his face.

Both of them glanced around the restaurant as if to make sure no one was watching. Then the man removed a small white packet from his coat pocket. He held the packet with his right palm facing the window so the restaurant patrons wouldn't see it, but it was clearly visible to Matt.

The kid reached out. They shook hands. The kid palmed the white packet and slipped it into his pocket. The man made an emphatic gesture with his forefinger as they spoke for a few seconds. The kid got up and left.

Sparks of anger roiled Matt's brain. He was more surprised than shocked that kids had easy access to drugs, even in this remote area. If the man was a drug dealer, Matt understood why Allyson wanted to avoid him. But was that the only reason for her fearful reaction?

The familiar aroma of McDonald's overpowered Matt's senses when he entered, not as pleasant as he'd remembered. He'd only eaten at the Halcyon since his return to civilization, but his craving for fast food had gotten the better of him. He preferred McDonald's thin and crispy fries to the Halcyon's thicker, home-style cut. He placed his order, then glanced over his shoulder at the man, who sipped a cup of coffee.

When their eyes met, a look of recognition combined with irritation came over the man's face. Matt's order was called, and he turned away to get his food. He went to the table farthest away from the man but sat so he could see everyone in the dining room as well as the counter help and doors.

A moment later, after he sampled his burger, shake, and fries, he looked up to see the man standing next to him. He stopped in mid-chew.

"We meet again." The man now spoke in a confident, pleasant voice that was easy on the ear. Different from his tone this morning. "But hey, small town, happens a lot. Right?"

Matt swallowed. "I suppose." He took another bite of his burger and studied the man for a moment. He seemed the nervous type, shifting his stance, eyes darting up and down, left and right. Taller and a bit heavier than Matt, his smile was disarming, but Matt remained wary because of Allyson's reaction earlier at the Halcyon.

"We got off on the wrong foot this morning, pal. I didn't mean any harm, just wanted to say hi to Allyson. She's an old friend."

"Really?"

"I'm Donnie Vossler."

Even the man's name sounded slimy. Donnie? Not Don or Donald? *Donnie* made it sound as though he assumed everyone was his close friend—or wanted to be his close friend.

Vossler extended his right hand.

Matt checked for a packet of white powder in Vossler's palm. Nothing, but he didn't extend his hand. "Matt."

"Just Matt?"

"For now."

"No offense, Matt, but you ain't the most sociable guy I ever met."

"None taken."

Matt had felt nothing but suspicion during their morning encounter and did so now too. Vossler looked like a glad-hander or a scumbag, someone who told lies for a living or operated in the gray areas of business.

"Can you tell me when I can connect with Allyson? I'd sure like to say hi before I go home."

"Where's home?"

"L.A."

It figured. Paradise for every kind of hustler known to man. Matt had played dozens of gigs in L.A. back in the day and recorded a few albums as a sideman. He couldn't wait to escape all the phony, backstabbing, social-climbing sycophants who haunted the entertainment business. People looking to hit it rich one way or the other without doing any real work.

"Where're you from, Matt?"

"Nowhere special like L.A."

Vossler puckered his face into a frown. "You sound like someone who ain't too eager for people to know much about you."

"Just people I don't know well enough to trust."

Vossler spread his arms in a pleading manner. "Hey, I'm a friend of Allyson's. Ain't that enough trust?"

"I hardly know her. I only work for her."

"How long?"

"Not long enough to trust her."

They stared at each other for a moment, then Matt took a slow, deliberate bite of his burger.

Vossler's expression darkened, and he sat down across from Matt. "Look, I don't have a lot of time, but I hope you can help me connect with her. I'm gonna level with you, so you know I'm legit."

Matt raised his eyebrows in a mock-impressed attitude. "I'm listening."

Vossler reached into his leather jacket and pulled out a four-by-six photo. "Her name ain't Allyson Clifford."

"Is that so?"

Vossler slid the photo across the table. "Her real name is Susan Vossler."

Matt studied the picture. Vossler and a woman stood on an ocean beach. She resembled a younger version of Allyson, maybe a sister. Close enough to be her. He subdued his surprise but couldn't fight down the surge of uneasiness pushing up from his gut. He'd stumbled into the Halcyon by chance a few days ago, started to build a fragile new life, and was rewarded with the claim that his employer also appeared to be someone else. Assuming Vossler was telling the truth, Matt now had more reason not to trust Allyson.

With great difficulty, Matt maintained an impassive expression. "Your sister?"

"My wife."

Matt sat back as if he'd been buffeted by a massive gust of wind. Allyson's panicked reaction this morning loomed in his mind's eye. Vossler seemed amused by his reaction. He smiled cynically. "You didn't really think a woman as hot as Allyson would be fair game now, did you?"

"Why'd you say you were an old friend?"

"Just being careful in case she was shacking up with some other dude. Didn't want him to go ballistic on her or me for no reason."

"I suppose not." If Vossler was her husband, it would be easier for Matt to suppress any romantic interest he might have developed for her and easier to leave after she hired a new chef. But since friction existed between the couple, Matt didn't feel right about leaving Allyson alone to fend off Vossler, either. As long as she didn't think he was trying to drive the couple apart, he'd offer to help her if she asked.

"I heard she was living here. I had some business in Duluth. Took a side trip up here. I wanted to see if there's a chance we can reconcile. I've changed. You tell her I've changed."

Changed like reformed or changed like a chameleon?

"On top of that," Vossler said, "we've got a son, Josh. You ever see her with an eight-year-old boy?"

Damn. Whatever Matt said would force him to take sides. Vossler seemed to be doing the honorable thing, trying to put his family back together.

"Do you have a picture of your son?"

Vossler appeared more annoyed, but he reached into his wallet, pulled out a snapshot, and tossed it onto the table.

The boy in the picture resembled Josh but was much younger.

"Back when he was three," Vossler said. "He might look a little different now. It's been five years. Seems like forever to me. Too long to be without a father. A boy needs his father in his life more than anything these days, don't you think?"

Matt thought of what a train wreck his relationship with his father had been after his mom had died. "Yeah, I suppose that's important." If Josh had been three years old when Allyson—or Susan—took him away, he probably had only some vague recollections of his father.

"Between you and me," Vossler's tone took on a dark, bitter edge, "Sue wasn't the greatest mother in the world." He leaned over the table. "She had problems."

What Matt had seen of Allyson and Josh together showed a loving, caring mother and an adoring son who seemed well adjusted, happy, and bright. Warning bells clanged in his head. "What sort of problems?"

"Just problems. You got kids, Matt?" Now Vossler was evasive.

"Do you have a picture of them together?"

Vossler glanced away, scowling, then looked back at Matt. "Why're you asking all these questions?" He kept his voice low enough to keep the conversation private. "I know she's here. If she's here, Josh is here."

Matt crossed his arms and lowered his chin. "You roll into town with this crazy story and expect me to believe everything you say. Maybe you're running some sort of fraud. Maybe Allyson only resembles your wife?"

Vossler spoke through clenched teeth. "All I'm asking is if you've seen her with my son."

Decision time. Chance had stuck him here with Vossler at this moment, and he couldn't rewind the past several hours to before Vossler showed up. The voice took over that had spoken to him daily for nine months in the wilderness when he'd relived the nightmare of last spring. *Stay out of other people's lives. Don't get involved.* But one part of his mind objected. Allyson was a beautiful, intelligent, successful woman with an adorable son—the kind of son he'd love to have someday. Once he got to know her better, she might be a woman for whom he'd willingly fight.

Vossler continued staring at him like a bull eyeing a matador behind a red cape.

Matt studied his fries. Why should he care about the Vosslers? The guy was trying to put his family back together. Still, Vossler seemed like trouble—trouble with which he wanted no part. "Maybe."

"Why only maybe?"

"Five years is a long time. She's got a kid, but I won't swear to you he's the one in the picture."

"Fair enough," Vossler said with a smug smile. "When you see Sue ... I mean, Allyson, tell her I'll come to the Halcyon tomorrow to see her and Josh. I got my shit together now. Business is good. No more debt. We need to be a family again. Josh has been apart from me way too long."

Vossler stood and left, leaving Matt to sulk. How could a man have changed for the better if he apparently dealt drugs to strangers? Matt finished his meal and hiked to the gas station on the corner, looking for a pay phone, and was directed to Marge's General Store. He presumed Marge greeted him since she was the only one working. She certainly looked like a Marge: middle-aged, cheery face, doughy physique, perhaps a youngish grandmother. She pointed him to the phone on the back wall.

The store was smaller than most convenience stores but stocked floor to ceiling with an impressive variety of goods, reminiscent of an old-fashioned five-and-dime store. He worked his way down the narrow aisles, then checked around to make sure no customers loitered nearby. He placed his call and tried to calm his roiling nerves while scanning the store for possible eavesdroppers.

A young male voice answered. "Hello?"

"Zach, this is Matt."

After a pause, Zach Perez said in a tight, covered voice, "*Madre Dios.* I thought you were dead. How are you? Where are you?"

"Still alive and free. That's why I called. I was hiding until recently. I'm back to civilization. What have you heard since I disappeared?"

"Oh, man, it was weird for a while. All those deaths hit the paper in a day or two. People were going crazy. Thought some serial killer was on the loose."

Taken aback for an instant, Matt laughed at the idea that anyone might believe he was capable of psychotic, murderous behavior. "Are you one hundred percent sure you erased all traces of your connection to that Millennium Four data?"

"You kidding? I couldn't erase it fast enough." Mild irritation laced his voice. "Then I smashed the hard drive and tossed the whole computer into the Mississippi River late one night."

"Good. I guess if no one's connected us in nine months, you're safe. I should've thought things through better, but I was exhausted and scared out of my wits."

"Me too," Zach said with a somber chill in his voice. "I still get nightmares. Bad ones."

Matt winced, anguished at what he'd done to Zach's life last April. He'd enlisted the computer genius in Minneapolis to help an old friend save her farm from foreclosure, but accidentally uncovered a massive real estate conspiracy masterminded by real estate tycoon Leland Smythe and aided by a group of associates calling themselves Millennium Four.

Their goal was to coerce, swindle, or steal farmland from families living along Interstate Highway 35, the major north-south corridor through the heart of America. Millennium Four believed a transcontinental superhighway built by the Federal government along that corridor was inevitable. They were trying to snatch up prime real estate from unsuspecting landowners at fire-sale prices and eventually resell it to the feds at grossly inflated, sweetheart-deal prices. Smythe alone stood to make billions of dollars. The scheme and all its fallout were so unbelievable, Matt still occasionally thought he'd dreamed the whole thing.

Matt had been shot at, injured his hand from flying glass in a staged house explosion, and been the target of a hit-and-run. Zach sustained a broken leg after he pushed Matt out of the car's path at the last second. Not long after that, Matt had pretended he was going to shoot the poor boy to fool Smythe into trusting Matt so he could somehow stop Smythe. That ploy hadn't worked. He and Zach barely escaped with their lives. Guards at Smythe's estate had shot at them as they fled. That had sent Matt on the run and probably messed up the young computer genius forever. Another casualty, just not a death.

"I get nightmares too," Matt said. "I dream I somehow outrun the bullet and shield her with my body. But then it still goes through me and kills her." He felt a small bit of relief that he could talk to Zach about their shared hell.

Matt had fired the shot that killed his ex-wife, Diane Blake, but that bullet was intended for Steven Crossley—Smythe's co-conspirator and the governor's chief of staff. However, Matt had killed Crossley with his second shot. In Matt's mind, it was self-defense. Crossley, an abusive bastard if there ever was one, had kidnapped Diane, driven her car to Duluth, and attempted to kill Matt before he could expose Millennium Four.

"I talked to a hacker friend after you split," Zach said. "He likes to snoop on law enforcement emails. The police checked Smythe's security tapes at his office building. They ID'd you the day you went to see him."

Matt put his hand to his forehead and squeezed his temples, unable to ease the sudden pounding in his brain.

"When it came out you'd been married to Diane, the guano hit the rotating blades big time. The media think you killed her and Crossley in a lover's revenge thing. Smythe slithered out of any suspicion of ordering Crossley to kill you. He also downplayed any connection he and Crossley had as normal political business dealings."

Matt leaned against the wall to keep from sinking to the floor in a heap. "I'm probably on everyone's ten-most-wanted list." Smythe's story was a gigantic pile of bullshit, barely plausible, but juicy enough for the media to jump all over it.

"Things have died down in the last few months because you did such a great disappearing act, but I'm pretty sure every cop in the state is driving around with a picture of you in his squad car."

"Do you still believe me?" Matt asked. If he ended up in jail, Zach was the only person still alive who could corroborate the conspiracy and testify on his behalf.

"Your disappearance didn't look so good," Zach said. "I know you explained why you pretended you were going to kill me to get close enough to stop Smythe. And I guess I buy that, but it was a crazy thing to do. Maybe you went loco and killed Diane and Crossley because you were crazy, not because you were trying to stop Millennium Four."

"The thing is," Matt said, "if I turn myself in, I don't see how I stand any chance of staying out of prison. No evidence can be corroborated. If I had pressed charges, we never would've gotten them convicted. They were too smart."

"Man, if I were you, I'd move to another country. You won't stay alive more than a few months any other way."

"Thanks for the advice. I'm good in the short run. I found a small town, quiet, out of the way. I doubt many cops will snoop around this neighborhood anytime soon."

"I hope you're right. But information travels at the speed of electrons now. Someone takes a cell phone video or pic with you in the background, it gets on YouTube or Facebook, and before you know it, some cop surfing the web recognizes you."

"Nah, I'm safe. Got a mustache now."

"Funny dude."

"Hey, gotta keep my sense of humor, right? That's all I've got left."

"Yeah."

"I need one favor. That's why I called."

The silence on Zach's end whooshed in Matt's ear. He imagined Zach clicking his computer mouse rapid-fire, one of his nervous habits.

Zach said, "What?" with dread in his tone.

"Check on someone for me. Donnie or Donald Vossler. Says he lives in Los Angeles. I need to know if he's got a criminal record or any sort of checkered history."

"Oh, is that all?" Zach said, the sarcasm dripping through the phone line.

"I've got his license plate number too. Probably a rental. If not, he might live in Minnesota, and the L.A. story is a lie."

"I dunno, dude. After our Don Quixote act last year, I quit the hacking business."

"Zach ... I ... it's important. Vossler came to town today, and he's already passing out drugs like Halloween candy. He claims he's in a custody fight with his estranged wife over their son. I just want to make sure the kid's going to be okay. He doesn't need to get mixed up with someone like Vossler."

More hesitation hung over the connection before Zach said, "You had to say the magic word—kid."

"Thanks. I owe you one."

"You mean one more."

"Right." Matt gave him the license plate data, then asked, "You still in school?"

"Graduating this spring. Double major. Computer Engineering and Computer Science."

"Your folks must be proud."

"I guess. They still think it could all vanish in a moment, like a dream." A pause indicated Zach wanted to say something else. All he said was, "I gotta go, amigo. Watch your ass."

"You too."

Chapter 18

Ben sat shivering at the old wooden desk in his closet-sized office, sipping the last of his morning coffee while doing triage on his bills. Number One: phone bill. Referrals generated most of his meager business. Number Two: utilities. Weather forecasters had accurately predicted—so far—the coldest, snowiest winter in decades, and it was only January. He'd already turned down the thermostat as much as he dared and not risk frozen pipes. As the stack of six other late bills stared back at him, he sagged into his chair and massaged his eyes with both hands.

The phone rang. He slowly lowered his hands and sighed. Another bill collector? He picked up and tried to mask his weariness. "Nowitzki Detective Agency."

"I'm glad my offer piqued your interest, Mr. Nowitzki," said the caller from yesterday's message. He glanced at the clock and immediately perked up. One minute past ten.

"How do I know this isn't some lame teenage prank?" Ben said, not ready to get his hopes up for this possible windfall assignment.

"Simple. I don't participate in ... pranks. This is a legitimate offer. Although, I should think a man in your financial situation would even entertain business offers from teen pranksters."

Ben was unnerved that this man knew about his dire financial straits. Then he realized anyone who looked him up and drove past his house could guess he wasn't working in corporate espionage or spying on wealthy Duluth socialites for their jealous husbands.

"Okay, let's say you're legit. Anyone who offers me an exorbitant fee out of the blue sounds crazy. How do I know you'll pay?"

After a pause, the caller said, "I'm sorry. I seem to have wasted your time. I'm looking for someone with a blunt and singular focus, someone looking for a challenge, someone not afraid of a little danger. I apparently overestimated you. Good—"

"Hold on," Ben said, too eagerly. "I'll hear you out. I'm suspicious by nature. Makes for an investigator."

"Very well then. But let's make one thing clear. If by the end of this conversation, you haven't convinced me I'm hiring the right man for this job, I'll take my business elsewhere. Understood?"

Ben's neck went hot. "Understood. But you understand this. If by the end of this conversation, you haven't convinced me I'm not risking my life to verify your nutcase hunch that aliens abducted your wife and impregnated her with Martian sperm to start a new race of beings, I'll hang up."

To Ben's surprise, the man chuckled. "That's the attitude I wanted to hear. Your reputation, no matter how tarnished, still follows you."

Now Ben was intrigued. This guy had done his research. Ben had been a rising star in the Minneapolis Police Department, partly for his outstanding detective work, but in large part due to his ability to cut through bullshit with nearly everyone—victims, criminals, his police bosses, citizens, even the local politicians. The combination of keen intellect, brilliant analytical skill, and a sharp tongue made for quick success and quotable sound bites for reporters who covered his crime solving.

He was primed for a fast-track career until he'd busted the wrong politician for the wrong crime. The crime, soliciting a homosexual prostitute, was a career-breaker for the politician, the wealthy son of a prominent Minnesota family. He'd offered Ben a healthy six-figure sum to avoid arrest. Several years pay on a detective's salary.

Ben had never imagined being tempted by any amount of money to break the law, but he'd never imagined being bribed by a millionaire, either. He had intended to invest the windfall and build a nest egg. Then he could retire early and lie on a beach some place warm where his biggest worry would be what to eat for dinner rather than if he would get shot at today.

Unfortunately, the male prostitute was later arrested for a different solicitation and squealed on the politician, which led to the discovery of the bribe. Because the family of the wayward politician was so powerful and well-connected, the patriarch imposed on the governor to intervene and cover up both the solicitation and the bribe. Disgraced, but grateful he hadn't been charged and convicted of a felony, Ben had escaped with a quiet resignation and the loss of his accrued pension. He had crawled back to Duluth, obtained his private investigator's license, and started over.

"What's the job?" Ben said.

"I want you to find a man wanted by the police for multiple homicides. They seem to have given up on the search for him. Recent news events lead me to believe he has been forced out of hiding."

"News events?" Ben racked his memory for news items he'd seen or heard lately that had anything to do with a wanted criminal.

"Yes," the man said. "Before I give you the details, I want to know if you'll accept the job. Discretion is paramount, and if you decline, I want the man I hire to know he'll have no competition from someone trying to cherry pick this case."

"How about you start by telling me who you are?"

"You may call me Mr. Jones."

"I didn't ask what I can call you. I asked who you are."

"I heard you," Jones said with a tinge of irritation. "For security reasons, my name and identity, as far as you're concerned, is Mr. Jones."

Ben chewed on his lower lip. *Fucking semantics*. "It's customary for me to sign a confidentiality agreement with prospective clients. I can assure you I will honor that agreement even if you don't hire me."

"Sorry, not enough. I can't risk any security breaches in this matter."

Recalling the deadbeat husband against whom he'd just won his court case, Ben said, "I also like to know with whom I'm dealing, so I can make sure I get paid."

"Payment will be all cash. I've arranged to send a retainer to your office immediately if you accept my offer."

"What sort of arrangements?" This was sounding way too cloak-and-dagger for Ben's liking. He half expected the man to tell him the code name for this job would be Operation Blind Obedience.

"A messenger will deliver a package containing an advance payment of twenty thousand dollars."

"How long do you expect this case to take? Six months?"

"I expect it to take as long as possible. I want it to take a matter of days. Every minute wasted is more time for the man I want to disguise himself or find a new place to hide. I've chosen one week as my target goal. I'll pay you another eighty thousand dollars at the end of that week. If it takes longer, I'll only pay your current hourly rate starting on day eight."

Ben let out a low, barely audible whistle, sat back in his chair, and ran trembling fingers through his hair. One hundred thousand dollars would solve his immediate financial woes, plus ensure a profitable year. And it was only January. Hell, with that sort of money in the bank, he could take a month off and fly to Florida for a winter vacation.

His cynicism kicked in. "Sorry, Jones, but your offer sounds too good to be true. What aren't you telling me?"

Without hesitation, Jones said, "He's killed two people in cold blood. Perhaps others. If he's approached by anyone who seems to recognize him, he might panic. You must be prepared to risk your life."

Although it was the catch Ben expected, the mention of lethal danger quickened his pulse. "If he's been able to hide this long, what makes you think one man can find him now?"

"He's an amateur, not a career criminal. I'm certain he was on foot when he was flushed from hiding. Logic dictates he'll head for civilization if only to survive the weather. My best guess is he's somewhere on the North Shore. I want someone to check every town on or near Lake Superior for a man who may have been walking or hitchhiking and looking as if he'd been in the wilderness for a long time. You're based in Duluth, you're familiar with the Arrowhead region and the North Shore towns, and you were a brilliant investigator. If I'm wrong, we'll know in a week, and I'll try another location with another agent."

"Why not call the local cops or the State Patrol?"

Jones cleared his throat. "Again, for security reasons. I have a personal stake in this case that would be severely compromised by law enforcement knowing my identity."

More cryptic bullshit. Ben was confident he could handle the legwork. Something deep inside gnawed at him, warning him this job was trouble no matter the amount of money involved. "I don't know. Can I think about it for a day?"

"I'm not prepared to wait a day. As I said, time is everything right now. Perhaps a bonus will convince you."

Greed had gotten a claw into Ben. "What sort of bonus?" The idea of a windfall on top of his once-in-a-lifetime fee intrigued the hell out of him.

"I'll only say this once. If the man I want ends up dead before you can bring him to me, I'll pay you an extra one hundred thousand dollars. Two hundred thousand if his death is ruled accidental."

Ben's stomach did a back flip and goose bumps skittered across his arms. Jones wanted a hit man. "Even if he gets hit by a bus or has a heart attack? Why should I get paid for an accident?"

Jones sighed. "Figure that out on your own. Do we have a deal?"

Ben wiped a bead of sweat from his forehead and glanced around his cluttered office. Frost coated the cracked inside window. Decades-old wallpaper was peeling in several places. His desktop was marred with cigarette burns and coffee stains. Three generations removed from being current, his computer was so slow he didn't surf the net. He waded. Ben tried to pick up a pen and tap it on his legal pad, but his fingers trembled so much he gave up. Kill a man and make it look like an accident for three hundred thousand dollars? He envisioned a cozy little woodworking shop down at Canal Park.

"Mr. Nowitzki?" Jones' tone implied it was decision time.

Ben swallowed hard. "We have a deal."

"Excellent." Jones sounded pleased. "I'll send a messenger immediately. He'll have two envelopes. Once you sign the contract in the first envelope, assuming it meets your requirements and accurately represents the money we've discussed, he will seal the contract inside that envelope. The second envelope will contain a twenty-thousand-dollar advance fee, a dossier of the man you will find, and instructions for contacting me. All contact will be via phone. I'll have a new phone number every day. None of my numbers will be traceable. Is that understood?"

"Perfectly."

"However, once you commit, I expect you to follow my instructions precisely and give me daily progress reports. I won't require you to use purely legal means to find this man, but if you choose to disregard the law and the authorities arrest you, the contract becomes invalid. You will be on your own with no intervention from me. Is that understood?"

"Understood."

"If you change your mind by the time my messenger arrives, simply write the word *refused* and your initials on both envelopes, and we'll pretend this discussion never happened."

"Fair enough."

"Thank you and luck, Mr. Nowitzki. I suggest you pack an overnight bag. Your seven-day clock starts at the moment of signing, and I don't think you'll want to waste any time." Jones hung up before Ben could open his mouth to reply.

His insides were a jumble of roiling tension, but his mind was surprisingly clear as the reality of this job hit home. He'd risk prison and his life for an anonymous client, with the reward being the biggest payday he'd ever imagined. Considering his pathetic life situation, he could live with that. *So this is what it feels like to sell my soul to a devil.*

Chapter 19

Two minutes after Allyson opened the Halcyon the next day, Donnie Vossler strode through the door. His glance darted in every direction, checking who was present, taking in the restaurant's layout. She saw him from her office, and a red-hot vision immediately flashed in her mind, vivid enough that her hands involuntarily dropped to her abdomen.

To her surprise, the overwhelming urge to kill him had faded. Cut off his balls, maybe. When he spied her and flashed his lady-killer smile, her heart fluttered, just as it always had in the past. She cursed her weakness when confronted with his charm. Breathing deep to calm her nerves, she forced hatred to the front of her mind. No matter what he said, she wouldn't tell him anything about Josh. She'd entrusted him to Pauline Allen to hide at her home while Donnie was in town, and now desperately hoped she could keep that fact from him.

She rose from her chair and went out to meet him. The smile she forced was more an attempt to restrain her contempt than an attempt to be a cordial hostess.

Before Allyson could speak, Donnie spread his arms wide and crouched slightly. "Surprised to see me, Baby Doll?"

"One for lunch today?" There was still a chance she could feign ignorance and convince him she wasn't Susan Vossler. The minor surgery she'd had, along with her new hair color and style, gave her a different aura, a more confident manner.

"Susie Q, come on, it's me, Donnie. You think I don't recognize you?"

"I'm sorry sir, but my name is neither Baby Doll nor Susie Q. If you'd like lunch, I can seat you at a window table. The view of Superior is magnificent today." She held her smile, tried not to look in his eyes.

Donnie glanced to the side, then huffed out a short chuckle. He tried to catch her gaze with his, but she kept focused on his shoulder, still able to see his face in her peripheral vision. He gestured toward her with both hands. "You're Susan Danforth Vossler." He gestured to himself. "I'm Donnie Vossler, your husband." His voice dropped a notch in pitch and friendliness. "We have a son, Joshua James Vossler."

"I'm sorry. You mistake me for someone else. I'm Allyson Clifford, the owner. If you care to eat, I'll do everything I can to make your meal an enjoyable experience."

He frowned and looked down, then cocked his head sideways. His eyes were angry, yet bright. "Cut the bullshit, Sue. You think I don't recognize you? You think a nose job and a new hair color's gonna fool me? I've known you since you were in high school." His voice rose in intensity with each word, but he kept the volume low. "I'm the guy who saved you from that hellhole, otherwise known as Gunnison, Colorado. Got you out of that dead-end town, dead-end life, away from your dead-end parents. We were together five years. You can change your appearance to look like Minnie fucking Mouse for all I care, but you can't change your damn voice." His face reminded her of a volcano ready to erupt, churning with restrained anger.

Allyson stood taller and tried to appear confident, but she couldn't see a way out of this. He wasn't going to leave just because she wouldn't confirm her former identity. But there was no way he'd get to see or talk to Josh. She glanced over her shoulder toward the kitchen. Matt was prepping vegetables and hadn't noticed Donnie yet. Hannah and Brent were working too. At least she possessed strength in numbers if Donnie became agitated and did something stupid.

He must have seen her waver. "Sue? I just want to talk." His tone turned to cool silk. "Nothing more."

She allowed herself to lock eyes with him.

His face softened. The snake-charmer smile came back. He raised an eyebrow.

After a sigh that was meant more to relax her body than to show resignation, she capitulated. "Talk about what?"

"That's more like it, Baby Doll." He seemed to loosen completely. That damn swagger returned to his body. "I'm a changed man. Worked for a car dealer, bought the guy out a few years ago. I'm a respectable business owner. No debts, cash in the bank, life is good. I want to share it with you and Josh again. It'll be ten times better than before." Donnie could charm the panties off any woman he wanted, and he knew Allyson still knew it. "I need time to convince you. Show you. I brought, whatcha call 'em, corroborating documents about my dealership. Josh needs a father. I need him ... and you. Can we go somewhere more private?"

"I have a business to run. I can't talk right now."

"When, then?"

She hesitated. She didn't dare be alone with him anywhere. He'd manipulate her, as he used to, into giving in to whatever he wanted. But she couldn't avoid him now. How he could have tracked her to the middle-of-nowhere still baffled her. She was two thousand miles away, almost in a different culture from Southern California.

It didn't matter now. She'd have to give him the time. See what he wanted. Tell him no as gently and firmly as possible and hope he would go away. "Come back at three. It's quiet then. We can use my office."

"Sure, Baby Doll. Anything you say." He reached for her arm to caress it, but she flinched away. He held up that hand in surrender. "Sorry. Old habit. You still are a prime piece of woman, Sue." Initially, he had restricted his eyes to her face. Now he stared at her breasts, her legs, back to her breasts. "Fine, fine, fine." His smile morphed into a subtle leer.

That look. An alarm buzzed Allyson's spine, and she shivered. She remembered it from so many times, so many years ago. When she'd been desperate for a fix and he always took his sweet old time. Then, when he finally obliged her, she went from wanting to kill him to wanting to please him any way he desired. That was the problem. He had controlled her mind, body, soul, instincts. She was truly a baby doll then. A toy for him and his friends to play with. *Resist, Allyson, resist.*

"You okay, Sue?" He sounded concerned.

She forced her memories down. "Oh ... sorry. And please don't call me Sue anymore."

"Gonna be hard, Baby Doll. That's all I know you as."

"I legally changed my name to Allyson Clifford. Get used to it." A slight bit of control returned. "And you can drop the Baby Doll line too." *Resist*. She could beat him this time. Could this be the closure she never dared to imagine? Listen to what he wants to say, pretend to consider it, tell him to leave, and get on with life. She could be that strong, that determined, that inspired, to resist all the slimy charm and guile Donnie shoveled at her.

The door opened, and Allyson was never more relieved to see two customers walk in. "I'll see you at three, Donnie." Her tone was full of false bravado and energy. She turned to the newcomers. "Hi, welcome to the Halcyon. Two for lunch?"

When she saw his eyes widen, first in surprise, then appreciation, she knew he noticed she'd switched to her sultry charmer voice with the customers. She'd used that voice in his service so many times. So many times.

He headed for the door. "See you at three ... *Allyson*." he backed out, leaving her with *the look*, trying to control her again.

She forced her knees to lock, then led the couple to a table.

Chapter 20

Stopping first to pick up his Ford Taurus at the body shop, Ben next went to the bank to deposit ten thousand dollars into his account. He'd put eight thousand in his home safe and the remaining two thousand in his wallet. Ben's first destination on his job was the county courthouse in downtown Duluth. He requested the police records of the homicides last April in the Boundary Waters, Ely, and Duluth that involved a man named Matthew Raymond Lanier.

A thorough study of the hospital security tapes confirmed that the man who'd brought two wounded men to the Ely hospital looked similar to Matt Lanier's driver's license photo. Lanier was taller than average and had no distinguishing facial features. Brown hair, brown eyes, neither obese nor thin, no moles, tattoos, or piercings. He was an Everyman.

Three of the four men who died in or near Ely had one thing in common. They were from Lanier's boyhood home, Straight River, Minnesota, a small farming town south of Minneapolis. One was the chief of police; another was a sergeant on the force. The third was a farmer who lived next to the farm of Matt Lanier's father. No way was that a coincidence.

The fourth man was an enigma. He appeared to be a career thug but couldn't be connected to the other three in any way except he also was killed on Big Island, somewhere in the Boundary Waters, with one of the other three men.

Shortly before two of the men were murdered in the Ely hospital, the emergency room doctor in Ely had repaired a few sutures on Lanier's back and rebandaged the fingers on his left hand, but Lanier refused further treatment and left immediately. Not coincidentally, a few weeks before the Ely deaths, Lanier's boyhood house had exploded from a gas leak, killing a police officer and putting Lanier in the hospital with a concussion, severe lacerations on his back, and a mangled left hand.

A computer search for Matthew Lanier yielded several different results, but the man Ben was looking for turned out to be a very successful jazz and classical bassist who lived in Minneapolis. Ben visualized a bassist playing his instrument. His eyes widened when he realized most bass players used their left hands for fingering the notes. A severely injured left hand that hampered or ended a performing career might be the reason for revenge murders. Why murder four men, two of whom were cops Lanier had initially tried to save? What about the double homicide at the Thompson Hill Rest Area on Interstate 35 in Duluth? Lanier's former wife and her recent boyfriend were the victims. A possible love triangle?

So, Ben was looking for an average-looking white man from a small farm town with a ruined career and a failed marriage. All wrapped up in anger management issues. If Lanier had actually killed six people, Ben might be risking his life against a deranged psychopath who had snapped under some unseen pressure.

Chapter 21

When Donnie returned shortly after three o'clock, Allyson led him to her office. Donnie had apparently showered and dressed up for the occasion. He looked the epitome of a GQ model. Stylish open-collar mauve shirt, black slacks, black leather coat, Gucci shoes, and his usual cologne applied too heavily.

As she passed the kitchen where Matt was prepping food, she said, "Watch the front please, Matt. I'll be talking with Donnie for a few minutes." She emphasized *minutes* enough that both men noticed. She tried to exude confidence, but her stomach churned like Lake Superior in a November gale.

"Sure," Matt said, sounding concerned as he studied her face.

In her office, she pointed Donnie to the lone chair in front of her desk, closed the door, and sat in her chair behind the desk. Laying her palms flat on the leather-edged blotter, she engaged his eyes. "Okay, start talking. Make it fast."

He recoiled in his chair. "Christ, Sue—I mean, Allyson. You're making this feel like a fucking job interview you don't have time for. Let's talk like mature adults, okay?"

"Sorry." Her defensive wall was too big for an innocent conversation. She calmed her voice. "Tell me about this business you own."

He flashed his trademark self-assured smile. "That's more like it." He pulled a folder out of the attaché he'd brought and passed it across the desk.

She opened the folder. On top of a thin pile of papers lay a newspaper article and photo showing a Chamber of Commerce welcome to Vossler Motors. Donnie wore a more formal smile in this picture, not the seductive smile he used on women. Half a dozen earnest looking Chamber members posed around Donnie, the newest member of the Greater Los Angeles Chamber of Commerce.

"Vossler Motors is one of the fastest growing dealerships in Southern California." Donnie started in with his hands the way he always talked when he was interested in a topic, usually himself. "Got a bank statement in there too," he said, pointing to the folder. "Three straight years of increased profits. I employ five salespeople, four mechanics, a receptionist, a finance guy, and an administrative assistant. Used to be called a secretary, but she's one of those politically correct chicks who thinks the word *secretary* is demeaning." He shrugged. "So I play along."

Allyson scanned the official-looking bank statement. Vossler Motors listed assets over one million dollars, liabilities less than half that amount. Inventory as of the statement date showed fifty cars in stock. "Looks impressive." She narrowed her eyes as if to focus on any minuscule flinch or tic that might betray him. "Why do I think these could be fakes? Take a newspaper article, Photoshop your face into the picture, rewrite the article to say Vossler Motors instead of an actual business, then concoct a fake bank statement and pretend you're Mister Upstanding Businessman." She closed the folder and tossed it across her desk.

His face registered mild surprise. "I know you're skeptical. Considering our past, I would be too. But I've changed, S—" He caught himself with an annoyed purse of his lips and shook his head. "I mean, Allyson."

"Talk is always what you did best. I've heard it all before. Why now?"

"I'm older. Wiser. Figured out what's important. Being away from you for five years made me realize how good we were together."

She suppressed the shock from her expression. "Good? You call what we had good?" Her face heated. "For me, it was a nightmare!" She gripped the armrests of her chair, restrained the urge to go for his throat and scratch him to death.

He held his hands up. "Hey, hey, hey. Easy now. I'm not saying all of it was good. But the you-and-me part was good early on when we first met. You can't deny that, can you?"

She relaxed her talon grip. Their initial years together had been spectacular. Donnie had been the suave, handsome stranger who rescued her from a hellish childhood.

In her first life, as Susan Danforth, she had been drowning emotionally in a home with an alcoholic mother and a minister father who enabled his wife as much as he condemned the sins of alcohol in his sermons. Of course, she'd rebelled against his strict discipline, while her mother gave her no support because of the perpetual alcoholic haze in which she lived.

The Danforths didn't even know their only child was now Allyson Clifford. She'd changed her name when she left Donnie, but had never told them. They didn't know about Josh either. It may have seemed cruel to keep her parents' grandson from them, but she saw no advantage in subjecting Josh to the toxic environment of an alcoholic and her enabler.

Her only nod to her past life was her new name. She'd never liked Susan or Sue very much. Changing her name gave her an immense feeling of power and control. Allyson was a derivation of her mother's name, Alice. She borrowed Clifford from her father. Yet she wasn't honoring her parents in any way. Allyson Clifford sounded like a good, solid name. She was finally who she had aspired to be all her life: free, independent, capable, in control. Now Donnie wanted to get back into her life. Wanted to take some of her control.

"Yes," she said, "we had a couple of happy years, but we had three disastrous years that wiped out the happy years and then some."

"I'll admit we made some mistakes, but—"

"We? We made mistakes?" Her temples pounded like thunder, and her body went rigid. She wanted to throw him bodily out of the Halcyon. "How dare you blame me for anything? You were the one who got us into debt, messed me up, and used me."

He raised his hands in a defensive gesture, palms out, repeatedly pushing against the air. "Sorry, sorry. You're right." He softened his voice to an apologetic tone. "I was an absolute asshole. But not anymore. From now on, I'll treat you like a queen."

She shook her head. "I would have believed you ten years ago. Today, I know what a fool I was for believing anything you ever said."

Donnie looked away and massaged his mouth and chin with one hand before turning back to level a laser-powered stare at her. "What about Josh? Doesn't he deserve a father in his life?"

The mention of Josh shot bolts of pained fear into her heart. He had a point, but she feared the kind of father he'd been to Josh in his first three years. She wished more than anything she'd been mentally there for her son during that time. She could only guess at what damage Donnie might have done to Josh's development. The fact he hadn't mentioned their son until now made it seem like his primary goal was to reconcile with her.

Yesterday, her first instinct upon seeing Donnie standing outside the Halcyon had been blood-chilling panic. A knot grew in her stomach as yesterday's emotion collided with today's intellect. She went with emotion.

Allyson shook her head. "No." She placed her palms on her desk, stiff arming herself into the back of her chair.

"He's my son. I have a right to see him."

"That's never been legally decided. Maybe you should take me to court. See what a judge thinks."

His eyes widened when she said *judge*. He forced a pained smile. "That shouldn't be necessary. We can work this out ourselves, can't we, S—Allyson?"

Touché. For whatever reason, he wasn't keen on getting any authorities involved. Neither was she, but Donnie didn't need to know that. "If you want to see him, talk to a judge."

His jaw tightened, and his face showed a hint of red under the L.A. tan. "Okay, Baby Doll, this is your last chance." His tone became dark, menacing. "If I walk out of here without some deal to see my son," he paused for dramatic effect, "I'm through being nice. Understand?"

Allyson tensed as if his words were piercing her body like so many darts. Ugly memories flooded back of the times he'd used that tone to force her to comply with his orders once again. Do what he said or start going through withdrawal for the hundredth time. Her blood ran like ice water. The long dormant pain in her lower abdomen flared up, and she slid her palms down her stomach as if trying to hide it from Donnie. She slowly drew in a deep breath, not wanting him to notice, hoping the extra oxygen would calm her trembling hands.

Locking eyes with her husband, she said, "I understand. Goodbye, Donnie. You know the way out."

He tensed his face into a scowl, looked down, shook his head, then reconnected his gaze with her eyes. "Big mistake, bitch." His tone was low, angry, predatory. "Big mistake." He stood and walked out, slamming the door hard enough to rattle her office window.

Allyson should have been proud of herself, but all she felt was a worse dread, a deeper fear, and a greater sense of foreboding. What might he do to her? How could he possibly find Josh if Josh was hidden at Pauline's? She contemplated calling the sheriff, but Donnie hadn't verbally threatened her or Josh in specific words. Just veiled threats.

Matt turned when he heard the office door slam.

"You got a toilet in here, fry boy?" Vossler said in the tone of a lord berating a serf.

"Down the hall."

Vossler walked down the hall, paused outside the two restroom doors, and glared back at Matt. "What're you looking at, pervert?"

Matt slowly turned away after a short stare down but moved to where he could stand between Vossler and Allyson's office when Vossler returned.

Two minutes later, Vossler came down the hall from the restrooms, adjusting his belt and collar. He reminded Matt of the kind of guy who knew he was looking and expected everything to fall into his lap because of those looks. He walked past Matt, veering enough to graze him with a shoulder.

Matt held firm, resisting the urge to body block the jerk into the wall.

When Vossler was outside, Matt tapped on Allyson's door.

She opened it seconds later. "What?"

"You okay? Your conversation got a little loud there at the end, and Vossler seemed royally pissed off when he left."

She nodded. "I'm okay." But her lips quivered, and her voice was on the verge of cracking.

Chapter 22

Ben Nowitzki's next stop was in Ely to interview a guy named Ferdinand S. Olson. He ran a canoe outfitting business that had been a focal point of the murder cases last spring and the rescue of a trapper in the Boundary Waters Canoe Area by some sort of hermit last week. He found Olson's address—a small bungalow one block off Ely's main drag, Sheridan Avenue—and parked on the street in front of the shoveled path to the sidewalk.

He hadn't called ahead to arrange a meeting, preferring to catch Olson off guard. Give someone time to prepare a lie, and he'll do so if he has something to hide.

After Olson had answered the door, Ben introduced himself and explained he was a private investigator working for the family of one victim of last spring's homicides in the Ely hospital. The simpler the lie, the better.

Olson looked puzzled but invited Ben inside and beckoned him to sit in a plaid covered armchair. He seemed much too old to operate a wilderness canoe outfitting business, let alone any business, perhaps because of his weather-beaten skin that added years to his appearance. But he dressed the part—a fisherman-knit wool sweater over a flannel shirt, faded jeans, ankle-high work boots. Olson's teeth were yellow brown, probably due to decades of smoking Camel unfiltered cigarettes, one of which he held between his thumb and forefinger. The smoke accosted Ben's nose as they sat in Olson's small, dusty living room.

Heat emanated from a cast iron wood stove in the corner, but Ben still felt a chilling draft from the window behind his chair. He got right to his questioning, acutely aware of the looming time pressure Jones had put on him.

"Last spring, five men in three separate canoes allegedly paddled from your boat landing to Big Island in the Boundary Waters. There, authorities found two men dead from gunshot wounds a few days after one of the five brought two other men to the Ely hospital with gunshot wounds. The wounded men were apparently killed later that evening in the hospital by an unidentified man who somehow snuck past security."

Olson sat motionless except for a narrowing of his gray eyes. "That's what I heard from the news."

"I also understand someone brought the injured trapper, Joseph Backstrom, to your outfitting business, then called an ambulance."

"Yeah. So?"

"Any suspicion about the identity of the rescuer?"

"Nope."

"Do you find it strange that the only common fact in these two incidents is you?"

Olson shook his head as he sucked on his cigarette. "Not me. My business. I'm on one of the busiest lakes in the BWCA. Lotsa folks go through there all times of the year, legal or not. I wasn't open last April, and I ain't open in winter."

Ben checked his notes. "The doctor who treated the fifth man at the hospital said he resembled a photo of the single suspect in the double murders of Steven Crossley and Diane Blake in Duluth a few days after the hospital deaths."

Olson seemed to tighten a little. He took a drag on his Camel and stared out the window as he exhaled.

Ben pulled a picture from the dossier. "This is the only suspect in all those murders. His name is Matthew Lanier. Do you know him?"

Olson gave the picture a cursory glance. "So what if I do? I ain't his father. He ain't my responsibility."

Ben caught a flicker of emotion in Olson's expression.

Olson looked away. He took an extra-long drag on his cigarette, flicked the butt into the glass peanut butter jar he used for an ashtray, and exhaled slowly, directing the smoke toward the ceiling. "A kid named Lanier worked for me for five summers. Ain't seen him in maybe fifteen years."

He nodded at the photo. "Could be him, but I ain't swearing on any Bible that this guy and the kid I knew is the same person."

Olson's stubborn reluctance to offer any new information or insight frustrated Ben. He tapped his pen against his notepad. Olson probably knew something, but didn't want to rat on a former employee.

Letting Olson fidget in the silence, Ben reviewed his impressions of the case to this point. He quickly dismissed a botched drug deal as a reason for the murders. Who in their right mind would paddle miles into the wilderness to buy or sell illegal drugs? There must have been some sort of chase. But who flees from deadly pursuers in a canoe? A sane man wouldn't run from danger in a canoe, but he might hide from danger using a canoe. And that same man might hide from prosecution in the same place—the middle of a nearly inaccessible wilderness—with the added protection of a brutal Minnesota winter as a deterrent against anyone searching for him.

Olson gave him a sidelong glance, which prompted Ben to speak. "The police think the man who rescued Backstrom was living as a hermit in the Boundary Waters. Do you buy that possibility?"

"Lots of hardy folk live around here. Winter's winter. We just deal with it."

"Yes, but living here in a modern house with heat, electricity, and plumbing is one thing. Do you know anyone tough enough to survive one of these winters with none of those conveniences?"

"And what if I do? Just 'cause someone's a tough guy, now he's guilty of killing people?"

Ben's heart raced. *Gotcha!* "Mr. Olson, I haven't implied Lanier is the man who rescued Backstrom. I only mentioned him in connection with the murders."

Olson froze for a second, clearly unnerved. "You mentioned both incidents. I figured you're only looking for one man, but you think he was in on both deals."

Ben suppressed a satisfied grin. "I was. Now I think you do too."

Olson lit another cigarette. "The Lanier kid I knew wasn't violent. He would've never shot no one unless someone was shooting at him first."

"Was he the kind of kid who could've saved an injured man from freezing to death?"

"You bet." Olson didn't hesitate. "In a heartbeat. Years ago, two idiot canoeists capsized a mile offshore from the lodge. Couple old farts who couldn't swim. Only sense they had was to wear their life jackets.

"Matt was working the dock. Nobody else was around. Saw 'em tip. It was fishing opener. Water was so cold it was barely liquid. He grabbed the nearest canoe, paddled out in a few minutes, hauled 'em into his canoe without capsizing himself, then made 'em paddle their asses off to keep warm until they got to shore. None of my other workers was that quick-thinking or that strong with a paddle. He had that canoe moving like a fishing boat." Olson puffed on his cigarette, held the smoke for a few seconds, and blew it toward the ceiling in a long steady stream. Then he eyed Ben. "Doubt I could've saved 'em myself."

That settled one question for Ben. He didn't believe in coincidence in a situation like this. "So Matt Lanier saved the trapper?"

"Didn't say that," Olson said with ire in his voice.

"But—"

"But nothing. Think what you want. I'm done talking." Olson stood.

Ben eased out of his seat, took a breath to protest, but Olson was already walking to the door. Best to back off in case he needed to question the old man later. "Thanks for your time," he said and stepped out into the cold.

As Ben started toward his car, Olson said, "The Matt Lanier I know ain't a murderer. He was one of the finest young men I ever met."

Ben stared at Olson for a moment, nodded, got into his car, and headed for the northernmost town on Minnesota's North Shore, Grand Portage. He'd called ahead to book a room because he figured with luck and roads he'd arrive before midnight, some twelve hours into his search.

Chapter 23

To Allyson's relief, the rest of the day passed without Donnie return-ing to the Halcyon. She feared he was plotting to steal Josh while she worked. She'd considered keeping Josh with her at all times, but quickly changed her mind. Donnie might cause some sort of scene. Fast-talk her into submission the way he'd been able to do so easily years ago, and walk out with Josh while she stood there bewildered and ashamed. Leaving Josh with the Allens was much safer, provided Donnie didn't find she and Pauline were best friends.

Allyson stood behind the bar cleaning up after her last two customers had finished their Scotches and left. The couple in the dining room, done with their dessert and coffees, stood to leave. Brent swooped in to clear the vacated table. Hannah was rolling silverware inside napkins. Matt was elbow-deep into cleaning the grease trap.

Matt was a curious one, an extreme sports enthusiast who never dis-cussed extreme sports. Most of those guys seemed eager to brag about their latest death-defying stupidity to anyone within earshot. Matt never bragged about anything.

He also seemed to be smarter than a typical jock. Every time he caught himself talking about the finer things in life—polar opposites of extreme sports in the wilderness—he clammed up as if he were hiding his knowl-edge. All those contradictions intrigued her.

Despite his secretive nature, Matt's agreeing to stay was a blessing, even if only for two weeks. He was temporary insurance that Donnie wouldn't try to use force against her when she was at work. He was slow in the kitchen but followed direction well and worked hard. Enough for the immediate future. Nevertheless, her first want ad for a new chef would hit tomorrow's edition of the *Arrowhead Times.*

Done with his work, Matt walked out to the small bandstand in the far corner of the dining room, against the wall opposite the fireplace. He studied the electric bass the jazz-pop trio's bassist had entrusted Allyson with overnight, then glanced around the dining room. In the low light, he didn't notice Allyson behind the bar. He picked up the bass, sat on the adjacent stool, gingerly placed his hands in position, and began to play.

The amplifier was off, so Allyson came out from behind the bar to hear the music better.

Matt played some scales, plucked and fingered his way through an intricate pattern, did some walking bass lines, then a blues riff at a slow tempo. He was good—better than most of the bassists in the bands she'd hired—but he stopped when the injured fingers on his left hand couldn't keep up with the plucking of the fingers on his right hand.

Grimacing, he looked as if he might throw the bass against the wall. Instead, he took a deep breath, wiped down the strings with the cloth that lying nearby, and set the instrument back into its stand.

He turned toward the bar, saw her standing close by, and instantly became red-faced. "Oh, sorry. I didn't think anyone would mind."

She waved a hand dismissively. "No big deal. Something tells me you're pretty good. Or *were* pretty good."

He wiggled the fingers on his left hand. "A winner on the second guess."

"Life get in the way of a music career?"

His expression became drawn, more tired than she'd seen him. "Actually, death got in the way."

The unusual statement caught her off guard. As Matt's boss, she was reluctant to pry. As a woman, she was dying to know more about this mystery man.

She said in a Mae-West-as-femme-fatale tone, "So what's your story, Johnson?" as if they were two strangers sharing a long bus ride searching for a discussion.

He looked away, then down, then at her again. "You're better off not knowing. A real cook will come here looking for a job in a few days, and I'll be on my way. Let's keep it simple, avoid any personal involvement."

"Let's call it bartender-customer involvement instead. You look like you need a drink. I listen to men's woeful tales almost every day, and I never violate a customer's confidence. I'll even spring for the stuff."

"I could use a drink. One thing I missed on the trail."

She led him to the bar. He followed far enough behind to watch her. She had a sexy walk and wasn't afraid to show it because she felt confident when she walked. The walk of a feline. The powerful, gliding swagger of a tigress on the hunt. Reflected in the mirror over the bar, she saw a hint of lust in his expression. She suppressed a smile. Few men could hide their libidos. A corner of her heart warmed because she'd finally seen a real but tiny piece of him.

He sat on a bar stool as she slid two brandy snifters out of the wooden glass rack hanging from the ceiling. Then she reached to the top shelf and pulled down the bottle of Louis XIII Cognac. "I don't sell much of this, but I keep it around in case a millionaire comes in."

His eyes widened, and he nodded appreciatively when he recognized the distinctive crystal decanter. "You weren't kidding when you said stuff."

She poured. They saluted each other with small tips of their snifters and drank. Matt studied her face with more than casual interest. She watched him as she let the smoky, elegant liquid coat her tongue before swallowing.

He held the brandy in his mouth for a moment, then swallowed. He closed his eyes, and his face relaxed as the hint of a smile crossed his lips. He puckered as if he was preparing to whistle, then inhaled slowly. He was inhaling the vapors to get a secondary hit of the aromas. The sign of a connoisseur.

"The fact you appreciate high-quality liquor proves you're not who you pretend to be."

His eyes flickered with the guilt of someone on trial who's just been nailed during a cross-examination. "I'll plead the fifth." His edgy tone implied he'd shared enough for the moment.

"Everyone's got some sort of regret," she said, "lost love, failure in business, family estrangements."

He cocked an eye. "Okay, I'll bite. What's your sob story?"

She stared him down for a few seconds, smiling enough to show a narrow slice of teeth, then took a tension-relieving breath. "I married the wrong guy."

"Vossler?"

She nodded. "Today I stood up to Donnie for the first time ever. That's my small victory." *Wow. Over five years of submission to that bastard. Why did I let it happen?*

He rubbed his chin. "That's funny. I married the right woman. Still blew up in my face."

"Oh ho, you leaked another secret."

He looked past her. His eyes took on a dead, regretting-the-past stare. "Yeah, but it's connected to the music thing." He swirled his snifter. "Why'd your marriage go south?"

She stared past him at the darkened windows overlooking the Lake. "He changed after we had Josh." Her thoughts were far from Castle Danger. "Things got tense. Money got tight. I had some ... personal problems. Donnie was the main reason."

He recoiled on his bar stool because he hadn't expected even a small bit of detail. "Fair enough," he said. "Bad marriage. I get it. I ended up divorced too, even though it wasn't my idea. How long were you and Donnie married?"

"Still are."

"Oh." Matt shifted on his barstool. "I see."

"I wasn't in a position to file for divorce and still keep Josh. So I just left with him." Her insides tightened. "I think we've shared enough misery for one night."

"I'll drink to that." Matt tossed back the rest of his cognac and Allyson followed suit.

Their eyes met as they both swallowed. Allyson stifled a shudder from the impact of the Cognac. Or had a small thrill of attraction shivered her spine?

Chapter 24

The next night, the Halcyon was full, and the joint vibrated with sound. After a lukewarm performance the night before, the jazz-pop trio caught fire and inspired a few couples to dance in the narrow space between tables and bandstand. The band was swinging, enjoying themselves, and transmitting energy to the crowd, who ate it up.

Matt listened from the kitchen and tried to cook. He struggled to keep from tapping his toes, playing air bass, singing backup lyrics. Heck, whom was he kidding? He struggled with not going on stage and elbowing the bass player out of the way so he could play.

He knew what those musicians were feeling—the unique connection with an audience that happens once in a hundred performances. Everyone connected to the same wavelength. Nothing else mattered but the music and the moment. More than anything, he wanted to be the bassist in that band and lead them to a higher musical plane.

He was visualizing himself playing on the bandstand when he was roused by stinging in his eyes and the smell of smoke. He glanced down and jumped back from the sauté pan as the venison steak he was searing went up in flames. He quickly tossed a lid on the pan to douse the fire, but even more smoke filled the kitchen.

Hannah, who was waiting at the pass-through for another order but watching the band, started coughing. This drew Allyson's attention from the hostess stand. She glared at Matt, but sat the new arrivals first, then stormed into the kitchen.

"What the hell's wrong with you tonight?" she said with an angry edge, just soft enough that no customers heard her.

Although shorter than he by several inches, she stepped so far into his personal space it seemed as though they were eye-to-eye. She ticked off his errors on her raised fingers. One-two-three. "You forgot the fries for one order. A Halcyon burger came to table barely hot. A lamb shank was so salty the customer almost had a fatal coughing spell because he could hardly swallow." Strident brass colored her tone.

Her eyes were dark cores of fire, and she'd never looked at him with as much anger and frustration. It almost scared him coming from such a beautiful woman. It was as if she had assumed the persona of a tyrannical business tycoon and was cussing out an incompetent employee who had cost her firm a multi-million-dollar deal.

He backed away, returning the gap between them to a less intimate distance. "Sorry, boss. I'm a little distracted by the music and the crowd. Haven't been this busy since I started here." He looked at the floor. "Need to get organized." He put aside the scorched meat and started over with a fresh sauté pan.

"Do it fast, or you'll be getting organized out on the highway as you snowshoe to the next town."

"Yes, ma'am." His cheeks burned, and he chastised himself for being distracted.

Allyson stared him down for a moment, then turned and listened to the band, which was finishing a fast, furious, swinging-their-asses-off version of "Cherokee." She turned back to him with an expression of triumph.

"Oh-h-h, I get it now. You were more than a talented musician." She waggled her finger at him. "You were a pro. These guys gave you a reminder of what used to be, and you couldn't help yourself. I watched you a few times tonight, cooking with your eyes closed, head bobbing up and down as if you were playing with them. I've seen other musicians get that look. You were in your own little sound world."

Whatever he said now wouldn't fool her into thinking she was mistaken. He glanced over at the band but said nothing.

"I'm not going to fire you. Yet." She softened her tone to her sultry hostess voice but kept a tense edge. "Just make sure the food comes first.

Maybe we can talk the band into staying until after closing so you can jam with them."

His blood surged at her patronizing tone. As if a half-hour jam session could make up for a ruined career that might have had thirty great years left. He would rather she fired him than humiliate him. He didn't need her to make special arrangements so he could get his music fix. "No," he snapped. "I'm fine. It won't happen again." He shot her a withering glare equal to the look she'd given him earlier.

She immediately sensed she'd gone too far and withdrew to the bar.

Watching her walk away this time did nothing for his libido. It only made him regret the random choice he'd made that landed him in Castle Danger. After nine months of feeling no emotion other than the desire to survive for some unknown reason, this flood of conflicting feelings messed up his head big time. If only she could hire a new chef. Then he could leave with a clear conscience.

Back at the bar, Allyson stayed busy pouring drinks, but checked on him every few minutes. Her stare felt like prickly thorns in his skin. He forced himself to concentrate on each order and tried to ignore the music. After enduring musical agony for ten minutes, he heaved a huge sigh when the band announced a fifteen-minute break.

Allyson returned to form and charmed everyone who came in, effortlessly schmoozed the customers at the bar, and made each one believe she was their own special friend. When the drinkers had been served, she worked the dining room, gliding from table to table, making sure each meal was perfect, and each diner was pleased with the food, service, and ambiance.

She was a natural restaurateur. Serving customers seemed as effortless for her as music had been for him. The difference came when she wasn't in front of a customer. Then she became withdrawn, firm with her staff, not gregarious, barely even friendly. She turned her personality on and off like a light switch. The way she'd acted with him just now—commanding, in charge, showing no weakness. In front of customers—effortless grace, charm, and hospitality.

He was coming out of the walk in when he heard a commotion from the front of the restaurant. He leaned under the top of the pass-through and looked toward the bar. A customer had grabbed Allyson with both hands as she walked past him, desperate to get a kiss. The man was lumberjack large and wore a flannel shirt, blue jeans, and work boots. He wobbled on his feet as he tried to mash his lips into hers. She struggled to wrench herself free, but he wouldn't let go.

The other men at the bar were having a laugh, and probably a vicarious thrill, as they watched the drunken lout manhandle a beautiful woman.

"C'mon, baby, jus' one lil' ol' kiss." The drunk puckered up and pressed his face toward hers.

The man's voice felt like barbed wire in Matt's ear. Discordance. Anger. Cruelty. Serious trouble was seconds away. He tensed and instantly assessed the situation. One opponent. The others only enjoying the show. They'd never respond in time if the situation escalated. He strode toward the bar.

The lumberjack wrapped his arms around her, still going for a kiss, and she pounded her fists on his back.

"Let me go!"

"I thought you and me'd have some fun in a back room."

"Get the hell off me!" She stomped on his foot.

"Oww!" He let go, and his expression turned ugly and angry. "God damn it!" In a flash, he backhanded her across the face, and she shrieked in pain.

Matt sprang at the drunken lumberjack with the power and quickness of a lion.

Two other customers had stopped laughing and protested at the drunk. Matt flew past them, went for the lumberjack's throat, and tore him away from Allyson. The man gagged and sputtered as Matt ran him toward the wall. He dropped one hand to the man's belt, keeping the other around his throat, and shoved him upward against the wall. The man's feet dangled six inches above the floor.

Barely able to speak through his rage, Matt said, "If you ever do that to a woman again, I will snap your neck like a pencil."

The bug-eyed man gaped at him as his face reddened. He started gurgling like a fish out of water.

Allyson shouted. "Matt, I'm all right. Let him down."

Hearing her voice should have calmed him, but the tension in his arms flowed to his hands, and he tightened his grip on the man's throat.

The drunk's feet kicked feebly against the wall.

Allyson grabbed Matt's chokehold arm. "Put him down, please." Her voice was soft yet pleading.

He recoiled from attack mode and relaxed the fingers around the man's throat, then lowered him to the floor.

The man sagged against the wall, gasping, then slid to the floor in a heap.

Matt turned to Allyson and studied her face. She had a red welt on one cheek. "Are you sure you're okay?"

"Thanks to you, yes." Her shaken expression was a mix of relief, fear, and awe.

She sat on a bar stool and ran a trembling hand through her tousled hair. "It happens occasionally. The cost of doing business."

"The what?" He gaped at her. "Getting assaulted isn't exactly an itemizable business expense."

"Besides," she said, "it looked worse than it was. He probably had a fight with his girlfriend and was lonely." Her eyes pleaded with him to calm down.

He was still panting, not from exertion as much as from a thrill-of-the-hunt excitation. He hadn't realized nine months of intense, daily physical labor outdoors had built his body to a level of strength and agility he'd never imagined he could possess. He forced a slow, deep breath into his lungs.

Two bar patrons stood guard over the drunk. "Want us to call the sheriff?" one of them asked. Several people had pulled out cell phones—one ready to call 911, the others eagerly filming the melee.

She waved down the cell phone holders and regarded the man on the floor. "I need to show him I can take care of myself and my business."

Surprised at her comment, Matt was also relieved she didn't want the authorities involved. He didn't want any interaction with any cop, anywhere, anytime.

"Anyone know him?" Allyson said as she looked at the people at the bar.

"I've seen him around the area," said one man. "Works construction somewhere."

Allyson knelt next to the lumberjack, grabbed a fistful of his curly black hair, and lifted his head up as much as his neck would bend. "Listen carefully." Her voice was back to the tone she'd used with Matt when he burned the venison. "As you can see, plenty of men around here are willing to defend my honor. And in case you ever try to catch me alone, I own a gun and know how to use it. Most importantly, I don't give second chances. Do. You. Understand?" She tugged his hair on each of the last three words.

The lumberjack muttered a painful "Yeah."

"So this is what's going to happen. These men will escort you outside, you will drive away, and you will never again set foot in my parking lot, let alone my restaurant. If I see you around town and you don't immediately turn and walk the other way, I will shoot your balls off one by one, then slice off what's left of your dick and feed it to the wolves that hang around the woods by my house." She tugged on his hair again for emphasis. "Is that clear?"

"Ow! Yeah." The drunk had suddenly sobered up.

"Good." She released her grip and the two men standing guard dragged him to his feet.

The drunk rubbed his bloody lip with one hand and his hair with the other. As the two patrons manhandled him to the door, he gave her a wicked leer and muttered, "Fuckin' cockteaser. Heard you were the friendly type." The patrons shoved him out into a pile of snow.

A second later, Matt comprehended what the drunk had said. He charged out the door and hauled the man to his feet by his coat collar. "Who told you she was the friendly type?"

The drunk swayed as he brushed snow off his face. He exhaled sour whiskey aromas. When he recognized Matt, he cowered and said, "I'm going, I'm going. Leave me alone."

Matt shook him hard by his coat lapels. "Who told you the bartender was looking to party?"

"Hey, man, fuck off. You got the hots for her yourself?"

Matt grabbed the man's windpipe with one hand and squeezed. "Want some more of this?"

The drunk's eyes bugged out, and he rose up on his toes to ease the pressure. "No, no, no!" he gagged. "I'll tell ya."

Matt released his grip. "Who?"

"Some leather-jacket punk hanging out at McDonald's. He asked if we was looking for some tail. We said we was always looking for tail. He said Allyson up at the Halcyon puts out for anyone. Figured I'd check her out."

Matt's throat clenched and his head instantly ached. He let go of the drunk and inhaled deeply to try to ease the pain. "Get out of here," he said with knife-edged coldness.

The drunk staggered to his truck. Matt walked back inside. Allyson the town slut? Sure, she flirted with customers, but that was so controlled and orchestrated. She never let it go past harmless. Now all of a sudden, these Neanderthals think she's loose and easy?

Allyson had regained her composure. "What was that about?" She nodded toward the door.

"Nothing. Just reinforced your message. You sure you're okay?" He put his hand on her shoulder. She flinched. He removed it quickly.

"I'm fine. Get back to work." She turned to the two men who had tried to come to her rescue. "Who wants a refill on me?" Her voice was back to its honeyed voluptuousness. She flashed her brilliant smile, and all seemed right in her world again. But as she poured the drinks, she couldn't hide her trembling fingers.

The restaurant returned to normal, but traffic thinned over the next hour. After she'd seated a customer, Allyson drifted over to the kitchen and leaned against the stainless steel counter at the pass-through. She had a quizzical expression that unnerved him when he realized she was scrutinizing him.

"What'd I do now?" he asked with caution.

She stared at him a moment longer before speaking. "How did you recognize the problem with the drunk so fast?"

Matt shrugged. "I'm not sure. Never reacted that way before. But I don't have much experience breaking up sexual assaults, either." He, too, was puzzled by his quick reaction.

"You knew he was trouble even before I did."

"I guess it's my musical training."

Allyson's eyebrows shot upward. "Say what?"

"The average listener has no idea what goes into a musician's training." Matt gathered his thoughts. He'd never put them into words before. Now they were flooding his brain to escape. "We spend thousands of hours practicing the most intricate musical passages until we can do them from memory a hundred times in a row without making a mistake. We're trained to sight-read a brand-new piece of the most complicated music nearly perfectly the first time. We adjust our intonation and tone quality unconsciously to stay in tune with the other musicians. We listen to our fellow performers and respond to the slightest nuances, changes in style or mood, sometimes getting to where we have an actual conversation through the music. The greatest improvisers have that gift in abundance. I'm not—I wasn't—a great improviser, but I was damn good."

"I still don't see how that applies to responding instantly to danger."

"I'm trained to see, think, and hear the big picture. I can look at one page of a symphonic score and tell you in five seconds the composer and the name of the piece. I don't see individual notes on my music. I see full measures, complete lines, sometimes even the entire piece, like it's all communicated in one sentence."

Merely talking about music in this much depth released a burst of endorphins that energized Matt. He didn't see an equal excitement in her, just curious puzzlement. He searched for a simpler explanation.

"I sight read better than almost any other musician because I'm always looking four or five measures ahead of what I'm playing, which gives me extra time to rehearse, if you will, for what's coming, no matter how intricate or up-tempo the music. I know what's coming because I've so deeply internalized what's happened up to—" He snapped his fingers. "—this moment."

Her blank expression changed to one of realization."Now I understand. It's like your senses are super in tune with ... everything."

He nodded. "My eyes and ears told me the lumberjack was trouble as soon as I focused on him. He wasn't going to take no for an answer. I was five measures ahead of him."

"Whatever the reason, thanks again." She turned to leave but stopped and looked over her shoulder at him with a look that was part bedroom eyes, part deep admiration. "I'm really glad you're a great musician."

Matt had to brace himself on his side of the counter from the burst of emotion he felt for her at that moment. All because she hadn't said, "You *were* a great musician."

Chapter 25

Winter tourist traffic had returned to normal thanks to all the fresh powder snow that had fallen to entice the ski crowd. The Halcyon was about half full. The jazz-pop trio was halfway through its last set. Matt was prepping an appetizer plate in the kitchen. Hannah and Brent were handling the tables. Allyson tended bar.

Six tables were occupied, most by couples, but a trio of young men who'd ordered the appetizers sat at one. They had made some raucous noise earlier when they'd coerced the band into playing a mini set of their favorite outlaw country music singers: Waylon, Willie, and Merle Haggard.

Matt plated the shredded leg of lamb pot stickers and rang the bell. "Order up."

Hannah was cleaning a wine spill at one of her tables, so Allyson came over. "What table?" she said.

"The three overgrown frat boys."

She took the plate. "Oh, right. I think they started drinking before they got here." She walked to their table and set the plate down. "Here you are, gentlemen." Her voice purred like a cat basking in the sun.

"Thanks, gorgeous. Wanna help us eat these?" said the taller, darker of the three.

"Sorry, gentlemen, I don't eat with the customers." She leaned in as if to share a secret. "I know what's in the food, and it'll make you think you've died and gone to heaven. But I need to keep my head on straight."

"Why don't you join us for a smoke of something that'll make you think you've died and gone to heaven?"

Allyson stood, and the purring left her voice. "No." She shook her head. "I'll sell you booze up to what I think is your limit. Anything else you do at home."

"Right," the leader said. "I know you gotta sound all legal and proper like, but I know lots of places that have special customers, back rooms, cops looking the other way." He winked at her, then slithered his tongue across his lips. His half-drunk buddies egged him on with conspiratorial snickers and inaudible comments.

Allyson's voice shifted into boss mode. "The cops don't look the other way around here. So take my advice and save your toke for home." She turned and walked back to the bar.

All three men leered at her. One made a crude gesture with a forefinger inserted into a circle formed by his other forefinger and thumb. Matt clenched his teeth and resisted the urge to say something that might incite worse behavior.

The leader, whom the other two had addressed as Rocky, stood up.

"Gotta see a man about a horse, dudes." Rocky jerked his head toward the men's room.

A second man said, "Yeah, me too," and stood.

The third glanced around the room nervously before following the other two down the hall.

Hannah came up to the pass-through with an order. "Pulled pork sandwich, apple-fennel slaw, onion rings." Then she called to Allyson, "Coors Light."

"Coming up," Allyson said and reached for a glass.

Matt was busy with the order as Allyson delivered the beer. As she returned, she stopped and intently sniffed the air. A look came over her face that reminded Matt of the expression on the mother bear he'd encountered last fall, ready to kill him to protect her cub, who had wandered too close to him.

Allyson stormed behind the bar, reached down, and pulled out a major league-sized Louisville Slugger baseball bat. She marched past him without looking and said through clenched teeth, "Follow me. Bring a meat cleaver."

Unsure if Allyson was serious, he looked at Hannah, whose puzzled expression said she also didn't know. He shrugged, picked up the biggest cleaver in the rack, the one used for hacking beef shanks and turkey legs, and walked after his employer.

He was five steps behind her in the hallway to the restrooms when he smelled the sweet, pungent aroma of marijuana. The smell brought him back to his musician days. He had never been into pot as much as most of his bandmates. It was just something to do, usually after a gig, sometimes before a big date, to relax a little. Harmless for the most part.

Allyson reared back and opened the swinging door to the men's room with a vicious karate kick. She raised the bat as if to prepare for batting practice and stormed in, then took a full swing against one of the stall doors. The sound in the tight space was like a gunshot. The door swung backward into the stall and hit the sidewall with a crunch. A split second later, the clank of metal echoed as the broken door handle hit the tile floor.

Matt stepped into the doorway. The three dopers stood frozen in mid-pass, mouths agape. Rocky dropped the glowing joint on the floor.

"What the fuck did I explicitly tell you not two minutes ago?" she demanded.

Rocky stiffened. "Whatever the fuck you said don't apply to me." His haughty manner instantly changed to panic when she swung the bat in front of his head and dented the side of the stall whose door she had mangled.

Matt flinched and his eardrums stung with pain. The cornered men clapped their hands over their ears.

Red-faced, she gritted her teeth. "Whatever the fuck I say especially applies to you, dickbrain!" Enough of a crazed smile formed on her lips to suggest that whatever Rocky said next might well result in her using his head as a baseball.

He held up his hands and stepped back against the sink next to the stall. "Whoa, whoa, whoa. We thought you were cool with this." He couldn't keep the terror from his voice.

"Who served you that plate of bullshit?"

"We heard it around town."

Her voice added ten decibels and went up an octave. "Around town?" Her face became a darker shade of red than her lipstick. "*Around town?*"

Punctuating each sentence with a quick thrust of the bat, resembling a practice swing, her voice changed to a tiger-like hiss. "Listen carefully. Nobody around town tells me what I'm cool with. This is my business. I make the rules."

The men flinched in unison with each practice swing.

"I decide who to serve. I decide what goes down, and this—" She smashed the smoldering joint with the barrel end of the bat, which produced a resounding thud. "—is *not* going down."

Fully panicked, the men looked at Matt for help.

He raised the cleaver as if preparing to chop off the nearest enemy limb and scowled to show he was serious. After all, the odds were still three men against the two of them, even though he and Allyson had the ready weapons.

"If I ever so much as see you look at my building when you drive by," she said, "I will do to your vehicle, and then to you, what I've done to this stall. You have five seconds to get the hell out of the Halcyon forever."

Allyson and Matt stepped aside, and the men shuffled toward the door.

She unleashed a mighty swing and put another dent into the stall wall. "Five!"

The men jumped and stampeded to their table to get their jackets, then bolted out the front door.

She trailed behind them with her arms taut as she gripped the bat, poised and ready to knock someone's head into the Lake. Matt followed her out the door. She took a menacing step toward them as they drove past in an oversized pickup truck.

Rocky, who was driving, gave her the finger and yelled out his open window, "Suck my tailpipe, you cockteaser!" He revved the engine and spun the tires for a ten seconds down Halcyon Drive toward Highway 61.

When the truck was out of sight, she broke from her stance and relaxed her grip on the bat enough to let the barrel end bounce on the step. She stared out across the parking lot toward the Sawtooth Mountains silhouetted against the starry sky.

Matt let out a low whistle and relaxed his viselike grip on the cleaver. He couldn't remember ever hearing or seeing a woman as angry and menacing as she'd been in the men's room. Her switch from sweet, sensuous hostess to venom-spewing business owner was as instantaneous as flipping a light switch. He stepped next to her. "You okay?"

Still shaking with rage, she breathed deeply and continued staring into the sky.

He figured talking any more wouldn't do any good, so he stood silently, trying to wrap his mind around this unexpected side of this remarkable woman. The only reason he could think of why she went ballistic on three customers smoking pot in her men's room was to protect Josh from the evils of illicit drugs, as a parent should. However, Josh was still in the Allen household, so her demonstration wasn't meant to be a lesson to him.

His mind flashed back to their recent conversation over Cognac. She'd mentioned personal problems. That could mean anything. Health, relationships, depression, drugs. *Drugs.* Something in her past had triggered her reaction. Perhaps an unresolved addiction issue? Someone with drug problems usually attracted the law. He wasn't ready to assimilate back into society with a new identity and the heavy load of baggage he'd been keeping secret for nine months and also deal with someone in a less-than-squeaky-clean situation. Too risky.

He tried again. "What just happened, boss?" She looked at him, still upset but now with an expression that suggested he was too dense to understand. She turned and brushed past him into the Halcyon. Seconds later, he heard a muffled chorus of cheers and clapping.

He followed her to the bar. "Talk to me, Allyson. If you have a super strict policy about pot or anything else, shouldn't I know about it? I work here too. I can tell guys like them to take a hike as easy as you can if that's what you need me to do."

She fussed behind the bar, dried glasses that were dry, washed glasses that were clean, wiped spills that were nonexistent. Then she stopped and faced him with eyes full of deep hurt and pain. She looked past him to make sure no one was within earshot. "I'm not a prude. Of course, I don't want to lose my liquor license, but it's not that. It's my problem."

"If people are doing drugs in your restaurant, call the cops if the dopers look dangerous. Otherwise, we tell them nicely to take it off the property. Potheads are a pretty agreeable bunch by definition." He smiled, hoping that last line would smooth her ire a little.

She shot an exasperated look at the ceiling. "I've never given anyone in town reason to believe anything illegal goes on here. If even one person thinks that doing drugs in my restrooms is cool, then I haven't convinced anyone it's not cool. I don't want to own that kind of business." She inhaled deeply. "How can I stop people from believing what they want? How many more drug users are going to come here to get high after dinner?" She turned away and hung her head. "I want Josh to be proud of me. Someday I want him to run the place if that's what he wants to do. But not a place like this." She pointed toward the door and the departed potheads.

He had no reply.

They worked in silence for the rest of the evening, blessedly short because the last bar patrons left before last call and the dining room had emptied thirty minutes earlier.

After Allyson locked the front door and turned off the exterior lights, Matt called from the kitchen. "Go home, boss. Hannah and Brent too. I know the drill. I'll lock up."

Hannah and Brent both sighed with relief and said, "Thanks."

Allyson gave him an enigmatic look that suggested she appreciated the extra time alone, but also hinted that someday she might tell him the whole story.

As she walked out the back door, Matt wondered why this stupid incident with the potheads had increased his attraction to her.

Chapter 26

Early the next morning, Allyson descended the path behind her house down to the gravel beach along Lake Superior some fifty feet below. She often woke early to sip coffee and watch the sunrise from there. A cold front was pushing the last few dark gray clouds toward the eastern horizon. The clouds glowed luminous orange and pink as they framed the rising sun. She meditated in the frosty air for several minutes until the sun completely cleared the horizon. Once the water had changed color from steel gray to slate blue, she climbed the path back home and drove to Pauline Allen's house, arriving in time to help wake and feed Josh.

Josh's teacher had given his homework to Pauline's son, Lucas, to bring home, so Allyson ate breakfast with Josh, then tutored him for an hour or so. Josh liked school and kept up with his homework despite being hidden at the Allens' house.

Shortly after nine o'clock, she hugged and kissed him goodbye, then drove to the Halcyon. Thankful for a loyal friend such as Pauline, Allyson could devote all her energy to dealing with Donnie while he was in town making her life miserable. He'd come to the Halcyon for dinner every day but said nothing to her in the hour he took to eat. As unnerving as that was, every time she looked at him, he stared back with a confident smirk, as if he knew he'd win their battle. She didn't know why he was harassing her in that way, other than he'd not given up trying to take Josh from her.

Arriving at the Halcyon, she went in the back door and set to work. Today's first tasks were some ordering and working on paychecks. It was too early for the staff to arrive, and she found this time period the best for concentrating. Shortly after she'd sat at her desk, a loud knock at the front door startled her. Her first thought was of Donnie back to harass her. Who she saw when she went to the front door made her heart race.

Sheriff Roy Hotchkiss, a tall, thick man with gray, stubbly hair and a rugged, weatherworn face, tipped his hat when she opened the door. "Ms. Clifford. Sorry to bother you this time of day."

"What's wrong? Is it Josh?"

"Ah, no." The grim-faced Hotchkiss looked away, then over her shoulder. "I need to discuss something with you. Mind if I come in?"

Allyson gestured him in and stepped back as he entered.

He removed his wide-brimmed uniform hat and thrummed it with his fingers. "I don't know how to break this to you since everyone in town seems to like you, but someone left me an anonymous note this morning. Said drug deals were going down in your establishment."

The statement curled her hands into fists, and she widened her eyes in surprise. Her mind flashed on the dopers she'd chased out of the men's room last night. She shook her head. "Impossible, Sheriff. I had some trouble with three men who tried to smoke pot in my restroom, but I chased them out. I didn't call you because I felt I should handle the situation immediately. I assure you I don't condone drugs, use drugs, or sell drugs in the Halcyon or anywhere, nor do I allow anyone else to sell drugs here. The Halcyon is my livelihood. I wouldn't dare risk losing my liquor license."

He nodded. "All the same, I'd like to check it out."

"Check out what?"

Hotchkiss fondled his hat's crown. "According to the tip, a buyer hides money somewhere in the restaurant. The dealer comes in, takes the money, replaces it with the drugs, and leaves. Soon after that, the buyer comes back and takes the drugs. Could happen in the coatroom, the restrooms, maybe a back closet. Hell, even under a table."

She pressed her palm against her forehead to suppress an instant headache. Dealing with Donnie and hiding Josh was bad enough. Now the Sheriff was telling her the Halcyon might be a drug clearing house. She studied Hotchkiss's face, pleading with her eyes for him to say this was all a bad practical joke.

He shifted his weight and studied her face with narrowed eyes and a tilted head. "I can't force you to allow me to search without a warrant," he said, "but I was hoping you'd let me poke around unofficially, then I can put this to rest."

"Okay." She shook her head slowly. "I have no idea who came up with this lame tip, but go ahead. Look anywhere you want. I have nothing to hide."

Hotchkiss walked around the perimeter of the bar and dining room, looking under tables, behind booths, under seat cushions. Allyson trailed behind him, growing more frustrated with each step. Her stomach rumbled, and her mind raced trying to imagine who might have done this to her.

Then Hotchkiss went down the hall to the restrooms. He checked the men's room first, looking inside the towel dispenser before stepping into each of the two stalls, feeling behind the fixtures and lifting the lids from the water tanks. Nothing.

Next, they entered the women's room. Hotchkiss repeated the search, but in the first stall he mumbled a startled, "Uh-oh."

"What?"

He held a tank lid for her to see. Duct-taped to the underside of the lid was a sandwich-sized plastic bag filled with a green, leafy substance similar to dried herbs.

Her stomach clenched, and her skin temperature shot up several degrees. She tried to speak, but all she could do was drop her jaw and stare incredulously at the Sheriff.

Hotchkiss cocked his head sideways. "We got us a little problem here, Ms. Clifford."

Her immediate thought was to get Josh and run as far away as possible. However, running would signal her guilt, and she wasn't guilty. For the first time ever, at least until Donnie had appeared, Allyson felt she'd achieved stability in her life. A blissful normal. She didn't want to lose that. *No. Stay and fight.* "I swear to you, Sheriff, I have no knowledge of any drug dealing."

He let out a noncommittal grunt and removed the baggie by peeling off the tape, taking care not to touch the bag itself. "Looks like marijuana." He sniffed the outside of the bag, then held it toward her. "Yep."

Her spirits sank toward her toes. She pointed at the bag and locked her gaze onto Hotchkiss's eyes. "That isn't my pot, Sheriff. None of my regular customers would do this to me. This must be some sort of setup."

"I want to believe you, but ..." He raised his eyebrows to emphasize the obvious.

"What are you going to do?"

Hotchkiss put on a latex glove, then hefted the baggie as if weighing its contents. "I won't press any charges since I have no probable cause, and the pot could've been put here by anyone. Might be able to lift some finger-prints. I'll confiscate this as potential evidence for a future prosecution."

The three dopers were her likeliest suspects, but they had been in the men's room, not the ladies' room. Might Hannah have something to do with this? Difficult to believe since she had proclaimed several times that any kind of drug users were losers. Allyson realized any customer who'd been in the Halcyon over the past month might be the culprit.

"Of course, if you have someone in mind who might have stored the pot here, I can keep an eye on that person." He pulled an evidence bag from his coat pocket and placed the pot baggie inside.

Allyson's fingers tensed into claws, but she hid them from Hotchkiss's view. "My only guess would've been my ex-chef, Gary Soukkala." She dismissed that idea immediately after she spoke. If the pot belonged to him, he would have stopped by for it before quitting. "But he and I had an understanding. He never brought pot or any other drugs to work, and I cut him some slack for being late or hung-over."

"Where is he now?"

"Long gone. He and his girlfriend moved to Arizona."

Hotchkiss rubbed his chin. "Hmm. What about your new cook?"

She hadn't considered Matt as a possible drug dealer or user. Then again, what did she really know about him? "He's an emergency sub. Temporary. I don't know him well enough to form much of an opinion, except he's a conscientious worker."

"Any reason to suspect him?"

She shook her head. "My gut tells me no. He's an extreme sports enthusiast. Training and all."

"Lots of athletes do drugs, especially pot. Could I talk to him?"

"He doesn't come in for a while. Stop back after the lunch rush if you want to talk to him."

"Okay. What's his name?"

"Matt Johnson."

Hotchkiss jotted notes in his notebook as they walked toward the front door. He stepped onto the front stoop and turned to face her. "Watch out for suspicious characters. If anyone looks like they're high or doing a deal, you call me right away."

"I certainly will, Sheriff."

Matt came into her view as they talked, walking around the bend in Halcyon Drive. When he saw the Sheriff's cruiser and Hotchkiss standing in the door, he ducked back into the trees lining the road. Allyson had opened her mouth to say Matt was coming, but stopped when he bolted. She caught herself too late because Hotchkiss noticed.

He turned to see what had startled her. "Something wrong, Ms. Clifford?"

"Oh, uh, no. Thought I saw a deer." She forced a weak smile.

"Okay. Sorry to ruin the start of your day." He donned his hat and left.

Allyson closed the door and stared out the window to see when, or if, Matt would emerge from the trees. Had she made a huge mistake in asking him to stay and help? If so, should she confront him? Ask him to leave and not give him a reason? Lie and say she found a new chef? But if he left, who could she get to take his place?

Chapter 27

Seeing a sheriff at the Halcyon changed Matt's mind about breakfast there, so he headed for the local coffee shop, Dangerous Grounds. He first thought Allyson had suspected him of something and called the authorities. But she'd seen him as he approached the Halcyon and didn't alert the sheriff. Still, the sheriff might have seen his wanted photo and was going door to door looking for Matt Lanier. Was she covering for him?

Inside the coffee shop—a comfortable-looking room with a half dozen ancient wood tables and local artwork on the brightly colored walls—he ordered oatmeal, a breakfast sandwich, coffee, and orange juice. He sat at a corner table away from the window.

His morning took another turn for the worse when Donnie Vossler and the kid in black he'd been talking to at McDonald's the other day stopped outside the coffee shop. After they had talked for a moment, the kid nodded. Vossler patted him on the back. The kid continued in the same direction while Vossler walked in. He stood in the doorway, scoping the room as Matt imagined a crook would—shifty eyes looking for enemies or easy targets for some sort of con.

When Vossler saw Matt, his face froze in a half-smile. He looked away, then sauntered to the counter and ordered coffee in a loud, confident voice.

Matt grabbed a section of the newspaper from an adjoining table, opening it high enough to cover most of his face but still allowing him to see Vossler in his peripheral vision. The barista brought him his meal. Seconds later, Vossler appeared beyond his newspaper, holding his coffee cup at his waist.

"Yo, Matt," Vossler said. "How you doing today?"

Matt put an annoyed look on his face, nodded, and started to eat, hoping Vossler would take the hint.

Vossler sat at an adjacent table. He slurped his coffee and sat back in his chair. "Ahh, not bad for Nowheresville coffee."

Matt glanced up. Vossler was staring at him.

"Too bad about Allyson, huh?"

Matt didn't see a way to ignore this annoying jerk without the other patrons noticing. No sense attracting attention or stares in case the sheriff was looking for him and had notified the entire town to be on the lookout for Matt Lanier. "What about her?"

"The sheriff busted her for drugs this morning."

"What?" Where had Vossler gotten that crazy idea? Had the Three High Amigos gotten revenge for last night by somehow planting drugs at the Halcyon?

Vossler smirked as if this were the most satisfying piece of news he'd heard in weeks. "Yeah, I hear he found a stash of weed in the place." His vocal tone was different today. Still a rumbling bass mixed with reedy bassoon but higher pitched now. Tighter.

"I hadn't heard." He didn't disagree because he didn't want to tip off his intuitive loyalty to Allyson. More importantly, he wanted to stay far away from anything remotely related to illegal, even if it was only a discussion.

"I'm not surprised." Vossler raised his eyebrows as if appraising Matt's worthiness of hearing more but also showing his eagerness to dish some dirt on his wife. "Typical Allyson."

Matt ate a spoonful of his oatmeal.

"I'm surprised she stayed straight this long, assuming this is the first time she's lapsed." Vossler must have decided his gossip was too juicy to save.

Matt sipped his coffee.

"Her habit goes way back. Maybe she started selling pot at the Halcyon to raise some dough for some serious stuff for herself. When we were married, I knew she liked to party, but wow, she got too crazy for me. She started flirting with bad boys, always the first sign of trouble. I figured all the money she spent was going for manicures, spa treatments, and shit like that. Turns out she was getting high on coke with some dealer.

She snorted for a year before I found out. Of course, we fought about it, probably the main reason we broke up. I worried more about Josh. She didn't seem to care much about him." His voice had crept up another half step. Something was different.

Matt subdued an are-you-kidding expression. Everything he'd seen about Allyson's relationship with Josh was that of a near-perfect mother. The fundamental flaw with single parenting was the lack of time with a child, but Allyson seemed to make up for the small quantity of time with excellent quality. Josh appeared to be the happiest kid he'd ever seen, well adjusted, confident, smart, thriving in school, and with a heart-melting personality. How could a drug-addicted mother raise her son so well? It didn't seem possible.

"Then, of course, she up and kidnaps him. I figured they'd arrest her within days. She must've fooled someone but good. Five years and no one's caught up to her?" Vossler made a motion as if to tip an invisible hat. "I doff my chapeau, but now I think she's cracking."

"Kind of ironic you think she's going back to that life right when you show up, eh?"

Vossler shrugged. "Coincidence, pal. What I hear, a junkie can only stay straight for so long. Once you're hooked, you stay hooked until you're in jail or dead."

"Are you saying this to get me on your side or to get me to spread rumors so Allyson loses in the court of public opinion?"

Vossler's face soured, and his expression took on a calculating coldness. "Fancy talk, fry boy. What's your story, anyway? You sound too smart for a short-order cook in this backwater."

Matt sensed Vossler would keep digging if he detected any fear or weakness. He stood and gulped the last of his coffee, but left the remainder of his oatmeal. "Excuse me. I have to go to my dead-end job."

Vossler glanced at his watch. "What's the rush? That dive bar don't open 'til eleven."

"None of your business."

Vossler turned as Matt walked toward the door. "You're one hell of a runner, Johnson. You must have quite the past you're trying to get away from."

Matt burned inside but said nothing. *Don't encourage the asshole by losing your own self-control, Matty.*

"I'm telling you, pal," Vossler raised his voice so everyone in the room could hear, causing Matt to look back at him. "She's an addict. Heroin, cocaine, 'ludes, bennies. You sell 'em, she'll buy 'em." Vossler spread his hands as if pleading for mercy. "What kind of mother can she possibly be to my son?" Not only was Vossler's voice pitched higher, but his tempo had also increased. Most listeners wouldn't have noticed, but Matt's hearing was trained to hear the difference between a violin tuned to A440 Hz compared to one tuned to A441 Hz, and he could discern tempo changes of as little as one or two beats per minute.

The eyes and ears of the half-dozen Dangerous Grounds customers were focused on Vossler. Matt envisioned these witnesses whipping out cell phones or scurrying to their neighbors as soon as he and Vossler left. "Do you live in a glass house, Vossler?"

"Huh?"

"Because all I see is you throwing stones at Allyson. What kind of father were you to your son?"

Disconcerted, Vossler blustered, "Hey, I'm not the addict." He looked at the customers, his expression appealing to them for sympathy.

Matt waved him off and left.

Outside, he filled his lungs with frigid air, glad to escape the suddenly suffocating coffee shop. He walked toward the Halcyon. As much as he was attracted to Allyson and totally enraptured with Josh, his gut roiled with a dull, churning ache. He needed to get away, keep moving, find a safer place. Sticking around, becoming a familiar face, might trigger a connection to last spring in someone's mind. He tried to force the dread from his body, but the feeling grew stronger each day since he'd returned from his self-imposed exile in the wilderness.

Vossler loomed up from behind, which caused him to flinch, but he kept walking. Vossler fell into step next to him.

"Forgot to tell you one thing, pal." Vossler sounded eager to tell him what probably amounted to more mud slung at Allyson.

"You told me enough. I get it." Matt forced a hard edge into his voice. "Some addicts turn their lives around. From what I've seen, she's clean and sober. We shared a cognac one night. That's all I've seen her drink. I've never seen her look like she was high in any other way since I've known her."

Vossler laughed, which surprised Matt. He'd expected Vossler to chastise him for being so naïve, so trusting, so gullible. Had he overlooked the warning signs because of his attraction to her?

"Ooh, Mister Experience. Known Allyson for what, two weeks? Gimme a break." Vossler's tone turned cold and hard, consistent with the image of him Matt wanted to believe. "How do you think she got money for all those drugs back then, found a pot of gold at the end of a fucking rainbow?"

"I'd have to believe you first before I'd considered it."

"Man," Vossler shook his head and laughed silently, "You really are a hick from the sticks. Figure it out, Gomer Pyle. Have you taken a good look at her?"

Matt stopped and faced Vossler, who stopped too. They locked eyes. "What's your point?"

Vossler thrust his hands forward. "She was a hooker. A damn one. Expensive too."

Matt froze, not wanting to give Vossler the pleasure of seeing he'd been surprised. He tried to swallow, but his tight throat choked off his saliva. Vossler's stare shifted back and forth to each of his eyes, looking for some clue of emotion: shock, anger. Arousal?

"And she'll hook again, guaranteed." Vossler's voice had increased another half step in pitch. Faster tempo. More tension. Why?

Prostitution. Addiction. Drug dealing. Child custody battles. Matt became so overwhelmed he got a sudden urge to return to his abandoned campsite at Solitude Lake, climb into his sleeping bag, and sleep off this developing nightmare until the spring thaw.

A cruel smile formed on Vossler's lips. "Ask her yourself. Maybe she'll even give you a new-customer discount on a blow job." He cackled at his wittiness, then got into his Cadillac Escalade and drove away.

Chapter 28

Ben Nowitzki spent most of his morning trolling the casino in Grand Portage. Since Lanier was an accused criminal, it made some sense he'd gravitate to criminal activities such as gambling. Not that the Grand Portage Band of Lake Superior Chippewa ran a questionable establishment. In fact, it was clean, modern, and well run, albeit sparsely attended on a frigid January day.

Ben wandered the slot machine aisles, studied the card players, played a few hands of blackjack so he wouldn't attract too much attention from the pit bosses, and checked out every man even remotely resembling Matt Lanier.

After dropping fifty dollars in thirty minutes at a blackjack table and waiting until he was the lone player, Ben said to the dealer, "I'm waiting for a friend of mine to show up. I think he might've come a day early, or maybe I'm a day late. Have you seen a guy near my age, about six feet tall, brown hair, decent looking, but not a movie star, with a bum left hand?"

"Nah," the dealer said. He was a black-haired Native in his twenties who was himself good-looking enough to be a movie star. "Just old folks this time of year. The gambling addicts."

"Okay, thanks. I'll try the restaurant." Ben took his chips and cashed out on his way to the buffet.

He tried the same approach with his server in the restaurant, the bartender at the adjoining bar, and the front desk clerk. No one had seen a man matching Lanier's description. While questioning the desk clerk, Ben learned the casino and hotel were essentially the only game in town. So he headed for Grand Marais, figuring he could get there and scout around a few hours before the town shut down for the evening.

Along the way, he stopped at every open gas station, gift shop, motel, and restaurant on Highway 61. He knocked on a few doors in the small settlements of Croftville and Hovland, asking if anyone had seen, heard, or taken in a stranger or hitchhiker for a meal or a bed. As expected, no one resembling Matt Lanier had stopped in during the past few days. He was beginning to feel foolish for hoping he might blunder onto one man among thousands of inhabitants and travelers along a remote highway.

At eight o'clock, Ben reached Grand Marais and found a room at the Best Western at the northeast end of the business district. Only a handful of the town's many restaurants were open in winter, so he made the short walk to Wisconsin Avenue and headed for the Gunflint Tavern for a meal and a much-desired beer.

Chapter 29

The Halcyon was empty before nine o'clock. Allyson feigned optimism for an hour, then finally caved and closed early, a first since Matt had been there.

Matt began his closing routine, all the chores that had become second nature to him in the two short weeks he'd worked as a cook. To his surprise, he enjoyed working in a restaurant. Check that. He enjoyed working for Allyson in her restaurant. What unnerved him was working for a possible drug addict. It might only be a matter of time before he was entangled in a drug bust as a potential witness. The aching lump in his stomach from wanting to leave steadily grew.

Vossler's preposterous story about Allyson being busted today was obviously false since she was here and working. He wanted to ask about it but hesitated to inquire into her sexual past. Vossler's linking the two sounded like bullshit, but it wasn't an uncommon occurrence—drug addicts selling their bodies for drug money.

After Hannah and Brent had left and Allyson was engaging the security system, Matt decided to broach the drug topic. As they walked toward the back door, he said, "I hear the Sheriff paid you a visit this morning."

She stopped and looked at him square-jawed. "Yes. Did you stash the pot in my restroom?"

He couldn't have been more startled. He recoiled in surprised shock, mouth agape. "What? Me? Where'd you get that idea?"

"You turned and ran when you saw the Sheriff."

"Vossler told me it's your pot."

She glanced skyward and let out a frustrated groan. "You're on his side now?"

"I didn't say that."

"You haven't answered my original question."

Anger and frustration welled up inside. She'd accused him without probable cause. "I'll make it simple for you. No. And as soon as I can pack up my gear, I'm outta here."

"You're quitting on me?"

His head snapped around to face her. "Isn't that what you want?"

"I don't want a drug user on my payroll. You decide what it means."

He exhaled through puffed cheeks. "Look, I haven't smoked pot in years. I've never done hard drugs. I don't deal, and I didn't hide any pot in your toilet. I've overstayed my welcome for my own reasons. You've had time to find a replacement. We agreed this arrangement would only last for a few weeks. I need to think of me first."

She unclenched and softened her expression. "You're right. But why did you hide from the Sheriff?"

It was his turn to unclench. "I had a different reason to hide."

"Such as?"

He shook his head. "I don't want you to get messed up in my problems."

"Fair enough. I guess I wanted to put the drugs on you to have an easy scapegoat for my problems."

"That kind of makes us even." He shook his head, disappointed he'd let her extract this much information from him. "I don't want to quit. I enjoy working for you. I get along well with the staff, and I—" He caught himself as he was about to say *love*. "—um, really like Josh." He also didn't mention how much he was attracted to her. No need to compound their relationship by implying he was trying to get to her through Josh, because he wasn't. Josh had simply charmed him off the hook. He was the kind of kid Matt had dreamed of having for a son.

"I won't beg you to stay, but Josh likes you a lot too."

"If I stay, your battle with Vossler might end up screwing me over." Matt took a deep breath, tried to soften the tension in his voice, the apprehension in his mind. "I see him dealing drugs, threatening—"

"Wait, what? Dealing drugs?"

"Yeah, to some kid at McDonald's, the day he showed up here."

"Oh my God," she said with hushed fear in her voice. "He's playing for keeps. Probably buying some information about me. I hope it wasn't that Pauline and I are friends. That would ruin her house as a hiding place for Josh."

Matt continued. "And then these bizarre incidents with the pot smokers in the can and the drunk who assaulted you at the bar. It's like watching a Fellini movie that even Fellini wouldn't understand."

She gazed out the door toward an unseen Lake Superior.

"What really happened between you and Donnie?"

Returning her gaze to him, she said, "It's not important now."

"Hey, I understand how relationships can implode. I lost the best thing that ever happened to me because she got tired of me not supporting her as much as she supported me." His voice dropped almost to a whisper. "Then I lost her forever, and it was my fault." He turned away when his voice began to quaver.

"How could you understand when I still don't?" she said. "I was a typical female victim who was conned by the man I loved into believing that everything he did to me, the way he used me, the lies he told me, was my fault." Her hands went to her sides, fists balled and emphasizing each phrase. "How foolish was that?"

"So why won't you tell me?"

She held his eyes, defiant, then looked away. "Josh. If he ever found out what I've done, it would ruin his life. That would devastate me."

He ran his fingers through his hair, wanting to grab a hank and pull it out in frustration. Whatever she was hiding must be pretty bad to fear ruining two lives. He muttered, "Sorry. I'm only trying to help," and walked out without looking back.

As he walked toward Allyson's house, the hair on the back of his neck prickled from her icy stare. He and she were similar in one big way—stubborn to a fault. Stubbornness had cost him his career, his boyhood home, his comfortable life, his friends, his wife. He hoped Allyson's stubbornness wouldn't explode her life the way his had exploded.

She called after him. "Are you quitting or not?"

He stopped in his tracks. The icy wind stung his face. After a moment, he half-turned toward her. "I'll decide in the morning."

Chapter 30

The Gunflint Tavern was nearly empty. A few men who looked like regulars sat at the bar sipping beers. Two older couples occupied window tables and ate their meals.

Ben went to the bar, leaving one barstool between him and the nearest local. He intended to play the stranger ready to engage in jovial bar banter instead of the stranger pushy enough to plop down next to someone and ask if he'd seen a wanted killer in the past few days.

The bartender, a young woman with blond hair pulled into a ponytail, took his order of a burger and fries along with a shot of Jack and a tap Budweiser.

After he'd downed the shot and taken a sip of beer, he glanced at the men at the bar and nodded. They nodded or tipped their glasses slightly.

"Sure feels good to get out of that wind," Ben said.

"You got that right," said the closest man. "We been let off easy the past three winters. I'm almost turning into one o' them southern Minnesotans who think twenty below zero is something to piss 'n' moan about for weeks."

Game on. Ben used his ploy from the casino about meeting up with a reclusive friend who had little regard for time or day. Over the course of his meal and two rounds for the men at the bar, he got the lowdown on what businesses were open, the best ice fishing lake within fifty miles, and the identity of the area's leading adulterers. They gave him the names and locations of lodging establishments where he could check to see if Lanier had possibly spent a night or two. But no one offered any information about a stranger matching Lanier's description passing through. All this took much longer than asking them directly, but Ben didn't want to arouse that automatic suspicion small-town folks get when private investigators come snooping around. Besides, he had to eat sometime. He might as well make it a working dinner.

Armed with this data overload, Ben made the rounds the next day. He first went to the lodging establishments where he could present his credentials and not arouse as much suspicion. Hotel and motel staffs were routinely asked about suspicious behavior by police, as well as having to deal with individuals who weren't breaking the law but were causing some sort of disturbance while renting a room.

He next stopped at the local coffee joints in case any early morning groups were there for their usual cups of whatever and gossip. The two groups he encountered were older and cordial enough, but none recalled seeing any notable strangers in town recently.

At noon, he stopped at the Angry Trout for lunch, inquired about any suspicious-looking men who might have recently eaten there, then checked the other restaurants in town before heading over to the sheriff's office.

His tactic with law enforcement was to describe Lanier but not give them a name because the man he was looking for had many aliases and would not likely use his real name. He explained the lack of a photo by saying his client told him the man grew his hair and beard (probably true) so a photo wouldn't help. They'd have to make do with the description Ben gave them, which was a detailed description of the photo used by law enforcement when the murders Lanier allegedly committed were first being investigated last spring.

After striking out with the sheriff, Ben finished the afternoon by canvassing the rest of the open retail businesses. He returned to his motel room around six p.m. He'd been working the case for fifty-four hours. He wasn't surprised that he'd found nothing, but it still demoralized him because he was sensing the impossibility of finding someone who didn't want to be found. He called Mr. Jones with his daily report, then went back to the Gunflint Tavern for dinner.

Chapter 31

An hour before opening the next day, Allyson arrived at the Halcyon in a hopeful mood. Certainly, all the crap that had come down lately was merely a string of coincidental bad luck. She called the *Arrowhead Times* advertising department and set up a two-for-one entrée coupon to be published in the next four weekly editions and an ad listing a week's worth of daily specials and half-priced bottles of wine Tuesday through Thursday. When in trouble, cut prices. Some people will vote with their wallets instead of their moral outrage.

A few minutes after she started working out the day's menu, Matt tapped on her open office door.

"You decided to stay?" she said with a tinge of hope.

"For now." His tone and expression were neutral as he walked to the kitchen.

"Thank you." She was genuinely relieved for the moment, even though his commitment to her now stood at zero. It wouldn't surprise her if he changed his mind and left in the next five minutes.

When Hannah and Brent arrived, Allyson walked into the dining room and called her staff together. "Business has sucked for a while now and doesn't look like it'll pick up anytime soon. Hannah and Brent, I want you to know your jobs are safe."

As expected, their expressions showed relief.

"Matt is only temporary, so if business is still slow when he leaves, I'll handle the kitchen the best I can." She looked at Matt, who pursed his lips into a flat smile in acknowledgment of their tension. "I'll put off hiring a new chef for now."

"Is there anything we can do to help?" Hannah asked.

"Just give the customers your usual excellent service, sweetie." Allyson put her hand on Hannah's shoulder and smiled. "Don't give them any reason to go somewhere else next time they eat out."

"I won't," Hannah said, beaming from the compliment.

Brent stared at his shoes. "If it helps, Ms. Clifford, you can have my share of the tips."

Allyson felt a pang of affection and put her hand to her heart. "Oh no, Brent honey, I could never take your tips. You work hard for me every day. Just keep on doing the best job you can." She gave him a long, tight hug.

Noting the time, Allyson said, "Let's get ready to open, guys. Today might be the day we get back to normal." She forced a smile as the others left to prepare.

The first customer didn't come in until almost noon. Today would not be the day business returned to normal.

Around one o'clock, Sheriff Hotchkiss stopped by for a club sandwich and a cola. When Allyson brought his drink, he said, "Any more suspicious activity to report?"

"Happily, no."

"I've arranged for an extra drive-by every night. Increases the chance I—or one of my deputies—will be close in case of an emergency."

"I appreciate that, Sheriff."

Business until then had been barely average compared to the past week, mainly a few travelers at lunch who didn't know to avoid the scandalized Halcyon. Charlie and Grace Simpson, owners of Dangerous Grounds, stopped in to give her some moral support. Allyson comped them cups of coffee even though she suspected they were there only to gauge whether they'd need to hire another barista for the expected influx of lunch customers if the Halcyon permanently closed.

The dinner rush consisted of two foursomes on ski weekends who were tired of cooking dinner in their rental condos. They'd all been served, and no one sat at the bar, so Allyson wandered the restaurant, trying to look busy or pausing to schmooze the diners.

A few minutes after she'd given up hovering over the dining room and retreated to her office, a long horn blast sounded from the parking lot and startled everyone inside.

Brent, who was stocking the bar with glasses, went to the front window and looked out. "Ms. Clifford, it's a Winnebago."

Allyson joined him. A small Winnebago motor home had parked against the back curb, taking up three spaces by parking perpendicular to the space lines. A car was parked behind the motor home. She was about to turn away when she noticed the Winnebago moving rhythmically up and down.

She sagged forward and leaned against the window frame with her forehead. "I'm going outside for a minute, Brent. Be right back."

"Okay," he said and returned to his duties.

Allyson donned her coat and gloves and stepped gingerly across the icy asphalt. After rapping on the front door of the RV, she heard muffled voices followed by footsteps.

The door opened a crack and part of a woman's face appeared. The single eye Allyson saw was covered in too much black mascara and eyeliner. A lock of white-blonde hair curled above her eye. "Yeah, what?" Her voice was hard-edged.

Allyson got a whiff of a musky perfume so dense she thought her nose hair might curl. She held down her anger and disgust with difficulty. "Sorry to bother you. I own this restaurant, and I noticed you were, um, having sex in my parking lot."

"So?"

"Will you please move somewhere else?"

A wall of heat wafted out of the RV as the door opened wider and the woman moved to fill the opening. Her features were as coarse as her voice. She had an average, but doughy, figure and wore flame red lingerie under a filmy peignoir.

"Honey, we're inside, and the shades are down. It ain't like we're doing it outside." She brought a lit cigarette up to her lips, inhaled, and flicked the long ash into an unseen receptacle on the counter next to the door. She exhaled slowly and defiantly.

Allyson tried to keep her voice cheery but assertive. "Yes, I know, and thanks for that." *At least.* "But I don't want my customers seeing you. It's bad for business. Besides, you're on my property. If you don't leave, you're trespassing."

The woman maintained a blank expression except for raising thickly penciled eyebrows. "Oh, so you want a little cash in exchange for me taking up three parking spaces."

"What? No, I don't want money. Why do you think I want anything from you except to leave?"

"The cost of doing business, honey. But hey, maybe I can send a few of my customers your way when they're done. I'm booked full tonight."

Customers? Booked?

Realization hit her like a slap across her cheek. A sick feeling welled up in her stomach, raced up her throat, and put a sour taste into her mouth. A mobile hooker in her parking lot? This cannot be happening. Getting her baseball bat and pounding on the Winnebago until the hooker left seemed like the best solution, but she didn't want her customers to see her lose her cool again. Allyson tried to calm her jangled nerves, but still spoke through clenched teeth. "You've got five minutes to get off my property."

"Or what, you gonna call the cops?" The blonde stood up to her full height and crossed her arms under her breasts, forcing the flab further up and out from the lacy top. Despite her attire, she looked ready for a catfight.

"No, because unless a deputy's in the vicinity, you'll be long gone by the time he gets here. But one call to my friend Pauline and within five minutes she'll have everyone in town here with torches and sledgehammers to trash your RV ... *Honey.*"

"Well, goody fuckin' gumdrops for Pauline. When I see them torches out my window, I'll leave. Until then, I'm busy." She slammed the door.

Allyson flapped her arms upward in frustration. When she heard a feminine giggle and observed the back half of the motor home bouncing rhythmically up and down again, she kicked a tire as hard as she dared. Even though the occupants of the Winnebago were probably breaking some arcane law, she felt powerless to do anything, so she went back inside the Halcyon.

Matt was busy in the kitchen, but Hannah and Brent stood by the front door windows. Their faces showed bemused puzzlement.

She started to explain the situation when the phone rang. At last. Maybe a customer was calling to place a takeout order or reserve a table for a late dinner.

"Thanks for calling the Halcyon Bar and Grill. May I help you?" she said in her most professionally pleasant voice.

"Yeah, Baby Doll, it's me."

A chilling wave of dread washed from her head to her feet. "What do you want?"

"Just calling to see how my son is doing." Judging by his tone, he wasn't the least bit concerned about Josh.

She made sure no customers were within earshot, then said with venom in her voice, "Bullshit, Donnie. What do you really want?"

"You're right, Baby Doll. I also wanted to know if you're getting any extra business from the Winnie in your parking lot."

Allyson almost dropped the phone. God damn him to hell. One second after she'd recovered from that surprise, she almost screamed into the phone, "You bastard. Why are you doing this?"

Donnie chuckled in the condescending way a husband does when his wife is irrationally afraid of spiders in the basement. "Doing what?"

The stark reality of the past several days finally hit home. Donnie was behind everything—the pot stashed in the ladies' room, the tokers in the men's room, the attempted sexual assault on her, and now the mobile hooker. He was sabotaging her business in order to get Josh. He must have been planning this moment since he first appeared in Castle Danger, and she wouldn't let him see his son.

Her knees buckled, so she groped for a barstool to sit on lest she collapsed to the floor.

Matt had come from the kitchen to get a club soda from the gun tap at the bar. As she staggered, he sprang toward her to provide assistance.

She waved a hand to signal she was okay and sat.

Donnie said, "You were always too smart for your own good, *Sue*." The emphasis on her given name was obvious. He wanted to regain control of her. "I want my son. I don't care if you're part of the bargain or not. You want to come back to me? I'm cool with that. You'll be way better off in L.A. No more scraping a living from a glorified roadside tavern, believing you're some modern fucking independent single mom who can manage fine without her man, her husband, the father of her child."

Her face numbed, and her blood chilled as he spoke. The day she'd taken Josh and left Donnie for good, her only goal was to live a life free of him, no matter how horrible it might turn out. Donnie was the ocean, more than willing to swallow her, dissolve her, destroy her. Josh was her life preserver.

In five years, she'd built the foundation for a decent life. A few more years of business success and she'd have considered her mission complete—stable home, steady income, Josh growing up in a safe place with people and quality schools.

"You will never get Josh, Donnie. I—I—" Her confidence dissolved. A thought flashed through her mind, quickly dismissed, that she'd kill Josh and herself before she let Donnie back into her son's life. She shuddered as if shocked by a plunge into Lake Superior.

She couldn't beat him if he'd so easily caused all these problems. Even though going to the police would be futile because she had no proof Donnie was behind all the mischief, she'd never go to the police for fear of Josh learning about her past with Donnie. She couldn't let Josh suffer from the weight of those facts while he was so young.

He laughed, evil and cruel. "It's fun making you squirm, Susie Q, but I'm getting bored. Make it easy on yourself. Give up now. I'll even hire a nanny for Josh, so you and me can go out and party like we used to. I might talk to some of our old clients, you know, the producers and directors. I'm sure I can persuade them to put you into one of their movies. I gotta say you've only gotten more gorgeous in five years. More mature. Like Julia Roberts in Pretty Woman compared with Mystic Pizza. You got so much more elegance. Hell, we could go back into business together. I'm sure we'd make twice as much as the old days."

The thought of returning to her old, nightmarish life and all its downsides was too much to comprehend. She blindly tossed the phone aside and buried her head in her arms on the bar. The phone clattered and landed keypad side up.

Donnie's voice sounded through the phone receiver—tinny but still sinister. "You can't ignore me. You can't win. I have all the time in the world and a dozen more ways to dump on your business."

She heard Matt pick up the phone.

"Who is this?" he asked.

Pause.

"Listen, Vossler, why can't you leave her and Josh alone? Don't you understand she's done with you?"

Allyson raised her head. Matt's expression was one of a big brother looking at a little sister who's been bullied at the neighborhood playground. She groaned. She could see this blowing up into some sort of love triangle thing, even though she thought she'd sufficiently suppressed her attraction to Matt.

"Drop whatever you're doing to Allyson, or you'll find the police knocking on your door. Understand?"

She sat up, waved her hands, signaling *Don't get involved* to Matt, and put a look on her face that implied this wasn't as big of a crisis as he seemed to think it was.

Matt raised his hand to a stop position.

Pause.

His face registered complete surprise. He slowly hung up the phone.

"Matt, you don't need to fight my battles for me."

"I'm not so sure I want to after what he said."

"What?" her body felt as if it were wrapped in a weighted tarp immobilizing her muscles.

He shuffled his feet and glanced around the room for a few seconds. "He said to ask you why he's not worried about any police."

So that was Donnie's trump card. Her belly churned and the urge to flee shot through her muscles. Running was the last thing she had told herself she would do. Indecision pulled at her as if she were the rope in a tug-of-war. She went into her office and slammed the door.

Chapter 32

A confused Matt stepped outside to get some air and clear his mind. His thinking was as chaotic and discordant as music by Arnold Schoenberg or Ornette Coleman. Allyson had said Vossler was a crook. Vossler should have been worried about Allyson complaining to the cops—unless he was so powerful he had the police bought and paid for. But why buy off a county sheriff's office two thousand miles from Los Angeles?

Then again, if Allyson feared the police more than Vossler feared them, perhaps sabotaging her business was a calculated gamble to force her hand. What terrible crime had she committed that put her custody of Josh at risk?

Matt went inside. A blast of heat enveloped him. A second later, another blast hit him, this one of revelation. Vossler's voice had sounded different at the coffee shop because he was lying. Matt raced past Hannah and Brent, who loitered by the bar. Matt knocked on the office door, paused, and entered.

Allyson sat in her chair, staring out the window into the black night.

"Allyson, I'm convinced Josh belongs with you. I want to help."

She turned enough for him to see one eye. Her expression indicated she didn't care what he wanted. After a long moment, she said in a lifeless tone, "Oh goodie. Everything will be peachy keen from now on." She turned back to the window.

"Vossler's been lying to me from the start. I'm not looking to get mixed up in a dispute that might get the law on my ass. If I'm going to help you, I need to understand your relationship with him."

Swiveling to face him full on, Allyson set her jaw, and her eyes caught fire. "Don't you dare patronize me. Believing my side of the story is an ocean away from doing anything about it." Her voice became quiet and bitter. "I survived all sorts of shit long before you showed up. I'll fix this myself."

Matt's temper warmed. "I wouldn't call what you've done so far fixing the problem." He thrust his arm toward the outside in the general direction of Vossler. "Unless you've got some secret battle plan you're not sharing, Vossler will win. He's turning the entire town against you with all the lies he's spewing and the mini dramas he's staged here since he showed up. I suggest you take help from anyone who offers."

The fire in her eyes subsided. Her head drooped and she sunk into her chair. "If I confide in you, I want to know one thing in return."

"What?"

She looked up. "Why are you using a fake name?" Her eyes were alert for his reaction.

Matt blanched with panic and stiffened to keep from bolting out the door. She *had* found his wallet that first night. He forced himself to meet her gaze. "It's complicated."

"Are you hiding from the cops?"

A wave of exhaustion hit him. He hadn't realized how stressed out he'd been from living a lie since returning to civilization. Maybe confiding in someone would reduce that stress. If she was hiding something too, who better to trust than another fugitive? He nodded and softly said, "Yes."

"I guess that puts us on even footing."

"Maybe we can help each other."

A slight smile curled the corner of her mouth. "Let's close up. I'll send Hannah and Brent home if you get rid of the Winnebago."

"The what?"

She briefed him on her encounter with the Motor Home Madam.

He laughed aloud for the first time in almost a year. A bit of tension left his body.

She glared at him down. "It's not funny."

"Sorry, but it is."

Allyson cracked a smile as they walked to the dining room. While she dismissed the staff, Matt stepped behind the bar and pulled out a new bottle of Johnny Walker Black Label. Holding it up, he said, "Think this will work as a bribe?"

She appraised the bottle and shrugged. "Worth a try."

Matt went to the parking lot and knocked on the Winnebago's door. It took less than a minute to complete the deal. After the Motor Home Madam had driven out of the lot, he returned to the Halcyon.

Allyson waited at the bar. She picked up two glasses filled with red wine from the bar top. "Bring the bottle. I might need to be drunk for this."

He picked up the bottle, one of the Halcyon's better pinot noirs. "Good choice."

She nodded toward the fireplace. "Let's sit by the fire and get comfortable."

Each sat in an easy chair angled toward the other. A white maple end table stood between their chairs.

Allyson sipped and stared into the fire.

Matt's insides churned, resembling the red wine he swirled in his glass. This was the first time they'd truly been alone as friends with a baseline of trust.

With a half-chuckle, she said, "This is going to be hard. I've kept the stuff about Donnie and me bottled up for five years ... well ... five years, six months, and twenty-three days, but who's counting?"

"Why not start at the beginning?"

She gave him a condensed version of her childhood: normal except for a bible-thumping minister for a father and an alcoholic mother. Clifford, Alice, and daughter Susan Danforth were a textbook dysfunctional family. The bitterness in her voice was unnerving. It was as if her alter ego were speaking.

Matt asked, "Why'd you change your name?"

"I never liked Susan Danforth. I wanted to be my own person, not their daughter. I changed it after I left Donnie."

They both took sips of wine.

"We kept up appearances. Didn't want it known that Mama was a boozehound. Daddy looked the other way, bought her booze, lied to the congregation. As long as she kept her drinking inside the house or outside the county, he was happy. But Gunnison, Colorado, is a small town. People talked. Everybody knew."

Allyson's tone changed to faux-cheery with an angry, sarcastic edge. "Then she got sick. Some intestinal bug. Lasted for weeks. I thought she'd die. Hoped she'd die. But she kept drinking. The alcohol must've killed the damn bug. I cleaned up her shit a dozen times."

Matt shifted in his chair, unnerved by her casual tone and visions of Susan cleaning up Mama's messes.

"I'd throw up from the smell and the mess and my disgust for her. My mother literally made me sick to my stomach." She gave him an I-dare-you-to-top-that glare. "Then I'd go to school and pretend God loves me, and we were one big happy family." Her voice became leaden and disembodied.

"Every day, every single damn day, I asked God why Daddy was making me do this, why he allowed Mama to be so weak and selfish, but I never got an answer."

"Must've been rough," was all Matt could think to say.

Allyson stared into the fire. "I thought about killing them once." Her tone was nonchalant, still in her light Colorado twang.

A shiver ran down Matt's spine, and he tensed.

She drained her glass and reached for the bottle. He held out his glass, and she refilled both.

Matt rested his elbows on his knees and ran a hand through his hair. He couldn't imagine hating his mother at all, let alone wanting to kill her.

"Of course, I never could've pulled the trigger. It just made me feel in control of my life for a few seconds. Besides, if I murdered them, I'd be stuck in hell with them after I die. I'm not a violent person by nature. I just get scared and act like I'm capable of killing as a defense." She studied him with her head tilted down, as if she didn't want to face him. "So, how you likin' m' life so far?" The wine had kicked in, and her speech was slightly slurred, but her eyes were luminescent and haunting in the firelight.

"I've heard worse. Tell me about you and Donnie."

She'd been facing him, but a look of discomfort came over her, and she turned away to face the lake, invisible in the blackness. Then she perked up and turned back to face him. "Wait a sec. You said we'd trade secrets. Let's hear some o' yours."

He pondered a moment. "Okay. Mom died of cancer when I was twelve. Dad took it hard. He started lashing out at the kids. I'm the oldest, so I took the most crap."

"Sorry."

"He'd been an okay dad until then. One of those stoic Minnesota Lutherans Garrison Keillor talks about. After Mom died, the only emotion he ever expressed was anger. I was grounded, whipped, smacked around, verbally abused, you name it. I rebelled by getting into juvenile delinquency stuff, which made our relationship that much worse. Nothing major—smoking, vandalism, shoplifting—but I got busted once and paid big time. He whipped me so badly I couldn't go to school for three days."

Allyson listened with a blank expression.

"The last straw was my decision to become a musician. All Dad wanted me to do was take over the farm. No way was I going to do that. So he pretty much disowned me. We hardly spoke until he had a stroke last spring. Unfortunately, going home to care for him was the catalyst that started the disaster that got me to where I am today. If I hadn't been the obedient, responsible son, I never would've ended up here talking with you."

"I'm kind of glad you did." She gave him a mysterious half-smile that reminded him of the *Mona Lisa*.

He lifted his wine glass and gestured toward her. "Now tell me about Donnie."

She studied him with an intensity he hadn't felt before. A palpable wall of tension filled the space between them. Part sexual, part crossing the line of how much personal information to share with a near stranger. He forced his hands to refrain from drumming on his thighs. Even so, his fingers felt electrified. No music played in the background of his mind.

"I thought it would be easy to spill my guts about him." She swiveled her head to gauge his sympathy, then turned back, but her head lolled slightly. "With Donnie, a lotta shit was my fault. He did nasty things to me, but every day, up to a certain point, I could've told him *no*. Stepped away. Told him no. I thought I was strong enough to maintain control. Hah."

"I guarantee whatever you've done isn't nearly as despicable as what I've done."

She gave him a we'll-see-about-that look and took a deep breath. "I worked part-time as a waitress in a local diner. Donnie came in one day when I was a senior and I waited on him. I flirted like I did with most of my male customers. Made me feel special, you know, valued for something as simple as givin' 'em a friendly smile and a flattering word or two."

She swirled the wine in her glass, slopping some over the rim. "Whoopsie daisy." She licked wine off her fingers. "He fell for me. I was eager to get out of Gunnison, so the day after I graduated, we split for Los Angeles."

"Love at first sight?" Matt asked.

"Eh, I guess. I was in high school. He's a few years older. What did we know about love?"

He couldn't imagine anyone not falling for her at first sight.

Allyson resumed her story. "Anyway, we partied a lot. Donnie always seemed to have extra money, although his job didn't pay much better than mine did. I was too naïve to understand. He always knew where the parties and drugs were because he was dealing a little on the side. The strange thing is, other than pot, he never did any harder drugs, and he didn't let me do any, either ... at first."

"I partied pretty hard in college too," Matt said, "mainly because that's what jazz musicians are supposed to do. I also played in the University of Minnesota Orchestra, which was as straight-laced as it gets. I decided I couldn't behave like the jazz cats and still succeed in classical, so I scaled way back my senior year."

She narrowed her eyes, appraising him again. "I guessed you were Joe College, but I never figured you for a party boy." She pursed her lips. "I thought musicians were mostly average body types, more egghead than athlete. When did you switch to extreme sports?"

He debated how much more to tell her, then decided only to explain his presence in Castle Danger. "I didn't. I've been playing hermit in the Boundary Waters for the past nine months. Decided to—"

"Wait. What?" Her expression was one of total disbelief. "You've been living outside all this time, in this winter?"

"I did what I had to do."

"My God, you're certifiable. Did you finally come to your senses when the temperature dropped to thirty below?"

"Nah, I had other reasons. I picked Castle Danger at random and because of memories. Picked the Halcyon because your light was on and I was five minutes from dead."

She raised her eyebrows in acknowledgment of his confession. "I was skeptical of the extreme sports story, but for some crazy reason, I believe this one."

"Whatever I say tonight will be the truth. Promise." He made his expression as open as he could to show his sincerity. "Your turn again."

She started talking, but his attention drifted as he studied her face. He liked her lips. They seemed eminently kissable. But her eyes were her salient feature. Deep, expressive, blue in enough light, dark but shiny at night, she could show any emotion with only her eyes. He saw it every time they conversed or when he observed her talking with someone else. It was like reading a book in a foreign language. You could get the gist of the words if you knew some basics of the language. He could look into those eyes for hours and never get bored.

A pause in his thoughts got his attention back to her story.

"... Then Donnie got a better sales job at a car dealer that specialized in luxury rides and sports cars. We started earning enough to make plans for the future. After a year, I got pregnant with Josh, so we got married. Vegas, of course. That was Donnie's style. He always looks for the easy bucks, legal or not. He never told me the dealership he worked for was connected to the Mob."

A spike of adrenaline shocked Matt's spine, and his face stiffened with instant surprise. "The Mob?"

"You're quick, Mr. Lanier."

Hearing his real last name unnerved him, and he shifted in his chair.

"Don't worry." She winked. "Our lil' secret."

"Thanks." He hoped she would keep that secret now that she was confessing her past to him.

"They bought stolen cars from the Mob boys, changed the VIN, reregistered the car, and sold it as if only a little old lady from Pasadena had owned it—a rich little old lady. The profit on those cars was twice that of the legit cars they sold. That's why I don't buy his respectable business owner crap now.

"Donnie thought he could run the scam bigger and better. He tried to line up a bunch of Hollywood folks with stolen cars. The deals went sour. He ended up on the hook for the two hundred thousand dollars he would've grossed from those sales. He owed half of that to the Mob, but somehow my clever-assed husband wiggled out of a pair of cement shoes."

"Maybe he's not as cunning as you think."

She shrugged. "Then Josh was born. Then Donnie got fired. Fucking perfect timing, huh? The shit sack officially exploded when that happened. No job, new baby, debts up to our neck to the Mob." She shook her head slowly, heavy with regret.

Matt shifted in his chair and took a large gulp of wine.

"We started over, sort of. Only this time, we owed the Mob and had Josh to take care of. Donnie got another job with a car dealer, not as much money. He didn't tell me, but I figured out that's when he started dealing drugs big time. He's a salesman, but not that good. We barely earned enough to keep the Mob off his ass. Our asses."

"They threatened you too?"

She shook her head. "Just a lot of scary hints. Having Josh put extra strain on me. I had a part-time job, but I struggled with motherhood. Donnie noticed and started giving me some cocaine. A short line helped me stay awake at work after a long night with Josh crying, or sick, or whatever. Then he started getting me high on a regular basis. Coke is great for giving you temporary energy, so it helped me cope. I didn't think I had a problem until—"

She turned her head away, put her hand to her forehead as if she had a sudden headache. Matt waited, unsure if he should speak. Was there something worse she couldn't talk about?

After a minute, Allyson studied him from under her shielded forehead. "Huh. I just gave you a chance to split. You stayed." She paused, presumably giving him another chance to leave.

He shrugged. "Drugs, debt, a smooth-talking crook for a husband. Nothing new. Well, the Mob's a nice twist."

"One beautiful Saturday in June," she said, "we were invited to a super fancy party, some of the biggest players he'd ever met. He'd been working hard to expand his business. We went to the party, and it was glam city. The best Champagne, caviar, gourmet food, movie stars, a band, the whole deal.

"Donnie introduced me to this movie director customer of his—older man, butt-ugly, overweight, Type A personality. Donnie said if I'm nice to him—" She formed air quotes as she said *nice*. "—he might consider me for a movie part."

Matt looked askance at her.

"I told the guy I was flattered, but I just wanted to go to a back room and snort some more coke. Donnie said, 'Sure, Baby Doll, right after you fuck the director.'"

She shook her head and engaged his eyes for the first time in a long while. Her expression was hollow, betrayed, disbelieving. Then she broke down into muffled sobs, curled into the easy chair, hugging her knees, her head buried in her forearms.

Matt had tried to keep an open mind to that moment, but regarded whatever she might say with skepticism. Even though he'd figured out Vossler had lied, the actual truth probably sat midway between versions.

She raised her head. "After that night, he made me quit my job and took over my whole life. Said we'd make more money with me being a call girl than him selling drugs, and it was much safer. Hah. He didn't mind risking my health or my life, but by then, I was too hooked to resist.

"I became the sexual equivalent of a world-class athlete. I trained several hours a day—aerobics, weights, stretching, organic foods, lots of vitamins and minerals. Then, of course, he wanted to sculpt me in the image of the ideal woman, so he bought me a boob job, injections so my lips would be fuller, sent me to the best hairstylists and makeup experts."

Matt recalled the night he'd seen her naked in her bedroom. He would have never guessed she'd had breast augmentation. She must have had a first-rate plastic surgeon.

"The silver lining was he paid off the Mob in less than a year. Business got so good we rented a big house in the San Fernando Valley. Very secluded. We had a guest wing with a bedroom, bathroom, wet bar, sitting area. My office. I walked a lot on my down time. Quite peaceful ... on the surface. Underneath the façade, it was tricky. Keep me addicted but also keep me in perfect physical condition."

She got a wistful look in her eyes. "My life seemed so glamorous when you deleted the sex and drugs. I felt like a queen, a movie star. He turned me into one hell of a high-priced—and high—call girl. I became Susannah. Sounded classier than plain old Sue or Susan. The clients probably felt justified in paying a couple thousand for Susannah, but might've bitched to Donnie about two thousand for plain old Sue."

A low whistle escaped from Matt's lips. "How long did this last?"

"Almost three years."

Matt pushed backward into the leather chair, stunned into silence.

"I had a few clients who paid me five thousand dollars a night. That stroked my ego like nobody's business. One day, I computed five grand a night, five nights a week, for a year." She looked at him as she said the last sentence, looking for a reaction.

He did the math in his head, and his jaw dropped in disbelief.

She smiled the smile of someone incapable of being shocked or surprised. "That's right. Allowing for a two-week vacation, one point two five million dollars a year."

Back in his days with a touring band, he'd heard from band mates that going rates were from twenty bucks for a quickie up to more than several hundred for an entire night. But five thousand?

"I suppose you're wondering how anyone would pay that much for a night of sex."

"Well, not being a connoisseur of call girls myself, then yeah."

"You won't believe me, but my price had almost nothing to do with sex." She took a sip of wine but spilled a few drops on her hand when she set her glass down. "Of course, I had many specific job skills that cost extra, if you know what I mean."

As if to illustrate, she licked wine off her index finger by slowly inserting it completely into her mouth and withdrawing it in a manner so erotic that Matt was mesmerized nearly into incoherence. For the capper, she languorously twirled her tongue around her fingernail, then blew across her fingertip as if blowing the smoke away from the barrel of a pistol. During the entire show, she tilted her head and narrowed her eyes into a come-fuck-me expression. He'd never been so aroused by such a simple act as licking a finger.

"More skills, more money," Allyson continued. The playful fire in her eyes suggested that had she stayed in the business, she'd just closed another sale. "Most importantly, I made those men feel more special and more desirable than in their own fantasies. When I was with them, they were Brad Pitt, Bill Gates, Michael Jordan, and Arnold Schwarzenegger all rolled into one superman."

Matt expelled another low, highly impressed whistle. He was beginning to understand the torment Allyson endured that made her leave Donnie.

"I did the girlfriend experience a hundred different ways. Southern belle, femme fatale, powerful businesswoman, country girl, Goth, English accent, French accent, shy, retiring type, slave girl, dominatrix, nymphomaniac, eager young virgin—*that* was a biggie."

She gazed at the flames dancing around the logs. "At the time I blew town with Josh, I was booked solid for the next two months, nearly five nights a week. Donnie was kind enough to give me a day off every few days to recover. What a considerate asshole."

Matt's brain reeled as he focused on the lakeside windows. A thin edge of light appeared over the black water of Lake Superior. One question throbbed at the forefront of his mind. "Let me get this straight. You were hooking after Josh was born?"

Allyson averted her eyes. "Yes." Her voice was barely audible, not quite a stage whisper.

He turned his head and massaged his face with his hands.

"Am I the biggest loser in the world or what?"

He let his fingers slide down his face. "No. Donnie did all that to you. He found your weak spot, cocaine, and exploited you." He met her eyes, which broke his visions of Vossler lying dead at his feet with a bloody red hole in his chest where his heart had been.

She stared at him, as if reading his thoughts. He tried to erase the thought of killing Vossler from his mind.

The tense silence was broken by the whoosh of a gas flare that momentarily doubled the size of the flame in the fireplace.

Allyson relaxed and broke eye contact. "All I need to do is visualize his smug grin, and I start looking for my chef's knife." She drained her half-full wine glass, raised her eyebrows, and smiled tightly. A warning expression. "It gets worse."

He opened his palms and shrugged. "You've come this far."

After a deep breath, she said, "One client, let's call him John, was a movie director about to break through with a big movie deal. He liked to play rough, and usually I was fine with that. One night, he spiked my club soda. I had a few sips and started to feel funny—weak, dizzy, barely able to talk. He got rougher and rougher. I tried to fight him off, but John just got hornier, as if it turned him on to dominate me. We struggled, and I ended up splitting his head open with a steel pipe I kept under the bed for emergencies."

Her eyes took on a faraway look as if she were watching the slow-motion replay of that night. "He hit me at the same time I hit him. I remember both of us falling down, but then I hit my head on the nightstand and blacked out."

"Lord, you poor thing." Matt struggled to comprehend all she'd confessed to him tonight.

"The next day, when I was coherent, I asked Donnie what happened. He said he wrapped a bandage around John's head, drove him home, and dumped him on his lawn."

"Why didn't Donnie call an ambulance or the police?"

"What, and tell the cops that his wife, the most expensive call girl in Southern California, got hit by one of her customers and she hit back?" Her look contained mild contempt for his naivete.

"Oh, yeah. Did John call the cops on you?"

"That's what bothered me. I expected a visit from the cops any minute. I would've been relieved in a way. Would've put a stop to that life, for sure. Then a few days later, I read in the newspaper that John was found dead in the woods near his house."

Matt couldn't keep the shock from his expression.

"I killed him, and Donnie got rid of the body for me."

"To keep it all a secret so you could stay in business?"

Allyson nodded, staring blankly at the fireplace. "Donnie swore up and down that John the john was conscious when he dropped him off. He was so smooth at telling me everything was okay. He gave me a week off. Kept me high on coke. After a while, I didn't care anymore. I didn't think I could sink much lower than a murdering whore."

"So, John the john was the last straw?"

She looked away. "Actually, no. It was Josh."

"Josh?"

She stared at the fire for a long minute. Her hands shook. "One day, Josh said, 'Mama, why do you act so funny all the time?'" She used a childlike voice for his words.

"I said, 'What do you mean, Joshie?'"

"He said, 'You don't see me.'"

"What do you mean, I don't see you?"

"When you're in the room with me, you look at me, but you don't know who I am. You don't see me."

She trembled. Her voiced cracked. "I was so spaced out on cocaine, or so desperately looking forward to my *next* high, I didn't know my own son was in the room. Didn't acknowledge his existence. Well, I fucking lost control. I fell on my knees and begged him to forgive me for being the worst mother in the world."

She blew her nose into a tissue from a box on the coffee table and dabbed tears from her cheeks. "I took one last hit of cocaine, so I'd have the energy to leave Donnie. Then I withdrew twenty-five thousand dollars from our joint bank account and took Josh to a shelter for abused women. That's when I changed my name and Josh's last name too. I wanted to make it impossible for Donnie to find us."

"Hold on," Matt interrupted with a raised hand. "Don't you need both parents to consent to a name change for a minor?"

She appraised him with seeming new respect as if she were surprised that anyone, let alone a supposed airheaded jock and part-time cook, might be literate in that area of civil law. "I, uh," she hesitated, and her expression turned downward into a guilty gaze at the floor. "I called in a favor. From a former customer. A Hollywood lawyer."

Matt looked askance at her. "What sort of favor?"

Her eyes flashed when she comprehended his tone. "I didn't bribe him with sex." She sat up straight and held her head high. "A year before, when he *was* a customer, we were out in public, role playing the stressed-out boss and his smoking hot secretary. His wife came into the restaurant we were at just before I started the hot groping under the table scenario. She immediately got suspicious because he'd told her he was working late at the studio. I deftly covered for him by saying I was a newly arrived Broadway theater actress who wanted his advice on a movie contract I'd been offered, and that he was consulting me during a quick dinner break as a favor to his boss."

Matt smirked. "A secretary knows how to cover for her boss, doesn't she?"

Allyson nodded with a subtle smile and lowered eyelids. "I told the lawyer to use whatever legal magic or manipulation it took to ensure that Donnie never found out. I insisted on paying him for his time, with the reminder that if he ever told anyone about my and Josh's name change, his wife would be number one on my speed dial list the next day." She crossed her arms and sat back.

Matt couldn't hold back a smile. "Very resourceful, Ms. Clifford."

"Anyway," she continued after a sip of wine, "we stayed at the shelter for a month. I quit cocaine cold turkey, even though at first I thought I was going to die. Every time I thought about scoring some coke, I visualized Josh's face the moment I realized he was desperate for me to be his mom. I never want to be in that situation again, never want to screw for money again, never want to touch cocaine again, never want Donnie to see his son again."

Judging from her faraway expression, she seemed to be reliving that decisive moment.

"There's no way being a call girl would end well, not with Josh, not with Donnie using me and corrupting him. Donnie was teaching Josh how to act like himself—an abusive, entitled, chauvinist pig. I don't want to give the world another man like Donnie Vossler."

"You won't. Josh is terrific. He'll turn out just fine." Matt was genuinely encouraging. He'd seen enough of the relationship between mother and son to know it was based on unconditional love. "How'd you end up in Castle Danger?"

Allyson sniffled, dabbed a corner of her eye with a tissue, and breathed deeply. "Got out a U.S. atlas, looked for faraway places where Donnie would never think of looking for me. I liked the ocean when we were in L.A., so I figured the biggest lake in the world was a substitute. Bought two bus tickets to Duluth. We stayed in a motel for a week, then I answered a want ad for the waitress job here."

"I chose Castle Danger for the water too."

"Donnie trying to take Josh away scares the hell out of me. I don't have any leverage. He can call the cops anytime he wants, tell them I killed John the john, and I go to prison for years. There's no way I ever see Josh again. Donnie might not get him either, but he's built up this successful businessman façade and could probably bribe a judge to give him custody and overlook his pimping and dealing."

"Am I missing something?" Matt said. "If Donnie has so much leverage, why didn't he call the police as soon as he found you here?"

"He mentioned getting back to our old life again. I suppose he'd rather keep the john's death secret so he can pick up with my old clients."

That made marginal sense to Matt, but something else didn't click. "How could anyone have gotten away with murdering a wealthy, nearly famous movie director?"

"Beats me," Allyson said. "Donnie was always pretty good at covering his tracks. The worst part is he can hold our past against me forever. Even if

Josh and I went back to him, he might decide he wants more and blackmail me for the rest of my life." Her eyes pleaded for some magic wisdom he didn't possess. Then she curled her knees to her chest and buried her head in her arms.

Matt felt impotent because of his own situation. All he wanted was to get back to a normal life, but Allyson and Josh Clifford were also not living normal lives as long as Vossler was trying to claim Josh. He didn't see how he could help her and help himself simultaneously.

"I ... I'm sorry, Allyson. I wish I could help, but I don't know what I can do."

She lifted her head. Her eyes had a glazed look, cold and empty of emotion. Her pleading look changed to defiance. "Oh yeah," she said and turned to face him. "You owe me your story now. Not that it makes any difference to my situation since you're obviously hiding from something too."

"My story will take as long, and believe me, it's worse. It's also the reason I can't help you." Saying that made him feel like a fraud because of what he'd said earlier about helping her.

Looking away, she said in taut, low tones, cold and emotionless, "Story or not, I figured once you found out the truth, you'd run for cover. Why would a near stranger stick his neck out for this?" She pointed her thumbs at herself. "At least it felt good to unburden myself."

The brightening eastern sky cast an orange-pink glow onto the walls. "It's late," Matt said. "Why don't we get some sleep and talk again later?"

Allyson pasted a mannequin's smile on her face. "Yeah, right. Gotta open in five hours." She stood and walked toward the door. "But if you show up for work, I'll be one surprised ex-junkie hooker."

Chapter 33

etween the lunch and dinner periods that afternoon, Matt asked Allyson for an hour off to go for a ski. He hadn't exercised much since arriving in Castle Danger, and the drop off in physical activity from his Boundary Waters exile compared to now was so extreme he'd put on a few pounds. He wasn't eating more, but he wasn't burning thousands of extra calories each day chopping wood, paddling a canoe, hunting, or preparing his shelter for winter.

He stopped by the house to grab his skis, then hiked down Halcyon Road to Highway 61. A local had mentioned a ski trail a few enthusiasts in town maintained so they could ski from their homes up the shore to downtown Castle Danger as an alternative to driving.

Matt skied away from town for thirty minutes to the end of the trail, then headed back. Lost in the hypnotic rhythm of skis and poles crunching the packed snow, and paced by fast, rhythmic breathing, he had almost reached Halcyon Road when he caught sight of a figure standing on the edge of a clearing in the woods just off the trail.

The figure was Vossler. He held a black object raised to his eyes. Binoculars. Vossler was spying on Allyson at the Halcyon.

Matt started toward him.

Vossler saw him approach, showed him a gloved middle finger, and hurried to his SUV parked alongside the highway on the other side of the ski trail.

Matt watched him drive off, then skied into town, where he stopped at Marge's General Store to call Zach and find out what he'd dug up on Vossler. That information could help him determine if Vossler was seriously dangerous or merely a prick causing trouble for his wife.

Zach answered after two rings.

"Hi, it's Matt. Anything on Vossler?"

"Matt. Hi. Actually, yes. Let me get my notes."

Matt's spirits rose, hoping Zach had found some huge piece of information he could wave in Vossler's face and send him scurrying back under the rock from which he'd crawled.

After a brief moment of rustling paper sounds, Zach said, "Here we go. Vossler, Donald Gordon. Age thirty-three. Had some minor run-ins with the law in his late teens. Possession of narcotics, intent to sell, an assault arrest that was dismissed because the victim declined to press charges. Also, a DUI that was pled down to community service and addiction counseling."

"Is there a bottom line here?" Matt wondered if he was dealing with a hardcore criminal or just someone who liked to party a little too hard?

"He wasn't a Boy Scout," Zach said. "Plenty of hombres have been busted for a small amount of pot or gotten into a street fight and never did jail time. I've known some of these dudes since I was a kid, and I'd trust a few of them with my life. They aren't evil, just wired differently than most people."

"Anything recent?"

"Yeah. The cops questioned him about a guy who died under suspicious circumstances five years ago. Vossler and that guy ran in the same social circles. The cops were trying to piece together the dead dude's last days. Vossler was at a party with him and a hundred other people a few days before the guy died."

Matt's spine tingled. "Was the dead man a movie director?"

"Yeah, a guy named Robert Wright," Zach said with surprise. "How'd you know?"

"Was Wright found in the woods with a big gash on his head?"

"What are you, psychic?"

"Vossler's wife told me."

"Ah." Zach paused. "Are you and her—"

"Don't go there, kid. We just talked."

"Sorry. It's just that it's been a while for you, assuming you really did hide in the woods for nine months, and—"

"I said—"

"I know, I know, just messing with you, old man. If I were in your situation, I'd about explode." Zach was no doubt getting a laugh at his expense.

"Any details on Wright's death?"

"I hacked the police report and also checked out the newspaper coverage. Wasn't a big deal since mysterious deaths happen every day in L.A. The police suspected homicide but never connected anyone to it. My guess is someone knew, and either was afraid to rat out the killer, or the killer threatened them or paid for their silence. Maybe to prevent some sort of scandal."

"Thanks, Zach. You confirmed a huge piece of the puzzle." Matt smiled, proud of his genius friend and ally who came from the wrong side of town, had the wrong color skin, and defied cultural stereotypes to excel at being a computer genius.

"Hmm, I must be better than I thought."

"I'd be screwed without you, kid."

"True dat."

Matt hung up, buoyed by the certainty Vossler either had killed John the john—presumably this Robert Wright person—or had covered up the death, thinking that was the simplest, neatest way to preserve his lucrative prostitution business. Calling the police would have resulted in the facts coming out that Vossler had been pimping out his wife to wealthy friends and acquaintances.

If Wright had lived, he might have pressed charges against Allyson—Susannah at that time. It would have been a *he said, she said* situation. Susannah would claim self-defense. Wright could claim Susannah was the one who'd gotten violent, maybe tried to rob him. And when he stopped her, she became desperate because of her addiction and killed him, intending to get his money one way or the other. Donnie had done the smart thing—eliminated the sole witness for the prosecution and pretended nothing had happened.

Even if Susannah had confessed to justifiable homicide and gotten a light sentence, Vossler would have been guilty of dumping Wright's body. He would have gone to jail too. He certainly had the most to lose of the two of them. Either way, Josh would have been removed from their custody.

Proof of anything would be impossible to obtain, short of a confession from Vossler or hiring a hypnotist to figure out what Susannah heard and saw that evening with Wright. Even then, if she had been unconscious for any part of that time, her story would be incomplete.

As Matt muddled through that train of thought, his body tensed, and his temples pounded. Vossler was pure scum to abuse his own wife in that way. Worse was letting her believe for over five years that she had killed a man. Susannah could have never been sure of what happened. She'd been on cocaine and had been given another drug by Wright, probably Rohypnol, the date rape drug.

At least he knew why Vossler hadn't sicced the police on Susannah then or Allyson now. Vossler feared police involvement more than Allyson did, and perhaps as much as Matt feared them.

Chapter 34

Over the next two days, Ben Nowitzki worked his way down Highway 61—first through the parts of Grand Marais he'd missed the day before, then Lutsen, Tofte, and Schroeder. He stopped at every open business on Highway 61, especially the hotels, motels, and eateries. Then he checked each small town thoroughly by walking the main streets, inquiring at the local post offices, coffee shops, libraries, and any other place people gathered. He hoped someone would say, "Yes, I saw that guy hitchhiking south on sixty-one yesterday," or, "A man matching that description stayed in my motel two days ago."

Nowitzki even went so far as to check the State Park campgrounds along the North Shore for any signs of winter camping, since Lanier presumably had camping experience. The Ely police had told him the Forest Service search plane found an abandoned campsite ten miles from Olson's Outfitters. The reasonable assumption was Lanier had been living there and ran when he realized he was a search target. Ben doubted he'd camp somewhere else, but he might be trying to outfox his pursuers by going where they least expected him to go.

Ben hit Silver Bay in the late afternoon and immediately went to the local sheriff's office. He asked whether anyone in the county had reported a stolen vehicle in the past few days. To his relief, no one had, which confirmed what he'd learned from the other local law enforcement agencies. This meant either Lanier had hitchhiked, or stayed on foot and therefore likely holed up somewhere nearby.

Personally, Ben would have hitchhiked, if only to get as far away from Jones as he could. He could see the clever logic of hiding in so-called plain sight. Jones maybe knew something about Lanier he wasn't telling, which is why he had insisted on such a thorough search of the North Shore.

The Silver Bay deputy had no information on any strangers passing through town, but he directed Ben to a coffee shop downtown that was the hub of all the gossip in the area.

Nadine, the rustically attractive middle-aged woman who owned the place, prepared a turtle mocha for him—extra whip—which was delicious. He was immediately attracted to her saucy attitude and coarse sensuality, although the rock on her ring finger told him she probably wasn't the fooling around type. So he limited his conversation to a few minutes of flirty banter, then asked about strange men passing through town.

"Nope," Nadine said in a silky voice as she leaned over the counter, letting the tank top under her cardigan open enough to expose some cleavage. "Just the usual folks in town, plus a few ice fishermen and snowmobilers. But all in groups, no singles. Sorry."

Ben fought the urge to stare at her chest and locked on her brown eyes. "I figured. Thanks."

"Is this guy someone special?"

"A friend of mine. He's kind of a wanderer. Said he'd be up along the Shore somewhere, and he'd like to see me some time. Unfortunately, he lives off the grid, which makes contacting him a hit-or-miss deal."

"We got a few of those types around here," Nadine said, but her expression indicated she didn't really believe him.

"Thanks, anyway," Nowitzki said as he tossed a dollar into the tip jar and left. Back in his car, he checked the next locations on the map. Beaver Bay first, then Castle Danger. He had a few hours of daylight left and decided he'd at least have dinner in Castle Danger at that award-winning restaurant, the Halcyon something or other.

Chapter 35

Now that Matt knew what Vossler had been up to in L.A., he needed to exercise caution. His best option might be to tell Allyson what Zach had found, then take off and let her deal with Vossler. If there was any chance Vossler had finished off Robert Wright, Allyson might be able to keep him away from Josh, or perhaps come to some sort of agreement. He also needed to warn Allyson that Vossler was spying on her.

An hour before the dinner rush, Matt stepped out the back door of the Halcyon with a trash bag for the dumpster, and his suspicions about Vossler crystallized. At the corner of the building, smoking either a cigarette or a joint, stood the black-leathered punk from McDonald's.

"Hey," he called in a loud, low-pitched voice, adding menace to his question. "What're you doing?"

The punk whirled to face Matt, and he reflexively put the hand holding the smoking stick behind his back. That answered Matt's question. Marijuana.

Matt shouted, "I said what're you doing, punk?" and walked toward him. The punk backed away, then turned and jogged toward Halcyon Road. Matt let him go and returned to the back door.

Allyson stood there with a concerned expression. "Anything wrong? I heard shouting."

"Yeah." He pointed at the punk walking up Halcyon Road toward town. "Vossler set him up with free drugs so he'd do Vossler's dirty work. He was lurking out back, maybe looking for a chance to sabotage the Halcyon again. He might be the one who planted the drugs in your ladies' room toilet, left roaches under the booths and by the front and back doors, and has been badmouthing the Halcyon all over town."

From that distance, Allyson couldn't have seen the kid's face. The leather jacket must have been the identifier. "Greg Rippe?" She scowled. "The little putz. Pauline warned me about him." She thrust her fisted hands forward. "I thought he only talked tough. You know, small town, big ideas, bigger ego. He's harmless ... or seemed harmless."

Matt hesitated, not wanting to ruin her day further. "Speaking of spying, Vossler was spying on you this afternoon."

Her eyes widened, but a second later, her expression sagged along with her posture.

"He's impatient," Matt said. "Probably trying to get a glimpse of Josh so he can confront you. Maybe grab him by force. All this submarining of your business is him getting you frazzled so you'll let down your guard."

"That bastard. Does he think I'd allow him to even see my son again in a million years?"

"I know it sounds ridiculous, but that's the part. He's not in a position of power anymore. He can't or won't call the cops and turn you in for killing the movie director, Robert Wright."

"How do you know his name?"

"I have a friend in the Cities. A sharp college kid. Excels with computers."

She nodded and looked at him, mildly impressed.

"They questioned Vossler soon after they found the body. If he didn't turn you in then, he won't now. He wants you to think you're guilty so he can manipulate you."

Allyson seemed puzzled, then clarity released the tension in her expression. "I hadn't considered that. All these years, I assumed I killed him when I hit him with the steel pipe. I was a coward, too afraid of losing Josh to go to the police." She'd been looking over his shoulder toward the Lake, but now refocused on his eyes. "As the months went by and no one arrested me, I figured there was no sense in being noble and ruining a young boy's life."

"Don't get overconfident. We still aren't positive he killed Wright or dumped his body. Maybe Vossler is protecting you so you won't turn against him. He can still go to prison for pimping and maybe also as an accessory to murder or some sort of homicide."

"You seem to know a lot about the law."

He shook his head. "Only what I absorbed from my ex-wife. She worked for—"

Matt caught himself just in time. Allyson already knew his real last name. He didn't know if she was aware he was wanted for murdering his ex-wife, Diane Blake, who had worked for the state Attorney General. It made no sense to give her another piece of that puzzle.

"Worked for who?" She cocked her head as if she hadn't heard.

"Just a big law firm." He turned away so she wouldn't see the lie of omission in his expression.

She shrugged. "Okay. Let's get back to work. I need to digest all this."

He followed her in and headed for the kitchen. He needed to digest the new information too. Staying or leaving depended on Allyson's vulnerability, which had noticeably lessened today. He was sure now that his best move was to leave, and soon. Perhaps tonight.

Chapter 36

Later that afternoon, as Matt prepared ground elk for Halcyon burgers, his head ached from overanalyzing his situation with Allyson and how much of a threat Vossler posed to his freedom. The pressure of deciding to leave or stay was compounded by whether she knew he was an accused murderer, Vossler's motives, and Allyson's motives if they differed from what she'd told him.

Dealing with Vossler was his biggest risk. He might get nosy and turn his criminal resources toward discovering Matt's identity. After all, Zach had mentioned that an innocent cell phone picture of him in the background might trigger recognition by anyone who recognized a wanted killer. If that happened, the manhunt would resume with full force. He'd be no match for helicopters, planes, snowmobiles, and bloodhounds. With the search narrowed down to this small, isolated corner of Minnesota, they'd catch him in a matter of days.

If he stayed and helped Allyson, what could it hurt? His life as he'd known it was gone. Vaporized last spring. If freedom meant struggling to survive in the wilderness or taking on assumed names and working for minimum wage in the middle of nowhere, always looking over his shoulder, then how free was he? If he somehow succeeded in helping a woman who had been used, abused, and wronged beyond comprehension to live a normal life with her son, that satisfaction might be worth giving up his last hope of freedom.

The memory of her unknowing R-rated show several nights ago further compounded his confusion. How could he think logically with visions seared into his brain of the statuesque, oiled work of living sculpture that was Allyson Clifford's nude body? He'd be stupid to let emotions, especially sexual urges, affect his decision to leave or stay. He wanted to help her simply because she was the injured party in this fight. If she were an ugly old grandmother wronged by a crook such as Vossler, he'd still be compelled to help. But deep in the selfish part of his soul, he wanted to be the powerful knight on the white horse who rescued the beautiful maiden.

He wanted to live a normal life, find a wonderful woman, have children, and rise above his past as well as Allyson had risen above Susan Vossler's past. He wanted peace and happiness again, what he once had with Diane. Was there any possible way to regain a new normal and stay out of both jail and the morgue?

The dissonant music in his mind still disrupted his thoughts, but it had switched to the more palatable Charles Ives and Igor Stravinsky instead of Schoenberg and Coleman. Was he inching closer to a decision?

The first evening diners who came in weren't locals. Typical of the past week or two—occasional travelers, very few regulars, very light compared to what Allyson had described as normal business traffic. He kept to himself in the kitchen, and whenever a lull hit, about every ten minutes, he sliced onions for onion rings.

In between slices, he studied Allyson without her noticing him. He felt a bond with her because she was also an outsider. She and Josh had lived in Castle Danger for five years, but he'd seen the polite treatment of her by the locals turn off fast when the Vossler-orchestrated sex and drug issues began to plague the Halcyon. He'd heard conversations about *that drug hangout* and comments such as *Don't go unless you're not afraid of dining in the middle of a prostitution ring.* He initially laughed them off but wised up fast. Castle Danger was the same as the small town in which he'd grown up, Straight River. After five years, Allyson Clifford was still a stranger in town, not to be trusted, not to be given the benefit of the doubt. Rather than rally around an upstanding businesswoman who'd provided excellent food, friendly service, fair prices, and a boost to the economy, the locals deserted her, and the gossip flew like snowflakes in a blizzard.

"Ordering-g-g-g-g," Hannah shouted, holding the last syllable as if imitating a telephone ringer.

Matt jumped because he stood five feet away from her across the pass-through and hadn't noticed her approach. He flushed hot and glanced around to see if anyone else was watching.

"This is my third attempt." Frowning, she folded her arms across her chest. "Are you even on the planet right now?"

"Sorry, just thinking too hard."

"I tried thinking too hard once. Didn't like it." She chomped on her chewing gum, then expelled an exaggerated sigh. "Halcyon Burger, hold the tomato, extra cheese, sweet potato fries."

"Got it." Matt turned to prep the meat for the grill. Allyson stood there, silently watching, and he flinched again. "Lord, why is everyone sneaking up on me today?"

She scrutinized his face. "You wear your emotions on your sleeve, Mister Open Book. There's no band, so I know you're not wishing you were performing with them. Is something else bothering you?"

He avoided her eyes and forced his expression into neutral. "Nothing for you to worry about."

She glanced at the counter behind him and nodded toward the mountain of sliced onions. "Whatever's on your mind caused you to slice enough onions to last a month."

Matt whipped his head around. He must have sliced fifty onions, half the giant bag. "Sorry, boss. What should I do with the excess?"

"Put them in a brining tub and store them in the walk-in. Maybe we'll run a special on French onion soup if you can figure out a recipe." She glanced over her shoulder to make sure Hannah was out of earshot, then looked at Matt and stepped closer. "You've been acting strange all night, even for you. Has Donnie somehow gotten to you?"

"No."

"You sure?"

"Why is it your business?" Matt put some edge in his voice to discourage her inquiry.

"Because he wants my son. Anything he does or says is my business, because he's working on some sort of plan to get Josh. So help me God, if you lift one finger to help him, I will scratch your eyes out, deep fry them, and shove them down your throat on the point of a knife."

Matt shuddered with that vision, then held up his hands in mock surrender. "Hold on a sec. Donnie's not using me in any way. Trust me. Nothing has changed concerning my allegiance. I'm still on your side."

Allyson retracted her verbal claws. "Sorry. I'm just tense. The lack of business is hurting. I can't stay open much longer if business stays this bad. I used to net a few dollars a day on average because I did great business on the weekends. Now I'm barely breaking even on weekends and losing money every weekday. Four losing days, two flat days. You do the math." She hung her head and put a hand to her forehead, shielding her eyes as if she had a sudden headache. "I tapped into my savings for the first time since the first year I owned this place and had a bad week right before payday."

"I understand. I wish I could do more, but Donnie has you over a barrel."

"That's what hurts most." She looked up. "My big weakness is an addictive personality. I only made one mistake—well, two if you count marrying Donnie—but he compounded my mistake by a hundred, and now he's playing me to his advantage."

"Think hard. Could anyone have witnessed Donnie hauling away Wright's body? Did anyone else know Wright was coming to your house that night? Another customer? A friend of yours?"

Hannah appeared at the pass-through.

Matt and Allyson each pulled back a foot from their previous conversation distance and angled away from each other.

Hannah eyed them suspiciously. "How's my order coming?" The look on her face was annoyance bordering on an outburst.

He'd forgotten to start her order. Slapping his forehead with his palm, he said, "Oh damn. Sorry, Hannah, really." He put the burger on the grill and set about preparing the sweet potato fries.

Allyson turned to Hannah. "It's my fault, sweetie. Apologize for the delay and offer the customer a free dessert or a drink." She jerked a thumb toward Matt and smiled wanly. "I forgot this guy can't talk and cook at the same time."

Hannah nodded and left, grumbling under her breath.

Allyson faced Matt. "Let's talk later." She headed for the bar.

After finishing the food order and handing it off to Hannah, Matt had more time to think. He feared he'd try to help and somehow make the situation worse. He'd done the right thing by rescuing the trapper, which hadn't turned out well because he'd been forced from his hiding place. He possessed no special skills or knowledge to combat Vossler. Any action he took on behalf of Allyson might subject him to exposure by Vossler, if not someone else who happened to see his wanted mug shot and identify him as a killer. What if doing the right thing—helping Allyson and Josh—brought disaster for everyone?

Chapter 37

Jones answered Ben's daily call on the first ring. "What have you to report, Mr. Nowitzki? News, I hope." Jones spoke in his usual stiff, formal tone, discouraging any familiarity between employer and employee.

"Maybe," Ben said. "I'm in Castle Danger. A local at the coffee shop told me about a guy who staggered into town only a day or two after the trapper was rescued. But I can't believe he's Lanier."

"Why not?"

"If Lanier walked out of the Boundary Waters, based on the weather at the time, it should've taken him three or four days to reach Castle Danger. The Forest Service said they found no snowmobile tracks or other signs of a snowmobile other than the trapper's machine. But if this guy is Lanier and somehow rode out on a snowmobile, why was he on foot when he was rescued?"

"Excuse me. Rescued?" Jones asked, surprised.

"Yeah, the woman I talked to said he was found outside a local restaurant late at night, almost dead."

"Such a pity nature couldn't do my dirty work for me," Jones said with mock sincerity.

"Anyway, I'll check out the restaurant tonight."

"See this lead through completely. I have a feeling he's our man."

"I hope so. Do you know how stupid I feel asking people if they've actually seen that needle in the haystack?"

"Your feelings are none of my concern. Call me tomorrow." Jones hung up before Ben could ask if he still wanted Lanier killed. And if so, did he want proof?

Chapter 38

After the last lunch patron had left and he'd finished his prep work for the dinner crowd, Matt poured a cup of fresh coffee and sat at the bar. He took a swig of too hot brew and let it scald his mouth, hoping to steel himself to tell Allyson he was leaving tonight. Business was so slow she wouldn't need him to cook. Josh was safe with Pauline. Vossler hadn't made any overt moves to get his son. Maybe he was all talk. She'd find a way to deal with Vossler herself. Millions of separated couples argued over who got the children and resolved the conflict peacefully. And if the situation became serious, Allyson would certainly call the cops.

Matt was enjoying the picture window view of a Lake Superior sunset one last time when Allyson emerged from her office. He studied her face as she walked toward him—furrowed brow, tight lips, eyes shifting from side to side.

"That was Pauline," she said as she walked behind the bar. "The fifth- and sixth-grade classes have been exposed to a student who came down with influenza. The principal warned all the parents that if their kids haven't been vaccinated, they might come down with influenza too. Josh hasn't been vaccinated. She thinks it's best if he doesn't stay with her anymore." Serious tension permeated her low-register flute tones.

Matt pivoted his bar stool to face her. "Hmm, not a development."

She grimaced and sucked air through her teeth. "I know I should take Josh back, but I don't want to risk having him with me. If Donnie sees us together, he might pull a gun and kidnap us, then shoot me and dump me in the woods on his way back to L.A."

"How do you know he won't dangle you over the cliff outside and demand you take him to Josh or he'll drop you into Superior?"

That comment hung in the air like the aroma of rancid frying oil. At first, her face lit up with panic. But she recovered by standing straight and looking defiant. "Because I'd never tell him where Josh is, not even to save my life. His life is more important."

Her bluntness surprised him. Or was it bravado? "You serious? That's easy to say now. Might be hard to back up when you're staring at ice-crusted boulders one hundred feet below you." He'd had a similar mindset the first time two armed men tried to kill him last spring in the Boundary Waters. Once they started shooting, his tough attitude evaporated. He'd fired back and wound one man, but had been shaken to the bone by the fear of a violent death.

She braced her hands on the bar top. "Donnie wants Josh more than he wants to be rid of me. Until he can take him without killing anyone or having witnesses around, I stay alive. Josh and I risk much more together than we do apart."

"Speaking of Vossler, did you notice he didn't come in to eat yesterday? That's a first since he showed up."

"I noticed." Her expression was not hopeful. "I don't know if that's a good or bad development."

Matt shook his head. "I don't trust the bastard. The best plan is to get yourselves lost again. Donnie will get frustrated and go home because he can't find you."

Tight-lipped, she shook her head. "No running. I've put my heart and my soul and most of my money into the Halcyon. This is Josh's home. My home. I won't start over somewhere else. I don't have the strength. I might relapse into drugs ... or worse." She gave Matt a look that told him what she meant by worse. "When I left L.A. with Josh five years ago, I promised myself I would find a place to raise him and be a family. I got lucky. Castle Danger is a wonderful place to raise my son. I'm staying."

The brave single mom defending her precious son from a no- crook of a father against all odds worked great in books and movies. In real life, naïve women often ended up dead. She was stubborn. Too stubborn? She was lucky she'd escaped Vossler the first time.

Matt studied her eyes. "I don't know. This is a small town. It's hard to hide a little kid and keep him close enough where you can take him out of here fast in an emergency. Is there anywhere else you can send him? A distant relative?"

She exhaled hard through her nose. "Not a chance. You already know why my parents aren't an option. I'm an only child. Either my aunts, uncles, and cousins are more fucked up than my parents are, or I don't know them well enough to trust them with Josh."

"A friend other than Pauline?"

Another sharp exhale. "How many close girlfriends do you think a high-priced hooker ever made? All I ever met were other hookers or serious party girls climbing the Hollywood social or career ladder. Those bimbos wouldn't know how to make a peanut butter sandwich for an eight-year-old, let alone be a decent mother." She slumped onto her elbows and stared at the shine on the bar top.

"The county social services?"

"If they start asking questions about my past, I lose Josh for sure. I'll run from them before I ever run from Donnie."

Matt shook his head, sad and frustrated. "You haven't made things easy for yourself."

A sarcastic twist formed on her lips. "Oh right, I forgot. You're an expert in making life easy. Nine months in the Boundary Waters to hide from your past? Yeah, real easy."

His face muscles tensed. He believed he could bite through a steel pipe from the frustration he felt about this whole situation. All he wanted was a few weeks of anonymity after returning to civilization. Instead, he found himself in the middle of a potentially explosive child custody battle.

She looked at him through a lock of hair that had fallen across her face. "Okay, Mr. Fixit, what do you suggest?"

"Sorry, I've got zilch." *Let her figure things out.* He shrugged and retreated to the kitchen. Leaving tonight was the right thing to do. He leaned over the prep counter, bracing himself with his hands, and eyed her from under hooded brows.

She idly wiped the bar, avoided his stare, then sliced some limes and lemons. Then she pulled out her cell phone, hesitated, and held it in her palm as if she were trying to guess its weight. She scowled and stalked toward the kitchen.

Matt braced for more acrimony.

"I'm sorry," she said in a conciliatory tone. "Too much pressure. I'm not used to it."

A little tension flowed out of his body. "I'm sorry too. Neither of us knows enough about the other to be making snap judgments."

She offered her right hand, and they shook. Her hand felt warmer than he'd expected, or his was colder than usual. This felt more intimate than their previous handshakes. The spark he felt wasn't static electricity. It reminded him of one of the salient features of females—personal warmth. The kind of warmth that helped on cold winter nights, or when the rest of the world was cold and cruel and a man needed someone to care.

She started to pull her hand away, but he squeezed tighter as if to ask, *Is this okay?*

She glanced away, then wiggled her hand free, but returned her gaze as a light blush came over her face.

He let go, disappointed the moment had ended. "Um, yeah, well, I should ... not ... slice some onions."

She smiled at his lame humor, then glanced from side to side and fidgeted with her hands. "I need to ask you something first."

"Anything."

"Will you hide Josh for me?"

Matt couldn't keep his eyes from bugging out. *No, no, no, don't ask me this.* Sharp stabs of guilt attacked his brain. "Me? How? I'm bunking at your place. I work for you. How can I hide him and do my job?" He hated to lie, but he needed to stall until he figured out how to tell her he was leaving.

"I own an unfinished cabin not far up the shore. Bought it for a song but didn't tell anyone. Very secluded."

"What about work?"

"Business stinks. I can handle the kitchen for a few days. Who am I kidding? I could work the whole place myself." She forced a weak smile. "Maybe I'll get a hit on my want ad soon."

His resolve weakened. He visualized laughing and playing with Allyson and Josh down by the Lake on a hot summer day, wading into the inland ocean up to their knees, then sprinting back onto shore as their legs went numb in a matter of seconds. Perhaps they'd have a picnic on the rocks, watch lakers cruise by, hunt for agates. After the picnic, they'd put Josh to bed and then cuddle by the fireplace, discussing the endless possibilities ahead.

Then he visualized Josh screaming in terror as Vossler dragged him away to California as Allyson wailed in despair. He ran his hand through his hair, over his face. Fatigue hit him for the first time since he'd rescued the trapper. Not physical fatigue. Mental fatigue so intense his limbs felt as heavy as lakeshore boulders.

"Just for a few days?" She sensed his reluctance and her pitch raised a few notes. Her tone morphed into a seductive violin solo passage, and the storyteller's *leitmotif* from Rimsky-Korsakov's *Scheherazade* popped into his mental CD player. "A week tops. If Donnie's still trying to get Josh by then, I'll call the authorities for help."

Her pleading look melted his resistance. He took a huge breath, slow, measured, and exhaled upward past an extended lower lip. "What the heck. As long as you don't expect much more from me than keeping him out of Vossler's sight, I'm in."

Her face brightened for the first time in days. "Thank you so much."

Matt refilled his coffee and poured a cup for Allyson. They sat at a window table, the only people in the place. They worked up a game plan for keeping Josh hidden, including how to feed him, keep him occupied and entertained, and most of all, not be concerned about why he couldn't sleep in his own bed at night.

No one except the realtor, seller, and county recorder knew she owned the cabin. Not even Pauline. The shell had been constructed, and most interior walls were finished, but the heat, electricity, and plumbing hadn't been connected. Allyson planned to finish it after she saved enough money and turn it into her cozy little retirement dream home. Its key selling point was a spectacular, one-of-a-kind view of Lake Superior.

The lone access road was carved through dense woods from Highway 61. The cabin was invisible for a half-mile in every direction except to someone in a boat on the Lake, but no one would dare to venture there in winter.

Josh would sleep in the cabin with Matt, and they'd spend most of their time there together. Allyson owned a pair of walkie-talkies with enough range to reach from the Halcyon or her house to the cabin. Any outside movement Josh did would happen after dark. Thankfully, in the dead of winter, darkness covered the landscape some fifteen hours per day.

They'd make it a game for Josh, a camping trip in a cabin instead of a tent. Allyson would visit and bring supplies early in the morning or after the restaurant closed. If Josh were outside at all, it would only be to go from the cabin to Allyson's house and back, or to play around the cabin within Matt's sight. All she had to do was make sure Vossler wasn't spying on her when she walked the fifty yards from her house to the trail in the woods that led to the cabin.

When they'd finalized their plans, both sat back and were silent. Matt stared at Allyson long and hard, not studying her, just worrying about his new responsibility for her son.

She'd been looking out the window at the Lake, idly rotating her coffee cup, but turned back to face him. When she noticed his blank expression of concentration, she tapped his shin with her toe under the table. "What's on your mind?"

He refocused, locked eyes with her, tried to look deep into her conscience. "I'm wondering why you trusted me, a near stranger who you initially assumed was the world's biggest fool, and who you've suspected of hiding drugs in your restaurant, with the safe keeping of the most important person in your life."

A wry smile formed on one corner of her mouth, but her eyes took on a look of intimacy that felt as if she were looking clean through his body. "Two reasons. One. You decided to leave several times but never did because helping me out was more important to you. Two. You're the only man who, once he found out I had been a call girl, didn't start treating me like one."

Matt's face heated and he shifted in his seat. He wasn't comfortable receiving such sincere compliments, but his heart raced as it never had for a woman since the day he'd met Diane.

Chapter 39

Ben pulled into the Halcyon Bar and Grill parking lot shortly after seven p.m. Three cars were parked near the entrance. Not exactly the sign of a highly rated restaurant. He parked and went inside.

Warm smells of onions, garlic, and roasted meat greeted him. He instantly got a relaxed, classy vibe from the muted colors, wood trim, and flickering fireplace. Smooth jazz played softly in the background. *Don't judge too soon.*

A stunning-looking woman glided in from the dining room to greet him with the most effortless smile he'd ever remembered seeing. She wore black slacks that hugged but didn't choke her shapely hips. A long-sleeved silver blouse set off her dark, shoulder-length hair.

"Welcome to the Halcyon," she said in a professional yet sultry tone. "Will you be dining with us tonight?"

Ben untied his tongue. "Uh, yeah, just me." He couldn't help thinking that if the food tasted half as good as this woman looked, he'd be in for one hell of a meal.

"You can sit anywhere," she said with a hint of disappointment as she glanced around the nearly empty dining room. "Perhaps near the fireplace since it's chilly tonight?"

"Sounds good."

She led him to a table for two set near the large double-sided fireplace. "May I get you a drink to start?" She placed a menu in front of him.

"Chivas rocks, please." *Might as well enjoy a little bit of my retainer fee.* "Is the owner or manager here tonight?"

She raised her hand and smiled. "Guilty twice. I'm Allyson Clifford."

"You are ... um, aren't you a bit young to own a restaurant?"

She shrugged as if her age was meaningless. "It sort of fell into my lap a few years ago. I started here as a waitress. The owners wanted to retire. They liked me, had faith in me, and sold the place to me. I've been the owner for three years now."

"Impressive," was all Ben could manage as he glanced around the room.

"What did you want to see me about?"

"I understand you rescued a man who nearly died on your doorstep."

Her face tensed, but she held a smile in place. "That's right."

"Did you get his name or know where he went?"

Instead of the harmless, matter of fact answer Ben expected, she said, "Why do you want to know?" He detected a slight annoyance in her tone, and her magazine-cover smile became less genuine. She obviously knew something and was reluctant to share her knowledge with him.

Ben's bullshit radar switched on. "Just curious. It's a great human-interest story."

Allyson hesitated. "Where are my manners? Let me get you that drink first."

He studied her at the bar as she prepared his drink. Her body language seemed neutral except for her eyes, which shot glances toward the kitchen several times. Ben followed her glances and noticed the cook—a tall man, medium build, mustache and a trimmed beard, baseball cap pulled down low on his forehead.

Allyson returned with his Scotch and set it down on his table.

"Thanks." He nodded and sipped. The warm smokiness coated his tongue and filled his sinuses with evaporating alcohol. *Nothing like the stuff.*

"About the rescued man," she said. "He stayed in my guest room overnight because the blizzard prevented us from getting him to a hospital or calling an ambulance." She was looking past him toward the darkened picture windows facing Lake Superior, instead of meeting his gaze like she had when he'd first come in.

"The fool was thru-hiking the Superior Hiking Trail, so once he thawed out, he went on his way. Wasn't even here twenty-four hours." She shrugged, as if rescuing a man from a blizzard was an everyday occurrence.

"Did you get his name? Where he was from? Anything?"

"He said his name was Tom. He didn't talk much. He seemed mad that he needed rescuing, like if he needed someone's help, he wasn't macho enough. You know how men are, right?" Her relaxed smile reappeared, as did the sultriness in her voice.

"So he came and went, and that's that?"

"Pretty much." She nodded at the menu. "Ready to order?"

"Oh, right." Ben pretended to scan the menu, focusing on the entrees. His local contact said Allyson had hired the man she'd rescued as an emergency chef after her regular chef bolted without giving notice. Allyson Clifford was lying through her teeth. The question now became why.

"I'll have the rack of lamb," he said after a long moment.

"Choice. For starters, I recommend the soup of the day—creamy wild rice with morel mushrooms. Really sets up your palate for lamb."

"Sounds delicious."

"If you're partial to wine, I have a seductive Bordeaux from Pomerol that picks up the rosemary *au jus* I serve with the lamb. I usually only sell it by the bottle, but I'll sell you a glass at my premium-glass price point."

Ben raised his eyebrows and pursed his lips. This woman certainly knew what made for outstanding customer service. "I like wine." He smiled and nodded. "Thanks."

Allyson went toward the kitchen and Ben watched. She gave the order to the cook, who looked up long enough for Ben to get a glimpse of his face. He'd studied the photos Jones had given him enough to believe the man in the kitchen fit the general description of Matt Lanier.

For the next hour, Ben ate his meal, sipped his glass of wine, then another, and watched Allyson and her cook. They were the only two staff on duty and did all the bussing, cooking, cleaning, and bartending for the handful of diners. Ben ordered coffee and a bittersweet chocolate mousse topped with crème anglaise and lingered until almost nine o'clock. When he started getting impatient looks from Allyson, he took his cue that she intended to close for the evening after he finished, so he paid his bill.

"Thank you. The food and service were far better than I expected," Ben said with sincerity as he stood and donned his coat. Having a beautiful, poised woman as his hostess and server only added to the pleasure.

A warm, appreciative smile formed on Allyson's lips. "I'm glad to hear that. Please tell your friends about us."

"May I compliment the chef?" Ben wanted to get another look at the man.

Allyson's eyebrows rose, but she said, "Sure," and gestured toward the kitchen.

Ben walked over and leaned in through the pass-through until he caught the chef's attention. "Hi," he said as he rapidly scanned the kitchen as a ploy to distract the man so he could get a look at his hands. "Just wanted to let you know that was one of the best lamb dishes I've ever eaten."

The cook shrugged and smiled. "Thanks, but Allyson's previous chef created the dish. I simply followed the recipe."

"Still, you executed to perfection. That takes skill too." A surge of excitement raced up his spine as Ben saw what he was looking for—a slight bending of two fingers on the man's left hand. He looked around the kitchen for two extra seconds to complete his deception. The smile that overcame Ben was mostly from the satisfaction of confirming the fugitive's identity, but he controlled it enough to be appropriate for the situation. He may have actually defied the odds and found a man who had been unfindable for almost a year.

After saying goodnight, Ben got into his car and exited the parking lot, but he turned around when he reached the highway and parked on Halcyon Road, facing the restaurant. From the back seat of his Taurus, he pulled a small duffel bag onto his lap. Then he took out his night vision scope and waited.

Chapter 40

After they'd closed the Halcyon and walked to Allyson's house, Matt and Allyson roused Josh from a deep sleep and bundled him, jammies and all, into his boots, coat, hat, and a warm blanket. She'd sent Matt to retrieve him from Pauline's and covertly bring him home earlier that day in case Vossler was watching Allyson's every move. Under a moonless sky, they stole out of the house toward the edge of the woods, where they'd pick up the trail to her unfinished cabin. Matt paused and scanned the landscape toward the highway, but saw nothing suspicious.

Allyson led the way with a flashlight that provided meager light. Josh slept in Matt's arms during most of the fifteen-minute walk. The going was slow through the powdery snow because no one had walked the trail that season.

Matt's primary concern was Vossler discovering their fresh tracks, following them, and stealing Josh at gunpoint. Allyson assured him Donnie was a city boy who would never consider walking anywhere outside other than on concrete, asphalt, or a sandy beach. Fortunately, once they'd gotten fifty yards away from the house, the trail curved behind a mound and became invisible from the yard, driveway, or the street in front of her house. An added bonus was her house wasn't in a neighborhood but sat alone on two acres.

When they reached the cabin, Allyson opened the door with her key. She went in first, shining the flashlight beam downward so they could see where they walked.

Matt roused Josh and set him down, then lit the Coleman gas lantern they'd brought. While Allyson hugged Josh to keep both of them warm, Matt got a fire going in the large stone fireplace. The biggest problem would be keeping the place warm with only fire. No electricity meant no portable heaters. It was risky enough having the gas lantern indoors since it emitted noxious fumes that became noticeable after burning for an hour or two. They decided to obtain a battery-powered lantern first thing tomorrow.

"Mama, where are we?" Josh said in a sleep-soaked voice.

Allyson shot a concerned glance at Matt, who nodded to reassure her Josh would believe their cover story. She knelt in front of her son and held his shoulders with outstretched hands. "We're at the cabin, Joshie. How would you like to camp here with Matt for a few days?"

Josh didn't seem to understand the question at first because, in northern Minnesota, camping meant outdoors in a tent. But his eyes lit up when he heard Matt's name mentioned. "Camping with Matt?"

"Yes. Except it's too cold to pitch a tent outside so you men can camp here, inside, and pretend you're outside."

He pointed to the crackling flames. "Can we have a campfire in the fireplace every day?"

"May we?" Allyson said as she glanced at Matt. She seemed relieved now.

"May we have a campfire?" Josh said, mildly chastened.

At that moment, Matt knew Josh would adjust. In his limited experience with children, he'd observed they were much tougher and more flexible than most parents believed. He knelt beside Josh. "Yeah, buddy, just you and me roughing it for a few days. We can go outside in the daytime, then build a toasty fire inside every night. I'll teach you how to build a fire, so when you're older, you can go camping by yourself."

Josh considered that idea. "Yay! I want to build a fire. Can you teach me now?"

Matt chuckled. "Not tonight. I already started this one. It's late, and we need to go to sleep."

"Is Mama going to sleep with us?"

A rush of blood went to Matt's face. Out of the corner of his eye, he saw her face brighten in color too. "No, she's going to sleep at your house because she has to work at the restaurant."

"Oh."

"I'll come and see you before work and after work," Allyson said, "and maybe in the afternoon between lunch and dinner."

"What if I want to play Hot Wheels?"

"I'll bring them over tomorrow, Joshie. Tell Matt what else you want us to bring over here, and he'll make a list."

"I want all my toys." Now fully awake, Josh seemed eager about this new adventure.

"I can't bring all your toys, just your favorite ones. And we'll bring your schoolbooks over too."

"Aw, Mama."

"No complaining. Schoolwork first, then you can play."

"Why can't I do schoolwork at school?"

She looked at the ceiling with mock exasperation. "We already discussed this. You can't go to school because a bad man might try to take you away from me."

"Oh yeah. I forgot."

Allyson opened the large duffle bag she'd brought and pulled out a sleeping bag, pillow, and a small toiletry kit with Josh's toothbrush, washcloth, soap, and a full water bottle. "Let's get you settled in."

Matt said, "We have two choices where to bunk: up in the loft or here in front of the fire like cowboys do." He smiled, hoping Josh would go for the second suggestion.

Wide-eyed and open-mouthed, Josh blurted, "Let's sleep like cowboys."

"Okay then." Matt turned to Allyson, smiling the way co-conspirators do when a plan succeeds. He switched to a cowboy drawl. "Us cowpokes'll be fine, ma'am. You mosey on home, and we'll pertect the cattle from them thar rustlers."

When Josh did a double take at Matt's change of voice, Allyson covered her mouth to stifle a laugh, then put the back of her palm to her forehead for melodramatic effect. "Thank you, kind sir."

"There's no cows around here," Josh said in a tone that implied the adults were clueless.

"We're joking, Josh," Matt said.

"Oh."

Allyson knelt again and bear hugged her son, smothering his face with kisses. "Be good, sleep tight, and mind what Matt says. He's the boss now."

"Okay, Mama," Josh said as he squirmed in her arms. "Are you gonna give Matt a hug and kisses too?"

Matt forced his hands to refrain from doing a drum roll on his thighs, then glanced sidelong at Allyson. Her expression became coy but hesitant. She stood and stepped toward him.

"Just a hug for now." She embraced him and put her cheek against his shoulder. "Thank you," she whispered.

Matt gingerly put his arms around her. Even through a thick winter jacket, she felt soft and warm. He expected her to end the hug quickly, but she held him several seconds longer. As she pulled away, he squeezed enough for her to notice, and their eyes met.

Those eyes. So much depth, so much passion. Now he saw the pain in them he'd only sensed before she confessed to him her life with Vossler five years ago. He felt as if he were looking through those dark pupils straight into her soul. Despite her troubled past, he liked what he saw.

Physically she seemed to have endured the hundreds of sexual encounters she'd been forced into with little damage. She had recovered from her addiction quite well too. Maybe there were a few more lines in her face than normal for a woman her age. Vossler's insistence on her staying in top physical condition back then was the one good that had come of that time. He would never have guessed she was a former call girl and cocaine addict.

She pulled back, not smiling, but with more of a wondering, open-to-possibilities expression on her face as she slid her hands down his arms and grasped his hands in a thank you squeeze.

He smiled. "We'll take it from here. Sleep well."

"G'night, Mama." Josh turned to his sleeping bag and unrolled it.

Allyson and Matt walked to the door. When he whistled "Happy Trails to You," she immediately elbowed him in the ribs. More of an affectionate nudge than an annoyed thrust. He opened the door and watched her walk away. After taking ten steps down the road, she looked back. He held up a hand to indicate she shouldn't worry. She turned left onto the trail and disappeared.

Chapter 41

I t didn't take long for Ben's stakeout to pay off. Within fifteen minutes of his leaving, the lights of the Halcyon clicked off. Two figures appeared from behind the building, walking toward Lake Superior. The night scope confirmed the figures were Allyson Clifford and her cook. Ben eased his car into drive and crept down Halcyon Road with his lights off.

The pair entered a modest house about one hundred yards away. Ben parked near the Halcyon and watched as lights turned on, shadows moved across shaded windows, lights clicked off, and the two appeared outside again. The cook carried a large bundle. What the hell were they doing?

They walked away from the house toward a wooded area and disappeared into the moonless, starlit night. Torn about how to proceed, Ben got out of his car, zipped up his coat, donned gloves and a hat, and followed the footprints into the woods. He pulled a small flashlight from his coat pocket and used it to ensure he didn't trip on a hidden rock or tree root. He also patted his inside coat pocket to make sure he'd brought his .38 caliber revolver. Flashes of a heaping pile of Jones' money converted into the image of the state-of-the-art woodworking shop he'd dreamed of ever since being booted from the Minneapolis Police Department.

Ten minutes later, the trail ended and broadened into a narrow road running perpendicular to the trail. Fifty yards to his right stood a log cabin, dark save for a faint glow of light from the window nearest the Lake. Ben hid behind some trees off the trail that offered him a view of the cabin.

Fifteen minutes later, the Clifford woman exited the cabin and walked back to the trail, passing barely ten yards from him, and headed back the way she came. A small jolt of panic heated Ben's body when he remembered he'd parked his car next to the Halcyon. Allyson might see it and get suspicious, but then again, he doubted she'd noticed his car when he'd been dining there. He decided to take his chances with that, since he might be able to eliminate Lanier in the next few minutes and leave before she became suspicious of anything.

Ben crept to the cabin window with the faint light and peered over the edge into a bare-walled, unfurnished great room. Lanier and a young boy were unrolling sleeping bags and tending a small fire in the fireplace. *A boy?* They appeared to be bedding down for the night. An impromptu camping trip that began at ten o'clock? Ben's mind raced. Why would those two sleep in the cabin while Allyson Clifford slept in her house? Was the child in danger from something or someone? If so, why was Lanier acting as a bodyguard? Or was it his kid, and he was the husband? The dossier on Lanier said he'd never had children.

Too confused to think clearly, and not wanting any witnesses when he did his hit on Lanier, Ben retreated down the trail back to his car. En route to his motel, he worked out a plan of action that would get rid of Lanier with no witnesses and no harm to an innocent child or his mother.

Chapter 42

Twenty-three hours later, Allyson locked the back door of the Halcyon after Sunday night closing and turned to make the short walk home.

A dark figure stepped around the corner of the building. "Hiya, Baby Doll," Donnie said with his trademark sliminess.

She gasped and stopped short, then glanced around to see if anyone else was in the vicinity. No one. Her throat tightened. "What do you want?" She wrapped her arms around her torso, clutching her purse under her arm. Heat rose through her jacket collar.

He looked and sounded nonchalant. "Just to talk."

"I have nothing to say." She tried to walk around him.

He sidestepped and blocked her path.

Don't show fear. She channeled the churning ache in her stomach into as stern a look as she could muster. "Please move." Her voice wavered, and she cursed her weakness.

He pulled a pistol from his pocket and pointed the barrel at her chest. "This time, I insist."

The sight of the gun shocked her worst nightmare into reality. She was defenseless except for a can of mace in her purse. "Do you think you can take Josh at the point of a gun?" She tried to sound haughty, but her voice trembled with fear. "I'll call the police to save Josh from you, even if it means I lose him."

He snorted. "Stupid bitch. You ain't getting the chance to call the cops. I'll get Josh one way or another, and however I get him won't involve the law."

Desperate, she blurted, "I sent him to my parents. They'll never let you within a mile of Josh, and they'd love to call the police if you try."

He laughed long and hard. "One, Susie Q. Ain't no way you asked your parents for help. You hate them more than I do."

Donnie knew her too well. She'd actually written into her will that if she died before Josh turned eighteen, he'd go to a distant cousin rather than to her parents.

He waved his free hand in a wide circle. "You've hidden him in this dead-end town because you need to run your precious restaurant. I'll get him sooner with you or later without you. You got one last chance to come with us, the way it should be. After all, a boy needs his mother. Not as much as a strong father, but he'll need a shoulder to cry on after his first fight or when I whip his butt for misbehaving." His voice turned icy and cruel. The real Donnie Vossler.

She locked eyes with him, trying to divert his attention while she eased the flap off her purse and attempted to reach her mace can.

He noticed the slight movement in her shoulders. "Don't," he said and cocked his revolver.

Allyson lowered her hand. Her spine felt as if it would collapse.

"I'll take your purse. Trying shit like that again might result in you falling into the lake by accident." He cracked a one-sided smile.

She started to hand over her purse but instead shoved it at his face.

He flinched and threw up his gun hand to block the purse.

She sidestepped him and sprinted for her house.

"Son of a bitch," he said and ran after her.

She reached the foot of her driveway thinking she had a chance to get inside and lock the door. As she planted her foot to turn right onto the drive, she slipped on an icy patch covered with loose snow. She went down hard on the iced asphalt, absorbing the fall with her knee and elbow. The sharp pain of impact stunned her, but she scrambled to get up. As she stood, Donnie reached her and shoved the muzzle of the gun against her temple.

"You stupid bitch. Try that again, and you *will* go into the lake." He grabbed her wrist and wrenched her arm behind her back.

She winced with the added pain. "Oww!"

"Let's go." He shoved her forward, and they started back toward the Halcyon.

She stumbled along, trying to walk in such a way as to relieve the wrenching pressure Donnie was applying to her arm. She was afraid he might dislocate her shoulder.

As they reached the parking lot, Donnie shouted, "Galvin, get out here."

A hulking figure emerged from the lone vehicle in the Halcyon's parking lot.

"Get her other arm," Donnie said.

Galvin grabbed her shoulder and elbow with a stronger grip than Donnie's.

When they reached the SUV, Donnie said, "Get in the passenger seat."

She obeyed as he stood outside the door until she sat and closed it.

Galvin stood outside her door until Donnie had gotten into the driver's seat.

Galvin got in the back seat behind her. "Pretty stupid trying to run, Susannah," he said with a lurid undertone.

His voice clicked in her memory. *La-la land. New Joisey accent.* She turned in her seat to identify the man. "You!" He'd been at the Halcyon's bar that night a few weeks ago. He'd said she looked familiar, asked if they'd met in Las Vegas. He must have tipped off Donnie. That lousy coincidence put a knot in her gut.

Donnie said, "You remember an old customer of yours, Bobby Galvin."

Galvin smiled, almost drooling. "Donnie here said I'll get another night with you if everything goes as planned. Makes it well worth my while to spend a few days in this frozen shithole. I think I'll take you back to the Black Opal in Vegas."

The reference to the Black Opal Hotel and Casino triggered instant recognition in Allyson's memory of three horrendous days back when she was Susannah. She turned back and stared out the windshield, shivering with disgust. The road trip, as Donnie had called it, was to repay a favor to some low-level mobsters from Vegas. The payoff had been Susannah for the entire weekend. "Anything goes," a jovial Donnie had told the mobsters, "except don't leave any scars."

Donnie had kept Susannah higher than usual from the start. She took on four men for an hour each, with some rest, water, a bit of food, and a snort of cocaine between each session. After she'd been allowed to sleep until noon on Saturday, the fun started with gusto. The men brought in two other call girls. One was a tall, Amazonian black woman with huge breasts, a generous behind, and a shock of straight black hair that was tinted purple. The other was short, petite, and nearly flat chested. She had long, white-blond hair, and with her pale complexion, resembled an albino. Neither could match Susannah's sultry, star-quality allure.

The group tried every possible combination of three women and four men. The one constant was Susannah. That day finished with a seven-person gang bang in which she starred.

Bobby Galvin stood out as particularly lascivious and crude. He was a square, oafish brute who had to be reined in from getting too violent more than once during his solo hour with her and again at the start of the seven-body main event. Donnie had come close to shooting him, but Galvin's boss had interceded and cut Galvin out of the party soon after the orgy began.

Passed out from exhaustion because of screwing until dawn the next morning, and aggravated by too much cocaine, Susannah slept for almost twenty-four hours. By the time she woke up enough to be coherent, she was lying in the back seat of Donnie's Lexus, and they were almost home. She was too stiff, sore, and hungover to do anything but eat and sleep for three days.

Allyson shuddered, shocked that so much of that weekend had leaped into the forefront of her conscience. Until now, she'd only had occasional vague nightmares. She refocused her concentration on how to escape, retrieve Josh, and run as far away as she could from the bastard. With Galvin's pistol trained on the back of her head, she was helpless. Certainly, two small-timers like these would eventually slip up. She remained alert, all senses tingling, looking for the smallest chance to escape.

After they had turned onto Highway 61, Galvin pulled his pistol away but quickly slipped a blindfold over Allyson's eyes. She sank into the seat, defeated for now.

While they drove, she tried to keep track of the elapsed time, the turns made, hills climbed or descended, hoping to get an idea of where they were going. All she knew after several minutes was they had gone uphill, meaning they'd left Highway 61 and gone inland, up into the Sawtooth Mountains, a weak excuse for real mountains, but which still rose more than one thousand feet to the glacial plain of the Arrowhead region. After a few minutes, Donnie pulled into what sounded like a gravel driveway, the tires crackling on the ice-covered rocks. The men got out.

Galvin opened her door, grabbed her arm, and yanked her out of the seat. His breath stank of garlic and cigarettes. He led her away from the SUV. After taking five steps, they stopped.

A key unlocked a door, and Galvin shoved her into a room that smelled of bathroom disinfectant and cheap, pine-scented air freshener. A motel or rental cabin. Probably on a back road. Based on their estimated driving speed and time, they were only a few miles from Castle Danger.

A light switch clicked, and she sensed light through her blindfold. Galvin led her a few feet into the room and pushed. She staggered forward, groped in front of her to find support, and fell onto a sofa. His rough hand pulled the blindfold from her face.

They occupied a small, dingy cabin decorated in a rustic style. The cabin measured about twenty-by-twenty feet. A small bedroom and bath filled three-fourths of one side, with a kitchenette tucked into the remaining five feet. An electric fireplace cast a dim, flickering orange light into the room. Besides the sofa on which she sat, the cabin contained a threadbare recliner and a 1950s-style laminated Formica table with four steel, vinyl-padded chairs surrounding it. An old TV, circa the 1980s, sat atop a low, well-worn credenza. A small desk and chair were crammed into one corner. It was too dark to see any identifying signs or landmarks through the front window.

Allyson slumped against the cushions, feeling springs push up under her back and butt. She focused her hatred and contempt on Donnie. "You're wasting your time. I'll never tell you where Josh is."

Donnie sat at the Formica table and trained his pistol on her. "I beg to differ, Baby Doll. The only question is *when* you'll tell me." The grin on his face was too confident, too smug. He had an ace up his sleeve, and she felt like a rookie trying to beat a pro at high stakes poker.

With a nod from Donnie, Galvin tied her hands behind her back with a short piece of cord and tightened it so much her fingers immediately went numb.

Now that she was more restricted from running, she could only bluster. "You can threaten to kill me, and I won't tell you. If you're stupid enough to kill me, you'll never see Josh. I've left instructions with someone who will protect him from you at all costs." She thrust her chin forward, strong, defiant, playing her last meager bluff.

Donnie pulled out several vials and a rectangular velvet pouch from an overnight bag on the table. He laid the vials on the table and opened the pouch, revealing a length of rubber tubing and several syringes. Smiling, he nodded toward the vials. "Your only weakness other than me. I even sprang for the stuff—heroin."

The realization that he intended to get her hooked again hit her like an anvil dropped from the ceiling. Her heart pounded, and her head became heavy with dread. Years ago, during those nightmarish years with Donnie, she'd been willing to suck and fuck anything with a pulse when she'd been hooked on cocaine. He must figure he could get her high and she'd sell out her son for another hit. She'd been strong enough to kick her habit once, but she'd be powerless if he gave her enough of either drug to make her desperate for more.

"The beauty of my plan is," Donnie said, full of himself and glancing at Galvin before turning back to her, "once you're hooked, ready to sell your soul or spread your legs for another hit, and finally sacrifice Josh for one more high, I give you an overdose. I take Josh back to Los Angeles, and when they find your body here in a day or two, they'll conclude you died from a self-inflicted overdose."

Feeling as if her chance of escape was gone forever, she said, "What about the owner of this place? You gave him your name and address. He'll know you left me here. They'll arrest you five minutes after they discover I'm dead. You might get Josh for a day or two, but then you'll spend the rest of your life in jail."

Donnie glanced at Galvin, whose expression reminded him of a trained dog waiting for a treat. Then Donnie mimed a bored-looking yawn. "Give me some credit, Sue. Do you know how easy it is to get a stolen credit card, a fake driver's license, pretend you're someone else?" He gave her a look of mock realization. "Of course you do. You've been doing it for five years."

"I changed my name and Josh's legally." She tried to sound defiant, but the words came out as desperate. "I wasn't hiding from anyone but you."

"I'll simply tell the owner we came here hoping to reconcile," Donnie said. "We tried to give it a go but couldn't. Then you decided you wanted to stay here and think for a while, alone. In my innocence, I believed you, forgetting you had a history of serious drug addiction. I'll pay for a couple extra days. Tell him I'm thoughtfully helping my beloved wife by allowing her to stay and work things out in her mind."

He walked over and sat next to her. "Of course, you won't want to be disturbed, even by the housekeeper. When the owner comes for his money for the extra days, he'll discover you lying on the bed, needle marks in your arm, syringe in your hand, dead as dead can be."

He caressed her cheek, which made her flinch. "You couldn't live without me, so life wasn't worth living. But before I left, you signed a document giving up your parental rights to Josh and naming me sole guardian and custodian."

With every sentence Donnie uttered, Allyson's world crumbled a little more. Her resolve to protect Josh, no matter what, seemed futile. He'd planned this abduction carefully, anticipated all her responses.

She looked up at him with downcast eyes. "All the drug activity at the Halcyon was to set me up as falling back in with the rest of the potheads and crackheads, right?"

A smug, satisfied grin curled upward to show his bright white teeth. He tapped his temple. "You always were smart, Sue. Lousy grades in school, but damn good street smarts for a small-town girl. Gonna miss that." The last sentence dripped with feigned wistfulness.

She imagined he was already planning his new life with Josh back under his thumb. He'd find a new, clueless beauty for his bed who would fall for his slimy charm because she lacked enough self-respect to kick him in the balls and run for her life. Then he'd proceed to turn Josh into Donnie Vossler junior. Desperation closed in like fog rolling across Lake Superior. Hopelessness weighed her down as if she were slowly being buried alive.

Donnie stood and walked into the bathroom.

Allyson lowered her head to hide her face from Galvin's ogling. She closed her eyes and prayed for some sort of deliverance to whatever god might be hovering above this backwoods cabin.

Sunday night would soon become early Monday. The Halcyon was closed on Mondays. No one would notice her absence except Matt, because on Mondays she usually caught up on paperwork, food ordering, menu designing, or minor repairs. The key word was *usually*. She'd told him she would either sleep in late or take a walk along the lakeshore for some much-needed exercise. Then she'd stop by the cabin to see Josh around noon.

More than twelve hours would pass before anyone worried about her. Donnie could administer several doses by then. She'd tried heroin once but didn't care for it because the high was a little too intense. Allyson swallowed hard to hold back her growing nausea. She wouldn't give up her son for all the highs in the world, so she prepared to die. Matt would have to figure out what to do with Josh.

Donnie returned and began prepping the syringes and heating the heroin. He said to Galvin, "Cuff her ankle to the bed."

From a canvas bag on the floor, Galvin pulled a set of handcuffs connected by a long chain, similar to shackles used on prisoners. He pulled her into the bedroom. In less than a minute, he'd chained one of her ankles to the bed and removed her wrist restraints.

After a few minutes, Donnie came over from the kitchenette. Galvin pushed her to her back and straddled her, then held her arms still while Donnie wrapped a rubber tube around her right bicep. She knew the drill and averted her eyes. She didn't want to watch the needle plunge into her arm.

The shame of weakness flooded over her like a tsunami. She saw her mother, maybe alive, maybe not, floating above her in the room, laughing derisively. *A chip off the old block,* Mama said and cackled like a frail chicken as she took a long pull from a bottle of gin. Allyson grimaced and squeezed her eyes shut. This was her last chance.

"No-o-o-o!" she wailed—a primitive, guttural sound from deep inside—and thrashed her arms up and out. This caught Galvin off guard, and he fell off her onto the floor. Donnie backed away as she stood and lunged at him, trying to get the syringe, to break it, anything to avoid getting high. Donnie stayed just out of her range as she lunged again. She managed to move the bed a few inches, but collapsed to the floor when she realized her efforts were futile.

Galvin tossed her onto the bed and climbed astride her again in a flash. He made a fist and started it toward her face.

"Stop," Donnie commanded.

Galvin dropped his fist, looking puzzled.

"No bruises, Galvin. She's doing these drugs on her own, remember?"

After a moment, a comprehending look came over his face. "Sorry, boss." He grabbed her wrists and slammed them down on either side of her head. His heavier weight and overpowering strength felt as though they were squeezing the willpower from her body.

Allyson couldn't stop her tears. All she could hope was maybe, just maybe, if she conserved her strength, she'd catch them off guard one more time before they gave her a second or third dose of heroin. Then she could sneak out, run to her cabin as fast as she could, and disappear with Josh forever. If not that, then dying from hypothermia in the woods was preferable to succumbing to Donnie.

Donnie wrapped the rubber tube around her arm tightly, waited, and appraised the bulging veins on her forearm. "Okay, she's ready."

Galvin wrenched her arm into a flat position, palm up, and held it immobile.

Donnie leaned over, syringe in his right hand, poised to stick her. "One last chance to save yourself, Susie Q. No need to get hooked again. No need to die. I'll get Josh either way. You can come live with us. You don't even have to be a call girl if you don't want to."

She breathed deep and tensed. If she held out long enough, maybe someone would rescue her. Josh was the most important factor in the equation. If there were any chance of Josh staying out of Donnie's grasp, she would sacrifice herself. She shook her head emphatically. "You're not getting my son."

"Okay then. Lay back and relax, Baby Doll," Donnie said in a soothing, mellow voice. "This'll be over soon." He stuck the needle into a vein in the crook of her elbow.

She flinched. Adrenaline shot through her in anticipation of the battle her mind was about to engage in with her body.

A few seconds later, Donnie removed the needle.

Galvin loosened the rubber tube.

The room swirled out of focus, and Allyson Clifford was overcome with a wonderful, hateful sensation of euphoria.

Chapter 43

When two hours had passed beyond the time Matt had expected Allyson to come to the cabin to see Josh, he sensed something was wrong. He called her via the walkie-talkie. No answer. He and Josh snuck to the house and then the Halcyon to look for her. No signs at either place. Matt commandeered her Suburban, told Josh to lie down in the back seat, and drove toward downtown.

They made a quick drive around Castle Danger, stopping at Marge's general store, Dangerous Grounds, McDonald's, the post office, and the hardware store. No one had seen or talked to Allyson, so they drove to Pauline Allen's house.

She came to the door in a bright red sweater and yellow sweat pants, looking haggard and warm, but perked up and smiled her coquette smile when she recognized Matt.

"Hi there, handsome." She placed her hands on either side of the door and leaned forward.

Matt stifled a groan when she fluttered her eyelashes.

She leaned to one side, spotted Josh, and changed her smile to one more motherly. "Hi, Tiger."

"Pauline, we've got a problem." Matt glanced at Josh, who'd been standing silently with one fist clamped onto Matt's jacket hem.

She turned back to Matt. "What's wrong?"

"I can't find Allyson."

Her hands snapped to her mouth, her eyes widened, and she glanced at both of them. Furrows etched her brow. "Are you sure? Where'd you look?"

Matt recapped the search route as Pauline nodded approval. "I don't know where else she might've gone. Any ideas?"

She contemplated for barely a second. "She might be at someone's house here in town. But after all the issues at the Halcyon, I doubt anyone would invite her in for coffee."

"She didn't call you this morning?"

Pauline shook her head. "No."

"When's the last time you saw her?"

"Yesterday afternoon at the Halcyon. I came in for coffee as usual."

"Did you two talk on the phone after that?"

Again, she shook her head, then pursed her lips.

He ran his hands over his face, then exhaled long and slow through puffed-out cheeks.

Pauline looked past them at the road. She gestured and stood aside. "Come in for a bit. No need to stand here in plain sight for ... him ... to see you."

Matt glanced over his shoulder and guided Josh inside. "What about your kids?" The warmth of the house felt good, although the air smelled vaguely of sickness.

She waved her hand dismissively. "Definitely influenza, but don't worry. I've kept the boys in their rooms. Only let 'em out to use the bathroom. Josh'll be safe for a few minutes." She turned to Josh. "How about some cocoa with marshmallows?"

The boy's eyes widened, and he nodded but didn't speak.

While Pauline prepared a cup of cocoa in the microwave, Josh took a seat at the kitchen table and watched the adults. He swung one booted leg back and forth under the table. His eyes had an agitated, faraway look.

Pauline noticed Josh's nervousness and beckoned Matt to lean toward her. "Should we call the sheriff?" she whispered in his ear.

That was the last thing Matt wanted to do, but he didn't dare explain his reason. "I don't think they start a search until someone has been missing for forty-eight hours." The whirring hum of the microwave helped mask their conversation, but he still kept his voice *pianissimo* and faced away from Josh. "Allyson's only been gone two hours. Maybe we could stretch that to fourteen if we say Josh and I were the last ones to see her last night after the dinner rush." If only Allyson had left some message or indication of where she'd be. They'd never discussed this possibility when deciding how to keep Josh away from Vossler.

"He has her, doesn't he?" she said.

Matt barely nodded. "Most likely." He glanced at Josh, who looked at them with a frown and hooded eyes but didn't show any sign he'd heard them discussing Vossler.

"We'll certainly help," she said. "I'll have Darrell check a few other places. I'll call some friends too. What's your cell number so we can call if we hear anything?"

"I don't own a cell phone."

She forced down the typically surprised bemusement most people exhibited when Matt confessed to being a techno-social caveman. "How long did you say you were on that trail?" Her eyes sparkled with teasing humor. "Two weeks or two decades?" Her voice had changed back to its flirty tone—all trilling flute and piccolo.

Not now, Pauline. He forced a *mea culpa* smile. "I was never much of a techie."

"We've got an old prepaid cell phone we keep for backup you can use. I think there's an hour left on it unless one of my little monster darlings used it without permission."

"Thanks. If you show me how and don't expect me to get on the Internet, I'll remember how to use it."

Pauline gave Josh his cocoa. "I'll get the phone."

After she had left, Matt studied Josh as he sipped cocoa and swung his feet under the table. How was he handling the loss, or rather the misplacement, of his mother?

He thought back to when his own mother became sick, and the unknown illness turned out to be cancer. His father had sat him and his siblings down at the kitchen table and explained that Mom was going to die soon. He remembered the frustration of wanting to make her better but not even knowing what cancer was. The fear of knowing most people died from it back in those days. The despair he'd felt one much-too-short week later when she left his life forever.

Were Josh's frustration and worry anywhere near that level? How would he react if the worst case for his mother came true? Matt then wondered how he himself would react. The cold jolt of dread in his heart told him all he wanted to know.

Pauline returned with the phone and gave him a quick lesson. It was easier than he'd expected, considering he'd never owned a cell phone and had first used one only last year. He keyed in Pauline's cell number to practice. Her phone rang seconds later.

She smiled. "See how easy? I'll keep my phone with me. If I don't answer for some stupid reason, leave a message."

Matt nodded. "Got it."

She took the phone from him and studied the screen. "Leave it on until we find Allyson. The battery's fully charged, so it'll last for several days if you only make a handful of short calls." She held the phone up for him to see and showed him how to monitor the battery level. "Call me if it's getting low and I'll recharge it."

"Thanks, Pauline," Matt said. "Come on, Josh, let's go find your mama."

"Luck," she said from the doorway as they walked to the Suburban.

After Matt and Josh had entered the vehicle, Matt realized he could call Zach Perez on the cell and stay in closer contact with him than before.

"Stay in the car, Josh. I need to call someone right away," Matt said and got out of the car. He dug Zach's phone number from his pocket and punched it in on the keypad. He was pleased to hear a ring tone on his first attempt and stepped a few feet away from the vehicle so Josh wouldn't overhear.

After three rings, he heard a click and then Zach's voice. "Hello?"

"It's Matt. Things are getting worse."

After a pause, Zach said with annoyance in his tone, "What now?"

"Allyson's missing. I'm certain Vossler's got her and wants Josh next."

"Oh, man, sorry." His tone changed to somber and concerned.

"I borrowed a cell phone from a friend. I might need to call you and have you send in the authorities."

"Why not call the cops now?"

Matt shook his head even though Zach couldn't see him. "Too risky. It's bad enough for me, but if Allyson's past goes public, she loses her kid for sure. That won't happen if I can prevent it."

"*Yo comprendo*," Zach said.

Matt gave him his phone number. "I'll call if I need you, and if you find out any more about Vossler, call me."

Chapter 44

The sky was the bluest blue Allyson had ever seen. And the air ... She inhaled as fully as she could, stretching her lungs against her ribcage, wanting to absorb the soothing pine scent, the fresh green grass, and the flowers. *Oh my God, there must be a hundred different flowers blooming all around.* The gentle breeze swirled and mixed the aromas into a cocktail with perfect amounts of rose, jasmine, gardenia, lavender, hyacinth, magnolia, lilac, oriental lily. Each scent filled a part of her lungs. She felt the aromas glide past her ear on the breeze. Each one caressed her cheek and weaved scented tendrils through her hair. Birds serenaded her, occasionally floating across the sky, leaving small puffy clouds in their wakes.

She felt weightless, pain-free, relaxed beyond the meaning of the word. All seemed right with the world. Josh frolicked as only eight-year-olds can. Her parents were with her too, and they were wonderfully happy, thrilled to dote on both their grandson and their only child. Life was perfect.

Allyson opened her eyes, and the sky turned dingy white, the color of the ceiling. She closed them again, but it was too late. The flowers died. The wind ceased to blow. The birds fell from the tree branches with small, sickening thuds. Josh ran off. Her father immediately began preaching about the evils of sex, drugs, rock-n-roll, and Donnie. Her mother cackled and swigged from a gin bottle. Her body sagged into the bed on which she lay. She was back in the cabin with Donnie, coming down from her latest high. The relaxed feeling drained away. Her mind fogged over. Thinking hurt her brain.

Worse, pain racked her bones, muscles, ligaments, even her skin. Tension returned with a ceaseless throbbing in her head. Each heartbeat raced through her temples and pounded in her chest. Her fingertips thrummed. She needed to move, to run, to sprint, to fly until exhaustion overcame her and dragged her down into an abyss of nothingness.

"Please, Donnie," she tried to say, but it came out as a croak. Her throat was dry, scratchy as sandpaper. Her tongue felt twice its normal size. Donnie would fix things. He always took care of her, took care of everything. He'd make her feel good again. Wonderful again. Orgasmically blissful again.

On the periphery of her vision, Donnie sat in a chair, motionless.

Through the haze in the room, in her eyes, in her brain, she knew she couldn't last. Swallowing, she tried again to speak and almost gagged with the effort. "Donnie, help me."

Donnie moved. His hand came toward her. In it, he held a syringe. "You mean help you with more of this?" His tone was cold. Allyson shivered as if his exhaled breath was flash-freezing the air.

She nodded even though her head felt as if it weighed a hundred pounds. "Yes, more." As soon as she said those words, she knew Donnie would win, just as he always used to win. Her stomach dropped. Nausea boiled inside. Cold sweat broke out all over her skin. Her mouth dried even more. The effort to breathe felt as if her torso were encased in a tight steel tube.

"I'd love to give you another fix, Baby Doll, but you know the deal. First, you tell me where you've been hiding my son. Then you can have as much as you want."

One tiny thread of sanity shot into her mind. "Never." She sounded defiant, but she'd only be able to withstand one more fix. The first three doses of heroin were small enough and increased gradually enough that she had maintained a minimal amount of composure. The highs were pleasant, sunny, cool, effortless. Reminiscent of taking a nap under a warm blanket in a soft bed on a chilly day. Coming down was unpleasant. She'd vomited, had a runny nose and watery eyes, and gotten intensely painful muscle cramps.

Donnie probably didn't want to go too fast initially, since she'd only tried heroin once before, years ago. What a guy, faking concern for her well-being as he shot her up with one of the deadliest drugs in the world.

The chills intensified, and her legs started to spasm. Sweat trickled into her eyes. She dragged a hand to her forehead. Her skin felt hot. "I need water," she blurted. Swallowing was nearly impossible. The cold sweats were so intense she felt like she was floating in ice water. She turned her head toward Donnie and croaked out, "Water."

He stared back with an impassive smile fixed on his face. Like a billboard smile—frozen, unfeeling, humorless. Just a pose on a mannequin. His sole movement was to waggle the syringe back and forth like a pendulum. Back and forth and back and forth and back and forth ...

Allyson breathed deep, hoping a huge lungful of air would clear her head, expel some toxins, allow her to think straight. The extra oxygen only made her dizzy. "Please, Donnie, just a little sip of water."

"Where's Josh?"

She turned away. "I'm dying of thirst. Please." Her words sounded syrupy, viscous, ugly.

"Josh first."

I can resist. Someone will find me soon. She closed her eyes and concentrated. *Don't give up Josh.* She remembered the hike they took last fall through the aspen, birch, and maple grove in nearby Gooseberry State Park. Crisp and clear weather, leaves bursting with color, warm sun, laughter, playing, teasing, hugging. That was the best day they'd had since running away from Donnie. A day she'd remember forever. She willed that memory and others to block out her physical discomfort. She remembered the first time Josh said, "I love you, Mama." Remembered his first day of school.

Just one more injection. Then she'd be satisfied and wouldn't crave the drug anymore. Just one more. Back and forth. One more. Back and forth.

"What's it gonna be, Baby Doll?" Donnie's cruel voice interrupted her concentration.

She forced her eyes open again, felt her eyelids scrape across her corneas. More sandpaper. Her lips quivered. She couldn't stop the tears. She sniffled, now aware her nose had been running so badly that snot had crusted around her mouth. As miserable as she felt physically, mentally, she wished for death. *I can't take this anymore.* Sandpaper tongue licked sandpaper lips. She tasted salty snot. After a deep, labored breath, she forced out the words, "My cabin."

"And where's that?" Donnie said through the fog of her brain.

"Just north of the Halcyon. Private road. Chain blocking entrance. Not plowed."

Donnie said nothing for a minute, probably deciding if she was telling the truth.

"Who's watching him?"

"Just ... my cook ... Matt Johnson."

Donnie snorted. "This is gonna be too easy."

"Please, Donnie, I need a fix." She turned to him, hoping he'd see her sincerity.

"If you're lying, Sue, it's gonna get real bad. You know that, don't you?"

She nodded and held out her arm, palm up, almost tasting the relief she'd get with another heroin high.

Donnie put on his coat and walked toward the door. "Shoot her up, Bobby."

"You got it, boss," Galvin said as he scraped out of a chair in the main room.

"Watch her close," Donnie said. "Don't answer the door or talk to anyone. I'll check out this hidden cabin and return in thirty minutes. I trust you to keep your hands off her too."

"Don't worry, boss. I can wait for my turn in Vegas."

Allyson would have fucked Galvin as much as he wanted instead of giving up Josh to Donnie, but it was too late to make that offer. She didn't care what Galvin did, as long as he did it after she'd gotten her fix.

Galvin appeared in Allyson's field of vision, holding the rubber tube and the small leather case she knew contained syringes and heroin. She was so desperate she wanted to inject herself, but didn't think she could hold her hand steady enough to hit a vein.

As Galvin tied the rubber tube around her bicep, she lay back in bed and closed her eyes. The disgust she felt for herself was exceeded only by the anticipation she felt for getting high again.

Chapter 45

Donnie drove into Castle Danger, checked the main streets for any activity possibly involving his son, then continued on to the Halcyon. The lights were off. No cars were in the parking lot, so he continued to Sue's house and checked through the windows for signs of life. The lights were off as well, and no cars were in her driveway. He drove back to the highway and turned right, looking for the private drive just north of town.

A reflective post signaled some sort of road, so Donnie pulled into the turnout. A chain drooped between two wooden posts on either side of the driveway and blocked the unplowed road. "Great," he muttered. "Gotta get my feet wet." He'd underestimated Minnesota winters and had only bought a pair of cheap rubber galoshes that barely covered his ankles. Any snowdrift deeper than a foot would leak snow into his shoes.

He struggled down the narrow driveway with his flashlight turned on. The snow glowed luminescent bluish white, but the scattered cloud cover allowed little moonlight to light his way. As Donnie rounded a curve in the driveway, he saw a building one hundred yards ahead. The alleged cabin. A curl of smoke drifted out of the chimney top, barely visible against a patch of dark sky. He saw no light through the windows facing him. As he neared the cabin, he observed a path through the woods to his right with fresh footprints.

Creeping closer, Donnie went to the front door and gently tried the knob. Locked. He walked around one side to the first window and peered inside. Nothing to see. Moving to the second window, he could see through a large central room to the other side of the cabin. The inside appeared to have two stories, or at least a loft. Glowing embers in the fireplace illuminated two dark shapes. Moving a few steps to change his angle, Donnie realized the masses were two bodies—one large, one small. His new view also revealed that the fireplace chimney went up two stories, so the second floor was indeed a loft. He recognized the faint outline of a steep staircase leading upstairs.

The two figures had to be Josh and the cook, Johnson. He decided against shining his flashlight through the window for fear of waking them and losing the advantage of surprise. He'd return with Galvin and take Josh with no trouble. Not only did he want to snatch Josh cleanly, but he also wanted to eliminate the possibility of Johnson following him and rescuing Josh in a noble, yet misguided, attempt to win his wife's favor and get her into his bed.

He wanted to laugh uproariously. His plan was coming together so perfectly. He limited his outward emotions to a tight, satisfied smirk. Nevertheless, an energetic vibration coursed through his body that reminded him of the jolt right after a snort of quality cocaine.

As he turned to leave, his foot slipped on a patch of ice under the snow, and he fell, dropping roughly and bouncing off the cabin wall. He swallowed a cry of pain after his kneecap took the brunt of the impact on the rock-hard ice. Searing agony radiated from his kneecap and coursed up his leg, hitting every nerve between there and his brain. He gritted his teeth, desperately forcing back the urge to groan. "Shit," he muttered, then silently cursed cold, snow, ice, winter, and Minnesota.

He glanced over his shoulder at the window, expecting Johnson to appear and see him sprawled in the snow. After fifteen seconds of silence, Vossler rose and brushed the snow off his clothes. He picked up his flashlight and limped back down the driveway to his Cadillac through the falling snowflakes that were being stirred up by an intensifying wind.

Chapter 46

Matt slept fitfully, waking and dozing as he considered all plausible reasons for Allyson's disappearance. He'd try to figure out what to do with Josh in the morning. If he'd ever had his own child, he might've been prepared. To be thrust into this situation, with his life already in enough disarray, merely added to his uncertainty.

Sometime in the depth of the night, a soft thump against the cabin wall roused him fully awake. He felt the vibration more than he heard the noise. Josh hadn't moved since falling asleep. Matt held his breath, listening for more noises. He was accustomed to the dead silence from his nine months in the isolated wilderness. He'd gained a sharper sense of hearing due to constantly being on the alert for predators who smelled his food and tried to steal it. The cabin was nearly as quiet as the Boundary Waters except for the constant low whistling of the strengthening wind through the pines.

After no other sound registered in that breathless minute, Matt rose and looked out each window of the main room. He saw little except the dark shadows of the trees and the dull white of snow. He walked to the front door of the cabin and opened it a crack, trying to keep out as much cold air as possible. He saw no sign of life, animal or human, until he glanced down and saw tracks in the snow coming in from the road and moving to the side of the cabin where the noise had come from. Human footprints. His blood chilled, and his face radiated heat.

In three quick strides, he was around the corner of the fireplace wall to make sure Josh was still safe and no one had snuck in the back door. Matt put on his boots, pulled his Glock 17 from under his pillow, and crept outside. The cold air shocked his exposed skin, but he ignored it and followed the footprints to the side of the cabin. Falling snow began to cover the tracks. They went in two directions, ended at the second window, and left the same way they came in. A small area of disturbed snow showed what appeared to be where the intruder had slipped and fallen. That had caused the thump he heard. Vossler? How could he have known to come here? Checked every property in Castle Danger? Played a hunch? Scariest of all to ponder, Allyson might have told him.

If she'd confessed for an unknown reason, why hadn't Vossler broken in and tried to take Josh? Maybe he wanted to have his Escalade handy to make a fast getaway. Whatever the reason, it was time to act. He needed to either take Josh and leave or prepare to fight. He had a slight advantage if a battle took place at night, being more familiar than Vossler with the cabin and surrounding woods. Lack of light would make it difficult to see Vossler and any allies he might have. *The Rippe kid? No.* Matt doubted the teenager was tough enough or trained enough to fight an adult, let alone inflict lethal damage. But maybe Vossler had one or more real goons in his service.

Conversely, if he and Josh ran, they'd need to leave immediately in case Vossler returned in the next few minutes. And this could be a trick to get them to return to the Clifford house. Vossler may have set up an ambush to facilitate an easy grab of Josh and an easier getaway.

Matt went inside. He turned on a flashlight and checked his ammunition. One magazine of seventeen bullets. Not much firepower if Vossler came back with support. Could he do a preemptive strike? Should he? What if he fired in the dark at whoever came down the road and it wasn't Vossler? Did Vossler deserve to die merely for wanting to get his son back into his life?

Any sort of shootout was a lousy idea for all those reasons, but the worst reason was Josh being caught in the crossfire.

Chapter 47

Vossler pulled into the driveway of the Lakeview Hideaway and looked around as he parked in front of his cabin. The single light pole barely lit the area, but all was quiet and dark except for his unit. The snow and wind had intensified and covered the footprints he'd made when he'd left earlier. No other cars were visible. He was the only tenant tonight. One positive thing about the middle of nowhere—no witnesses.

He got out of his car and tapped on his cabin door.

After several seconds, Galvin spoke from the other side of the door. "Yeah?"

"It's Vossler," Donnie said.

The door opened, and Donnie slipped inside. "Getting nasty out there," he said as he shivered. Swirling snowflakes blew into the main room as he closed the door.

Galvin nodded toward the open bedroom door. "I think she's still high, boss." Sue was lying on the bed, faced away from them. "She moaned and hummed and mumbled shit for a few minutes, but since then she's been a good little addict." He smiled the smile of a man who could hardly wait to rip her clothes off and defile her in several different ways sexually.

"Excellent," Donnie said, mildly surprised she hadn't tried to escape while he was gone. Maybe she secretly wanted to get high, wanted him to take command of her life again. Maybe she was tired of being a single mom, running a restaurant, working herself to the bone just to get by. Maybe this was her way of saying, "I give up, Donnie. Take me back to L.A., and I'll never leave you as long as you take care of me."

Galvin said, "What's the lowdown on that cabin?"

Donnie cocked his head and grinned. "Bitch told the truth. My son is with Johnson in a log cabin not far from town. It's in a forest thicker than spics crowded around a goddamn piñata. Can't see it from the highway. Probably can't hear anything from the highway either, like gunshots or screams of pain."

Galvin gave a guttural laugh and rubbed his hands together. "Ooh, me likee this plan."

Donnie held back a barbed retort aimed at Galvin's maturity. "We won't have any trouble. They're both asleep. But I want to go out in style."

"How's that?" Galvin asked.

Donnie allowed the inspiration to crystalize in his brain. "We've got one more piece of the plan to fit into place."

Galvin stared at him, uncomprehending. "What's that?"

It was above Galvin's intelligence or creativity to understand, but it was one of the more brilliant parts of Donnie's plan. He checked his watch. A self-satisfied grin spread across his face. After five long years, he would reclaim his son within the hour. So much lost time to make up for. So much to teach Josh about being a man. So much his mother had done that needed undoing. He looked at Galvin, whose expression always contained a glimmer of stupid. "Sue—I mean Allyson—is going to make a phone call."

Chapter 48

"Wake up, Josh." Matt knelt and shook the little boy's shoulder.

"Huh? What?" Josh mumbled.

How could he tell Josh they might have to fight for their lives tonight? "Get dressed. We might have to leave soon." He switched on a flashlight, risked being seen for a minute while Josh got oriented.

Josh groaned and squinted at him with uncomprehending eyes. "Why? It's not morning."

A pain churned in Matt's gut for an innocent child who didn't deserve to be in the crossfire of a parental battle that might turn deadly. "The bad man might come here tonight and try to take you away from your mama."

Josh gulped, and his eyes widened with fear. "Can we go find Mama right now?" His voice was whiny. "She said she'd protect me from him, but she can't protect me if she's not here." His lips quivered.

Matt squeezed Josh's shoulder, willing assurance to travel from his hand into Josh's mind. "I'll protect you as much as your mama would if she were here. We'll find her as soon as it's safe. So get dressed—jacket, boots, mittens—in case we need to leave fast."

Josh sat up but said in a voice closer yet to tears, "I don't wanna leave. I want Mama."

Matt grabbed Josh's shoulders with both hands and turned him so he could lock his eyes with the boy's eyes. "You have to act like a grownup and do whatever I say. The bad man might shoot me. Do you want me to get shot by a real gun with real bullets?"

Despite Matt's intentions, that comment sent Josh over the edge. The boy's expression dissolved into heart-wrenching tears of desperation.

Matt hugged Josh firmly yet gently and spoke in an intense whisper. "I know you're scared, buddy, but I also know you can be strong. You're smart, you're a hard worker when you help at the Halcyon, and you love your Mama more than any little boy ever loved his mother. All those things make you the strongest boy I've ever met. If I had a son, I'd want him to be exactly like you."

Josh pushed away and looked up with wide eyes, wet cheeks, and quivering lips. "Really?"

Matt smiled down at his pint-sized ally and formed the Boy Scouts salute. "Scout's honor."

Josh hugged him twice as hard as Matt had hugged him.

"This'll be over soon, and then you and your mama can be together, and everything will be normal again." He struggled to sound sincere. He hardly knew Vossler. Maybe the guy was a ruthless murderer. Maybe he had an army of goons to do his dirty work, and a task force would show up in riot gear, wielding AK-47s, and Matt would be powerless to do anything but surrender.

They both dressed for the outdoors, then doused the nearly dead embers in the fireplace with water from Matt's canteen. Even a small glow might illuminate him enough to become an easy target.

Josh sniffled, his crying done for the moment. "What do we do now?"

"We wait." Matt checked his Glock once more to make sure it was loaded and ready.

Josh stared at the gun with wonderment and awe. "Is that a real gun?"

"Yes."

"Are you going to shoot the bad man?"

He put forward a confident façade. "If shooting him means saving you, I will."

Josh looked up at him with all the innocence every child should possess. "Have you ever shot someone?"

That was the last question Matt expected to hear from the boy. His stomach did a back flip in sync with his brain flip-flopping on whether the truth was better than a lie. He stared out the window toward the

Lake. "Yes." He glanced down at Josh, who showed no reaction other than holding his gaze with penetrating eyes.

"Good, that means you know how to shoot the gun if you have to, right?"

From the mouths of babes.

Matt's heart ached, dejected that this little boy might witness something tonight about which no eight-year-old should even have nightmares. His sole consolation was the practical side of Josh accepting the peril of the situation and figuring it would be better if Matt shot the bad man rather than the other way around.

"Right. But I'll only shoot if there's no other way to keep you safe." He tousled Josh's hair.

After checking the locks on both doors, Matt climbed up to the loft to look out the windows and gauge sightlines, vantage points, anything that might give him an edge inside the cabin. He checked and re-locked the operable skylight—another entry point for invaders—just in case. He wanted no surprises.

Although the corner of the empty loft would initially be safe from ground level gunfire, it would become a death trap once an attacker with more firepower discovered he and Josh were up there. The best he could hope for was a standoff, which they would lose with no food or water and only seventeen bullets in the Glock.

He climbed down the ladder.

Josh watched his every move.

Matt tried to determine the safest place in the bare, unfurnished, unfinished ground floor should a gunfight ensue. The fireplace wall stood in the center of the cabin but didn't span the entire width of the structure. The left side formed the start of a hallway to the front door, the other side opened up to the kitchen. The large fireplace box would protect them from three sides, but two picture windows on the back wall provided clear sight lines for a shooter. A pantry off the kitchen area provided visual cover from all angles, but the drywall wouldn't stop a bullet if a shooter knew someone was inside. Anywhere else in the cabin, Matt would be a tin duck in a carnival shooting gallery. He checked the coals in the fireplace. They were dead. He kicked them to one side with his booted foot.

"Listen carefully," he whispered and pointed to the fireplace box. "Stand in the corner and don't say a word or move unless I say so. If I say *run,* or you see I'm hurt and can't walk, I want you to run out the back door and go for help. Understand?"

Josh's eyes widened with fear, but he nodded.

"That means take the woods trail to your house," Matt said. "As soon as you get home, call nine-one-one. Tell them a man named Donnie Vossler tried to kidnap you. The sheriff will come and get you, so lock the doors and don't open them until you see the sheriff's car, okay?"

Josh nodded. "Is Donnie Vossler the bad man?"

Matt hesitated. "Yes. Why?"

"I heard Mama say the name Donnie at school when she came to get me. She said he would try to take me away, and then she said he might hurt her but not me."

"No one's going to hurt you if I can prevent that."

"Is Donnie Vossler my father?"

Matt groaned internally. Should he lie? He hated to be the one to tell him the truth, so he equivocated. "He told me he's your father, but only your mama knows for sure."

Just then, snow crunched outside. Matt tensed and doused his flashlight. "Shh," he stage-whispered. The attack had begun.

Josh pressed against the fireplace wall.

Matt grabbed Josh's navy-blue sleeping bag and tucked it around Josh up to his neck. "This will cover your red jacket so no one can see you," he whispered. In the dark, the boy would blend into the fireplace like a large soot mark. It was just enough of an illogical, in-plain-sight hiding place that it might keep Josh safe. "Remember what I told you to do if I get hurt."

Josh nodded, too afraid to speak anymore.

Matt repeated his instructions to make sure Josh understood. "Cover all of you except your eyes with the sleeping bag. Don't move until either I come for you or I tell you to run. If you have to run, go to your house and call nine-one-one."

Josh nodded again.

Matt tossed his sleeping bag into the loft to get it out of his way, then crouched and crept to the nearest wall to eliminate any silhouette he might present. He hoped Vossler hadn't seen them lit up by the flashlight. Maybe he hadn't noticed the faint light at all. Matt tracked the footsteps with his ears, turning his head like a fox picking up sounds from a mouse under a foot of snowpack.

The footsteps were heading toward the back door. If Vossler were alone, he'd have come in through the front door, presumably to prevent them from escaping either down the trail to the Clifford house or down the road to the highway to find help. This meant there was at least a second person.

A soft, metallic scraping at the back door made his head swivel toward the sound. Someone was trying the doorknob. When it didn't open, he began picking the lock.

Matt stepped to the back of the room, opposite the fireplace and near the back door, at the spot against the wall where the door would open and provide him some cover. He readied his flashlight. A beam of light shining into an attacker's eyes might disorient him enough to either not shoot or fire wildly. He might gain a few seconds of advantage.

He glanced out the window toward the sky. Whirling snowflakes bounced off the window. The wind had increased to a strong, audible whoosh. A blizzard was on the way, which might provide extra cover for Josh if he had to flee.

Thirty seconds after hearing the click of the lock opening, the door hadn't moved. Matt hadn't heard any more footsteps, either. Was this a deliberate strategy to confuse him? The urge to look out the window was powerful, but he resisted. He had to keep Vossler off guard by not doing the expected. He leveled his pistol at the center of the back door.

When he'd almost lost his patience, he heard a soft creak at the front of the cabin. The second attacker had picked the front door lock. Smart strategy. Eliminate both barriers to entry first, then launch a coordinated attack from front and back.

He inferred they'd assume he and Josh were asleep and try to take them by surprise. He'd only have a few seconds to surprise them before they sprung their trap. Crouching to present a small target, he put his hand lightly on the doorknob, feeling for resistance, which would indicate a hand gripping the outside handle. Feeling none, he assumed whoever was outside would wait for the inside front man to make his move. Matt regripped his flashlight and felt for the switch with his thumb, pointing it toward the front of the cabin. Soft footsteps from that direction told him an enemy was walking toward the main room. He strained to see any motion.

When Matt thought he saw a body move into the room, he pulled open the back door and wedged himself between it and the exterior wall. Mouth dry, nerves sparking in his fingertips, he pointed his Glock toward the front, ready to fire.

No intruder was visible toward the front. No one came rushing in the back door. No curses. No shouts. No movement. No gunfire. All noise had been sucked out of the room except the whooshing wind.

At that instant, the rear intruder shoved hard against the partly open door. Matt took the brunt of the door's impact on his knee and yelled in pain as the intruder's pressing weight against the door immobilized him against the wall. Hearing noise from the front as well, he pushed back against the door, using the wall for leverage, as a bright light from the front-door assailant temporarily blinded him. Matt turned on his flashlight as a counter to the light in his eyes. A thud near the top of the door and a groan implied he'd inflicted some damage on the backdoor enemy, maybe a head knocking against the wall. He shoved forward and pushed his assailant off balance. They tumbled to the floor.

A gunshot rang out. A bullet whizzed past the spot his torso had been a split second earlier. He clicked off his flashlight, then scrambled to regain his balance and fire at the front-door assailant. But while grappling with the man who writhed under him, he couldn't free his gun hand. Helpless and exposed, he braced for the impact of a bullet penetrating his body.

Instead of a shot, a foot flew at his head from his right and caught him square in the temple, stunning him. In the next instant, the front man grappled for Matt's pistol. Matt fought to hang on, tried to point and shoot, only succeeded in shooting, but the bullet merely hit the cabin wall.

He lashed out with his legs, trying to scissor kick the man who'd kicked him, caught an ankle, heard a loud yelp, then Vossler's voice.

"Damn it, Johnson, give up!" Vossler was grappling with him for the Glock.

The man at the back door lay wedged between the door and the jamb, grunting, trying to free himself from underneath both Matt and Vossler.

Matt freed his left hand from under his body and lashed out toward Vossler, catching him with a glancing blow off his jaw.

The punch staggered Vossler enough that he let loose the grip on Matt's pistol. He staggered backward and turned off his flashlight an instant before Matt could aim and fire.

Matt shot into the darkness at where he thought Vossler stood, but had little hope he'd hit anything. He guessed Vossler had ducked behind the fireplace. It was now or never.

"Run, Josh!" Matt yelled as he fired another covering shot toward the front door. He heard a rustling sound as Josh tossed aside the sleeping bag. Matt fired again, high this time, to make sure he wouldn't hit Josh if he ran the wrong way. Josh brushed against him as he headed for the back door.

"Remember what to do," Matt called as he watched Josh's dark shape clamber over the back-door assailant and outside. He fired another warning shot toward the front door, then felt a sharp, heavy blow on the back of his head. As he fell to the ground, Matt heard Josh's footsteps crunch on the snow. Matt's last act was to fall against the door, wedging tight against the prone intruder and hopefully delaying Vossler long enough that he wouldn't see Josh duck into the woods and head for home on the trail. Then everything went dark.

Chapter 49

A lump formed in Donnie's throat as he watched his son dash out the door, running for his life. The kind of lump that comes when you realize you made the big mistakes that led to this craziness. Here he was, freezing his ass off, trying to rescue his son. Yet thanks to his wife's brainwashing of Josh for five years, Josh must have thought his father was the enemy.

He followed the footprints in the snow toward a copse of trees and found the start of a path. Unsure where it led, he yelled out, "Josh, come back! It's your father!"

It seemed impossible that Josh would hear him above the noise of the surf from Lake Superior and the increasing wind unless he was hiding nearby. Donnie took several strides down the path, but stopped when he realized where the trail headed. He smiled. Josh was running for home. He'd find his boy easily enough. He needed to deal with Johnson first, anyway.

The snow fell harder compared to when he and Galvin had arrived at the cabin. The wind gusts whipped the flakes sideways in a sheeting pattern. If this turned into one of those blizzards, it might delay his return to L.A. with Josh. A minor detail. His Escalade had four-wheel drive, whatever that meant. He high-stepped back to the cabin, cursing his numb hands and the snow in his shoes.

Inside he found Galvin awake but dazed, rubbing his head. "You okay?" All he cared about was if his muscle man could do the rest of this job. After that, the mook could drop dead.

"Yeah, fuckin' bastard caught me a lucky one," Galvin said. "Knocked me off balance. I hit the doorjamb square on with my head. Always thought that seeing-stars bullshit was bullshit. But I sure as hell saw some." Galvin examined his hand as if he'd never seen his own blood.

Donnie nodded toward Johnson, still unconscious from the butt of his pistol cracking the back of his head. "He move at all?"

"Nah. You must've whacked him pretty good."

"Let's work fast before he comes to. You get the accelerant. I'll drag him into position."

Galvin staggered to his feet, wiped his bloody hand on his pants leg, pulled out his flashlight, and went out the front door.

Donnie checked Johnson's limp body for signs of life. His breathing was steady. Close enough. They should have enough time. Setting his flashlight on the floor, Donnie aimed it at the center of the room and then dragged Johnson to the bottom of the ladder to the loft.

Galvin returned with a red plastic gasoline container and removed the cap.

Donnie glanced around the room and noticed a camp stove on the floor of the kitchen area.

"Hold on a sec." He thrust out his hand. "I just got a better idea." He examined the stove and its steel fuel bottle, connected by a flexible, metal-sheathed hose. He shook the bottle. It was nearly full. "This'll be perfect," he said. "The fucking idiot will die from his own stupidity." He smiled, confident that a fire caused by a leaky camp stove would seem less suspicious than one ignited by gasoline. "You know anything about these stoves?"

Galvin came over and studied the compact one-burner stove. "We had camp stoves sort of like this in Boy Scouts. Ain't seen one of these fancy new ones before. Probably works the same." He fumbled with the connector for a moment, separated it from the burner, and opened the fuel bottle a half twist. A sharp hiss escaped from the metal container.

Both men sniffed. Donnie smelled some sort of gas.

"Yep, it burns white gas like the old ones," Galvin said. "It's good to go."

"Set it up next to the woodpile," Donnie said, "but spill a little and make sure that connection is leaky."

"Okay, boss, but why don't we just cap the motherfucker."

Donnie could have sworn he'd heard rusty gears turning in Galvin's skull. He shook his head and chuckled. "Here's where the style part comes in, my man. If we shoot him or there's any other sign of foul play, the cops'll come looking for us because of all the witnesses who've seen me around town. Hell, he might've told someone about our little run-ins."

Galvin pursed his lips and nodded.

"And that stoner kid, Rippe, might sing if the cops so much as look at him. He was okay to help me with the easy shit, like spying and recruiting lowlifes to stage my little melodramas in the Halcyon. I doubt he'll keep quiet if he thinks he's an accomplice to murder. If Johnson dies in a fire, Rippe pleads ignorance. End of story. You and me are free and clear and long gone."

"Woulda been fun to mess him up a little first," Galvin said, "then blow his brains out. Or toss him off the cliff out back and watch him splat into a hundred pieces."

"I thought about the cliff. But if they don't know if he jumped or was pushed, the cops might treat it as a possible homicide, and I'm a suspect again."

"Won't a fire attract the cops too?"

"This ain't L.A., Bobby. They got volunteer fire departments. Bunch of guys get a signal on their cell phones or hear the town siren, run to the firehouse, load up a truck, and drive out here. Takes forever. By the time they turn on the first firehose," he pointed to the window, "this snow will have covered our tracks, and Johnson will be a charred piece of meat."

Galvin's puzzled countenance turned to one of comprehension. "Oh, yeah."

Donnie's face soured. Galvin only pretended to understand his brilliance, but at least he followed the general train of thought. "Enough jaw flapping. Get that fire going."

Galvin started a fire in the fireplace, then splashed some of the white gas from the stove's fuel bottle at the base of the stack of wood in the bin next to the fireplace. Then he poured the fuel in a long, thin trail around the cabin's perimeter. He appeared nervous as he scurried about, well aware he was a spark away from going up in flames himself. He finished without incident and set the camp stove near the firewood, leaving a few ounces of fuel inside the loosely capped bottle.

Donnie checked for any sign he and Galvin had been in the cabin. The bullet holes from the brief gun battle would most likely burn up in the fire. If anyone found empty shell casings lying around that he and Galvin hadn't retrieved, they'd presume someone had been using the vacant cabin for target practice—believable enough since half the highway signs he'd seen in this wretched county had been shot through with bullet holes.

He pulled a small orange cinder from the fireplace with the fireplace shovel, blew on it until it glowed red hot, and tossed it into the puddle of white gas. With a whoosh, the gas flared brightly, and flames crept onto the nearest piece of firewood in the pile.

They went out the front door, but Donnie stopped in the doorway. The flames grew to where the room was lit up as if a light was on, except the flickering flames made the shadows dance back and forth. He lit a cigarette and took a deep drag. Holding the burning match in front of him, he tossed it onto the white gas on the doorway floor. It caught fire and raced around the perimeter of the cabin. He gave Galvin a satisfied grin. "Let's go find my son."

They walked down the driveway to their car with their heads down and braced against the sideways onslaught of snow. By the time Donnie finished his smoke, Johnson would be dead.

Chapter 50

When his motion-sensing infrared surveillance cameras picked up a third burst of activity at the access road to Allyson Clifford's cabin, Ben assumed he'd see a deer, as he had the first two times.

He was wrong. One man was walking from a car down the access road toward the cabin. He was tall and wore what appeared to be a business-style overcoat. When the man passed out of the picture, Ben stepped away from his monitors. He went to the bathroom of his motel room, splashed water on his face to wake himself up, and checked his watch. Eleven-thirty p.m.

Ben was quartered at the AmericInn, some five hundred yards from the Halcyon. He'd set up the cameras the day before. He'd hidden one in the trees along the access road, fifty yards from Highway 61. He'd attached the second camera to a sturdy branch above the trail entrance nearest to Allyson Clifford's house. His plan was to wait until either Lanier took the child somewhere else and returned to the cabin alone, or Clifford came to get her child and left. If Lanier and the child left together, Ben would hustle down to a vantage point in his car where he could pick up the live trail.

Over the next hour, Ben drank coffee and watched his monitors. During that time, the first man returned from the cabin. Thirty minutes later, two men walked down the access road toward the cabin. One resembled the first man he'd seen, but since his images were infrared, he could only get an estimate of size and height. The second man was shorter and quite stocky.

After another fifteen minutes, the child stumbled out of the woods on the trail and ran past the camera, presumably toward the Clifford house. On the surface, that was a development. If the child was out of the way, it was only a matter of time before the two men left Lanier alone. But why wouldn't the two men have taken the child? Why was he running alone? Fleeing some danger? Ben's stomach tightened. If the boy feared for his life, was he fleeing Lanier or the two other men? Damn, this was getting confusing. He ran his hand through his hair, squeezing and pulling the strands, undecided how to proceed.

As he fidgeted and watched his monitors, two men emerged from the access road. He studied their forms and concluded they were the two who had walked in together. Lanier was finally alone.

Ben threw on his coat, hat, and gloves, checked that his revolver was loaded, and ran to his car. Minutes later, he parked on Halcyon Road near the Clifford woman's house and started down the trail toward the cabin with a flashlight in one hand and his revolver in the other.

Chapter 51

A loud crackling sound woke Matt from a black sleep. As he analyzed the sound, it grew louder and clearer. The smell of smoke hit him, and he sensed abnormal warmth. *Fire!* He opened his eyes. Flickering orange shadows danced on the log wall. Flames were mere feet from his body.

His head felt as if it were being squeezed in a vise. He rose onto one elbow. The room spun, but he managed to focus his vision. The wood-pile was well established in flames, as were the walls on either side of the chimney. Panicked, he gasped and drew too deep of a breath, which made him cough and retch. He closed his eyes and groped for support from the ladder to the loft. Gripping it tightly, he pulled himself to his knees and swallowed the dizziness and nausea.

He opened his eyes again. This time, he kept them open for several seconds. He looked around the cabin. Josh had escaped. But had Josh escaped Vossler?

His cook stove, the obvious source of the fire, was engulfed in flames and well on its way to melting. The fire burned all around the perimeter of the cabin. Flames and smoke obscured the doors and windows. The heat intensified and forced him to crawl away from the flames toward the center of the great room.

Fighting the fire was futile with no water source and no fire extinguisher. He needed to leave but wasn't sure he could walk. Rising to his knees, he coughed again as the smoke layer worked its way closer to the floor. *Running short on time. Must get out now.*

Over his shoulder, the woodpile of flame surged upward as it found a new foothold on the wood mantle and knotty pine walls. The noise from the blaze mixed with the whooshing in his head to create a cacophony. The smoke thickened to where he could barely see five feet away. He coughed, put his sleeve over his face, and dropped to the floor, trying to find a smoke-free corner. He ended up back at the base of the ladder to the loft.

His sleeping bag! It might still be in the loft. He had one chance to get out alive, and this was it.

He put his nose to the wood floor and inhaled as much air as he could, then stood and clambered up the ladder to the loft. Once there, he groped for his sleeping bag and found it in the middle of the floor. He wrapped the nylon and goose down bag around his body, covering as much of himself as possible and still maintaining the ability to walk. He slid down the ladder and stumbled toward the front door. In two steps, the sleeping bag caught fire. Heat radiated through the material to his back and arms. Crouching low, he crept crablike toward the front door. The smoke hung so thick he couldn't see anything.

As his lungs felt ready to explode from holding his breath, he bumped into a wall and reached up to feel for a doorknob. Nothing. He moved to his right. Nothing. He moved to his left. The metal doorknob seared his hand. He jerked back with a yelp, then used the corner of the sleeping bag as a potholder to turn the hot knob. Even with that protection, he scorched his hand again. Intense heat pounded his back. The sleeping bag had burned through, and he felt a searing pain on his back and arms.

He pulled the door open, then stood and leaped off the porch. In midair, he tossed aside the flaming sleeping bag, hit a snowdrift with a thud and a whoosh, and rolled in the snow for a full minute. The flames hissed as they were extinguished. The heat subsided on his body. He'd been burned but was still in the initial stage of shock where he felt little pain.

Matt hacked and wheezed as he rolled to put out the flames, but inhaled some snow, which made him choke even more. He had never coughed so painfully hard in his life. He retched as if the smoke had given him an upset stomach. When the last hiss of flames had stopped, he rolled onto his back. The coughs subsided to a tolerable level, and he opened his eyes, staring up into the blizzard as windblown flakes of snow landed on him, cooling his scorched body.

He was alive, barely, and had escaped with only seconds to spare. For a moment, he wondered if Vossler and his partner waited outside ready to shoot him on the small chance he'd escaped the cabin. But no gunshots came. Through the muddled haze in his brain, he reasoned they wanted him to die from the fire, not from a bullet. Smart of Vossler to cover his crime that way.

Matt had a serious burn on his left hand, lesser burns on his back and arms. The pain registered, and he grimaced and moaned. Arrows, stabs, lightning bolts shot through his nervous system. Desperate, he tore off his jacket and shirt and dropped back into the snow. The iciness shocked him, but soothed and numbed his burned flesh. After lying in the snow as long as he could tolerate, he stood and donned his shirt and scorched jacket.

Josh was who knows where. Vossler and Galvin were probably minutes away from finding him. Assuming Josh had called 911, Matt doubted the sheriff could get to Josh before Vossler could because the odds of the county sheriff either being in Castle Danger or close enough that his vehicle could still navigate Highway 61 were virtually nil. The county was large, and the roads were two-lane paved at best. With up to two feet of snow forecast to fall in this blizzard, no one in the Arrowhead was driving anywhere with any speed.

Matt would have to get back to Josh somehow. Find Allyson somehow. Stop Vossler somehow. All that with no weapon, a probable concussion, numerous burns, and smoke inhalation damage to boot. He did the only thing he could think of and staggered down the wooded trail to Allyson's house.

After ten steps he stopped short when a flashlight clicked on, blinding him for the moment, and a voice said, "Matt Lanier, I presume?" The question was punctuated with the click of the hammer of a revolver.

Chapter 52

Donnie felt a warm rush of anticipation at seeing his son after a five-year separation. Despite his eagerness, he drove cautiously to the Clifford house because the highway was nearly impassible. Galvin had to get out and push the car through a deep drift after they'd turned onto Halcyon Drive.

It was too cold and snowy to hide outside, so Josh's sanctuaries were limited. He would hide at one of two places: his house, or the Halcyon. But a scared boy will run to his mother before anyone else. He drove down Halcyon Drive toward his wife's house, where he pulled his Escalade into the Clifford driveway and parked.

As they exited, Galvin said, "Hey boss, whose car is that?" He nodded to a sedan parked across the street and facing toward Lake Superior.

Donnie studied the car, then turned toward Galvin. "Take a look. Could belong to some friend of Sue's."

Galvin walked to the car and peered in, then put his hand on the hood. "No one inside, but the hood's warm."

Donnie tensed and felt for his pistol. The last thing he needed was someone hanging around who wasn't supposed to be here. "Check it every minute or two while we search the house."

Galvin returned, and they went to the back door, out of sight of Halcyon Drive. No lights were on inside. Donnie tried the door. Locked. He nodded at Galvin, who threw a beefy shoulder into the door and popped the lock right out of the jamb. Wood splinters cracked and flew. The house shook from the impact. Donnie glanced at the parked car again, and his jaw clenched at this unexpected wild card.

When Josh saw a second pair of car headlights moving toward his house, his tummy gurgled and ached. The first car had parked across the street, and a man got out and went down the trail. He didn't recognize the car as belonging to anyone in town. But if the man was walking into the woods, it couldn't be the bad man.

Josh knew he shouldn't trust any car other than a sheriff's car. And neither car that approached his house had the cherry lights on top of the cars that the sheriff's car had. He wouldn't let anyone from the second car take him away, either. When the car stopped in his driveway, he hid behind the living room sofa near the front door. The sofa was his favorite hiding place because the back formed a shallow *V* that allowed him to slip in between the sofa and the wall but gave the illusion there was no room for even the smallest person to hide.

The loud crack of splintering wood made him flinch. His heart pounded in his ears. He thought of the gunshots he'd heard in the cabin. They were louder than any noise he'd heard other than fireworks. He hoped he wouldn't hear any more.

Donnie stepped inside and flipped on the kitchen light. "Josh," he called, "it's your father. Come on out. Don't be afraid. Your mother and I are back together. All three of us are going home to California. That's where you were born, sport. You loved it there. We'll go to the ocean and Disneyland as much as you want. And the weather is warm all year. You can play outside every single day."

He went downstairs to check the lower level while Galvin checked the attached garage and main level.

Josh recognized the voice of the man who yelled at him back at the cabin. *He said he was my father.* Weren't fathers supposed to be people who didn't scare you the way this man scared him? He was so confused, his head ached.

He would much rather have Matt for his father. Matt was cool and super nice and funny and played Hot Wheels with him every day.

When one man went down the basement steps and the other into the garage, Josh crawled from behind the sofa, eased the front door open, and ran as fast as he could to the Halcyon. He would watch for the sheriff from there and run out to get in his car before the bad men found him.

After a quick but thorough check of the basement, Donnie returned to the central hallway.

Galvin stood there with his palms open. "Nothin' up here. No activity in that car, either."

Pressure hit Donnie in the form of full-body tension. His sixth sense of knowing when something was wrong vibrated in his brain. He needed to find Josh fast before the driver of the mystery car returned. "Let's check the restaurant."

"Sure thing, boss," Galvin said, and they made the short walk to the back door of the Halcyon.

That door was locked as well, and much more solid than the door to the house. Galvin produced a small crowbar he'd brought for this eventuality, inserted it between the door and jamb, and pried. The door gave way with a loud crack of wood and a scraping of metal as he sprung the jamb and the deadbolt.

Near the front of the restaurant, Josh stifled a frightened cry. The bad men were already in the Halcyon's kitchen. Maybe they'd seen him running outside. His tummy ached more now. His hands were sore from repeatedly making fists as he glanced out the window, looking for the sheriff's car.

If he ran outside again, the bad men would for sure see him and catch him. He had to hide in the Halcyon, but there was only one hiding place the bad men might not find.

He'd bumped his toe against a panel under the front edge of one of the booth benches one day, which had caused the wood panel to pop out. The space was just big enough to stash several dozen Hot Wheels cars or one small boy. Mama said he could play there anytime the Halcyon was closed, as long as he replaced the loose panel before he left.

He hustled over to his Secret Super Garage, knocked the panel off with a quick pop of his hand, and rolled under the bench with his head closest to the front door. He pulled the panel back into place, which was hard to do because it didn't have any place to grab it just right. He finished a second before the bad men entered the dining room. Darkness scared him more than he ever admitted to Mama, but dark wasn't nearly as scary as having bad men chase him.

Donnie went in first, his flashlight guiding the way, and found a light switch. He turned it on. "Let's work fast. Someone sees a light on in here at two a.m., they call the cops, and the cops come looking for a burglar."

"Okay, boss," Galvin said.

They were near the kitchen, so Donnie said, "You check the front area, bar, and dining room. I'll check the kitchen, restrooms, and office. He's a little kid, so look in every nook and cranny. I'm sure Josh is scared and confused, what with all the shooting earlier. He won't know his dad's here to rescue him and take him back to a better life." He intentionally spoke those last words louder in case Josh could hear him.

After a few minutes of intensive searching, Donnie was ready to give up and head for the McDonald's on a desperation hunch when he had an idea. Motioning for Galvin to come close, he whispered, "Follow my lead."

Galvin nodded, and they walked to the front door.

While the bad men searched for him, Josh relaxed a little because of the clangs, bangs, and slams of pots, pans, and doors. If he coughed or made another sound right, they wouldn't hear him over the noise they made. But now he had to go to the bathroom. He squeezed his legs together and made fists. It was only pee, but he hadn't peed since he and Matt had been at the house before going to the cabin to sleep. He wasn't sure because it was so dark in his Secret Super Garage, but it had to be almost morning. He had to pee as badly as he usually did when he woke up each morning.

When one man stopped near his booth and stood for a few seconds, Josh held his breath as long as he could and prayed the loose panel wouldn't fall out. The man walked to the next booth, then the next, and the next, stopping and making some noise at each one as he searched.

Josh took another breath when his lungs ached so much he thought he'd explode. He didn't gasp or make any noise when he breathed, because if the bad men heard him, they'd find him.

The sounds from the kitchen moved to the restrooms, the bar, then the front, where the man called Boss said, "Where the hell did that damn kid go?"

Josh's ears burned. His ears always burned when he heard people swear. He wasn't allowed to swear. Once last year he said *hell*. Mama gave him a time out and scolded him about only saying polite words even if you're mad. Did Boss's mama ever give him time outs?

Why wasn't Mama here to protect him? He dug his fingernails into his fisted palms. She'd never left him by himself like this before. Sometimes he wished he could do more things by himself, without Mama watching and telling him to be careful or don't get dirty or play nice with your friends, stuff like that. Now that he was alone, he wished he wasn't alone. He wished Mama was here, even if she had to hide in his hiding place too. Being alone now wasn't fun. He missed his stuffed bear, Buddy, more than he could remember in his whole life. He wanted to cry, but crying made noise, and the bad men would for sure hear him cry.

He'd lain still and quiet for a long time while the two men searched the Halcyon. Besides having to pee, the lingering food smells made him hungry. *Why won't they leave?*

Josh heard the men walk toward the front door.

"Josh isn't here. Let's go," Boss said.

"Okay, boss."

The door opened, then closed, and the Halcyon was dead quiet. Maybe Sheriff Hotchkiss was outside. Josh pushed the panel open a crack and peered out into the darkness.

Donnie was mildly annoyed by Galvin's density. He'd been asked to do one small piece of acting, and he sounded like a robot. Donnie made a mental note to hire a better class of goon next time. He opened the door and motioned for Galvin to stay inside, then turned off the lights and slammed the door. The two men stood motionless, barely breathing.

A minute later, Donnie heard wood scrape on wood near the booths next to the windows overlooking the Lake. He readied his flashlight. Another scrape, then the rustle of nylon clothing. He clicked on his flashlight and guided the beam to the noise.

Josh Clifford gasped, threw his hand up to block the light beam, and froze.

"Oldest trick in the book, kid," Donnie said with a chuckle. "I learned it playing hide and seek when I was your age."

Josh bolted for the back door, but Galvin ran him down in a half-dozen quick strides. Holding him by the scruff of his collar, Galvin muscled the boy to the hostess station and held him in front of Donnie, who had turned on the lights.

"That's another thing I'll teach you when we get home," Donnie said, "seeing as how your mother couldn't be bothered to do that either. Might take a while, but I'll whip you back into shape and teach you how to be a real man."

Josh had been staring at the floor. At the word *whip*, he looked up with a mask of panic across his face.

Donnie experienced a minor pang of feeling. Love, he guessed, but immediately suppressed that as a sign of weakness, something else he'd retrain Josh to push out of his character. He glanced at Galvin. "Let's go."

As Galvin closed the door, Donnie grabbed his son by the arm and headed for his car.

Chapter 53

S tunned at the appearance of this new player, Matt threw up one hand to shield his eyes. Weaponless, he raised the other above his head in surrender. Either Vossler had captured his Glock, or it was melting in the cabin fire. Unable to identify his attacker through the flashlight's glare, he asked, "Who are you?"

"Not important. Are you Matt Lanier?"

"Did Vossler hire you?"

"Who?"

Matt became confused until he realized this man probably had nothing to do with Vossler.

"What's with the fire?" the man said and gestured toward the cabin with his gun.

"A weenie roast got out of control."

The man shoved the gun close to Matt's nose. "One last chance to answer before I toss you back into the fire."

Matt's head cleared enough to understand whom this guy was working for. "If you don't know Vossler, then you must've been hired by Leland Smythe."

"Never heard of him, either."

"I doubt he gave you his real name. Smythe is the only man other than Vossler and his muscle who wants me dead. If you're not working for Vossler, you're working for Smythe."

"All I know is the man who hired me pays extremely well." The man gestured with his pistol. "Let's head back to the cabin before the fire dies down. I don't want to miss my opportunity."

Frantic with the thought that this guy would probably shoot him and dump him into the blaze, hoping to burn his body beyond recognition, Matt turned and started walking.

Five steps later, he cried out, "Argh, my leg!" He grabbed his leg and pitched forward onto the snowy ground.

His captor said, "What the—"

Matt barrel-rolled and sprang into the dense thicket of pines at the edge of the trail.

The man fired several shots at where Matt had been a split second earlier, then began whirling his flashlight beam around in circles, looking for a moving body in the forest.

Matt slipped through the trees behind the man, recalling the previous months in the Boundary Waters when he'd hunted game with just a pistol. He had to get close enough for a clean kill shot because he lacked spare ammunition, and a pistol's range was much shorter and less powerful than a hunting rifle. He literally had to stalk his prey to within point-blank range.

Sneaking up on the man was easy because the human senses of hearing and smell aren't as keen as an animal's. After the man turned away, Matt silently stepped out onto the trail and sprang upon him like a wolf lunging for the kill on a deer.

Matt knocked the man down with a hard right hook to the head, followed by a leveraged throw across his body. In seconds, he'd seized the man's weapon and shoved the barrel against his forehead.

He was enraged that every minute he'd wasted out here was a minute lost in rescuing Allyson and Josh. A twitch from pulling the trigger, he stopped himself with a mighty internal effort masked by a deep, guttural, primal, animal-screaming howl of pain, frustration, and anger at this entire situation. Anger at his life for the last nine months.

The man cowered and exhaled a frightened whimper as the crazed man pinning him to the ground howled like a wild beast.

The release of emotions also released within Matt a flashback of the fateful events last spring: helping an elderly widow save her farm with Zach Perez's help only to stumble upon a bizarre land grab conspiracy called

Millennium Four. The house explosion that injured his hand. Fleeing to Big Island in the Boundary Waters only to be tracked down by two Millennium Four conspirators. His two best friends coming to his rescue but losing their lives along with the two conspirators. The rendezvous that never happened with his ex-wife, the love of his life, Diane Blake, at the rest area in Duluth because another conspirator had kidnapped her and tried to run over Matt with her car. The subsequent shootout ended when Matt killed the man but inadvertently killed Diane too.

And all for what? The ruined life of a fugitive. This current mess was rapidly devolving into another disaster.

He desperately wanted to lash out at the world by pulling the trigger on this stranger and blasting his brains into a red mess on the snow, but he thought of his mother and resisted. *Family helps family.* He still had a small chance to help Allyson and Josh.

"Get up," Matt said through clenched teeth. He stood but kept the gun aimed at the man's chest.

The man stood.

Matt nodded down the trail toward Allyson's house. "Walk."

Chapter 54

Prisoner and captor set off down the trail. Matt staggered and stumbled, nearly falling several times. His limbs tightened with cold even as his burns radiated heat. Fatigue rushed up through his feet into his brain in a frigid wave of lethargy. He concentrated on keeping the gun pointed at his prisoner.

With his mind foggy and getting worse, his sense of purpose began to wane. Why in hell was he risking his life attempting to save two people he barely knew? Josh might have lost his way and lay dying a slow, painful death from hypothermia all because Matt told him to run out into a fierce blizzard to escape from his own father. Allyson was missing too, perhaps dead. Had he spent the last few hours trying to help a dead woman keep her child safe?

The men exited the woods trail where it met Halcyon Drive as a car engine revved to life and the car's lights came on. The vehicle was parked in Allyson's driveway.

"Run!" Matt said and shoved his captive forward. They sprinted toward the house. As the car backed out of the driveway, he saw two silhouettes through the auto glass. When the car passed under the lone streetlight on that section of Halcyon Drive, he recognized the red SUV.

"Vossler!" A futile cry since he was too far away. "Back door," he said to his captive, and they ran to the house. If the door were locked, he'd break in because he feared he'd go into a coma from the hypothermia and die mere feet from safety.

"On the ground," he commanded. "Now."

The man prostrated himself.

As Matt fumbled with the knob and opened the door, he saw the splintered wood of the doorframe and stopped. Josh had tried but failed to keep Vossler out. If only he'd arrived a minute earlier. "Josh, it's Matt. Come out if you're here. You're safe."

Matt turned to the man. "Inside."

The man rose and entered the kitchen.

"Garage." Matt pointed the pistol at the door leading to the attached garage.

The man opened it and entered, followed closely by Matt holding the gun barrel to the man's back.

"Pull that rope from the blue pack."

The man complied.

"Back inside."

They returned to the kitchen, where Matt finally got a clear look at his prisoner.

"You were in the Halcyon the other day," Matt said with surprised recognition.

His prisoner's silence was confirmation enough.

Then the fact crystallized in Matt's brain. The man had pretended to compliment him to get a good look at his face. Matt's spirits sunk as he realized how unvigilant he'd been in watching for either the law or Smythe's men. He forced Smythe out of his mind for the moment. "Sit and tie your ankles with one end of the rope."

"Hey, if you're looking for the kid, I'll help," said the man. "We can call a truce. I promise I won't try anything."

"No chance, pal. Do it now." He shoved the pistol closer to his prisoner's face, and the man quickly tied his ankles with the nylon cord.

"Now wrap it around your thighs and the chair seat."

The man did as he was told and held out the rest of the rope, some ten more feet.

"Wrap it around one wrist several times. Tight."

The man followed instructions.

"Hands behind the chair back. Keep holding the rope."

After the man had complied, Matt walked behind him, lashed the man's tied wrist to one of the wood supports of the chair back, then put the pistol on the table and tied the man's other wrist to the opposite chair support. The tie job wasn't artistic, but it would do for the moment.

Matt stepped in front of his prisoner. "You just wasted five minutes of my time, buddy. So help me God, if Josh is kidnapped or killed because I was five minutes too late, this is the last sight you'll ever see." Matt put his face inches from the man's with a fierce expression he hoped would cow him into passivity.

"No problem," the man said. "You could've killed me on the trail, but you didn't. I owe you a little something in return. Where'd you learn to move that quick and sneak up on a guy?"

"Lots of practice in the woods hunting game. Now shut up. I'm busy."

Matt checked the house. Doors throughout were open, closets had hanging clothes swiped to one side, the lower level light was on, and the front door was ajar. He went to a window and looked up the road toward the Halcyon. No inside lights on. Had Vossler had been there first and then come here to capture Josh?

Still shaking with cold, but grateful to be warming up again, he went to the phone and dialed Pauline Allen's number.

She answered in a sleepy voice. "It's two in the morning. This had better not be a prank."

"Pauline, it's Matt. Vossler is after Josh and was just here at Allyson's. If he didn't find him here, Josh might be on his way to your house."

"What? Wait. Why?" She sounded confused and concerned.

"Vossler left here a few minutes ago. He may have kidnapped Josh. If not, he might go to your place if he thinks you've been hiding Josh. If he shows up, call the sheriff. Then lock your doors and get a shotgun ready." Matt glanced at his red, blistered forearms. "He's through playing nice."

"That doesn't make any sense," she said, now fully alert. "Allyson called me earlier tonight and told me she'd made up with Donnie. They're taking Josh back to California."

A split-second wave of relief that Allyson was alive was followed by disbelief that hit him like a slap in the face. "She what?"

"I didn't believe it either. I asked a couple of times if she was sure. She insisted things between them were okay now."

"That can't be. I've only been here a few weeks, barely know her or Vossler, but seeing her when he was around, it seemed she would've killed him instantly if she could've gotten away with it."

"That's how I feel about the slime ball now too."

"You're positive it was Allyson?"

"She sounded weird, but it was her."

"Weird? How?"

She hesitated. "Hmm, mechanical I guess. Robotic."

Matt's stomach bottomed out. "Robotic, as if she were on drugs?"

Pauline gasped and began talking so fast that Matt had difficulty understanding. "Holy mother of God I thought there was something phony about the whole story a woman doesn't change her mind about any man that fast especially if he's a sleaze like Donnie I feel so *stupid* for falling for his b.s.!" She strung the words together as if she were an old vinyl LP recording played at forty-five r.p.m.

"Hey, slow down," he said as calmly as he could. "Don't kick yourself. Vossler's sharp enough to sucker anyone. Did you get any clue where she was calling from?"

"No. I didn't hear any background noise except Donnie talking to her. His voice was muffled, so I couldn't hear his exact words."

"Change of plans. Call the sheriff now. Ask if Josh had called them in the last hour or so. If he has, there's an outside chance they rescued him already."

"I'll call, but it might not help," Pauline said. "If a patrol car is more than a few miles away, they'll take forever to get here in this blizzard. And that assumes they're willing to risk driving."

Matt's mind raced, trying to think of what else he could do. "If Vossler kidnapped them both, he'd be stupid to drive tonight, so he's got to be holed up somewhere." His voice intensified with desperation. "I need to make another call. I'll get back to you in a few minutes."

"I'll wake up Darrell. He'll help us."

"Good. But both of you be careful. And make sure your kids are in a safe place. Vossler might not have Josh yet. In that case, you're in his sights."

"We'll be fine. You find Allyson and Josh, then we'll all be great."

"I apologize for getting you into the middle of this."

"Forget it. That's what friends do."

"Thank you, Pauline."

He hung up and called Zach Perez. As the phone rang, he prayed the kid had some sort of news for him: a lead, some insight, any dirt on Vossler that would help Allyson keep her son away from that scumbag.

"Hello?" Zach answered in a sleepy voice.

"Kid, this is Matt. I need your help again, I—"

"Dude! I tried to call your cell phone for hours. I finally gave up and went to bed."

Matt groaned loudly. He'd left the phone in the cabin, whereby now it was probably a molten mass of plastic.

"Let me guess," Zach said. "The battery ran low, or you turned it off by accident."

"No. It burned in the fire I just escaped from."

"Whoa." That stopped Zach cold. "Fire?"

"Yeah. Vossler doesn't like me very much. Plus, another guy tried to kill me five minutes after that." He glared at his prisoner. "I think Smythe sent him, but he denies knowing the name."

"*Madre de Dios.* You're crazy to mess with both these guys. One will kill you to get to his son. The other will kill you just for messing in his business."

"That's not important. Time's wasting. I'm pretty sure Vossler has kidnapped Allyson and her son."

There was a brief pause followed by, "Oh shit."

"Did you find anything on him? I need some leverage, need to know a weak point, how to deal with him when I find him."

"I've got some info on the dead movie director, but I've got another piece of information you might want to know." Excited urgency charged Zach's voice.

"Okay, shoot."

"This scoop is awesome even for me, *muchacho*."

"What?" Matt wanted to scream with impatience. Didn't the kid know how serious this was? Maybe not. He was three hundred miles away, living his own life, probably trying to forget he'd ever offered to help Matt Lanier navigate a computer for the first time on that raw, drizzly day last March at the University of Minnesota library.

"The smartest thing you ever did that I've seen is write down Vossler's license plate number."

"How so?" All a license number might tell him was Vossler's address or that he'd rented the car if he was from out of town.

"Rental companies found that putting GPS transmitters on their vehicles helps keep track of their inventory more carefully, find out if renters drive across international borders without permission, verify mileages, and help recover stolen vehicles."

"So Vossler rented a car. I still don't see how that helps."

"It helps a lot if a brilliant hacker gets into the rental car computer system and looks up Vossler's ride on the tracking screen."

"You mean—"

"That's why I've been trying to connect, dude. I can tell you where he's driven in the past few days and where the car has been stopped for hours at a time, like *o-ver-night*." The pride in Zach's voice was palpable.

"Kid, you are a genius. Where is he?"

"A place called the Lakeview Hideaway Motel and Cabins. Way the hell up the North Shore. Does that make sense?"

"Perfect sense. Give me the address."

"No address, just the name of a road and directions."

"Hold on." Matt found paper and pen and returned to the phone. "Go ahead."

Zach recited the directions. Matt had a vague idea of the motel's location but figured the Allens would know for sure.

"Honestly, Zach, you may have saved two lives."

"Really?" Zach's surprise sounded genuine. Matt could almost hear him blush through the phone line.

"Yeah. I gotta go. If I survive this and manage to keep out of jail, I'll buy you one helluva fantastic dinner to say thanks."

"*De nada, mi amigo.*"

Matt hung up and dialed the Allens.

"You're a popular guy, Lanier," his prisoner said. "You calling your girlfriend to make a date for later?"

"Shut up."

Pauline answered on the first ring.

"Any sign of Josh or Vossler?" Matt asked.

"The sheriff got a call from Josh, but they're snowbound way down south. Might take an hour for a snowplow to get through."

Matt was relieved Josh had at least made the call, but also glad he still had time to operate without the law breathing down his neck. "I know where Allyson is, but I need your help."

"Anything."

He explained the situation and his germ of an idea.

She instantly had a suggestion.

"Thanks, I'll be there as soon as I can."

After Matt had hung up, his prisoner said, "You just going to leave me here?" with more than a little concern in his voice.

"For now. Make yourself comfortable." Screw it if the man caught his sarcasm or not.

Matt went to the bathroom. The creature in the mirror scared him enough to elicit a double take. Soot covered most of his face. He stripped off his burned shirt and examined the raw red splotches on his arms. They didn't look too severe, but hurt like blazes. He recalled his first aid training and guessed none of the burns was worse than second-degree. He'd have to risk infection for now.

Removing his charred, wet clothes was painful and difficult. His fingers were numb and stiff. He shivered so much he had difficulty steadying his arms and hands enough to make them go where he wanted them to go. That was a positive sign because a hallmark of severe hypothermia was feeling so hot the victim would try to remove his clothes. Ironic, having burns and frostbite at the same time.

He toweled off gingerly and walked to Allyson's guest room closet. He donned his spare polypropylene long johns, blue jeans, and flannel shirt, then added a wool sweater, heavy socks, and spare boots. Gloves and a stocking cap completed his attire. He didn't have another jacket but hoped he could borrow one from Pauline's husband, who was about Matt's size.

He looked outside at the Halcyon to see if anyone, particularly the sheriff, had arrived yet. He saw nothing through the swirling snow. The rate of snowfall had intensified. The roads would be nearly impassible until plows had been at work long enough to gain the advantage. That might take hours.

Matt returned to the kitchen and checked the knots securing his prisoner to the chair.

"You letting me go?" The prisoner said with sarcasm now in his voice.

Matt replied with a yank of the ropes around the man's wrists.

"Oww!" the man said.

Matt flicked off the lights.

"Aw, come on, Lanier. At least keep the lights on."

Matt went to the garage and fired up the Suburban, hoping it could at least get him to the Allen residence. If not, his wild-ass rescue attempt would implode before it started.

Chapter 55

Visibility was near zero because of the ferociously blowing snow. With no streetlights to guide Matt outside of Castle Danger, the one-mile drive to the Allens' was slow but treacherous. He almost slid off the road twice because he wasn't sure where the road was and could only see about twenty feet ahead.

The Allens waved from their open garage as he pulled into their driveway and parked. Darrell was suited up in full snowmobile gear: snowmobile suit, heavy mitts, and insulated boots. A shotgun hung from the crook of his arm. Pauline was resplendent in a hunter-orange jumpsuit that tightly outlined her substantial assets even in the swirling snow and fluorescent glow of the garage light. Why she wore that now was a mystery. Maybe it was her usual around-the-house outfit.

Pauline gasped as he walked into the light of their garage. "What happened to your face?" She stared at his burns like a worried mother.

He dismissed her concern with a wave of his hand. "Just some minor burns." She might have panicked if she'd seen his arms.

"Heard you got some trouble," Darrell said as they shook hands. He sounded so nonchalant that Matt wondered if this guy were some sort of gun-slinging Nordic superhero who could single-handedly quash an army of bad guys before lunch and hardly work up an appetite.

"You could say that," Matt said.

Darrell Allen was a big, husky galoot who reminded Matt of his childhood friend, Dave Swanson. He'd met Darrell briefly at the Halcyon when he and Pauline came in for dinner last week. Darrell was slower on the uptake than Swanson was, and didn't light up a room when he entered, as Swanny had on his best days.

"Got your ride here," Darrell said and jerked his thumb over his shoulder to indicate the two Arctic Cat snowmobiles sitting behind him in the third garage stall.

"Thanks," Matt said. He pointed to Darrell's riding gear. " But with all due respect, this isn't your fight."

"Huh? But Pauline said we need—"

"No." Matt raised his hand in a stop gesture. "I can't ask a married man with two kids to risk his life for this. I'll take your logistical support, but there's no way you get anywhere near potential danger." He stared at Darrell with an expression intended to emphasize his decision was non-negotiable.

Pauline protested. "I'd do anything for Allie and Josh. Please let us help."

He shook his head. "Vossler tried to broil me tonight. He could've killed me with a bullet, but he didn't because he's vulnerable. He's trying to get away with three perfect crimes—kidnap Josh, murder Allyson, and murder me. If I show up again, he won't bother with perfect. He'll shoot to kill."

Pauline sputtered a weak protest, but fell silent when Darrell gripped her shoulder. He gave Matt a knowing look and a small nod.

Matt's respect for Darrell increased. A family man doesn't get involved in macho heroics with a virtual stranger. He understood the Allens' desire to help Allyson, but they were the last line of defense. "If I end up dead, someone needs to tell the sheriff about Allyson's situation."

He clapped Darrell on the shoulder and looked at both him and Pauline with as much confidence as he could muster. "Show me how to drive this sweet ride of yours."

Darrell gave him the rookie tour in less than two minutes. Driving a snowmobile was similar to driving a motorcycle—except for the large skis and a wide drive belt instead of two wheels. "Electric starter. Right hand, accelerator. Left hand, brakes. Lean into your turns." He locked eyes with Matt. "Most important, don't drive too fast if you don't know the road or the trail. If you hit something under the snow at fifty miles an hour, you'll go into orbit. When you land, you're probably dead."

Matt nodded and swallowed hard at the thought of becoming a human missile.

Pauline produced two walkie-talkies and gave one to Matt. "We got the idea from Allyson, who started using them with Josh when he was old enough to learn."

He examined the walkie-talkie. "Thanks. Might come in handy. What's their range?" He glanced at Darrell as he put the walkie-talkie into his jacket pocket.

"New batteries, about fifteen miles," Darrell said. "Only about three from here to where they're hiding Allyson and Josh. I'll trail you up there, stay out of sight. Call if you need me." He still seemed eager for a fight.

Matt shook his head emphatically. "No. Still too close. But if I'm smart and careful, and Vossler's as overconfident as I think he is, I'll be all right."

Darrell shrugged as if to indicate *your funeral, tough guy.*

Pauline's face was etched with worry lines. She clasped Matt's hands. "Are you sure we can't let the sheriff handle this?"

"We may be too late to save her if we wait. Also, Allyson won't let me get the authorities involved."

"Why? She's my best friend. She tells me everything." Pauline seemed annoyed that Allyson trusted this near stranger, but not her, with the juiciest gossip.

"She swore me to secrecy, but I had to confess some bad things I did in the past too. I also don't want the sheriff involved unless Vossler gets past me."

Pauline didn't seem mollified, but she ceased protesting. "One more thing," she said and darted to a storage locker against the far wall. She returned with a down jacket, a full snowsuit, and a helmet for him to wear. "Gets cold riding, even behind the fairing," she said.

The Allens helped him into the gear. The snowsuit fit well over his clothing. The visored helmet on his head gave him a secure feeling, as if he could merely flip down the facemask to block out all his troubles.

After one more review of how to run the Arctic Cat and a test run down the driveway and back, Matt was ready to go. He retrieved his snowshoes from the Suburban and bungee-corded them to the snowmobile's rear seat.

Darrell handed him the shotgun. "You familiar with this model?"

Matt examined the weapon, worked the pump, put the stock up to his shoulder, and aimed at a pine tree near the driveway. "Remington 870?"

"Yep."

The Remington packed plenty of firepower to stop a full-grown man. "First shotgun I ever owned," Matt said. "Hunted when I was a kid. Been a long time since I used one."

"Like ridin' a bike."

"Mag capacity?" He knew the answer, but wanted to make sure it hadn't been modified in any way.

Darrell seemed impressed that Matt talked the lingo of an experienced hunter. "Four plus the chambered round. Double-ought buckshot." He held out an extra box of shells. "Just in case."

Matt pocketed the ammunition. "Thanks."

Pauline handed him a headlamp. "In case you end up walking." She tried to smile but couldn't get past a tight, fretful pursing of her lips. She gave him an intense hug that lasted longer than seemed appropriate for the situation.

Darrell exaggerated a cough, and Pauline released her grip. "Are you sure you can't wait for the sheriff? You'll have no chance against two armed criminals."

After hearing the situation expressed that way, Matt chuckled at himself for his hubris. "Normally I'd agree with you, but I've got one ace up my sleeve." He cocked his head to the side and half-smiled at the Allens.

"What's that?" Pauline asked with a skeptical expression.

Matt started the snowmobile and revved the engine. "Vossler thinks I'm dead."

Chapter 56

Able to act instead of react, Matt wanted to finish his showdown with Vossler. His burns still radiated pain, but the constant movement as he drove the snowmobile numbed his nerves enough that the pain took a back seat to saving Allyson and Josh.

The luminous glow through the trees indicated an area with outside lights wasn't far up the private drive. Riding noisily into the cabin area would blow his advantage of surprise, so he slid the Arctic Cat behind a stand of pines for cover and turned off the engine. After removing his helmet and replacing it with a black wool cap, he strapped on his snow-shoes, slung the shotgun over his shoulder, and walked atop the deep snow toward the resort. The wind howled and blew the snow sideways. When the first cabins came into view, the scene reminded him of a real-life snow globe that had been shaken by a Paul Bunyan-sized five-year-old.

After he'd walked another ten paces, the door of the only occupied cabin opened and emitted a slash of light into the parking area. Matt moved to the edge of the trees on the left side of the road to better camouflage himself. Two figures emerged and began loading luggage into the red SUV in front of the unit. The figures were Vossler and his accomplice.

Keeping his profile low, Matt crept tangentially closer along the road and stopped when he'd drawn to within fifty yards of the SUV. During that minute, the men made a second round trip. As they exited the cabin, one man locked the door. The other cradled a large bundle in his arms.

Josh.

Matt's spine electrified with angry energy, which negated the pain from his burns. Every muscle tightened into fight mode. Despite the whistling wind, his heartbeat thudded loudly in his ears.

He clicked off the safety on his shotgun. If forced to shoot, he hoped five shots were four more than he'd need. Slow, clumsy reloading in the dark with cold, stiff, gloved hands might prove fatal. Not to mention he didn't want to risk shooting Josh or Allyson.

By now, Vossler and his man had buckled Josh into the back seat and gotten into the SUV. Vossler took the driver's seat. Where was Allyson? Had they put her in before he'd arrived? Was Vossler going to leave her in the cabin? Was she already dead?

Vossler started the engine. Its soft roar jolted Matt out of his thoughts. With only seconds left to act, he ran parallel to the driveway toward the cabin, virtually flying across the top of the snow in his snowshoes, partially concealed by the row of large boulders spaced decoratively along the road's edge.

The car backed out, tires spinning, engine whining, moving inches at a time. Vossler coaxed the vehicle backward far enough so he could turn and go forward. He accelerated gradually, gained some traction, and got up a small head of speed.

Matt knelt behind one of the small boulders for protection. He aimed the shotgun at the driver's side windshield, waiting for a sharp enough angle to minimize the risk of hitting Josh with buckshot or broken glass.

When the SUV hit a deep drift, Vossler tried to overpower the snow and failed. The wheels spun in place for a long moment before the accomplice got out and went to the back end. He pushed as Vossler gave the engine some gas.

Matt hesitated, then changed plans and ran toward the SUV. He was next to the man in an instant, aiming for his head with the butt of his shotgun. As Matt reached him, the man turned and threw up his forearm.

The rifle butt hit the man's forearm square and solid. He yelped and groaned. "Damn!"

Vossler stopped spinning the wheels. "What's wrong, Galvin?" he shouted through the open passenger door.

Matt and Galvin struggled to control the shotgun. The snowshoes gave Matt an advantage in traction but messed with his mobility. Galvin fell against the fender but pushed off from it against Matt. His much larger bulk knocked Matt off balance. Galvin grabbed the shotgun barrel as they tumbled into the snow and slid down a slight embankment.

"What the fuck's going on?" Vossler had stepped out of the SUV and was standing a few yards away from the grappling men.

The sight of Vossler looming above him in the whirling snow jarred Matt to summon his pent-up anger. He roared and pivoted, using Galvin's weight against him as he worked his way astride the heavier man and twisted the shotgun from his grip. Matt directed the recoil of that twist so the butt of the shotgun whipsawed back across Galvin's face, striking fleshy cheek, solid jawbone, and spongy ear cartilage.

Galvin shrieked and clutched his hands to his face. Blood darkened his skin. He rolled away and his momentum threw Matt to the ground.

A bullet whizzed past Matt's ear. He dove behind one boulder as another shot ricocheted off the rock. Matt scrambled to firing position and aimed his shotgun at Vossler.

Vossler stood at the open back door with one hand pointing a gun inside at the passenger—Josh.

The SUV shielded Vossler from his shoulders to his feet. "Go ahead, Johnson, shoot." He spoke with desperation in his voice. "I won't miss his head from point blank range even if yours is a kill shot."

Panic clenched Matt's heart like a vise. "Josh, it's Matt. Whatever you do, don't move."

"Save your breath. He's out cold."

Shock replaced panic in Matt's heart. "You drugged your son?"

"Sleeping pills. I used to give them to the boy all the time when Mama was working, and I'd had enough of the little rug rat for a day."

Matt became even more determined to stop Vossler. "The model father gives his son drugs? What the hell is wrong with that picture?"

Vossler shrugged. "All kids get drugs nowadays. Ritalin, Adderall, shit like that." An insane, manic laugh erupted from deep within Vossler. "Besides, you're going to surrender to me."

Matt tensed and regripped the shotgun in reaction to Vossler's bravado. "I'll drop my weapon only after you toss yours into the woods and I see your hands up." He blinked away snowflakes that had blown into his eyes.

Vossler stood upwind and several feet higher, which gave him both a visual and tactical advantage.

Vossler shook his head and sneered. "Seems we got us a stalemate."

He was right. Matt couldn't risk shooting. "All of a sudden, you're willing to kill your son. Doesn't sound like the father I first met, only concerned with raising his son the right way, as you called it."

"The only thing I love more than my son is my freedom. No way I go to prison for all this. If I can't bring Josh back to L.A. cleanly, then death is my best option."

Suicide by cop—or at least by the vigilante Matt Lanier. Great. Another twist. Matt hesitated, desperate for an edge, an idea, anything to get the gun away from Vossler. One absurd possibility came to him. It might buy some time.

He said, "I've got nothing better to do right now than stand here freezing my ass off in a blizzard. You keep your gun pointed at your son, I'll keep mine pointed at you, and we'll see who freezes to death first."

"Fine by me," Vossler said, surprisingly cheerful. "Didn't think you'd force my hand so fast. Hell, I didn't figure you'd escape the fire, didn't think you'd find me. And how the hell did you get up here, anyway? I don't see a car. You use them stupid skinny skis I saw you on the other day?"

"Since you were so sure you'd killed me at the cabin, let's just say I'm an angel and I flew up here."

"I'll admit the cabin fire wasn't a sure bet to kill you, but I was going for the accidental death angle. Either way, I always make contingency plans." He pulled something from his pocket and held it above the SUV's roof. "I was saving this for an emergency bargaining chip."

"Saving what?"

Vossler nodded toward the cabin. "My wife's inside. Alive, but not for long. I gave her an overdose of heroin. She'll be the first to die. You comfortable with that, tough guy?"

Matt fought down panic when his heart leaped into high gear, then suppressed the urge to charge Vossler and choke the life out of him just to wipe the smugness off his face. "You are one sick bastard. It'll be worth whatever happens to me for the pleasure of blowing your face off."

"I've got a proposition," Vossler said. "Everybody wins. Nobody dies."

Matt still believed he could distract Vossler long enough to get off a shot without harming Josh, but so far, Vossler had stayed focused. "I'm listening."

"I've got the antidote for heroin." He wiggled the object in his hand. "Brought some along so when I got *Sue*—" He emphasized her given name. "—re-addicted, I'd have some insurance in case I gave her the wrong dose before she caved and told me where Josh was hiding. It's called Narcan. Works like a charm. I'll give you the Narcan if you give me Josh."

"And I believe you because …?"

"Simple." Vossler did a one-armed shrug, keeping his pistol pointed at Josh. "You're too fucking noble. If you can prevent it, you won't let an innocent woman die. Besides, if you don't believe me, then everybody's dead. We can stand out here as long as you want to, but if I start to crack, I'll get desperate. My trigger finger might get a cramp, and …"

Damn him to hell. Vossler seemed to have anticipated the entire scenario. No matter what Matt did, he was going to lose a standoff. In either case, he'd only save one person. But if he agreed to let Vossler escape with Josh, there was still a chance he and Allyson could rescue Josh before it was too late.

"What's it gonna be?" Vossler's impatience sounded through the whipping wind. "You've got about five minutes before she dies."

The chances of Vossler reaching Highway 61, let alone driving to Duluth, in this blizzard were not great. However, he might get lucky and tuck in behind a snowplow or blindly creep through the knee-high snow on the highway without driving into a ditch. Matt had no choice but to play the odds.

"Deal."

They simultaneously lowered their weapons.

Dread overcame Matt. Vossler might be lying about the Narcan. Distracting him with Allyson to buy time would give Vossler a large enough head start that Matt might not be able to track him down.

Vossler raised the vial of Narcan high above his head. "I hope she survives. Maybe you two can go into business. I doubt she'll want to work for me again." He laughed. "She still has one hell of a body. Finest piece of ass I've ever had."

Galvin moaned and started to rise. Matt spun and aimed his shotgun at the snow-covered hulk, then whipped it back to aim at Vossler when it became apparent Galvin wasn't an immediate threat.

"Get in, Bobby," Vossler said with a calm, controlled tone.

Seeing Matt's shotgun barrel not five feet from his face, Galvin quickly opted for the warm interior of the SUV.

"If this is a trick," Matt said, "I will find you and smear you into the dirt like dog shit that got onto my shoe."

Vossler had ducked farther down behind his vehicle, so only his head showed. "The way I see it, you've got no choice other than to trust me." He tossed the vial high over Matt's right shoulder.

Matt tracked the vial through the swirling snow, watching where it fell. He sprinted for the spot but trained his shotgun on Vossler in case the whole deal was a ruse to give Vossler a clean shot at him.

When Vossler got into the SUV, Matt frantically dug through the snow.

The sheer weight of the heavy vehicle sitting in one spot for several minutes had compressed the snow, providing the tires with enough traction to break through the drift. The SUV lurched out of the parking lot, fishtailing as Vossler tried for maximum speed. He slowed, straightened, and disappeared into the snow-splattered darkness.

After a few seconds, Matt found the vial and ran for the cabin. The door was locked, but three powerful bashes with the butt of the shotgun splintered the flimsy doorjamb. He shoved the door open.

"Allyson!" He fumbled for the light switch, flipped it on, and scanned the cabin. Square from the outside, it was L-shaped inside with the lone bedroom filling in the crook of the L. No Allyson in the main room. He kicked off his snowshoes, went to the bedroom, and turned on the light. The eerie bluish glow of a compact fluorescent fixture illuminated her lying sprawled on the bed, arms out, one leg bent awkwardly, and a syringe across her open right palm. A short rubber tube lay under her left arm, and he saw the needle tracks below her elbow. Vossler had masterfully set the death scene.

"Allyson," Matt said, softer, anguished, panicked. He knelt beside her, cupped her face in his hands, patted her gently. "Allyson, wake up."

Her breathing was shallow and rapid. Her skin looked deathly gray under the morbid artificial light. He tore off his gloves and lifted one of her eyelids. Her pupil was dilated, but he had no way of knowing if it was fixed. He fumbled open the vial of Narcan with cold, trembling fingers. There was no clean syringe lying around, so he took the syringe from her hand and ran to the bathroom. There, he disassembled it, filled it with water, and shot it through to flush out any remaining heroin. His hands shook so much he feared he might stick himself with the needle. He drew some Narcan into the syringe and dashed back to the bed. He'd only been gone a minute, but he stopped short when he saw her lips had turned blue. Kneeling, he checked her pulse and put his ear to her mouth.

She'd stopped breathing.

Helpless panic slammed into him as if he'd been hit by a car. "Allyson, do *not* die!"

He performed CPR for a minute, ending with one last strong breath into her lungs, then pulled away and breathed long and slow to steady his nerves.

She was still blue, still not responding. No time left. Matt couldn't risk botching an intravenous injection, so he pinched her upper arm around the triceps with one hand, picked up the syringe with the other, and thrust the needle into her flesh. He pushed the plunger and watched the Narcan pass into her arm. How much was an appropriate dose? The vial was still half-full in case she needed more.

He removed the needle, rocked back onto his heels, and watched her for signs of life. Ten seconds passed. He leaned in and gave her another breath of air. Ten more seconds.

"Come on, damn it, wake up," he said through clenched teeth so tense he thought they might snap off in his mouth. Another breath, another ten seconds passed.

He closed his eyes, trying to think of a prayer to the god he'd long neglected, when Allyson gasped and sucked in a lungful of air on her own. The sudden noise in the deathly quiet room shocked his eyes open. He grabbed her shoulders and shook gently. "Allyson, it's Matt. You're going to be all right."

He wasn't sure what to do next. Was the antidote permanent, or did he need to worry about her relapsing into an overdosed state? Best to get her moving, like sobering up a drunk. "Move your fingers and toes."

She responded with minimal motions.

"Say something."

"Where's ... Josh?"

He swallowed hard. Was she physically or mentally up to hearing the news? "He's alive."

She formed a weak smile and raised a hand to his chest. "Thanks."

"Keep moving your arms and legs."

She moved her limbs a little, but then groaned. "Gonna be sick." She rolled over to the side of the bed.

"Hold on." He dashed to the bathroom and returned with the waste-basket, placing it under her chin, which hung over the edge of the bed.

She retched violently, but only a small amount of liquid came up. Vomiting was a hopeful sign, getting the poison out of her system. He caressed the back of her head until she finished retching and rolled onto her back, breathing hard, and wiped her mouth with the back of her hand.

"I'm ... I'm better now, thanks." She focused on him, seeing now, not just aware of light. "I thought you'd run for your life when I went missing."

His face burned hot like his real burns, and he glanced at the floor. "Almost."

"Can I see Josh now?" Her face brightened with anticipation.

Matt hesitated, felt his stomach knot. "Vossler has him."

She shrieked, "*Noooooo!*" and tried to rise from the bed. She grabbed his arm for support, but he wrenched his arm free and held her down. "You bastard. Why did you let Donnie take him?"

"I didn't let him take Josh. He tried to kill me, then kidnapped him."

She studied the soot remnants and red, blistered skin on his face and hands. Her eyes widened, and she put a hand to her mouth.

"I tracked Vossler here. He threatened to kill Josh if I tried to shoot him. He gave me the Narcan in exchange for Josh and a head start."

She covered her face with her hands and wept. "You gave Donnie my baby." Her tone became hostile. "You should've let me die and done whatever it took to save Josh. Donnie will ruin him. Turn him into a monster." She glared up at him with fiery eyes. "Do you understand?" She broke into wails of anguish as her body shook.

He dared to caress her shoulder. "I promise I'll get Josh back."

She stopped sobbing long enough to ask, "How?"

"We're in the middle of a blizzard. He can't drive fast. The only place he'll go is south toward L.A. Sixty-one's the only highway that'll get him out of here. He doesn't know I have a snowmobile. I'll catch him and stop him before he goes ten miles."

She pulled her hands down her face until her eyes met his. "Then bring me along. I want to kill Donnie, so he'll never be able to harm my son or me ... ever."

He shook his head. "Three minutes ago, you were dead. I still don't know how this Narcan works. You might relapse and die again."

As if on cue, she looked disoriented and clutched his hand. "Gonna be sick again."

He helped her to the edge of the bed above the wastebasket, then went to the phone. "I'm calling an ambulance. I'll go after Josh once you're out of danger."

After retching again, she shouted, "No," then sat up and swung her legs over the edge of the bed. Gripping the headboard tightly, she swayed with dizziness. "I don't care about me." She leveled laser-beam eyes at him. "I'm going to save my son."

"I won't let you die." He picked up his phone to dial 911.

"Then fuck you." She stood and staggered toward the door. "I'll save him myself." She faltered, stumbled backward, and sank toward the floor.

"Allyson!" He dropped the phone, lunged, and caught her enough to slow her collapse. They fell together, arms and legs tangled. She burst into another round of tears.

He pinned her arms to the floor. "I'm staying with you until help arrives."

She shook with anguish, mumbling, "You don't understand. You don't understand. You don't understand."

He let her cry, then relaxed his grip when she stopped struggling. "I don't understand what?"

She sniffled, wiped her nose with her sleeve, and unzipped her jeans.

He reached to stop her.

She slapped his hand away with a violent backhand.

He put his hands up in surrender.

She slid the jeans off her hips a few inches and grabbed the waistline of her panties, bright pink against her creamy white skin.

He flushed with embarrassment because he was quite confused and slightly aroused by her actions.

She pulled her panties down several inches with one thumb. "This," she said. Anger exploded from that single word.

He scanned from her eyes down to her waist, reluctant to look. Above her close-cropped pubic hair lay a dark reddish mark a few inches in diameter. It had a definite shape but was faded like an old scar. A tattoo that had been infected or removed?

"Read it," she said robotically.

Puzzled, he looked at her, but she turned her head away.

"Read. It." Her voice quavered on the edge of exploding into anger.

He leaned closer, embarrassed. She smelled faintly of perfume and perspiration. "Looks like letters."

"Which letters?"

He ran a hand over his jaw, unsure he was ready for whatever was coming. "A *D*." His heart thumped like a bass drum as the bottom dropped out of his stomach. "And a *V*."

She'd stopped crying. "It's Donnie's brand." Her voice sounded absolute-zero cold.

"His *what*?" Stunned, he looked again. Sure enough, the left side of the *V* overlapped the curve of the *D* and was about an inch lower. The indentations of the brand had softened over time, but it was as clear as a blue-sky January day.

Donnie Vossler had branded his wife.

"This proved to my clients I was the legendary Susannah." Her voice went lifeless, like a student reciting a history lesson. As it had when she'd first confessed her past to him last week. "He called it his seal of authenticity. The sick fuck got me high as a kite one night early on, strapped me down with my dominatrix ropes, and ..." She put a hand to her forehead and covered her eyes. "He had a branding iron made special by a blacksmith. Can you fucking believe that?" She spat out a sound similar to a bitter laugh. "I was a two-legged piece of meat to that bastard." She turned her head and broke down again.

He had no words of comfort, no rationalization, no comprehension of how one human could treat another so badly. He'd never heard of anything so blatantly heartless and cruel in his life. He imagined Josh being raised by Vossler, taught everything about being a man by Vossler. He choked back the vomit welling up in his throat.

She controlled her tears. "I refuse to have my son raised by a man who treated his wife like a brood mare. I'd rather jump into Lake Superior with him and drown us both. Being on drugs again, even for this short time, scared me. Part of me still likes the high, and I hate myself for that. As long as Donnie knows my weakness, he can control me. I can't let him near me ever again. I won't." She sat up and put her hand on his shoulder until he met her gaze. "Now do you understand?"

The rage he'd felt last spring was bad when he discovered he'd killed Diane. But this was a different rage. Toxic rage. Rage directed at the violent animal instincts that inhabit all men but are subdued by the vast majority. Vossler wasn't salvageable. He needed to be removed from the system. Permanently.

Matt stood, pulled out his walkie-talkie, and clicked it on. "Darrell, Pauline, this is Matt. Over."

Seconds later, he heard a hiss and click. "Darrell here. Over."

"Vossler left with Josh, but I've got Allyson. He overdosed her on heroin. I gave her Narcan, but I don't know if she's safe yet. I'll bring her to you, then I'm going after Vossler. Over." He studied Allyson's expression.

Her eyes contained a faint glimmer of hope, but she knew she wasn't strong enough to go with him.

Darrell responded. "An EMT in town maintains a state-of-the-art first responder emergency pack. I'll get him up here ASAP. Over."

"We'll be there in a few minutes. Over."

He reached down and helped her to her feet, then held her shoulders. Looking into her eyes, Matt finally saw the real Allyson Clifford. The fighter; the mother who would willingly die to save her child; full of love; full of spirit; strong enough to rebuild her life after surviving three years of hell that would have killed anyone else. She deserved a complete chance to raise her son, teach him well, leave a positive legacy.

Shaking with emotion himself, he struggled to speak. "I'll save Josh for you. I promise." He tried to exude confidence and sincerity but didn't know if he could keep that promise. If this were his last day of freedom from capture or his last day on Earth, he might as well die attempting to save an innocent boy from a toxic upbringing.

As he helped Allyson into her coat, hat, and gloves, his mother's voice echoed in his mind again. *Family helps family. End of story.* After only a few short weeks, Allyson and Josh were as much like family as his own blood relatives had ever been.

Chapter 57

To ensure Allyson's safety above all, Matt slowly drove the Arctic Cat away from the Lakeview Hideaway, with Allyson sitting behind him, holding on tightly. They reached the Allen house within minutes. Pauline and Darrell stood just inside their open garage, and they helped Allyson off the snowmobile.

Pauline embraced Allyson with tears in her eyes. "Oh, Allie honey, I'm so glad you're safe. We've been going crazy since Matt called."

"Thanks, Pauline," Allyson said, also teary-eyed.

Darrell said, "Rick, the EMT, should be here in a few minutes."

Matt stepped off the Arctic Cat and removed his helmet. "She seems okay now, but still was almost dead a few minutes ago." He faced Darrell. "Is there any other way to Duluth besides sixty-one?"

"Not unless you're a native and know all the interior county roads."

"Then I've got a shot at catching him." Highway 61 would be drivable at maybe twenty miles per hour. If Matt could drive *over* the snow-covered roads faster than Vossler could drive *through* the drifts, he would catch the bastard.

He offered his hand to Darrell, who shook it. "Thanks, you two. If I get Josh back, I'll give Darrell a big hug—" He turned to Pauline and clasped her hands. "—and you, an even bigger kiss."

The women broke their embrace, and Pauline's eyes lit up. "You're damn right you will, stud."

Darrell looked skyward and shook his head.

Allyson came over and hugged him, then whispered in his ear, "Be careful. Now you finally know what sort of brutal animal Donnie is."

Matt had spent nine months in the Boundary Waters competing with wolves, bears, moose, and eagles for his food. Swam and bathed in near-freezing water until the lake iced over. Worked for hours each day chopping wood, hauling water, preparing and storing food for winter. Hunted and fished as if his life depended on it, which it had. Survived through half of the coldest winter in decades in a primitive wilderness shelter he'd built alone.

He had seriously questioned his purpose on earth, his ability to recover a sense of hope, his will to live. His anger and frustration grew daily because his life had imploded for no reason. His anger toward Vossler became the tip of an iceberg of fury.

He let go of her but couldn't force a confident, devil-may-care smile. He met her gaze and stared deep into her eyes. "Compared to the animal I feel like right now, Donnie is a fucking bunny rabbit."

Allyson's reaction was a combination of fear and attraction. Her eyes assured him she wanted him to do whatever was necessary to bring her son back. She hugged him again—tighter this time—as if she'd finally found a man who put her welfare above all else. It felt so natural to embrace her. As much as he wanted her touch, wanted to hold her in his arms for hours, he wanted even more to crush Vossler.

Matt donned his helmet, fired up the snowmobile, and plunged into the raging snowstorm. Despite wind gusts that blew the snow sideways, the Arctic Cat ran easily between the still-visible tire tracks left by Vossler's SUV. Matt had time to think while he rode, mostly about how much his burns hurt. Were they getting worse, maybe infected? He might fall into shock if the adrenaline that had kept him sharp for the past several hours ran dry. For now, none of that mattered. He'd use every remaining bit of energy and strength he possessed to rescue Josh.

When he reached Highway 61, he stopped, but not for any traffic. Vossler might have driven north instead of south to throw Matt off his trail and evade any pursuit. However, based on Vossler's loathing of the North Shore's version of winter and a check of the freshest tire tracks at the intersection, Matt was certain Vossler was headed south.

Matt turned south onto the wide, deserted highway and gunned the engine. True to its name, the Arctic Cat leaped forward and raced along the snow-covered road. He wasn't sure of its range but figured it was better to push his speed and catch Vossler before the gas tank went dry rather than go slower and avoid the risk of an accident. The Cat cruised effortlessly at fifty miles per hour, so he nudged the throttle even higher. She responded instantly—this was one fine ride Darrell had loaned him—and he got up near what he thought was the limit of urgency plus safety, seventy miles per hour.

A few miles south of Castle Danger, he saw yellow flashing lights ahead in the distance, shielded by a rise in the road. He slowed and looked for a place to turn off. In a few hundred yards, he found a private drive and turned in. He doused his headlights and engine and manually turned the big Cat around so it faced the highway. If the flashing yellow lights indicated a snowplow, it might be leading a sheriff's deputy to Castle Danger. He didn't want to risk being seen and stopped.

Matt ducked behind the snowmobile as the plow lumbered past. As expected, it led an ambulance and a sheriff's SUV. He felt an incredible sense of relief that one thing had gone right. Allyson would live. Could he make it two? He started the engine and sent the Arctic Cat racing after Vossler again, more energized than ever to rescue Josh.

Minutes later, as he rounded a curve in the road, he spotted two red lights glowing in the distance. Vossler's taillights? Matt risked driving in the freshly plowed northbound lane so he could speed up. It was snow-packed enough to offer traction to the drive belt but still gave a decent cushion to the sled runners. He figured he could risk a higher speed but still swerve back into the southbound lane in case a vehicle approached from the opposite direction.

As Matt flew down the wrong side of the highway, Wagner's "The Ride of the Valkyries" from the opera *Die Walkure* began playing on his mental sound system. He hadn't heard or felt any music or rhythm playing or pulsing in his body since he'd whistled "Happy Trails" to Allyson the other night. He didn't see himself as grandly righteous as the legendary Nordic goddesses who decided who lived and died in battle. Neither did he envision himself as a chopper pilot flying into battle during the Viet Nam War for a nebulous geopolitical reason. He was simply a man trying to right one small, unspeakable wrong in a world overflowing with unspeakable wrongs. A man trying to reunite a boy with his mother.

When he'd closed to within a half-mile, he noticed Vossler was also driving in the left lane. Matt formulated a plan of attack. The snowmobile couldn't run the much larger Cadillac Escalade off the road by brute force. But maybe, just maybe, he could use the element of surprise along with a bit of finesse. Vossler probably didn't expect Matt to be following him this soon, if at all, and certainly not in a snowmobile.

As he and Vossler rounded another bend and came into a straightaway, Matt recognized this part of the highway from many previous trips along the North Shore. Straight and flat for more than two miles. Rare on this winding scenic byway. No better time to make his move.

He switched off his headlights and accelerated until he was less than ten yards behind the Cadillac Escalade. Then he flipped his headlights to high beam and laid on the wimpy excuse for a horn the Cat possessed.

Vossler's Caddy swerved into the right lane and slowed drastically, presumably to let the maniac pass him who was driving too fast for the road and weather conditions.

Instead of passing, Matt turned off his headlights and followed Vossler into the right lane. In total darkness other than his own headlights reflecting off falling snow, Vossler would have no idea where Matt was or what he was doing. Once both vehicles were going straight, Matt aligned the Cat so its skis straddled the right rear tire. Accelerating, he drove the sled into the vehicle. The crunch of fiberglass was audible above the howling wind and engine noise. Upon impact, he gunned the engine full throttle and pushed the sled hard against the back right end of the car for a few seconds, then released the throttle and backed off.

As Matt had hoped, Vossler was unaccustomed to emergency driving in deep powder. He over-steered. The Escalade fishtailed, threw up a huge spray of snow, spun one hundred eighty degrees, and drifted off the road into the ditch. It bounced a few times as it slid down the embankment, then the driver's side slammed into a massive rocky outcrop.

Matt stopped the snowmobile on the shoulder, dismounted, and unslung his shotgun. He leaped into the ditch, churning through the thigh-high snow as fast as he could, hoping to surprise Vossler and Galvin before they recovered from the impact.

Because the SUV's lights were still on and pointed obliquely toward him, Matt couldn't see any movement inside the car. He stopped and aimed the shotgun. Time froze for an instant, and for some crazy reason, he recalled duck hunting as a boy with his father. The one lesson Dad had drilled into his head filled his mind: Aim low to compensate for recoil. With two quick blasts, he knocked out the headlights. He'd traded the element of surprise for a visual advantage.

Metal thunking against rock told him Vossler was unsuccessfully trying to exit via the driver's door.

Matt's vision adjusted to the sudden darkness, and he saw Galvin opening his door. Matt knelt to provide a smaller target. He was off to the side of the SUV, but Galvin was looking forward to an area the headlights had been illuminating.

Galvin's raised right hand appeared to be holding a gun. Matt waited until Galvin had stood and stepped away from the door.

"Drop it," Matt demanded as snow whirled around him.

Galvin spun and fired blindly toward the sound of Matt's voice.

Matt flinched at the sound of the gunshot, but immediately steadied his nerves. *Aim low.* He got off a shot an instant before Galvin fired high and wide for the second time. Galvin toppled backward into the snow.

An instant later, Matt saw movement from the passenger seat. Vossler had climbed over the center console and exited the car with his pistol drawn, using the door as a shield. Matt spun and fired.

Vossler ducked as the buckshot hit the passenger door, then stood and took aim.

Matt's cold, stiff fingers fumbled the re-chambering, so he dove for the front driver's side of the SUV, hoping to use the vehicle as a shield.

Vossler fired.

Simultaneously, Matt heard the crack of the gunshot and felt the whiz of a bullet near his head as he flew through the air. The shotgun in his outstretched arms hit a large rock under the snow and knocked the weapon from his hands. He was out of Vossler's sight, but groped frantically for his weapon, knowing he only had a second to retrieve it.

Vossler and Galvin had both shot to kill, so it was obvious Vossler didn't care about covering his ass anymore. If Matt wanted to live, he'd have to do the same. Survive first, or at least make sure Josh survived. Deal with the law later.

Matt found his grip on the shotgun and rolled onto his back as he aimed toward the spot he expected Vossler to be. Snow covered Matt's visor. So Vossler was only a dark vertical blob next to the lower horizontal outline of the SUV. He only had one shell left in the chamber. If he missed, there'd be no time to reload. *Aim low.*

Both men pulled their triggers, and two bright flashes ten feet apart lit the black night.

Matt's head snapped backward into the snow. He felt intense pain. White light filled his vision, then faded to black.

Chapter 58

Matt awoke dazed and confused. His head throbbed as he sat up. He tried to raise his helmet visor to see clearly, but it jammed. He removed the helmet and examined it. The entire top above the visor was shattered to bits. If he hadn't been wearing a helmet, Vossler's shot would've plugged him dead center in the forehead. He shuddered uncontrollably and retched.

After wiping his mouth, Matt focused his eyes. The snow had stopped. The sky was clearing. Bright moonlight illuminated two dark figures in the pure white snow next to the Escalade. Vossler lay below the fender. Galvin lay a few feet past Vossler.

Matt fumbled another shell from his pocket into the shotgun chamber in case he needed it. He struggled to his knees and shuffled toward the bodies, pilgrim-at-Mecca style, using the shotgun as a crutch.

A light coating of snow covered both bodies. When Matt had aimed low, he envisioned blowing Vossler's genitals into a thousand pieces. He hadn't aimed quite low enough. A large, dark spot glistened on Vossler's chest. He poked a shoulder with the shotgun barrel. No response. No breath vapors. Galvin's neck and lower face were a bloody, jagged mess. Matt had almost aimed too high, but Galvin was equally dead.

All Matt felt was emptiness deep in his gut. His rage at what Vossler had done to Allyson hadn't been sated. Maybe it was because a million other Vosslers skulked around the world and he couldn't eliminate all of them. He forced the bile back down his throat. Shaking from cold and shock, he struggled to his feet and opened the backseat door.

"Josh, wake up." He shook Josh's shoulder as if he were waking the boy after a long drive home late at night.

Josh responded with a listless moan. Matt said a silent prayer of thanks. The SUV's engine was off, and the interior felt almost as cold as the outside. Matt had been exposed to the cold longer than Josh, but only now realized his extremities were stinging numb. He'd been unconscious for less than fifteen minutes; otherwise, he'd be severely hypothermic if not dead.

Before Matt could attend to his throbbing head, he needed to make sure Josh stayed warm. He climbed over the center console into the driver's seat, started the Escalade, and turned the heater and fan to *high*.

He turned on the dome light and examined his head in the sun visor mirror. A large welt had formed, red and ugly. No blood, just a baseball-sized lump. Combined with the conk on his head back at the cabin, he was sure he had more than a minor concussion.

Josh remained unresponsive to any of Matt's noise or motion, so Matt climbed out and switched on his walkie-talkie. "Pauline or Darrell, this is Matt. Over." Barely a second went by before he heard a crackle.

"Go ahead, Matt. Over," Pauline said.

"I've got Josh. He's unconscious but safe in Vossler's SUV. Vossler drugged him back at the Lakeview. He's still asleep, but he seems stable. Over."

"Thank God, Josh is okay. Thank you, Matt. Over."

"We're about five miles south of Castle Danger on sixty-one. How's Allyson? Over."

"She'll be okay. The EMT says you gave her the Narcan in time. And the ambulance just pulled into the drive. I'll send it back to you. Over."

"I know the sheriff is there too. Tell him ..." He stopped himself from confessing to manslaughter, if not murder. "Tell the ambulance to hurry. I'm still concerned about Josh. I don't know what sort of sleeping pills Vossler gave him. Over and out."

Another chill ran through him, followed by another wave of nausea. He'd briefly considered driving Josh on the Arctic Cat to meet the ambulance. But if he passed out and crashed or dropped Josh from the moving sled, the boy might die.

He returned to the Escalade and checked the gas gauge. Half full. The heater blew hot now, and the inside felt comfortably warm. Assuming the ambulance arrived soon, Josh wouldn't freeze to death.

The whistling in Matt's ears intensified. He breathed deep, trying to force himself into lucidity. He got out and mounted the Arctic Cat. Still shivering and dizzy, he drove south, away from Castle Danger. In less than a quarter mile, he found an access road to the Gitchi-Gami Trail, a recreational trail for hikers and bikers that ran alongside Highway 61 for a good deal of the length of the North Shore.

Matt took the trail back toward Castle Danger and stopped parallel with the accident scene, watching the Escalade, making sure Josh didn't wake up and wander away before the ambulance arrived. A few minutes later, he heard the cry of sirens and saw the pulse of flashing lights on the treetops. He turned off his headlights and motored forward about five hundred yards. The ambulance and sheriff's vehicle drove past, barely visible through the thicket of birch trees that shielded the trail from the highway. When they were out of sight, he resumed his drive, keeping his headlights off and navigating by moonlight.

Blurry vision and a pounding head that throbbed every time he hit a bump in the snowpack forced him to drive slowly and cautiously. When he arrived at Allyson's house, he parked in the driveway. The house was dark, just as he'd left it. He entered through the back door and flipped on the kitchen light.

"You save the kid?" asked his prisoner, who looked as if he'd been roused from a doze by Matt's entrance.

"Yeah," Matt said, with no triumph in his voice.

"How's the woman, Allyson?"

"She's out of danger."

"You three going to live happily ever after now?" His tone dripped with cynicism, implying Matt was some sort of noble knight who'd saved the damsel.

Matt resisted the urge to slap the man's face. Showing any emotion about Allyson might give Smythe or his hit man the idea of using her somehow as bait in the future. "None of your business." He'd contemplated what to do with the hit man while on the snowmobile, but couldn't bring himself to kill someone who had no personal gripe against him. How ironic that he'd adopted some sort of killer's moral code. "What are you going to tell Smythe?"

"You mean Jones?"

"Whatever."

"None of your business," said his captive with a smirk.

"Fair enough." Matt assumed Smythe would keep sending hit men after him until one ultimately succeeded. "On second thought, tell Smythe I'm coming after him. See how he likes it."

"Your funeral," the man said and added a chuckle. "I gotta say you don't seem like the type of man someone would want dead."

"I'm not. Where's your wallet?"

The man glared at him defiantly.

Matt fumbled inside his prisoner's coat pockets and pulled out the wallet. He was surprised to find well over one thousand dollars in the bill compartment. He read the driver's license. "Well, Mr. Nowitzki, if this is all you're getting paid from Smythe, he's not as loaded as I was led to believe."

Nowitzki expelled a short, grunting laugh. "That's just part of my expense money."

"How much is he paying you to kill me?"

"Does it matter?"

"Not really. Just curious."

"Six figures. Another six if you have an *accident*."

Matt emitted a low whistle. "That explains why you wanted to roast me in the cabin instead of shooting me on sight." Smythe's largesse impressed Matt, as well as the seriousness of his desire to get rid of him. He immediately felt pleased to relieve Smythe of some of his money, even though Nowitzki had earned it.

Nowitzki's expression became wistful. "I was looking to retire after this score. I got greedy."

Matt pocketed all but twenty dollars and replaced Nowitzki's wallet. "Are you going to keep trying to kill me?"

Nowitzki gave him a puzzled look and hesitated. "When you first tied me up, I intended to. Now, I'm not so sure."

It was Matt's turn to look puzzled.

Nowitzki narrowed his eyes. "Did you rescue the trapper near Ely?"

Matt froze but held his composure until his heart calmed. What would it hurt to tell the truth? He had broken no laws. Smythe had already flushed him out, and the cops would soon be after him.

"Never mind," Nowitzki said. "You just told me. What I'm curious about is why. Especially with you being a fugitive. Pretty risky."

Matt's body tensed, and his stomach churned. He didn't expect a greedy, unprincipled hit man to understand. "None of your business."

That elicited a knowing smile from his captive.

"If I spare your life," Matt said, "will Smythe kill you for failing to kill me?"

"I doubt it. Wasn't in the contract."

"Contract?" Matt shook his head and smiled wryly. "Damn, that guy is a true businessman." He studied Nowitzki carefully for the first time that night. "What's your background?"

"Cop, then private detective. Obviously one with questionable scruples."

"Obviously." Matt hesitated. "I doubt you'll tell the truth to the authorities, but Jones' real name is Leland Smythe. He's one of the biggest real estate crooks in the country. If you don't end up in jail after tonight, check him out when you get back to wherever you came from. Then you'll find out what kind of psychopath you're doing business with. Dig deep enough, and you'll unearth a secret group called Millennium Four. Uncovering Smythe's Millennium Four conspiracy got me into trouble, not the fact that I killed my ex-wife and her lover."

Nowitzki tilted his head and studied Matt's face. "Why are you telling me this?"

"For your own benefit. Smythe may kill you, whether or not you kill me. And maybe so you'll reconsider coming after me."

"Because you're not the killing type, right?"

"That depends on who you ask," Matt said. A wave of frustration washed over him. Nowitzki's presence would confuse the cops for a while. Even if Nowitzki were arrested, Matt doubted he would reveal his employer's identity. Smythe would remain on his trail.

The Allens' account of the events leading up to the shootings would support him, along with Allyson's version of the story. However, if she revealed Matt's identity, the law would once again be on his trail. Matt was squarely back where he'd started nine long months ago—minutes from arrest or death.

He went into the garage to repack his clothes and the equipment that hadn't burned in the fire. He borrowed a few days' worth of food from Allyson to sustain him until he figured out a plan for the near future.

As he packed, his burns demanded attention. They'd been forgettable during all the action, but throbbed with every movement here in the quiet of the house. By his calculations, Allyson and Josh would be at the hospital for a while. The sheriff would be occupied with the crash scene and two men dead from gunshot wounds. Matt still had some time.

He went to Allyson's bathroom and rechecked his burns in the mirror. Raw red blotches covered most of his hands and forearms. Eventually, he'd need treatment, but he couldn't risk going to a hospital with Smythe back on his tail. The lump on his forehead had stopped growing but hurt twice as much now that all the adrenaline had drained from his system.

Allyson's medicine chest was atypically understocked with pain pills—with any kind of pills. She probably avoided drugs in general because of her addictive past. The best he could score were a bottle of extra-strength Tylenol and a half-bottle of Midol. He popped two of each with a glass of water, then packed both bottles with his gear. He went to Allyson's bedroom, closed the door so Nowitzki wouldn't hear, and dialed directory assistance on the phone on her nightstand.

When a female voice answered, Matt said, "Do you have the number of any free clinics along the North Shore?"

After a moment, she replied, "There's a clinic in downtown Duluth, but nothing farther up the Shore."

"Duluth will do."

She connected him. When a man's voice answered, Matt inquired about the clinic's address and hours of operation. The man gave him the information. He hung up and resumed packing. The phone rang a minute later. Matt flinched and stared at the phone as it rang again. The only people who might call at this hour were the Allens—or Allyson. He let the phone ring until the answering machine clicked on.

A few seconds later, Allyson said in a panicky voice, "Matt, are you there? If you are, please pick up."

After she'd asked twice more, he picked up and said, "I'm here," unsure of what else to say.

"Oh, thank God you're safe, but you were supposed to be with Josh. How could you leave him?" Anger now tinged her panicked voice.

He stifled his annoyance at her glossing over his welfare. Josh would always take precedence. "He was unconscious but safe and warm. No visible injuries. His breathing was normal. Ten more minutes alone in the SUV wasn't a risk. I was in no shape to take him on the snowmobile."

"Why not ride to the hospital in the ambulance with him?"

He tensed, unsure how to explain his paranoia. "The sheriff was escorting the ambulance. I wasn't ready to deal with him."

"Why not?"

"Remember the time we stayed up all night talking at the Halcyon?"

"Of course."

"I was supposed to tell you about my sordid past, but we never got that far. I've got a good reason—well, a reason anyway—to avoid the law. Vossler and Galvin aren't the first people I've killed."

"Oh." He detected a hint of fear in her voice. "Didn't you fire in self-defense?"

"The cops might see it differently."

"Did those people deserve to die as much as Donnie did?"

"The man, almost as much. My ex-wife, not in the least."

Allyson gasped.

He felt her shock through the phone. "I didn't know she was tied up in the passenger seat of her car. I fired several shots at the man who was driving and trying to run me over. One of them hit her. She died at the scene."

"Oh, Matt. I'm so, so sorry."

"The cops think it was a love triangle revenge thing. It's easier to sell to the media than a convoluted conspiracy even I don't believe at times."

"I believe you, and I'll tell the sheriff you killed Donnie in self-defense."

"Thanks." Her support meant more to him than the fact the authorities would no doubt call it manslaughter and redouble their efforts to find him.

"I'll also tell the sheriff you told me your last name was Johnson, and I had no reason to doubt you."

A lump formed in his throat. "Do what's in your heart, Allyson. I can live with that."

"Will you be up when I get home?" she asked. "The doctors cleared me to leave, but Josh is going to stay here until the sleeping pills are out of his system. The Allens will drive me."

The prospect of seeing her again, maybe embracing her, was a powerful deterrent to leaving. That conflict caused his head to throb and his vision to blur again.

"Matt? Are you still there?"

"Sorry, just tired after all the excitement tonight."

"So you'll stay up until I get home?"

His hesitation was shorter this time. "Sure."

Flushed with anticipation fired by her increased attraction to the man who had saved her and her son from her worst nightmare, Allyson fidgeted during the entire ride from the hospital. The plows had cleared the highway in both directions, but the remaining snowpack forced Darrell Allen to drive well below the speed limit.

When they reached home, Pauline helped her into the house. The lights were on. Allyson's heart sped up at the prospect of seeing Matt. "We're home."

No response.

She spotted the snowmobile helmet on the floor next to the door to the kitchen and bent to pick it up. When she saw the shattered top half, her heart surged up her throat, and she clamped a hand over her mouth. "Oh my God," she whispered.

Pauline saw Allyson's expression and picked up the helmet. Surprised dread showed on her face. "I think this was done by a bullet," she said as she ran her hand over the jagged plastic.

So there had been a gunfight. Matt had nearly had his head blown off. The shock and stark reality that he'd risked his life for her and Josh hit home. Hit hard enough that her chest tightened and breathing became difficult.

She stepped into the kitchen and gasped when she saw a man tied to her kitchen chair. "What the—who are you?"

Nowitzki smiled meekly. "Ahh, the fair maiden our friend rescued returns. You look like you've been through a bit of hell."

Allyson's confusion was supplanted by recognition when she heard his voice. "You were in my restaurant the other night." She glared at him. "Why are you tied up in my kitchen?"

He looked annoyed but sounded contrite. "I was outmaneuvered by a cunning hunter."

"Where's Matt?"

Nowitzki shrugged. "He apparently rode off into the sunset on a white horse."

Her face screwed up into incomprehension. "Call the sheriff, Pauline."

Pauline had been standing slightly behind her, no doubt speechless for one of the few times in her life. "S-s-sure, Allie." She pulled out her cell phone and tapped in 911.

Nowitzki said, "Save your questions, Ms. Clifford, because I'm not talking."

Allyson was about to ask another when she saw the note taped onto the refrigerator door. She pulled it off, walked into the hallway, and read:

Dear Allyson,

I want to stay more than I can express in words, but the fear of losing my freedom is still greater than any other emotion. I borrowed a few things—food, supplies, the Allens' snowmobile suit—but intend to pay you all back someday. In person.

Love,

Matt

Allyson's heart raced even as her body went numb.

Pauline hung up her phone. "The sheriff will be here soon, Allie. He said there must be a logical reason Matt tied up this guy. We're supposed to treat him as deadly and check that the ropes are secured."

With her mind in a fog, Allyson dropped the note on the floor.

Pauline picked it up, read it, and looked at Allyson.

Allyson blinked away a tear.

Pauline hugged her. "Oh, Allie. I'm so sorry."

"What'll I tell Josh?" She took the note from Pauline and went into her bedroom.

Matt stood in the backyard, ready to leave but battling the urge to stay. He was about to head south when he saw the car lights turn off Highway 61. He heard the car doors open and close and the back door to the house open and close. Her muffled voice called his name. A few minutes later, she appeared in her bedroom holding his note. He watched her for a moment until dizziness rattled him again, this time from remembering the night she had dried herself off and applied oil to her body.

After a deep, finalizing breath, Matt unstuck his feet, which had seemed to be frozen in the snow. He checked the bindings on his snowshoes and the ski pole harness he used for towing his makeshift sled loaded with gear. On his left, a thin line of light blue edged above Lake Superior. He trudged into the waning darkness. The wind whipped the freshly fallen snow into swirling vortexes, and Matt Lanier vanished into a gauzy curtain of white.

T hank you for reading *Castle Danger*. If you enjoyed it, please tell your friends and family who love to read. Also, consider writing a *brief* online review of the book on your favorite book website. Word-of-mouth advertising and online reviews are the keys to success for most authors. We don't have the advantage of national advertising campaigns, book tours, and other publicity that big publishers provide to their bestselling authors. Here are some popular online review websites for you to consider:

Goodreads.com (my favorite)
Bookbub.com
Amazon.com
Barnesandnoble.com

Simply go to your preferred website, type "Castle Danger" into the search box, and follow the prompts to write your review. Some websites may require you to sign up before posting reviews. Please follow me at chrisnorbury.com for news about upcoming events and future projects.

Sincerely,
Chris Norbury

Thank you to my outstanding group of beta readers: Jody Brown (who also consulted on the cover blurb), Paula Matsumoto, Margaret Mazzaferro, Polly Rodriquez, Val Rudy, Betsy Wade, and Daniel Williams. Their collective evaluations and critiques inspired me to bring this novel to reality.

Thank you to my editor and proofreader, Lauren O'Neil of Sharp Eye Edits. She took a chance on a rookie and treated me like a veteran.

I owe thanks to Kimberli Bindschatel for opening my eyes to the possibilities of independent publishing. Her success with her own writing motivated me to keep chasing my writing goals.

Dr. Jim Sheard, an author and avid golfer, provided me with wise counsel, encouragement, and friendship early in my writing efforts, often while we commiserated about our golfing woes and maladies.

Award-winning author Christine DeSmet, a writing instructor in the Continuing Studies Division of the University of Wisconsin-Madison, supercharged my resolve to finish this book. She provided me with a detailed critique of my first ten pages and said, based on what she'd read, "This is publishable." To hear those words from an expert was the catalyst for the stretch run of finishing the manuscript.

I couldn't have stayed awake through countless hours of writing, revising, and editing without the wide variety of coffees, teas, and delicious pastries offered by the friendly owners and baristas of the local coffee and sweet treat shops. For a small town, we have a uniquely excellent collection.

Finally, thanks to all the writing teachers, editors, bloggers, authors of books on writing, and writers—published and unpublished—whom I've encountered during my writing journey. Those involved in writing and publishing are among the most generous, caring people I know. Dozens of them shared their time, wisdom, and encouragement with me. Each has helped me shape and improve my writing in countless small ways.

Chris Norbury is the un-gainfully employed, non-bestselling author of four novels. Each book has earned various book awards most people have never heard about and probably won't remember, anyway. His Matt Lanier thriller series stars a musician hero who stumbles upon a violent, powerful conspiracy that ruins his life and nearly kills him because he's too brilliantly stubborn to let the bad guys win.

His newest book—*Little Mountain, Big Trouble*—is a middle-grade adventure novel inspired by his experiences as a volunteer with Big Brothers Big Sisters for twenty years.

Chris grew up in the Twin Cities where he earned a B.S. in Music Education at Minnesota. He's had careers as a public-school band director, financial planner, wine consultant, and day trader before taking up the challenge of being an author. He belongs to the Twin Cities and national chapters of Sisters in Crime and the Alliance of Independent Authors.

He lives in southern Minnesota with his wife, Sandra. For bizarre reasons even *he* can't understand, he's a lifelong golf addict. Another passion is canoeing in Minnesota's Boundary Waters Canoe Area Wilderness. He's taken dozens of canoe trips there, plus several other river trips over the decades. Many have been solo adventures.

After publishing his first book in 2016, Chris began donating a portion of all his book sales to Big Brothers Big Sisters of Southern MN. For more information, visit chrisnorbury.com.